西遊記

JOURNEY
TO THE WEST

西 遊 記

JOURNEY TO THE WEST

An Abridged Version

Written by Wu Cheng'en
Translated by W. J. F. Jenner

The Commercial Press

西遊記

JOURNEY TO THE WEST
An Abridged Version
Written by Wu Cheng'en
Translated by W.J.F. Jenner

First edition first published March 1994
© 1994 The Commercial Press (HK) Ltd.

Based on the unabridged version of JOURNEY TO THE WEST published by the Foreign Languages Press, Beijing, 1988
English translation © W.J.F. Jenner 1982, 1984, 1986, 1990, 1993.

Picture on the cover reproduced by courtesy
of Hilit Publishing Company Ltd., Taiwan and
The Prospect Publishing House, Beijing.

Published by: THE COMMERCIAL PRESS (H.K.) LTD.
           Kiu Ying Building, 2D Finnie Street,
           Quarry Bay, Hong Kong.
Printed by: ELEGANCE PRINTING & BOOK BINDING CO., LTD.
           Block A, 4/F, Hoi Bun Industrial Building,
           6 Wing Yip St., Kwun Tong, Kln.
ISBN 962 07 1148 3
Printed and bound in Hong Kong

Publisher's Note

This is an abridged version of the complete three-volume translation by W. J. F. Jenner of *Journey to the West* published by the Foreign Languages Press of Beijing, China in 1982–86 and reissued in 1988. This edition has 34 chapters which is about one-third of the original translation and contains the most entertaining and best-known parts of the story.

A well-known mythological novel based on folk tales, *Journey to the West* was probably put into its present form in the 1570s by Wu Cheng'en (1500–82).

The translation is based on the Chinese edition of *Journey to the West* (西遊記) in 100 chapters published in 1955 by the Beijing People's Literature Publishing House.

Many different editions of the novel have appeared over the past 400 years. The Chinese edition of 1955 was based on the earliest known edition, the Shidetang woodblock edition printed in Nanjing in the 20th year of the Wanli reign (1592) in the Ming Dynasty, and was further checked against six different editions from the Qing Dynasty.

Translator's Introduction

Journey to the West is one of the greatest treats in Chinese literature. It has been enjoyed by countless readers for almost four hundred years, and episodes in the book have been the basis for many a tale and an opera through which many more people have known the story than have read it. It has been adapted for the large and small screen and been turned into comic books. Every child brought up in the Chinese world wants to be Monkey, and would rather laugh at the greedy and idle Pig than be compared to him.

Of all the Chinese fantasy novels published in the sixteenth and seventeenth centuries it is the only one to have become so central to Chinese culture and remain so popular.

Pinning down this marvellous book and its appeal to the reader is not easy. The structure of the book is casual; the plots of its episodes all end in predictable success for the travellers; and there are only three fully developed characters in the whole vast story. And yet the book works, and works triumphantly well.

Before trying to answer the question of why it works, there is an even more basic one to deal with: what is *Journey to the West?* The question is not a new one: in one form or another it has been asked for nearly four hundred years, and the answers have been many and contradictory. Whenever anyone thinks that Monkey is caught by a formula he springs out of the trap on his somersault cloud. So rather than offer any single interpretation I prefer to consider the novel from a number of different approaches.

Can we call it a novel? In the sense that *A Dream of Red Mansions* or most of the great nineteenth-century European novels are novels, the answer must be no. They are, or attempt to be, integrated wholes, structures in which the component parts are all more or less interdependent and essential, the creation of a single mind (even if left incomplete to be tidied up by others, as was *A Dream of Red Mansions*). The *Journey* is no such thing. It is a string of stories that developed over many hundreds of years before being put into the definitive version we now have at some time in the middle or later sixteenth century. But if we take "novel" to mean an extended piece of fiction, that it certainly is, and it is in that more general sense that I use the word here.

The component stories of the full novel, which number between thirty and fifty depending on how one divides them up, fall into three main groups. Of the original book's hundred chapters the first twelve tell of the earlier life of two of the chief characters, Monkey and the Tang Priest Sanzang, and of the circumstances in which Emperor Taizong sends Sanzang off on his journey to the Western Heaven to visit the Tathagata Buddha and fetch the Mahayana scriptures. These chapters are represented by chapters 1–11 of this abridgement. By far the largest section, chapters 13–97 of the original and chapters 12–33 of this version, over five-sixths of the whole book, covers the journey itself. The earlier of these chapters include some episodes essential to the whole in which the lone pilgrim Sanzang acquires his three disciples, Monkey, Pig and Friar Sand, as well as his white dragon horse. The next seventy-five chapters, the adventures of the four travellers and their horse on their fourteen-year journey, are not one but dozens of stories, all self-contained and running from one to five chapters in length. In each episode the travellers are presented with a problem that they have to deal with before they can continue on their way. Once the problem is solved, as it always is, the place where it happened is left behind and a new episode immediately begins. Apart from the pilgrims themselves and some of their heavenly patrons who put in an occasional appearance, characters virtually never recur after the episode in which they feature. It is unusual for earlier episodes on the journey even to be referred to once they are over. Monkey, Pig, Friar Sand and the Tang Priest hardly ever talk about them; and while the monsters, kings and other characters met along the way have often heard of the pilgrims' general reputations and origins, they rarely know anything about Monkey's deeds along the way.

The third part, which is also the shortest, is only three chapters long. This is enough to deal with the travellers' arrival at the Thunder Monastery on Vulture Peak in India, their rather shabby treatment there, their return to China, and their final reward. Once the journey to the West is over there is little more to be said, and we have virtually omitted the cursory account of their return to China.

The structure of the novel is thus something like a pair of book ends, the opening chapters and the closing one in the present version, between which stand a number of booklets, each of which is a self-contained story or short set of related stories about the same group of pilgrims in a new location every time.

We can see something of how this loose structure developed by comparing the *Journey to the West* we now have with surviving parts of earlier versions of the story cycle.

The ultimate origin of the tradition was a real journey across central Asia to the Indian subcontinent by a most remarkable man, the Buddhist monk and translator Xuanzang, also known as the Dharma Master Sanzang, who died in 664. Xuanzang was brave and able, coping unaided with the difficulties and dangers of his journey, then becoming so expert in Mahayana Buddhist Pure Ideation theory that he could defeat rivals in public disputations in India. His own account of his travels and the biography of him written by a disciple bear very little relation to the pure fantasy of *Journey to the West*; and the real Xuanzang was nothing like the helpless idiot in the story who can scarcely take a single pace without his disciples. So although Xuanzang's journey was the starting point of the tradition, that starting point is so remote from the present book as to have very little direct relationship with it.

Even before the Tang Dynasty was over the legends that led to *Journey to the West* had begun to form. Among the many thousands of manuscripts found in a cave at Dunhuang earlier in this century is a tantalizing fragment from the ninth or tenth century of the story of how Emperor Taizong of the Tang went down to the underworld that appears in chapter 11 of the full novel (but is omitted from this selection).

In Hangzhou in the thirteenth century or thereabouts a book
was printed, only two tattered copies of which were preserved
in Japan till modern times, that is immediately recognizable as
an ancestor of the present *Journey to the West*: *The Tale of How
Sanzang of the Great Tang Fetched the Scriptures.*[1] It is far
shorter — about a fiftieth of the length of the *Journey* — and is
much simpler. In both plot and detail the *Tale* differs in all sorts
of ways from the vastly richer, more subtle and more mature
Journey. But it adds the fantastic Monkey to the historical Tang
Priest, and though he is not identical with our Monkey he is
evidently the same character in essence: the reformed king of the
84,000 monkeys on the Mountain of Flowers and Fruit who has
made mischief in heaven in the past and is now putting his
magical powers (which are much like our Monkey's) at the
service of Sanzang on his pilgrimage. It is generally accepted that
this monkey is closely related to the mischievous monkey king
Hanuman of Hindu mythology who led his monkey hordes to
help Rama. An earlier version of Friar Sand also appears; of the
essential characters only Pig is lacking.

In the *Tale* we can see an early stage of the development of
the *Journey's* great central section. Already it contains self-
contained adventures along the way to India in which Sanzang
would be lost were not Monkey there to save him with his magic
power and his intelligence.

The next fairly full version of the story that survives is a
stage one, probably going back to fourteenth-century performing
scripts though it was printed much later. *The Drama of the Journey
to the West*[2] is a musical play in twenty-four scenes that starts
with four of the disasters that befell Sanzang's parents and the
later retribution. Not till Scene 9 does Monkey appear, rebel
against Heaven, and submit to Guanyin. From then on he
dominates most but not all of the episodes on the pilgrimage,
which ends with Sanzang reaching Vulture Peak in Scene 22. As

---

[1] 大唐三藏取經詩話。

[2] 西遊記雜劇。

in our novel, the story is brought rapidly to an end after this. In this play script the white dragon horse, Friar Sand and, more important, Pig all appear. Pig tells us that he was the charioteer of Marici (a Hindu goddess taken over by Buddhism as a bodhisattva) in an earlier life. Although the story of his carrying a wife off to his mountain cave is clearly an earlier version of the story of how he is subdued in chapter 14 of our abridged *Journey*, he is not yet the marvellously rich character of the *Journey*, and in the few scenes that follow his submission he has no speaking or singing part. The central relationship in our *Journey*, that between him and Monkey, has not yet appeared.

We know for certain that there was at least one other written version of the story circulating about this time, *The Story of the Journey to the West*.[1] An excerpt is quoted in one of the few surviving volumes of an early fifteenth-century compendium, the *Yong Le Encyclopaedia*. Other excerpts are quoted, summarized or referred to in a manual of lively conversational Chinese published in Korea at about the same time. These include Monkey's battle of magic with the three Taoist immortals in chapter 25 of this version.

From what we can judge of this earlier *Story of the Journey to the West* it was well on the way to becoming the present novel. We do not know how long it was, and we cannot tell how many episodes or chapters it contained. The fragments that survive suggest that it was a lot closer to the present version than were the *Tale* and the *Drama*, but that it was far simpler and less elaborated. Clearly the individual episodes were much shorter than they are in the present text; and I am inclined to doubt whether there were as many of them. There were good reasons why the number of episodes along the way should grow and grow as the story developed over the centuries.

We have been looking so far at written versions of the story as it developed from about the thirteenth century onwards. Much of the real development of the story, however, was not on

---

[1] 西遊記平話, also referred to as 西遊記。

paper but in performances, sometimes on stage but especially by storytellers. In the cities of late mediaeval China drama and storytelling were commercialized: they were show business. Storytellers in Tang times had sometimes been Buddhist monks, using amazing tales that were often drawn or copied from the immensely wealthy storehouses of Indian fantasy to bring their listeners to share their faith. By the Song Dynasty storytelling was primarily a secular trade, though the professionals undoubtedly were influenced by some of the religious parables. The earliest known version of the present story, the *Tale of How Sanzang of the Great Tang Fetched the Scriptures*, still has a very clear Buddhist message that is put over hard in every chapter. Yet its publisher was from the entertainment quarter of the city of Hangzhou. It is thus at the transition from what is primarily preaching while also being fun, to what is primarily fun but still has more than a touch of religion to it.

Storytellers earning their living in a highly competitive market such as the city of Hangzhou had their work cut out to keep their customers. Their position was not unlike that of a television series competing in an open market with a number of rivals. Different storytellers specialized in telling different kinds of stories, and within their own fields each one had to be predictable enough for the audience to know more or less what kind of thing to expect, while also being original enough within those limits to keep the public interested and wanting to come back for more. Just as television viewers can switch channels, the would-be hearers of stories could always go elsewhere if they did not like what was on offer. And just as television executives like to stay with a series that has a successful formula, arranging for more and more episodes to be written and made until the audiences fall off, so did the storytellers in fourteenth-century Chinese cities enrich and develop the very simple formula of monk plus monkey they had inherited into the vital triangle of monk, monkey and pig facing a long series of troubles. The chapters in the book were equivalent to performances; new episodes could be freely added. It is during this century that wit comes into the tradition, and the stories become far richer in satire and invention. By the end of the fourteenth century the quintet of Tang Priest, Monkey, Pig, Friar Sand and the white horse were well enough known to the public for a manufacturer to market a porcelain pillow featuring them all on its design.[1]

Once the successful formula had been found it could be developed. Now that the audience knew and liked the pilgrims it wanted new stories and plays about them as well as the familiar ones repeated. And as the series became more and more popular in theatres, teahouses and bars, enterprising publishers, not restricted by copyright, brought out printed versions of the stories and plays that enabled the rich to enjoy them in private. There would always have been a demand for new, self-contained episodes. To return to the metaphor used above, as more and more booklets were added, the book-ends were pushed further apart.

Although we cannot be sure when the present novel was written there are reasons for thinking it almost certainly dates from the middle or later decades of the sixteenth century. The style is right for the period, and the theme of a deluded monarch under the influence of devilish Taoist magicians that is found in several episodes of the full novel, and in our chapter 25, would have had a special relevance during or soon after the Jiajing reign of 1522–1567. The Jiajing emperor was a devotee of heterodox Taoist magic, including some of a very unpleasant nature.

It may be that the author of the novel was the Wu Cheng'en to whom it is generally attributed by scholars, but the thin evidence for the attribution fails to establish it beyond reasonable doubt. Wu's official career took him to Beijing, where he would have learned much about palace politics, and to provincial postings; and the author of the book must have known a little about court life, though he shows scarcely any interest at all in the inner workings of bureaucratic politics. There is nothing about palaces in the book that a fairly well-read commoner could not have known, and one would not have needed inside sources of information to hear the kind of rumours

---

[1] Now in the Guangzhou Museum.

about the court that may lie behind some chapters of the *Journey*.

Another question about the authorship that is just as important and even harder to answer with confidence is this: how far did the person who wrote down the present version of the story create it, or was he only an editor? It seems reasonable to regard the sixteenth-century *Journey* as one man's reworking of material that had been accumulated, developed and improved by countless professional entertainers over many centuries. Did this final reworking include the invention of whole new episodes? This is a question that cannot yet be answered.

The style of the book is basically consistent throughout. So too are the characters of the four travellers, even when some of the adventures they undergo differ greatly from the normal pattern. The book's overall structure is casual — the result, as we have seen, of hundreds of years of lengthening the journey by adding new episodes — but the writing is not. Although the individual episodes are not all equally inspired, even the lesser ones are enlivened by the marvellous dialogue, especially the endless banter between Monkey and Pig, and by the acute observation of human foibles. Whenever we can compare a passage in the present *Journey* with a related one in a previous version of the story the present version is vastly superior.

Another reason for believing that the author of this version really did a lot to the material he inherited is that once this version of the story was published all earlier versions disappeared. All later editions of the story were reprints, adaptations or abridgements of this one; and though it gave rise to sequels it left no room in the market for rival versions of itself. Given the absence of copyright and the competitiveness of the Ming book trade, publishers would have been only too willing to bring out other versions of the story had ones as good as this been available. Wu Cheng'en (or whoever else the author was) produced something so superior to any other treatments of the story cycle that he gave it a definitive form. There was no further room or need for improvement.

Journey to the West was thus both a collective creation by professional entertainers who over many hundreds of years developed its stories and characters in response to audience demand and also the work of an individual writer of unusual quality who used the excellent material he inherited to make something even better. The author's personality never intrudes, but the reader can often feel it there.

The author of *Journey to the West* could not transcend the form he took as his basis, the storyteller's tale, but he could make the best possible use of it and adapt it to the printed page.

The storyteller's tale was the vehicle for a performance that had to hold its audience. A storyteller had no time for long descriptions except as poems or songs to vary the entertainment, keeping the audience in suspense at exciting moments, or commenting on what was happening. The many verse passages in the novel are, I believe, a development of storyteller's verse. As they are not essential to carrying the story line forward nearly all of them have been omitted from this abridgement.

Although *Journey to the West* was written to be read, it deliberately creates the impression of a storyteller's performance. From time to time the reader is addressed directly and told to wonder at something; at the end of each chapter, or session, we are urged to listen to, not read, the next instalment. Like a storyteller, the author does not tell us directly about his characters' personalities and motivations, but brings them out through their words and actions. Yet even though we are given the feel of a story being told, it is a book most enjoyed when read. One has the choice of reading it through from beginning to end or dipping in and enjoying an episode. Perhaps it is best treated as a serial and taken a few chapters at a time.

One thing the book does not try to do is to persuade the reader very hard that the fantastic adventures really are happening. As its original readers would all have known before they opened the book that the Tang Priest and his disciples were going to complete his journey safely there would have been little point in trying to create great suspense about whether he is going to be eaten by any of the monsters who capture him along the way. The interest of plot of each episode is not whether Sanzang will be rescued but how Monkey will do it this time.

Monsters doomed to failure cannot be all that frightening, and the author of the *Journey* does not really attempt to terrify his readers. They are of course wicked. Most of them, especially the ones who live in the mountains or rivers, eat people. The males are particularly eager to eat some of the flesh of the Tang Priest because he is so holy that it will make them live for ever; and the females among them want to attain immortality by mating with him. They all have amazing magical powers and most of them look terrifying. And yet apart from the ones in human form who masquerade as Taoist masters, delude kings and persecute their subjects, the monsters are not shown as being personally evil or loathsome. Some are even shown with a certain warmth, and the reader suspects that in some of the portrayals the author is satirizing powerful figures in the human society of his own day. We even feel a little sorry for Raksasi, the Princess Iron Fan who has been abandoned by her husband the Bull Demon King and whose son the Red Boy has been taken from her by the Bodhisattva Guanyin.

One might expect that a long series of adventures in which Monkey has to save either his master or a country from monsters and in which we know he is going to succeed would be of much less interest than in fact they are. Most of the episodes on the journey fall into two categories. The larger category is of episodes in which monsters who live in the wilds, generally mountains and sometimes rivers, capture the Tang Priest and at least one of the disciples, and are eventually subdued. These are the monsters who have to be dealt with if the journey is to continue. The smaller category is of episodes set in cities or other settled, civilized places. Here the danger is usually not to the travellers themselves but to human society, coming generally from misgovernment that results from fiendish influences. In the full novel the proportion of episodes in the wilds to ones in civilization is about two to one. These standard patterns are varied with unique episodes, such as the subduing of Pig and the trouble over the manfruit in the Wuzhuang Temple. The standard patterns themselves allow plenty of room for ingenious diversification.

When we first get to know Monkey as a monster himself on the Mountain of Flowers and Fruit we see him develop powers so tremendous that only the Tathagata Buddha can subdue him.

After he becomes Sanzang's disciple he remains a formidable and indestructible fighter capable of amazing magical feats. But his powers have their limits: after all, if he could beat all enemies with a couple of swings of his gold-banded cudgel there would be no story to tell. Although none of the monsters can kill him, he cannot beat the more powerful of them. The help of Pig and Friar Sand is rarely enough to tip the balance. This brings into play another of his talents that turns out to be at least as important as his strength, speed and power of transformation: his understanding of the ways of the human, the heavenly and the demonic worlds. Monkey's own fighting prowess makes him all but invincible, but it is his expertise in knowing the right people, and in knowing or finding out what everybody's background is, that enables him to beat the monsters. With that knowledge, his old prestige as a heaven-smashing rebel and his present status as the Tang Priest's escort Monkey can get past the underlings who would block anyone else's access and ask for help from whoever has the power to subdue the monster in question. It is not what Monkey can do but who he knows that gives him most power. He is a master of *guanxixue*, the art of knowing the right people (and, in his case, gods). Monkey the fixer, never at a loss whether he is dealing with humans, gods or demons, holds our interest long after the novelty of Monkey the fighter with amazing magic arts has worn off. The fantasy is firmly grounded in social reality.

Another way in which the novel is successful by being true to life is in the handling of the main characters. Two of them, Sanzang and Monkey, had been in the earlier versions of the story as far back as it can be traced, as we have seen, and Monkey had always been the dominant one. In order to set him off better, Sanzang became weaker and more useless over the centuries, until by the time the present *Journey* was written he had become a nincompoop. The only positive thing left about him is his unswerving determination to preserve himself so he can reach his goal and collect the scriptures. Apart from that, he is cowardly, self-pitying, easily deceived, stupid, petty, given to complaining when he is hungry or tired, and grudging in acknowledging Monkey's abilities and efforts. Monkey, on the other hand, is loyal, selfless to the point of risking the dreaded Band-tightening Spell being recited, unafraid, dauntless, cheerful and tireless, in addition to all the magic powers that make him so outstanding a fighter and a fixer. Monkey's attitude to his master, in which real loyalty is expressed with no respect for Sanzang's dignity, is utterly free from slavishness. But these two characters are not enough to build a great story on.

This gap was filled when Pig was brought into the tradition; it is he who provides the ideal foil for Monkey. He is the archetypal man of appetites, greedy, vain, jealous, boastful, and lecherous. Lazy when he can be, he also works hard when he must. Stupid though he is usually, he also knows a trick or two, as when he ties straw on the horse's hooves before the crossing of a frozen river. He is always the first to want to give up when things are going badly, but he can easily be talked round, just as he will restrain himself from pursuing a woman when reminded of his duty. When the novelist constantly calls him "the idiot" he is not being quite fair: Pig is not completely stupid. If he were there could be no rivalry between him and Monkey. Pig is not so much an idiot as an ordinary man.

That rivalry is the central relationship in the book. Pig envies Monkey's superior magical and fighting powers, while Monkey resents what he sees as the master's favouritism towards Pig. Pig brings out some aspects of Monkey's character, such a playful but malicious cruelty, that might otherwise be less noticeable. While Monkey won't let Pig die, he is willing to let his junior fellow-disciple suffer all sorts of unpleasantness short of death just in order to get one up on him.

The development of Pig into being a central figure in the story over the century or two before the present *Journey* was written also changed Monkey, making him more distinctive. In earlier versions of the tradition Monkey had a wife and chased women, behaving much more like an ordinary monster. Pig took over that side of the earlier Monkey, leaving Monkey free of appetites to be the pure intellect, the Mind-ape capable of infinite transformations, the potentially destructive and dangerous force that has to be controlled by the golden band round his head. While Monkey embodies the mind, Pig can represent the body with its appetites. Monkey is never bothered about food — the occasional piece of fruit is enough to keep him going — while Pig is obsessed with it. Monkey is always trying to find things out, and he moves with the speed of thought; Pig, though capable of flying, is a plodder who rarely thinks further ahead than the end of his snout. Pig cares terribly about what people think of him, whereas Monkey does not worry about his prestige or even refer to it except when it will help the cause. Pig is as essential to the journey as Monkey. Grumble though he may, he will do the heavy jobs such as carrying luggage or clearing the way across Thorn Ridge; and as even Monkey cannot be everywhere at once Pig can, provided he is kept under control, help guard the master and fight demons.

Monkey and Pig's dialogues are one of the greatest joys of the novel. Sometimes very warm, sometimes needling, sometimes getting at each other, sometimes discussing the situation, often joking, their talk is an unending source of pleasure. For many readers they are the heart of the novel; and because they are so true to human nature everywhere they give the book its immortality and universal appeal.

The triangle of Monkey, Pig and their master is the central structure of nearly all the episodes of the journey. This leaves little for Friar Sand to do in carrying the story forward, with the result that he remains a rather shadowy figure throughout. His main contribution to the stories is to be somebody to whom one of the three main characters can talk when the other two are away. One has the impression that he was too firmly established in the tradition to be got rid of, but that neither storyteller nor writer, neither hearer nor reader, found much of interest in him. For this reason he has been retained but placed in the shadows, leaving the limelight to Monkey and Pig.

The question of what the book's message really is has been argued about for over three centuries and is never likely to be finally answered because its archetypal symbols can be taken in so many ways. Part of the difficulty in interpreting it arises from the fact that what was originally a preaching story to encourage the general public to accept a rather simple Buddhist faith changed much of its content as it grew over the centuries while preserving the form of a pilgrimage to collect Buddhist scriptures. It is hard to disentangle what is simply time-honoured convention from the author's own thoughts. The Buddhism of the book is not very rigorous. Titles of sutras and of Buddhas and bodhisattvas are in places wrong; and the Buddhist verses contain the sort of teachings that were commonplace in Ming China, where they were taken for granted in much the same way that Christian values were in Western Europe at the time. The book is Buddhist, but not overwhelmingly so, just as much sixteenth-century European literature is Christian without being religious.

There is also a strong element of Taoism in it. Some commentators have argued that this is the book's main message, and presented it as a guide to finding the Way. It is true that there is much use of commonplace Taoist symbolism, such as the Five Elements that yield to each other. Obscure references are made to achieving the elixir of literal or metaphorical immortality through combining the elements and a long process of self-purification. In sixteenth-century China Taoist chemical and physiological alchemy were much in vogue, so that references to that kind of thinking were almost inevitable: but it is hard to see that it is meant to be taken very seriously. In addition, the hatred that the author felt for some Taoist magic is made very clear, particularly when it involved ruining a country by deluding its monarch. Yet Monkey himself acquired his powers through learning Taoist magic. The supernatural world of the novel is one in which Buddhas and Taoist deities co-exist as part of the same heavenly hierarchy. The Jade Emperor and Lord Lao Zi have their spheres of interest, and the Buddhas and bodhisattvas have theirs. Nowhere in the book do they clash. When in the early chapters Monkey is a rebel, he rebels against both, and they combine forces to put him down. Then, as later, the Tathagata Buddha is the ultimate authority; but he so holds back from intervening in worldly affairs that only in exceptional circumstances will he use his supreme power.

It seems to me that there is no need to choose between the Buddhist and the Taoist aspects of the book. Monkey advises the king of Tarrycart to combine the three teachings by honouring both the Buddhist clergy and the way of Taoism, and also by educating men of talent in the Confucian tradition. We cannot be sure that the author is speaking through Monkey's voice, but it certainly sounds that way.

Nor is the book a straightforward struggle between good and evil. Monkey himself has some ambiguities about him. In the book's exhilarating early chapters he is himself a great monster who rebels against Heaven. As he explains to the Tang Priest, he used to eat people too. Monkey as rebel has been made much of in China in recent decades, and this is understandable. But does that mean that once he becomes Sanzang's disciple he has surrendered? Not, I think, in the author's mind. The book does not end with the defeat of Monkey's rebellion: it is only the beginning of the story. An overall interpretation of Monkey has to give more weight to eighty-seven chapters than to seven, and treat the seven as a prologue to the rest. In the eighty-seven chapters Monkey's destructiveness and wildness are held under control, both by his loyalty to his master and by the threat of excruciating headaches. But he does not lose his spirit. Monkey's loyalty does not extend to toadying, whether to his master or to anyone else. In his frank speaking and impatience with protocol, hypocrisy, pomposity and tyrannical government he is the same Monkey as before.

For Monkey the obstacles along the way are just that: obstacles to be dealt with. Only the ogres in human form who bring misery to human society are seen as really evil to be eliminated for their own sake. Most of the monsters in the wilds along the way are themselves escaped heavenly creatures, whose masters and mistresses take them back and protect them from Monkey's avenging cudgel. All that matters is that they stop hindering the travellers. Whether Monkey and Pig exterminate them or not is not really important.

It is sensible, I think, to take the book's symbolism and message in as broad a sense as possible. There are besides a number of hints that the highest teaching is wordless. The quest could be any quest, any long and difficult undertaking in which patience, ingenuity and courage, together with an excellent understanding of the ways of the world, are essential for success.

The form happens to be a journey to fetch Buddhist scriptures, and it can be taken as what it appears to be if one wishes. Like all the best symbolism, it is very adaptable. Whatever the message may be, the best thing is not to worry about it, but simply to enjoy the book's wisdom, humour and endlessly rich observation and invention. This abridgement, for which I claim no responsibility, amounts to about a quarter of the original in terms of pages, and covers about half of the episodes that make up the whole *Journey*. The principle followed has been to retain whole stories while cutting out long passages in verse and stylized prose that embellish but do not advance the narrative. Only a minimum of rewriting has been done, and the language of the full translation has been retained as far as possible. This means that while the reader of this version will miss much that is in the original, virtually everything in this version is — within the limits of translation — to be found in the Ming novel.

Half a century ago the great translator Arthur Waley made· an even shorter abridgement of the *Journey* available to readers of English under the title *Monkey*. It was reading a secondhand copy of *Monkey* as a boy of twelve that first aroused my interest in knowing more about Chinese culture. If this shortened version of my translation of the *Journey* can be half as alluring as Waley's was to me a debt will have been repaid; and if anyone who has made the abbreviated pilgrimage would like to follow some of the full itinerary, the complete translation of *Journey to the West* is waiting to be explored.

W. J. F. Jenner
Beijing, September 1984
Canberra, July 1991

CONTENTS

2

4

CHAPTER 1
The Stone Monkey Is Born and Takes the Throne in the Mountain of Flowers and Fruit

Once, far beyond the seas, there was a country called Aolai. This country was next to an ocean, and in the middle of the ocean was a famous island called the Mountain of Flowers and Fruit.

There was once a magic stone on the top of this mountain which was thirty-six feet five inches high and twenty-four feet round. There were no trees around it to give shade, but magic fungus and orchids clung to its sides. Ever since Creation began it had been receiving the truth of Heaven, the beauty of Earth, the essence of the Sun and the splendour of the Moon; and as it had been influenced by them for so long it had miraculous powers. It developed a magic womb, which burst open one day to produce a stone egg about the size of a ball. When the wind blew on this egg it turned into a stone monkey, complete with the five senses and four limbs.

On this mountain the monkey was soon able to run and jump, feed from plants and trees, drink from brooks and springs, pick mountain flowers and look for fruit. He made friends with the wolves, went around with the tigers and leopards, was on good terms with the deer, and had the other monkeys and apes for relations. At night he slept under the rockfaces, and he roamed around the peaks and caves by day. As the saying so rightly goes, "There is no calendar in the mountains, and when winter's over you don't know the time of year." On hot mornings he and all the other monkeys would play under the shade of some pines to avoid the heat.

After playing, the monkeys would go and bathe in the stream, a mountain torrent that tumbled along like rolling melons. There is an old saying, "Birds have bird language and animals have animal talk." All the monkeys said to each other, "I wonder where that water comes from. We've got nothing else to do today, so wouldn't it be fun to go upstream and find its source?" With a shout they all ran off, leading their children and calling to their brothers. They climbed up the mountain beside the stream until they reached its source, where a waterfall cascaded from a spring.

The monkeys clapped their hands and exclaimed with delight, "What lovely water. It must go all the way to the bottom of the mountain and join the waves of the sea."

Then one monkey made a suggestion: "If anyone is clever enough to go through the fall, find the source, and come out in one piece, let's make him our king." When this challenge had been shouted three times, the stone monkey leapt out from the crowd and answered at the top of his voice, "I'll go, I'll go."

Watch him as he shuts his eyes, crouches, and springs, leaping straight into the waterfall. When he opened his eyes and raised his head to look round, he saw neither water nor waves. A bridge stood in front of him, as large as life. He stopped, calmed himself, took a closer look, and saw that the bridge was made of iron. The water that rushed under it poured out through a fissure in the rocks, screening the gateway to the bridge. He started walking towards the bridge, and as he looked he made out what seemed to be a house. It was a really good place.

He took a good long look and then scampered to the middle of the bridge, from where he noticed a stone tablet. On the tablet had been carved in big square letters:

HAPPY LAND OF THE MOUNTAIN OF FLOWERS
    AND FRUIT
CAVE HEAVEN OF THE WATER CURTAIN.

The stone monkey was beside himself with glee. He rushed away, shut his eyes, crouched, and leapt back through the waterfall. "We're in luck, we're in luck," he said with a chuckle. All the other monkeys crowded round him asking, "What's it like in there? How deep is the water?" "There's no water, none at all," replied the stone monkey. "There's an iron bridge, and on the other side of the bridge there's a house that must have been made by Heaven and Earth." "How ever could you see a house there?" the other monkeys asked. The stone monkey chuckled again. "The water here comes under the bridge and through the rocks, and it hides the gateway to the bridge from view. There are flowers and trees by the bridge, and a stone house too. Inside the house are stone rooms, a stone stove, stone bowls, stone plates, stone beds, and even stone benches. In the middle of it all is a tablet which says 'Happy Land of the Mountain of Flowers and Fruit, Cave Heaven of the Water Curtain'. It's just the place for us to settle down in — there's room there for thousands. Let's all move in, then we won't have to put up with any more nonsense from heaven."

The other monkeys were all so delighted to hear this that they said, "You go first and take us with you." The stone monkey shut his eyes, crouched, and leapt in again, shouting, "Follow me in, follow me in." The braver monkeys all jumped through. The more timid ones peered forward, shrank back, rubbed their ears, scratched their cheeks, shouted, and yelled at the top of their voices, before going in, all clinging to each other. After rushing across the bridge they all grabbed plates and snatched bowls, bagged stoves and fought over beds, and moved everything around. Monkeys are born naughty and they could not keep quiet for a single moment until they had worn themselves out moving things around.

The stone monkey sat himself in the main seat and said, "Gentlemen, 'A man who breaks his word is worthless.' Just now you said that if anyone was clever enough to come in here and get out again in one piece, you'd make him king. Well, then. I've come in and gone out, and gone out and come in.

I've found you gentlemen a cave heaven where you can sleep in peace and all settle down to live in bliss. Why haven't you made me king?" On hearing this all the monkeys bowed and prostrated themselves, not daring to disobey. They lined up in groups in order of age and paid their homage as at court, all acclaiming him as the "Great King of a Thousand Years". The stone monkey then took the throne, made the word "stone" taboo, and called himself Handsome Monkey King.

Taking control of his host of monkeys, apes, gibbons and others, the Handsome Monkey King divided them into rulers and subjects, assistants and officers. In the morning they roamed the Mountain of Flowers and Fruit and in the evening they settled down for the night in the Water Curtain Cave. They made a compact that they would not join the ranks of the birds or go with the running beasts. They had their own king, and they thoroughly enjoyed themselves.

CHAPTER 2
The Handsome Monkey King Becomes Sun Wukong

The Handsome Monkey King's innocent high spirits could not, of course, last three or four hundred years. One day he suddenly felt depressed during a banquet with his monkey host, and he started to weep. The startled monkeys crowded round, bowed to him and asked, "What's the matter, Your Majesty?" "Although I'm happy now," the Monkey King replied, "I'm worried about the future. That's what's getting me down." The other monkeys laughed and said, "Your Majesty is being greedy. We have parties every day; we live in a mountain paradise, in an ancient cave in a divine continent. We are spared the rule of unicorns, the domination of phoenixes, and the restraints of human kings. We are free to do just as we like — we are infinitely lucky. Why make yourself miserable worrying about the future?" To this the Monkey King replied, "Yes, we don't have to submit to the laws and regulations of human kings, and we don't live in terror of the power of birds and beasts. But the time will come when we are old and weak, and the underworld is controlled by the King of Hell. When the time comes for us to die, we won't be able to go on living among the Blessed, and our lives will have been in vain." All the monkeys covered their faces and wept as every one of them thought about death.

Suddenly a gibbon jumped out from their ranks and shrieked in a piercing voice, "If Your Majesty is thinking so far ahead, this is the beginning of enlightenment. Now of the Five Creatures, there are only three that do not come under the jurisdiction of the King of Hell." "Do you know which they are?" asked the Monkey King. "Yes," the ape replied. "They are the Buddhas, the Immortals and the Sages. They are free from the Wheel of Reincarnation. They are not born and they do not die. They are as eternal as Heaven and Earth, as the mountains and the rivers." "Where do they live?" the Monkey King asked. "Only in the human world," the ape replied, "in ancient caves on magic mountains." The Monkey King was delighted to hear this. "I shall leave you all tomorrow," he said, "and go down the mountain. If I have to, I'll roam the corners of the oceans and go to the edge of the sky to find these three kinds of beings and discover the secret of eternal youth that will keep us out of the clutches of the King of Hell for ever." Goodness! Because of these words he was to learn how to be free from the Wheel of Reincarnation and become the Great Sage Equalling Heaven. All the monkeys clapped with approval and said, "Great! Great! Tomorrow we'll climb all over the mountain and get lots of fruit to give Your Majesty a really big banquet to send you off."

The next day the monkeys set out to pick magic peaches, gather rare fruits, dig out yams, and cut Solomon's-seal. Magic fungus and fragrant orchids were collected, and everything was set on the stone benches and the stone tables, with fairy wine and dishes.

The host of monkeys ushered the Handsome Monkey King to the seat of honour and sat down below him according to age. Each of them took it in turns to bring him wine, flowers, and fruit, and they drank hard for a whole day. The next morning the Handsome Monkey King got up early and ordered, "Children, tear down some old pines and make me a raft. Find a bamboo pole to punt with and load it up with fruit. I'm going." He went aboard the raft all by himself, pushed off with all his might, and floated off towards the waves of the ocean. The wind carried him across oceans and seas to find the Way of Immortality.

He spent eight or nine years in his search. One day, he reached the Great Western Ocean and came to the Western Continent of Cattle-gift. He went ashore and made extensive and lengthy enquiries until he came to a high and beautiful mountain. On climbing it he saw a magnificent cave.

He saw that the doors of the cave were shut fast, and that everything was still, with no signs of any people. He turned round and noticed that there was a stone tablet about thirty feet high and eight feet wide at the top of the cliff. On it was carved in enormous letters:

SPIRIT-TOWER HEART MOUNTAIN, CAVE OF THE SETTING MOON AND THE THREE STARS.

The Monkey King exclaimed with delight, "The people here really are honest. The mountain and the cave I was told about do exist." He took a good long look, but did not dare to knock on the door. He climbed to the end of a pine branch and ate some pine seeds to amuse himself.

Before long the doors of the cave opened with a creak, and an immortal boy came out. In the nobility of his bearing and the exceptional purity of his features he was completely different from an ordinary boy.

When this boy had come out he shouted, "Who's making that row out here?" The Monkey King scampered down the tree, went up to him, and said with a bow, "Immortal child, I am a disciple who has come to ask about the Way and study under the Immortal. The last thing I'd do would be to make a row here." The boy laughed. "So you've come to ask about the Way, have you?" "Yes," the Monkey King replied. "Our master has just got up," the boy said, "and has now mounted the dais to expound the Way. Before he had started to explain about origins he told me to open the door. He said, 'There is someone outside who wants to cultivate his conduct. Go and welcome him.' I suppose he must have meant you." "Yes, he meant me," the Monkey King said with a smile. "Come with me," the boy said.

The Monkey King straightened his clothes and followed the

boy deep into the depths of the cave. He saw majestic pavilions and towers of red jade, pearl palaces and gateways of cowrie, and countless rooms of silence and secluded cells leading all the way to a jasper dais. He saw the Patriarch Subhuti sitting on the dais and thirty minor immortals standing below it.

As soon as the Handsome Monkey King saw him he bowed low and knocked his head on the ground before him many times, saying, "Master, master, your disciple pays his deepest respects." "Where are you from?" the Patriarch asked. "You must tell me your name and address before you can become my pupil." "I come from the Water Curtain Cave in the Flowers and Fruit Mountain in the land of Aolai in the Eastern Continent of Superior Body," replied the Monkey King.

"So you came here by stages," the Patriarch remarked. "What is your surname?" "I'm not surly," the Monkey King replied. "If people call me names it doesn't bother me, and if they hit me I don't get angry. I'm just polite to them and that's that. I've never been surly." "I didn't ask if you were surly. I wanted to know the surname you inherited from your parents." "I didn't have any parents," the Monkey King replied. "If you had no parents, did you grow on a tree?" "I grew not on a tree but in a stone," the Monkey King replied. "All I remember is that there was a magic stone on the top of the Flowers and Fruit Mountain, and that one year the stone split open and I was born." Concealing his delight at hearing this, the Patriarch remarked, "In other words, you were born of Heaven and Earth. Walk around for a moment and let me have a look at you." The Monkey King leapt to his feet and shambled round a couple of times. The Patriarch smiled and said, "Though you have rather a base sort of body, you look like one of the rhesus monkeys that eat pine seeds. I think I will call you Sun ('Monkey'). Apart from the 'animal' element, the character Sun has one part implying male and one part suggesting a baby, which fits in with my basic theories about children. Your surname will be Sun."

When the Monkey King heard this he kowtowed with delight and said, "Great! Great! Now I have a surname. I am

eternally grateful to you for your mercy and compassion, master.
I beg you to give me a personal name to go with my
new surname, then it will be much easier to address me."
"There are twelve words within my sect," said the Patriarch,
"which I give as names. You belong to the tenth generation
of my disciples." "What are these twelve words?" asked the
Monkey King. "Broad, great, wisdom, intelligence, true,
likeness, nature, sea, bright, awakened, complete and enlightenment. If we work out the generations of disciples, then you
should have a name with Wu ('Awakened') in it. So we can
give you the Dharma name Sun Wukong, which means 'Monkey Awakened to Emptiness'. Will that do?" "Marvellous,
marvellous," said the smiling Monkey King. "From now on my
name will be Sun Wukong."

CHAPTER 3
Sun Wukong Gets Rid of the Demon King of Confusion with Magic Transformations

After being given a name, the Handsome Monkey King jumped for joy. He studied under the Patriarch and learnt to cultivate his conduct. Six or seven years slipped by in the cave without his noticing them as Monkey succeeded in mastering the seventy-two transformations. Later, in addition, he was taught by the Master the excellent art of the somersault cloud. With one somersault, Monkey could go sixty thousand miles. From then on he was free from all restraint and he enjoyed the delights of immortality, living as he pleased.

On a day when spring was giving way to summer, all the students were sitting under some pine trees listening to lectures. Monkey's spiritual brothers urged him to give them a demonstration of the seventy-two transformations. At this suggestion Sun Wukong braced his spirit to show off his skills by transforming himself into a pine tree. When the fellow disciples saw it, they clapped their hands and chuckled aloud. The row they were making had disturbed the Patriarch, who rushed out and roared angrily, "Yelling and shouting like that is no way for those cultivating their conduct to behave. What was all the laughing and shouting about?" "Just now Sun Wukong did a transformation for fun. We told him to turn himself into a pine tree, and he did. We all praised and applauded him, which was why we disturbed you with the noise, master. We beg you to forgive us."

The Patriarch was angry and sent them all away except for Sun Wukong, to whom he said, "I shan't punish you, but you'll have to go. It will be absolutely impossible for you to stay here!"

Sun Wukong took his leave and went away. Making the spell, he summoned a somersault cloud and went back to the Eastern Continent. Within two hours he saw the Water Curtain Cave on the Mountain of Flowers and Fruit.

Sun Wukong put away his cloud and headed straight to the Mountain of Flowers and Fruit. As he followed the path there he heard the call of the cranes and the cries of the apes. The crane calls echoed beyond the Milky Way, and the ape cries were pathetically sad. Sun Wukong shouted, "Children, I'm back."

Big monkeys and little monkeys came bounding in their thousands and tens of thousands from caves in the cliffs, from the grass and flowers, and down from the trees. They all crowded round the Handsome Monkey King, kowtowed and said, "Your Majesty, you're a cool one. How could you stay away for so long and abandon us all here? We've been desperate for you to come back. A demon has been mistreating us terribly. He's occupied our Water Curtain Cave, and we've been fighting for our lives with him. Recently he's been stealing our things and carrying off many of our youngsters. We've had to stay awake all night to guard our families. Thank goodness you've come back! Another year without you, Your Majesty, and every one of us would be under his control, cave and all."

Sun Wukong was furious. "Who is this demon? What an outrage! Tell me everything about him, and then I'll go and give him what's coming to him." The monkey host kowtowed again and said, "Your Majesty, the wretch calls himself the Demon King of Confusion. He lives north of here." "How far away is his place?" Sun Wukong asked. "He comes and goes in cloud and mist with wind and rain, or thunder and lightning, so we don't know how far it is." "If that's how it is," Sun Wukong replied, "then don't worry. Just keep yourselves amused while I go and find him."

The splendid Monkey King jumped up into the air, and

as he somersaulted towards the north he saw a high and precipitous mountain.

As the Handsome Monkey King stood gazing in silence at this view, he heard voices. When he went down the mountainside to look he found the Cave in the Belly of the Water facing the cliff. Several minor demons were dancing around in front of the cave doors, and they ran away as soon as they saw Sun Wukong. "Wait a moment," Sun Wukong said. "I want you to take a message for me. I am the King of the Water Curtain Cave in the Mountain of Flowers and Fruit that lies due south of here. I've come to find that Demon of Confusion of yours, or whatever he's called, the one who's been mistreating my children and grandchildren, and have it out with him."

The minor demons scuttled into the cave and reported, "A disaster, Your Majesty." "What do you mean, disaster?" the demon king asked. "There's a monkey outside the cave," the minor demons reported, "who says that he's the King of the Water Curtain Cave on the Mountain of Flowers and Fruit. He says that you have been bullying his children and grandchildren, and that he's come specially to find you to have it out with you." The demon king laughed. "Those monkey devils are always going on about a king of theirs who renounced the world to cultivate his conduct; I suppose it must be him who's here now. Did you see how he was dressed or what weapons he was carrying?" "He hasn't got any weapons. He's bare-headed, and he's wearing a red gown belted with a yellow silk sash, and a pair of black boots. He isn't dressed like a monk, or a layman, or an immortal. He's bare-handed and empty-fisted, and he's standing outside the doors yelling." "Bring me my armour and weapons," said the demon king when he heard this. The minor demons produced them at once, and when he had donned his armour he went out of the door with all the demons, his sword in his hand. "Who is the King of the Water Curtain Cave?" he roared.

"You insolent demon," shouted the Monkey King. "Your eyes may be big but you can't see who I am." The demon king laughed at him. "You don't even stand four feet from the ground, you're still in your twenties, and you've got no weapon in your hand. What sort of mad courage makes you challenge me to a fight?" "You insolent demon," retorted Sun Wukong, "how blind you are. You may think I'm small, but I can grow easily enough. You may think I'm unarmed, but I could pull the moon down from the sky with my two hands. Don't worry, old Sun Wukong will sock you one." Sun Wukong gave a jump and leapt into the air, taking a swing at his face. The demon king put out his hand to stop him and said, "Look how big I am, you dwarf. If you use your fists, I'll use my sword. But I'd only make myself look ridiculous if I killed you with a sword. Wait till I've put my sword down and then I'll give you a display of boxing." "Well said," exclaimed Sun Wukong, "spoken like a man. Come on then." The demon king dropped his guard to throw a punch, and Sun Wukong rushed in towards him, punching and kicking. When he spread out his hand it was enormous, and when he clenched his fist it was very hard. Sun Wukong hit the demon king in the ribs, kicked his backside, and smashed several of his joints. The demon king seized his steel sword that was as big as a plank, and swung it at Sun Wukong's skull. Sun Wukong dodged the blow, and the sword only split air. Seeing how ugly the demon king had turned, Sun Wukong used his magic art of getting extra bodies. He pulled out one of his hairs, popped it in his mouth, chewed it up, and blew it out into the air, shouting, "Change!" It turned into two or three hundred little monkeys, who all crowded round him.

Sun Wukong now had an immortal body, and there was no magic transformation of which he was not capable. Since he had followed the Way he could change each of the eighty-four thousand hairs on his body into anything he wanted. The little monkeys were too quick and nimble for sword or spear. Look at them, leaping forwards and jumping backwards, rushing up and surrounding the demon king, grabbing him, seizing him, poking him in the backside, pulling at his feet, punching him, kicking him, tearing his hair out, scratching at his eyes, twisting his nose, all picking him up together and throwing him to the ground. They went on until they had beaten him to a pulp. Sun Wukong snatched his sword from him, told the little monkeys to get out of the way, and brought it down on the crown of his head, splitting it into two. Then he led his force charging into the cave, where they exterminated all the demons, big and small. He shook his hair and put it back on his body. The monkeys who did not go back on his body were the little monkeys the demon king had carried off from the Water Curtain Cave. Sun Wukong asked them how they had got there. There were thirty or forty of them, and they replied with tears in their eyes, "It was after Your Majesty went off to become an immortal. He has been fighting with us for the last two years. He brought us all here by force. All the things here — the stone bowls and plates — were stolen from our cave by the beast." "If it's our stuff, take it all out," said Sun Wukong. He then set fire to the Cave in the Belly of the Water and burnt it to a cinder. "Come back with me," he ordered the monkeys. "Your Majesty," they replied, "when we came here all we could hear was the wind howling in our ears as it blew us here, so we don't know the way. How are we ever going to get back?" "There's nothing at all to that spell he used," said Sun Wukong. "I can do it too, as now I only have to know the smallest bit about something to understand it completely. Shut your eyes and don't worry."

Splendid Monkey King. He recited a spell, took them riding on a hurricane, then brought the cloud down to the ground. "Open your eyes and look, children," he shouted. As soon as the monkeys' feet touched the ground they recognized their home. In their delight they all ran along the familiar path to the cave, and the monkeys who had stayed in the cave all crowded in as well. They divided themselves into age-groups and bowed in homage to the Monkey King. Wine and food was laid out to celebrate, and they asked him how he had defeated the demon king and saved their children. When Sun Wukong had told them the whole story the monkeys were full of admiration. "Where did you learn such arts, Your Majesty?" they asked insistently.

"When I left you," Sun Wukong replied, "I followed the waves and the currents, and drifted across the Eastern Ocean to the Southern Jambu Continent. Here I taught myself to take human form and to wear these clothes and boots. I swaggered around for eight or nine years, but I never found the Way, so I sailed across the Western Ocean to the Western Continent of Cattle-gift. After long enquiries I was lucky enough to meet a venerable Immortal, who taught me the True Result, which makes me as immortal as heaven, and the great Dharma Gate to eternal youth." The monkeys all congratulated him and exclaimed that his like could not be found in a billion years. Sun Wukong laughed and said, "Children, we should congratulate ourselves on having a surname." "What is Your Majesty's surname?" the monkey masses asked. "My surname is now Sun, and my Buddhist name is Wukong." The monkeys all clapped their hands with joy and said, "Your Majesty is Old Sun, and we are Second Sun, Third Sun, Thin Sun, Little Sun — a family of Suns, a nation of Suns, a den of Suns." They all offered Old Sun their respects, with big plates and small bowls of coconut toddy, grape wine, magic flowers, and magic fruit. The whole household was happy.

CHAPTER 4
Monkey Finds the Gold-Banded Cudgel in the Dragon King's Palace

We have related how the Handsome Monkey King returned home in glory, bringing a large sword he had captured when he killed the Demon King of Confusion. From then on he taught the monkeys military arts and practised with them every day.

One day they paraded as usual. Sun Wukong assembled all the monkeys, and they numbered over forty-seven thousand. This had alarmed all the strange beasts of the mountain — wolves, monsters, tigers, leopards, deer, muntjacs, river-deer, foxes, wild cats, badgers, raccoons, lions, elephants, orang-utans, bears, stags, wild boars, mountain cattle, antelopes, rhinoceroses, little dogs, and huge dogs. The kings of various kinds of monsters from seventy-two caves all came to pay homage to the Monkey King. They offered tribute every year and attended court in each of the four seasons. They also took part in drills and paid their seasonal grain levies. Everything was so orderly that the Mountain of Flowers and Fruit was as secure as an iron bucket or a wall of bronze. The kings of the monsters sent gongs, drums, coloured flags, helmets, and armour in great abundance, and every day there were military exercises.

One day, amid all this success, the Handsome Monkey King suddenly said to the other monkeys, "You are now expert in the bow and crossbow, and highly skilled in other weapons; but this sword of mine is too clumsy for my liking. What shall I do about it?" The four veteran monkeys came forward and submitted a suggestion: "Your Majesty is an Immortal, so mortals' weapons are not good enough for you. We wonder if Your Majesty is able to travel underwater." "Since hearing the Way," Sun Wukong replied, "I have mastered the seventy-two earthly transformations. My somersault cloud has outstanding magical powers. I know how to conceal myself and vanish. I can make spells and end them. I can reach the sky and find my way into the earth. I can travel under the sun or moon without leaving a shadow or go through metal or stone freely. I can't be drowned by water or burned by fire. There's nowhere I cannot go." "If Your Majesty has these magical powers, the stream under our iron bridge leads to the Dragon Palace of the Eastern Sea. If you are willing to go down there, go and find the Dragon King and ask him for whatever weapon it is you want. Wouldn't that suit you?" "Wait till I get back," was Sun Wukong's delighted reply.

Splendid Monkey King. He leapt to the end of the bridge and made a spell with his fist to ward off the water. Then he dived into the waves and split the waters to make way for himself till he reached the bed of the Eastern Sea. On his journey he saw a yaksha demon who was patrolling the sea. The yaksha barred his way and asked, "What sage or divinity are you, pushing the waters aside like that? Please tell me so that I can make a report and have you properly received." "I am the Heaven-born Sage Sun Wukong from the Mountain of Flowers and Fruit, and your old Dragon King's close neighbour. How is it you don't know me?" When the yaksha heard this he hurried back to the crystal palace and reported, "Your Majesty, Sun Wukong, the Heaven-born Sage from the Mountain of Flowers and Fruit who says he is your neighbour, is coming to your palace." Ao Guang, the Old Dragon King of the Eastern Sea, leapt to his feet and went out to meet Sun Wukong with his dragon sons and grandsons, his prawn soldiers, and his crab generals. "Come in, exalted Immortal," he said, taking Sun Wukong into the palace where they introduced themselves, seated him in the place of honour, and offered him tea. Then the Dragon King asked him, "Exalted Immortal, when did you find the Way, and what magic arts did you acquire?" "After my birth," said Sun Wukong, "I renounced the world and cultivated my conduct, and thus obtained an immortal and indestructible body. Recently I have trained my sons and grandsons to guard our cave, but unfortunately I have not yet found myself a weapon. I have long heard that my illustrious neighbour enjoys the delights of a jade palace with gate-towers of cowrie, and I was sure that you must have some magic weapons to spare, so I have come especially to beg one of you."

Not wishing to refuse this request, the Dragon King sent Commander Perch to fetch a large sword and offer it to Sun Wukong. "I don't know how to use a sword," said Sun Wukong, "so could I ask you to give me something else?" The Old Dragon King then sent Colonel Mackerel and Guard Commander Eel to fetch a nine-pronged spear. Sun Wukong leapt down from his seat, took it, tried it out, then flung it down, saying, "It's too light, far too light; and it doesn't suit me. I beg you to give me another." The Dragon King smiled as he said, "Exalted Immortal, don't you see that this weighs three thousand six hundred pounds?" "It doesn't suit me, it doesn't suit me at all," protested Sun Wukong. The Dragon King, feeling frightened now, ordered Provincial Commander Bream and Garrison Commander Carp to bring out a patterned heavenly halberd for warding off spells that weighed seven thousand two hundred pounds. As soon as he saw it Sun Wukong bounded forward to take it. He tried a few postures and thrusts with it then stuck it in the ground between them. "Still too light, far too light." The Dragon King, now really terrified, said, "Exalted Immortal, that halberd is the heaviest weapon in my palace." "As the old saying goes," said Sun Wukong with a grin, " 'Never think the Dragon King has no treasures.' Have another look, and if you find anything satisfying I'll give you a good price for it." "I really have nothing else," the Dragon King replied.

As he was speaking, his dragon wife and dragon daughters came in from the back of the palace and said, "Your Majesty, by the look of him this sage must be really somebody. The piece of miraculous iron that anchors the Milky Way in place has been shining with a lovely rosy glow for the last few days, and creating a most auspicious atmosphere. Perhaps it has started to shine to greet this sage." "That piece of miraculous iron is one of the nails that Yu the Great used to fix the depths of rivers and seas when he brought the waters under control," said the Dragon King. "What use could it be?" "Never mind whether it's useful or not," his wife replied. "Just give it to him and let him do with it as he pleases. At least you'll get him out of the palace." The Dragon King did as she suggested and described the piece of iron to Sun Wukong, who said, "Bring it out and let me see." "It can't be moved. You will have to go and look at it yourself, exalted Immortal." "Where is it? Take me there," said Sun Wukong. The Dragon King took him into the middle of the sea treasury, where all of a sudden they could see ten thousand rays of golden light. Pointing at it, the Dragon King said, "That's it, where all the light is coming from." Sun Wukong hitched up his clothes and went to give it a feel. He found that it was an iron pillar about as thick as a measure for a peck of grain and some twenty feet long. Seizing it with both hands he said, "It's too thick and too long. If it were a bit shorter and thinner it would do." As soon as these words were out of his mouth this precious piece of iron became several feet shorter and a few inches thinner. Sun Wukong tossed it in his hands, remarking that it would be even better if it were thinner still. The precious iron thereupon became even thinner. Sun Wukong was taking it out of the sea treasury to have a look at it when he saw that it had two gold bands round it, while the middle part was made of black iron. There was a line of inlaid writing near the bands which said that it was the AS-YOU-WILL GOLD-BANDED CUDGEL: WEIGHT 13,500 POUNDS. Sun Wukong was delighted, though he did not show it. "I think that this little darling will do whatever I want." As he walked along he weighed it in his hand and said reflectively, "If it were even smaller still it would be perfect." By the time he had taken it outside it was twenty feet long and as thick as a rice bowl.

Holding his treasure in his hands, Sun Wukong sat down in the main hall of the palace of crystal and said with a smile to the Dragon King, "Many thanks, worthy neighbour, for your great generosity." The Old Dragon King humbly acknowledged his thanks, and Sun Wukong went on, "This piece of iron will be very useful, but there is one more thing I want to ask." "What might that be, exalted Immortal?" asked the Dragon King. "If I hadn't got this cudgel, that would have been the end of the matter, but as I have got it the problem is that I don't have the clothes to go with it. What are we to do about it? If you have any armour here, I'd be most obliged if you gave me a suit." The Dragon King said he had not any. "'A guest should not have to trouble two hosts,'" said Sun Wukong. "I won't leave without one." "Please try some other sea, exalted Immortal — you may find one there." "'It's better to stay in one house than to visit three.' I beg and implore you to give me a suit." "I really don't have one," replied the Dragon King. "If I had I would present it to you." "If you really haven't, then I'll try this cudgel out on you." "Don't hit me, exalted Immortal, don't hit me," pleaded the Dragon King in terror. "Let me see whether my brothers have one that they could give you." "Where do your brothers live?" "Ao Qin is the Dragon King of the Southern Sea, Ao Shun is the Dragon King of the Northern Sea, and Ao Run is the Dragon King of the Western Sea." "I'm damned if I'm going there: as the saying goes, 'Two in the pocket is better than three owing.' So be a good chap and give me one." "There is no need for you to go, lofty Immortal," the Dragon King replied, "I have an iron drum and a bronze bell. In an emergency we strike them to bring my brothers here in an instant." "In that case," said Sun Wukong, "hurry up and sound them." And indeed an alligator general struck the bell while a terrapin marshal beat the drum.

The sound of the bell and the drum startled the other three dragon kings, who had arrived and were waiting together outside within the instant. One of them, Ao Qin, said, "Elder Brother, what's up? Why the drum and the bell?" "It hurts me to tell you, brother," the Old Dragon King replied. "There's this so-called heaven-born sage from the Mountain of Flowers and Fruit who came here this morning saying that I was his neighbour, then demanded a weapon. I offered him a steel-pronged spear but he said it was too small, and a patterned halberd that he said was too light. Then he picked up the miraculous iron that fastens the Milky Way and tried a few movements with it. Now he's sitting in the palace and demanding a suit of armour, but we haven't got one. That's why I used the bell and the drum to call you here. You three must have some armour. Please give him a suit, then we can get rid of him." When Ao Qin heard this he said in a fury, "To arms, brothers. Arrest the criminal." "No! No! It's out of the question," said the Old Dragon King. "If that iron cudgel of his gets you you're done for, if it hits you you die, if it comes close your skin is broken, and if it so much as brushes against you your sinews are smashed." Ao Run, the Dragon King of the Western Sea, said, "Second brother, you must not attack him. Instead we should put a suit of armour together for him, then send him away. We can send a memorial about it to Heaven, then Heaven will of course punish him." "You're right," said Ao Shun, the Dragon King of the Northern Sea. "I have a pair of lotus-root cloud-walking shoes." "I've brought a suit of golden chain mail," said Ao Run, the Dragon King of the Western Sea. "And I have a phoenix-winged purple gold helmet," added Ao Qin, the Dragon King of the Southern Sea. The Old Dragon King was very pleased, and he brought them into the palace to meet Sun Wukong and present the equipment to him. Sun Wukong put on the golden helmet and the armour and the cloud-walking shoes, then charged out, waving his cudgel and saying to the dragons, "My apologies for disturbing you." The four Dragon Kings were most indignant, but we will not go into their discussions on the protest they sent to Heaven.

Watch the Monkey King as he parts the waters and goes straight back to the iron bridge, where the four senior apes can be seen waiting for him at the head of the monkey host. Sun

Wukong suddenly leapt out of the waves without a drop of water on him and gleaming with gold. As he came across the bridge the monkeys were so astonished that they fell to their knees and said, "How splendid you look, Your Majesty, how splendid." Sun Wukong, his face lit up with youthful vigour, climbed up to his throne, thrust his cudgel into the ground in their midst. The foolish monkeys all tried to grab this treasure, but it was as futile as a dragonfly trying to shake an iron tree: they were unable to move it in the slightest. Biting their fingers and sticking out their tongues they said, "Grandpa, it's so heavy, how can you possibly lift it?" Sun Wukong went over, lifted it with one hand, and laughed as he said to them, "Everything has its rightful owner. This little treasure has been lying in the sea treasury for goodness knows how many thousands of years, but it just happened to start shining this year. The Dragon King thought it was just a piece of ordinary iron, and said it was the miraculous treasure that holds the bed of the Milky Way in place. None of his men could move it, so he had to ask me to go and fetch it myself. It was more than twenty feet long then, and as thick as a peck-measure. When I picked it up I felt that it was too big, and it shrank till it was several times as small. I told it to get even smaller, and it did that too; then I told it to get smaller still, and it got many times smaller again. I hurried out into the light of day to look at it, and I saw that there was an inscription on it that read 'AS-YOU-WILL GOLD-BANDED CUDGEL: WEIGHT 13,500 POUNDS'. Stand aside, and I'll make it change again." Holding his treasure in his hand he said, "Shrink, shrink, shrink," and it became as small as an embroidery needle, tiny enough to be hidden in his ear. "Your Majesty," the monkeys cried out in astonishment, "bring it out and play with it again." So the Monkey King brought it out of his ear again, laid it on the palm of his hand, and said, "Grow, grow, grow." It became as thick as a peck again and twenty feet long. Now that he was really enjoying himself he bounded over the bridge and went out of the cave. Clasping his treasure he used some of his heaven and earth magic, bowed, and shouted, "Grow."

He became a hundred thousand feet tall; his head was as big as a mountain, his waist like a range of hills, his eyes flashed like lightning, his mouth seemed to be a bowl of blood, and his teeth were as swords and halberds; the cudgel in his hands reached up to the Thirty-third Heaven and down to the Eighteenth Hell. The tigers, leopards and wolves, the beasts of the mountain, and the seventy-two monster kings all kowtowed and bowed in terror, trembling so much that they went out of their minds. A moment later he reverted to his proper size, turned his treasure into an embroidery needle, hid it in his ear, and went back to the cave. The panic-stricken kings of the monsters all came to offer their congratulations.

The Monkey King named the four senior apes as his four Stalwart Generals: he named the two bare-bottomed apes Marshal Ma and Marshal Liu, and called the two gibbons General Beng and General Ba. He entrusted the stockade, questions of discipline and rewards to these four. Thus freed from cares, he mounted the clouds and rode the mists, wandering round the four seas and enjoying the thousand mountains. He practised his martial arts, visited many a hero, used his magical powers, and made a wide and distinguished circle of friends. He met with six sworn brothers of his: the Bull Demon King, the Salamander Demon King, the Roc Demon King, the Camel King, the Macaque King, and the Lion King. With him included as the Handsome Monkey King, they made seven. For days on end they talked about politics and war, passed round the goblet, strummed, sang, piped, danced, went off on days out together, and enjoyed themselves in every possible way.

CHAPTER 5
The Handsome Monkey King Is
Appointed Protector of the Horses

We now tell how one day the Supreme Heavenly Sage, the
Greatly Compassionate Jade Emperor of the Azure Vault of
Heaven, was sitting at morning court on his throne in the Hall
of Miraculous Mist in the Golden-gated Cloud Palace,
surrounded by his immortal civil and military officials, when the
Immortal Qiu Hongji reported, "Your Majesty, Ao Guang, the
Dragon King of the Eastern Sea, has presented a memorial
outside the Hall of Universal Brightness, and is awaiting a
summons from your Imperial Majesty." The Jade Emperor
ordered that he be called in, and the Dragon King came to the
Hall of Miraculous Mist. When he had done obeisance an
immortal page came from the side to take his memorial. The Jade
Emperor read it through. It was a complaint about how Sun
Wukong had bullied the Dragon King and disturbed the Dragon
Palace with his evil powers.

When the Jade Emperor had read this through he ordered,
"Let the Dragon God return to the Sea; we shall send generals
to arrest the demon." The Old Dragon King bowed till his
head touched the floor and took his leave.

His Celestial Majesty then asked all his civil and military
officials, "Which divine general shall we send to capture the
demon monkey?" And before he had finished speaking the
Great White Planet* stepped forward, bowed down, and
submitted, "I beg Your Majesty to remember your life-giving

---

* A name for the planet Venus.

mercy and hand down a sage edict of amnesty and enlistment, summoning him to this upper world and inscribing his name on the list of office-holders, thus keeping him here under control. If he obeys Your Majesty's heavenly commands, he can later be promoted; and if he disobeys, he can be arrested. This will both avoid military operations and be a way of winning over an Immortal." The Jade Emperor, delighted with the suggestion, ordered that it should be put into effect. He told the Wenqu Star Officer to compose the edict, and commanded the Great White Planet to persuade the monkey to accept the amnesty.

The Great White Planet left Heaven by the Southern Gate, and brought his propitious cloud down by the Water Curtain Cave, where he said to the little monkeys, "I am an envoy from Heaven, and I am carrying a divine edict inviting your great king to the upper world. Go and tell him at once." The little monkeys outside conveyed the message by relays into the depths of the cave: "Your Majesty, there's an old man outside carrying a document on his back. He says he's an envoy from Heaven with an invitation for you." The Handsome Monkey King was delighted. He said, "I'd been thinking of going up to Heaven to have a look round for the past couple of days, and now a heavenly envoy has come to invite me." "Ask him in at once," he shouted, hastily straightening his clothes and going out to meet the envoy. The Planet came straight in, stood facing the south, and said, "I am the Great White Planet of the west, and I have come down to earth with an Edict of Amnesty and Enlistment from the Jade Emperor to invite you to Heaven to be given office as an immortal." "I am very grateful to you, venerable Planet, for condescending to come here," replied Sun Wukong with a smile; then he told his subjects to prepare a feast to entertain the visitor. "I'm afraid I can't delay," replied the Planet, "as I am carrying a divine edict, so may I ask Your Majesty to come back with me now? We can talk at leisure after your glorious elevation." "Thank you for coming," said Sun Wukong. "I'm sorry you couldn't take some refreshments before leaving." Then he called for his four Stalwart Generals and ordered them, "Give my sons and grandsons a thorough training. When I've had a look round in Heaven, I'll take you all to live with me up there." The four Stalwart Generals accepted their orders, and the Monkey King made his cloud carry him up above the clouds.

The Great White Planet led the Handsome Monkey King to the outside of the Hall of Miraculous Mist. He went straight in to the imperial presence without waiting to be summoned, and did obeisance to the throne. Sun Wukong stood bolt upright beside him, not bothering with any court etiquette, but just concentrating on listening to the Great White Planet make his report to the Jade Emperor: "In obedience to the Divine Edict, your subject has brought the demon Immortal here." The Jade Emperor lowered his curtain and asked, "And which of you is the demon immortal?" "Me," replied Sun Wukong, only now making a slight bow. The faces of the officials went white with horror as they exclaimed, "What a savage monkey! He has the impudence to answer 'Me', and without even prostrating himself first! He must die!" In reply to this the Jade Emperor announced, "Sun Wukong is a demon immortal of the lower world who has only just obtained human form, so he is not acquainted with court procedure. We shall forgive him this time." "We thank you for your mercy," said the immortal ministers. Only then did Sun Wukong express his respect by bowing low and chanting "re-e-er" at the top of his voice. The Jade Emperor ordered his immortal civil and military officials to find a vacancy in some department for Sun Wukong. The Star Lord Wuqu stepped forward from the side and reported, "There are no vacancies in any of the palaces, halls, and departments of Heaven except for a superintendent in the Imperial Stables." "Then make him Protector of the Horses," ordered the Jade Emperor. All the ministers thanked him for his mercy, apart from Sun Wukong, who just expressed his respect with another loud "re-e-er". The Jade Emperor then told the Wood Planet to take him to the Imperial Stables.

The Wood Planet accompanied the delighted Monkey King to his post and then went back to the palace. The heavenly horses flourished in the Monkey King's care. At the sight of him they would prick up their ears and paw the ground. Thus more than a fortnight slipped by. On one morning that was a holiday all the officials of the stables held a feast both to welcome and congratulate the Protector of the Horses.

In the middle of the party the Monkey King suddenly put down his cup and asked, "What sort of office is this 'Protector of the Horses'?" "What the name suggests, that's all." "Which official grading does it carry?" "Unclassified." "What does 'unclassified' mean?" "Bottom grade," the others replied, going on to explain, "it is a very low and unimportant office, and all you can do in it is look after the horses." The Monkey King flared up on hearing this, gnashed his teeth, and said in a great rage, "How dare they treat me with such contempt? On the Mountain of Flowers and Fruit I am a king and a patriarch. How dare he trick me into coming here to feed his horses for him? It's a low job for youngsters, not for me. I won't do it, I won't. I'm going back." He pushed the table over with a crash, took his treasure out of his ear, and shook it. It became as thick as a rice bowl, and he brandished it as he charged out of the Imperial Stables to the Southern Gate of Heaven. As the celestial guards knew that his name was on the register of immortal officials they did not dare to block his path, but let him out through the gate.

He descended by cloud and was back on the Mountain of Flowers and Fruit in an instant. Seeing the four Stalwart Generals and all the kings of the monsters drilling their troops there he shouted in a shrill voice, "Children, I'm back." The monkeys all bowed to him, took him into the heart of the cave, and asked him to sit on his throne, while they prepared a banquet to welcome him back.

As they were drinking someone came in to report, "Your Majesty, there are two Single-horned Devil Kings outside who want to see you." "Ask them in," said the Monkey King, and the two formally-dressed devil kings hurried into the cave and prostrated themselves. "Why have you come to see me?" asked the Handsome Monkey King, and they replied, "We have long heard that Your Majesty is looking for men of talent, but we were unable to see you before. Now that Your Majesty has been given heavenly office and come back in triumph, we would like to offer you this yellow robe as a token of our congratulations. We also hope that you will not reject us although we are low and worthless, but will accept our humble services." An exultant Monkey King put on the yellow robe and his happy subjects bowed to him in order of precedence. The two devil kings were appointed Commanders of the Van, and when they had thanked the Monkey King for this they asked, "What office did Your Majesty hold while you were all that time in Heaven?" "The Jade Emperor has no respect for talent," replied the Monkey King. "He made me something called 'Protector of the Horses'." "Your Majesty has such miraculous powers: you should never have been feeding his horses for him. You should have been made a 'Great Sage Equalling Heaven', shouldn't you?" The Monkey King was beside himself with delight at this suggestion, and he kept saying how splendid it was. "Get me a banner made at once with the words 'Great Sage Equalling Heaven' in big letters on it, and put up a pole to hang it from," he ordered his four Stalwart Generals. "From now on I am to be called 'Great Sage Equalling Heaven', not 'Your Majesty' or 'King'. Pass this order on to all the other kings of the monsters."

CHAPTER 6
The Monkey King Fights with the Heavenly Generals and Becomes the Great Sage Equalling Heaven

When the Jade Emperor held his morning court the next day the Heavenly Teacher Zhang led the deputy and assistant superintendents of the Imperial Stables to the vermilion steps, bowed low, and reported, "Your Majesty, Sun Wukong, the new Protector of the Horses, left Heaven yesterday because he thought his office was too humble." Just as he was speaking the Heavenly King Virudhaka came from the Southern Gate of Heaven with his heavenly soldiers and reported, "The Protector of the Horses has gone out through the gate. We do not know why." On hearing this the Jade Emperor commanded, "Let the two divine officials return to their posts; we shall send heavenly soldiers to capture this devil." The Pagoda-bearing Heavenly King Li Jing and Prince Nezha stepped forward from the ranks of those attending the audience, and they memorialized, "Your Imperial Majesty, we beg you to command us, your incompetent servants, to subdue this fiend." The Emperor was delighted with this suggestion, and he appointed the Pagoda-bearing Heavenly King as Demon-quelling High Marshal, and Prince Nezha as God of the Three Mass Altars. He told them to take their forces down to the lower world at once.

Heavenly King Li and Nezha kowtowed, took their leave, went straight back to their own palace, and assembled their troops, commanders and officers. They put the Mighty Miracle

God in charge of the vanguard, and General Fishbelly in command of the rear, while General Yaksa was made adjutant. Within an instant they were outside the Southern Gate of Heaven, and they went straight to the Mountain of Flowers and Fruit. They chose a piece of level and open ground on which to construct a fortified camp, and ordered the Mighty Miracle God to issue the challenge to battle. On receiving this order the Mighty Miracle God tied on his armour firmly and went to the Water Curtain Cave, holding his flower-spreading battle-axe. When he got there he saw huge numbers of devils — wolves, tigers and leopards — wielding spears, brandishing swords, leaping around, fighting each other, and making a great noise outside the little entrance to the cave. "Accursed beasts," shouted the Mighty Miracle God, "tell the Protector of the Horses at once that I am a heavenly general come on the orders of the Jade Emperor to subdue him. If you make him come out and surrender immediately it will save the lot of you from being wiped out." The devils went rushing into the cave and reported, "Disaster, disaster." "What disaster?" the Monkey King asked. "There's a heavenly general outside who says he's come on the orders of the Jade Emperor to subdue you. If you go out and surrender immediately, he says he'll spare our lives." "Fetch me my armour," said the Monkey King. He then donned his golden helmet, tied on his golden armour, put on his cloud-walking shoes, and took his as-you-will gold-banded cudgel in his hand. He led his troops out of the cave and drew them up in battle array.

The Mighty Miracle God shouted in a harsh voice, "Insolent ape! Don't you recognize me?" The Great Sage Sun Wukong replied at once, "I've never met you before. How should I know which wretched little deity you are? Tell me your name at once." "I'll get you, you conceited baboon. So you don't know who I am? I am the Heavenly General Mighty Miracle, the commander of the vanguard for Heavenly King Li, the Pagoda-bearer. I have come here on the orders of the Jade Emperor to accept your surrender." "Stop talking so big, you lousy god," retorted the furious Monkey King, "and give that long tongue of yours a rest. Take a look at what's written on my standard." When the Mighty Miracle God heard this he looked hard and saw that a tall pole had been planted outside the entrance to the cave, on which hung a banner reading GREAT SAGE EQUALLING HEAVEN. "Heh, heh, heh," he mocked, "you ignorant ape. What shameless effrontery, to want to be a 'Great Sage Equalling Heaven'! Take that!" He swung with his battle-axe at the Monkey King who, quite unflustered, parried with his gold-banded cudgel.

The Mighty Miracle God was no match for his opponent. He hastened to block the Monkey King's first blow with his axe, which broke in two with a crunch. He fled for his life as fast as he could.

The Mighty Miracle God returned to his camp, went straight to the Pagoda-bearing Heavenly King Li Jing and told him about the fight. Prince Nezha, who was standing to one side, stepped forward, bowed, and said, "Do not be angry, Your Majesty. Let me go and do battle; then we'll see who's boss." When he had put on his armour and helmet, Prince Nezha charged straight out of the camp to the Water Curtain Cave. Sun Wukong, who was just going to pull back his troops, saw the ferocity of his onslaught.

Sun Wukong went up to him and asked, "Whose little boy are you then? What do you mean, charging up to my door?" "Stinking monkey fiend," shouted Prince Nezha, "don't you know who I am? I am Nezha, the third son of the Pagoda-bearing Heavenly King, and I have been commanded by the Jade Emperor to come here and arrest you." "You do talk big, don't you, little prince," said Sun Wukong, laughing at him. "But as you've still got all your milk teeth and are still wet behind the ears I'll spare your life and I won't hit you. Do you see what it says on my standard? Go and tell the Jade Emperor that if he gives me that title I'll call off my armies and submit to him once more. But if he doesn't do what I want him to, I'll surely attack the Hall of Miraculous Mist." Nezha looked up and saw the words "Great Sage Equalling Heaven". "You wicked monkey! How dare you give yourself a title like that, whatever your magic powers may be! Don't worry, all you're getting is my sword." "I'll take a few swipes, then," replied Sun Wukong, "I won't move." "Change," yelled Nezha in a passion, and at once he had three heads and six arms, which made him look most ferocious. In his hands he held six weapons, a demon-beheading sword, a demon-hacking cutlass, a demon-binding rope, a demon-quelling pestle, an embroidered ball, and a fire-wheel — and wielding all these he rushed straight at Sun Wukong. At the sight of him Sun Wukong exclaimed with astonishment, "Well, my boy, you certainly know a trick or two. But just behave yourself and watch what I can do." Our dear Great Sage shouted "Change", and he too had three heads and six arms. He shook his gold-banded cudgel, and it turned into three cudgels, which he gripped with his six hands to ward off Nezha's blows. It was a great fight, and it made the earth shake and the mountains tremble.

Prince Nezha and Sun Wukong both used their divine powers to the full as they fought thirty rounds. When the six weapons of the Prince turned into thousands and tens of thousands, so did Sun Wukong's gold-banded cudgel. The air was filled as if with drops of rain or shooting stars, and there was no way of telling who was winning. As Sun Wukong was deft of hand and quick of eye, he plucked one of the hairs from his body in the midst of the fray and shouted "Change!" It changed into his own double to mislead Nezha while his real self leapt round till he was behind Nezha and struck at his left shoulder. Nezha was in the middle of performing a spell when he heard the whistle of the cudgel through the air and twisted away as fast as he could. But he was unable to avoid the blow and had to flee wounded. He brought his magic to an end, put his six weapons away, reverted to his true appearance, and abandoned the field of battle in defeat. The prince, in pain and unable to go on fighting, went back to Heaven with the Heavenly King.

Heavenly King Li and Prince Nezha led their forces straight to the Palace of Miraculous Mist and made this request: "We, your subjects, took our forces down to the lower world, under your Divine Edict, to subdue the immortal fiend Sun Wukong. But to our surprise we found that his magical powers were too far-reaching for us to be able to defeat him. We therefore hope that Your Imperial Majesty will send more troops to exterminate him." "How could a mere monkey goblin have such great powers that you actually need more troops?" asked the Jade Emperor. Prince Nezha then came forward and memorialized, "We beg Your Majesty to spare us the deaths we deserve. That monkey fiend has an iron cudgel that he used to defeat the Mighty Miracle God and wounded me on the shoulder. He has set a banner up outside the entrance to his cave that reads 'Great Sage Equalling Heaven', and he says that if you give him this office he will stop fighting and submit; otherwise he will attack the Hall of Miraculous Mist." When the Jade Emperor heard this he asked in horror, "How dare that monkey fiend talk so wildly? Send all the generals to execute him at once."

As he spoke the Great White Planet stepped forward from the ranks of officials. "That monkey fiend knows how to talk," he suggested, "but he has no idea about real power. If more soldiers were sent to fight him, they might not be able to over-come him at once and their energies would be wasted. But if Your Imperial Majesty were to show your great mercy, you could send down a pacificatory amnesty and let him be a Great Sage Equalling Heaven. It would only be an empty title that he was given, just an honorary appointment." "What do you mean by an honorary appointment?" asked the Jade Emperor. "He would be called a Great Sage Equalling Heaven, but he would not be given any responsibility or paid any salary. He would be kept between Heaven and Earth, where his evil nature would be under control and he would be kept from wickedness. Thus Heaven and Earth can be at peace, while sea and sky en-joy tranquility." The Jade Emperor approved this suggestion and ordered that a new edict should be issued for the Great White Planet to deliver.

The Great White Planet left once more through the Southern Gate of Heaven and went straight to the Water Curtain Cave on the Mountain of Flowers and Fruit. The underlings of Sun Wukong rushed in to report, "There's an old man outside who says he's come from Heaven with an edict of invitation for you." Then the Great Sage, wearing his helmet, his yellow robe over his armour, and his cloud-walking shoes, hurried out of the cave at the head of his monkey host, bowed in greeting, and shouted in a loud voice, "Please come in, venerable Planet. Forgive me for not being here to welcome you."

The Planet walked straight into the cave, stood facing the south and said, "Great Sage, when you left the Imperial Stables because you found the post too humble, the officials of that department naturally reported the matter to the Jade Emperor. The Jade Emperor decreed that all officials have to work their way up from the bottom, and asked why you objected to its being humble. After this Heavenly King Li took Nezha down to the lower world to do battle with you. Your divine powers, Great Sage, were more than they expected, and they suffered defeat. On their return to Heaven they reported that you had set up a banner and wanted to be a 'Great Sage Equalling Heaven'. All the generals wanted to punish you; but I, Great Sage, ran the risk of punishment by suggesting that the armies should not be called out, and that Your Majesty should be given a post instead. The Jade Emperor approved my memorial, and that is why I have come here to invite you." "I am most grateful for this honour after the trouble I caused you earlier," replied Sun Wukong, "but I am not sure whether there is such a title as 'Great Sage Equalling Heaven' in the upper world." "After obtaining imperial approval for this title," said the Planet, "I came down bearing a decree. If anything goes wrong, I'll bear the responsibility."

A highly delighted Sun Wukong tried his hardest to persuade the Planet to stay to a banquet, but without success, so he went with him by propitious cloud to the Southern Gate of Heaven. The heavenly generals and soldiers all greeted them with respectfully folded arms, and they went straight to the Hall of Miraculous Mist. The Great White Planet did obeisance and said, "In obedience to the imperial edict your subject has summoned Sun Wukong, the Protector of the Horses, and he is present." "Let Sun Wukong come forward," said the Jade Emperor. "We do now proclaim you Great Sage Equalling Heaven. Your rank is now very high. Let there be no more mischief from you." The monkey simply chanted "re-e-er" to express his thanks to the Emperor. The Jade Emperor then ordered the two officials in charge of public works, Zhang and Lu, to build a residence for the Great Sage Equalling Heaven to the left of the Peach Orchard. In the residence there were to be two offices: a Tranquillity Office and a Calm Divinity Office. Both these offices were to have immortal clerks and senior and junior assistants. He then told the Star Lords of the Constellation Five to escort Sun Wukong to his post, and in addition gave him two bottles of imperial wine and ten golden flowers, and admonished him to settle down and keep out of mischief. The Monkey King accepted the order and went that same day with the Star Lords of the Constellation Five to his residence, where he opened the bottles of wine and drained them dry with the help of all present. He then saw the star officials off and returned to his own palace. From then on he lived in happiness and content, and enjoyed untrammelled pleasure in the Palace.

CHAPTER 7
The Great Sage Steals the Peaches and Makes Havoc in Heaven

When the Jade Emperor was holding his morning court one day the Immortal Xu of Jingyang came forward from the body of officials, kowtowed, and suggested, "The Great Sage Equalling Heaven is spending his time in idle travel, and is making the acquaintance of all the stars in the sky, calling them all his friends irrespective of their rank. It would be as well to give him some responsibility, and prevent his idleness leading to trouble later on." The Jade Emperor's response to this suggestion was to send for the Monkey King at once. He came in a cheerful mood and asked, "What promotion and reward have you summoned me here to receive, Your Majesty?" "Seeing that you are idle and have nothing to do," replied the Jade Emperor, "we are giving you a job. You are to administer the Peach Orchard, and you will give it your attention day and night." The Great Sage was overjoyed, and after expressing his thanks he withdrew.

In his eagerness to be at work he went straight to the Peach Orchard to have a look round. When he got there he was stopped by a local tutelary god who asked him, "Where are you going, Great Sage?" "I've been put in charge of the Peach Orchard by the Jade Emperor, and I've come to inspect it." The local god hastened to greet him formally, and he called the men who weeded, brought water, looked after the trees, and swept the grounds to come and kowtow to the Great Sage.

亂蟠桃大聖偷丹

Monkey Steals Elixir at the Peach Banquet

After taking a good look at the Orchard the Great Sage asked the local god, "How many of these trees are there?" "Three thousand six hundred all together," the local god replied. "The ones growing at the front have tiny blossoms and small fruits, and they ripen every three thousand years. Anyone who eats them becomes an immortal and understands the Way, and his body becomes both light and strong. The twelve hundred in the middle have multiple blossoms and sweet fruits, and ripen every six thousand years; whoever eats them can fly and enjoy eternal youth. The back twelve hundred are streaked with purple and have pale yellow stones. They ripen once every nine thousand years, and anyone who eats them becomes as eternal as Heaven and Earth, as long-lived as the Sun and Moon." The Great Sage was beside himself with joy on learning this, and that day he checked the number of the trees and looked over the buildings in the orchard before going back to his residence. From then on he went to admire them every three or four days. He dropped his friends, and made no more pleasure jaunts.

One day he noticed that the peaches near the end of the branches of one old tree were all but ripe, and he felt like trying one; but as the local god, the workmen, and the immortal clerks from his residence were close on his heels it was impossible. Suddenly he had an idea, and he said, "Go and wait for me outside the gates while I take a nap in this summerhouse." All the immortals thereupon withdrew, and the Monkey King took off his official hat and clothes, climbed one of the bigger trees, and chose some large, ripe peaches. When he had picked a good number he sat at his ease in the branches and ate his fill of them, then jumped down from the tree, pinned on his hat, put on his clothes, and shouted for all his attendants to go back to his residence with him. Two or three days later he thought of another trick to steal some more peaches, and he ate his fill of them.

One day the Queen Mother arranged a banquet, opening many precious pavilions for a peach banquet by the Jade Pool. She sent the Red Fairy, the Blue Fairy, the White Fairy, the

Black Fairy, the Purple Fairy, the Yellow Fairy, and the Green Fairy to the Peach Orchard with their baskets to pick peaches for the feast. The fairies first filled two baskets from the trees in front, and then they picked three basketfuls from the trees in the middle; but when they came to the trees at the back, they saw that peaches and blossoms were few and far between. Only a few unripe fruits with furry stalks and green skins were left. All the ripe ones had been eaten up by the Monkey King. The seven fairies looked everywhere, but all they could see was a single red and white peach on a southern branch. The Blue Fairy pulled the branch down, the Red Fairy picked the peach, and then they let the branch go again. This woke up the Great Sage, who had changed himself into this peach to take a nap on this branch. He resumed his own form, took his gold-banded cudgel from his ear, shook it till it was as thick as a ricebowl, and shouted at them, "Where are you from, you thieving fiends?" The seven fairies fell on their knees in confusion. "Please don't be angry with us, Great Sage. We're not fiends but seven fairies sent by Her Majesty the Queen Mother of the West to pick peaches of immortality and open the precious halls here for a peach banquet." These words turned the Great Sage's bad mood into a good one, and he said, "Please rise, Fairy Beauties." "Will I be invited?" asked the Great Sage with an ingratiating smile. "Not as far as we've heard," the fairies replied. "I'm the Great Sage Equalling Heaven, so why shouldn't I be an honoured guest?" said the Great Sage. "That was what happened before: we don't know about this time," the fairies replied. "You're right," he said. "Just wait here while I go and find out whether I'm invited."

Splendid Great Sage. Making a magic with his hands as he spoke the words of the spell, he said to the fairies, "Stay where you are! Stay where you are!" As this was an immobilizing spell, the seven fairies were left standing in a daze under the peach tree with their eyes wide open as the Great Sage leapt out of the orchard on a somersault cloud and headed for the Jade Pool. On his way he saw the Barefoot Immortal coming towards him. The Great Sage lowered his head and thought of a plan by which to trick the immortal and get to the banquet himself. "Where are you going, reverend sir?" he asked; and the immortal replied, "I'm going to the Peach Banquet by the invitation of the Queen Mother." "There is something you do not know, venerable sir," said the Great Sage. "As my somersault cloud is so fast, the Jade Emperor has sent me everywhere to tell all you gentlemen to go to the Hall of Universal Brightness for a ceremony before going on the banquet." As the immortal was an open and upright man, he took this lie for the truth, but wondered, "The thanksgiving ceremony is usually held by the Jade Pool, so why are we having the ceremony in the Hall of Universal Brightness before going to the Jade Pool for the banquet?" Nevertheless, he turned his propitious cloud around and went to the Hall of Universal Brightness.

As the Great Sage rode his cloud he said a spell, shook himself, took the form of the Barefoot Immortal, and hurried to the Jade Pool. He reached the pavilion there a moment later, stopped his cloud, and went quietly inside.

Everything was neatly set out, but no Immortals had yet arrived. The Great Sage had not finished looking when he smelt wine; and as he whirled round he saw under a portico to the right several immortal officials in charge of brewing liquor with some workmen who stirred the lees, a number of novices who carried water and some boys who looked after the fires. They were washing the vats and scrubbing the pots, having made jade liquor and a fragrant fermentation of the lees. The Great Sage could not stop himself from drooling, and he longed to drink some, but unfortunately all those people were there. So he performed a spell by pulling several hairs from his body, chewing them up, spitting them up, saying the magic words, and shouting "Change"; whereupon the hairs turned into sleep insects, which flew into the faces of all the liquor-makers. Watch them as their hands go limp, their heads droop, their eyes close, and they drop their activities and all fall asleep. Whereupon the Great Sage grabbed the rare delicacies and exotic foods, then went under the portico and drank from the vats and pots until he was completely drunk. Only then did he think, "This won't do at all. When the guests come for the banquet they'll be furious with me, and I'll be for it if I'm caught. I'd better get back to the Residence as soon as I can and sleep it off."

Our dear Great Sage staggered and swayed, charging about all over the place under the influence of the liquor, and going the wrong way. He arrived not at the Equalling Heaven Residence but at the Tushita Heavenly Palace. As soon as he saw this he sobered up and said to himself, "The Tushita Palace is the highest of the thirty-three heavens, where Lord Lao Zi of the Great Monad reigns. However did I get here? Never mind, I've always wanted to see that old chap, and I've never managed to come here before. I might as well go and have a look at him now that I'm passing this way." He straightened his clothes and rushed in, but did not see Lord Lao Zi. There was no sign of anyone. This was because Lao Zi and the Ancient Buddha Dipamkara were expounding the Way from a red dais in a triple-storeyed pavilion, and all the immortal boys, generals, officials and petty functionaries were standing to right and left listening to the lecture. The Great Sage went straight to the room in which the elixir was kept, and although he could not find Lao Zi there he saw that there was a small fire in the stove beside the range over which pills were made. Around the stove were five gourds, full of golden pills of refined elixir. "This is the immortals' greatest treasure," he exclaimed in delight. "I've wanted to refine some of these golden pills to save people with ever since I understood the Way and mastered the principle of the correspondence of the Esoteric and Exoteric, but I've never had time to come here. Today I'm in luck — I've found them. As Lao Zi isn't here I'll try a few." He emptied the gourds of their contents and ate up all the pills as if he were eating fried beans.

Before long he was full of pills and quite sober. "This is terrible," he thought, "this is a frightful disaster. If the Jade Emperor is shocked by this, I'm done for. I must get out of here. I'd be much better off as a king in the lower world." He rushed out of the Tushita Palace, avoiding his usual route.

Using a spell to make himself invisible, he left by the West Gate of Heaven, and went straight down to the Mountain of Flowers and Fruit by cloud.

The story returns to the seven fairies, who were only able to free themselves a whole day after Sun Wukong had immobilized them with his magic. They picked up their baskets and went back to report to the Queen Mother about what the Great Sage Equalling Heaven had done to them.

On hearing this the Queen Mother went to see the Jade Emperor and gave him a full account of what had happened. Before she had finished, the liquor-makers arrived with their immortal officials to report that an unknown person had thrown the Grand Peach Banquet into confusion. The Jade Emperor was filled with anger and astonishment. "The Miraculous Investigator is to find out at once what the wretch has been up to," he commanded.

The Miraculous Investigator left the palace in obedience to the edict, and by making thorough enquiries he found out all the details of what had happened. "The wrecker of the Heavenly Palace was Sun Wukong," he reported, and he went on to give a full account. The Jade Emperor was furiously angry, and he ordered the Four Great Heavenly Kings along with Heavenly King Li and Prince Nezha to mobilize a hundred thousand heavenly soldiers. They were to surround the Mountain of Flowers and Fruit, and capture the wretch Great Sage for punishment.

CHAPTER 8
The Handsome Monkey King Battles with the Gods

The gods called out their troops at once, and left the heavenly palace. They threw a watertight cordon round the Mountain of Flowers and Fruit. The Nine Bright Shiners were sent out to start the battle. They took their soldiers to the outside of the cave, where they saw the monkeys, big and small, leaping and fooling around. The star officers shouted in harsh voices, "Little goblins, where's that Great Sage of yours? We are gods sent from the upper world to subdue your mutinous Great Sage. Tell him to surrender at once — and if there's so much as a hint of a 'no' from him, we will exterminate every last one of you." The little monkeys went rushing in to report, "Great Sage, a disaster, a disaster. There are nine evil gods outside who say they've been sent from the upper world to subdue you."

The Great Sage, who was just then sharing the immortal liquor with the seventy-two kings of the monsters and his four Stalwart Generals, exploded after hearing the report: "The stinking gods! What bloody cheek! I never wanted a fight with them, so why should they come here to push us around?" He thereupon ordered the One-horned Monster King to lead the seventy-two monster kings into battle while he followed them with the four Stalwart Generals. The monster king hastily assembled the devil soldiers and sallied forth to meet the enemy. They were all stopped by a charge by the Nine Bright Shiners, who held the head of the iron bridge so that no one could enter to leave.

During the tumult the Great Sage came on the scene, and shouting "Make way" he raised his iron cudgel, shook it till it was as thick as a bowl and twelve feet long, and struck and parried as he came charging out. He whirled his gold-banded cudgel, parrying to right and left, and fought the Nine Bright Shiners till their muscles were weak and their strength was gone; then each of them broke ranks and fled, dragging their weapons behind them. They rushed to the command post of the central corps and reported to the Pagoda-Bearing Heavenly King Li that the Monkey King was so ferocious that they had fled from the battlefield, unable to defeat him. Heavenly King Li then sent the Four Heavenly Kings and the Twenty-eight Constellations into battle. The Great Sage, not at all frightened at this, ordered the One-horned Demon King, the seventy-two kings of the monsters, and the four Stalwart Generals to draw up their line of battle outside the gates of the cave.

The battle started in the morning and went on till the sun set behind the mountains in the west. By then the One-horned Demon King and the seventy-two kings of the monsters had all been captured by the heavenly hosts. Only the four Stalwart Generals and the monkeys had got away, and they were now hiding in the innermost recesses of the Water Curtain Cave. The Great Sage's solitary cudgel had fought off the Four Heavenly Kings, Li the Pagoda-bearer and Prince Nezha, who were all in the sky. After the battle had gone on for a long time the Great Sage saw that night was drawing on, so he plucked out a pinch of his hairs, munched it up, spat out the pieces and shouted, "Change!" They changed into thousands of Great Sages, all with gold-banded cudgels, who forced Prince Nezha and the five Heavenly Kings to withdraw.

The Four Heavenly Kings also withdrew their troops, thus ending the day's battle. They ordered the heavenly soldiers to surround the Mountain of Flowers and Fruit, ready for a great battle the next day.

We shall leave for the moment the Heavenly Generals making their encirclement and the soundly sleeping Great Sage. The story goes on to tell how the Compassionate and Merciful Miraculous Saviour from Suffering, the Bodhisattva Guanyin of Mount Potaraka in the Southern Sea, having been invited by the Queen Mother to the Peach Banquet, went to the precious pavilions at the Jade Pool with her great disciple Huian the Novice. She found the place deserted and the banquet ruined. The few immortals present were not sitting at their places but talking with great agitation. When greetings were over the immortals gave the Bodhisattva an account of what had happened. "If there is to be no banquet and no drinking," said the Bodhisattva, "you had better all come with me to the Jade Emperor." The Immortals were delighted to follow her, and when they arrived before the Hall of Universal Brightness the Four Heavenly Teachers, the Barefoot Immortal and many others were all there to greet the Bodhisattva.

The Bodhisattva went in at the head of the others, and when she had done obeisance to the Jade Emperor she greeted Lao Zi and the Queen Mother. After they had all sat down she asked what had happened at the Peach Banquet. "The banquet is held every year, and it is normally a very happy occasion," the Jade Emperor replied, "but this year that monkey fiend wrecked it, so that your invitation was worth nothing." "Where does this monkey fiend come from?" asked the Bodhisattva. The Jade Emperor told her all about him.

Guanyin put her hands together and said, "Do not worry, Your Majesty. I can recommend a god to capture this monkey." "Which god?" the Jade Emperor asked, and the Bodhisattva replied, "Your Majesty's nephew, the Illustrious Sage and True Lord Erlang, who is now living at Guanjiangkou in Guanzhou, enjoying the incense that the lower beings burn to him. In the past he exterminated the Six Bogies. He has the Brothers of Plum Hill and the twelve hundred straw-headed gods, and his magical powers are enormous. He will agree to be sent though he would not obey a summons to come here, so Your Majesty might like to issue a decree ordering him to take his troops to the rescue." The Jade Emperor then issued such a decree and sent the Strongarm Devil King to deliver it.

The devil king took the decree, mounted his cloud, and went straight to Guanjiangkou. He reached the temple of the True Lord within an hour.

The True Lord Erlang called the six sworn brothers of Plum Hill — Marshals Kang, Zhang, Yao, and Li, and Generals Guo Shen and Zhi Jian — together before the hall. "The Jade Emperor has just ordered us to the Mountain of Flowers and Fruit to subdue a monkey fiend," he said. "You are all coming with me." The brothers were all eager to go, and mustering their divine troops they unleashed a gale wind. In an instant they had crossed the Eastern Ocean, commanding eagles and dogs, pulling their bows and drawing their crossbows, and had reached the Mountain of Flowers and Fruit. The Four Heavenly Kings and Heavenly King Li all came to welcome him outside the headquarters. When the introductions were over he asked how the fighting had gone, and the Heavenly Kings gave him a full account of what had happened.

The True Lord Erlang went out at the head of the four marshals and the two generals — making seven sworn brothers with himself included — to challenge the enemy to battle; and he ordered his other officers to defend the camp firmly and keep the eagles and dogs under control. All the straw-headed gods acknowledged the order. Erlang then went to the outside of the Water Curtain Cave, where he saw the monkey hordes neatly drawn up in a coiled-dragon battle line. When the junior monkeys at the gate of their camp saw the True Lord Erlang they rushed back to report, whereupon the Monkey King took his gold-banded cudgel, and leapt out through the gates of the camp. He saw at first sight how cool and remarkable Erlang looked, and how elegantly he was dressed.

When the Great Sage saw him he laughed with delight, raised his gold-banded cudgel, and shouted, "Where are you from, little general, that you have the audacity to challenge me?" When the True Lord Erlang heard this he burst out angrily, "Damned monkey! Where are your manners? Try this blade of mine!" The Great Sage dodged the blow and instantly raised his gold-banded club to hit back.

After Erlang and the Great Sage had fought over three hundred rounds the outcome of the fight was still undecided. The Great Sage was suddenly appalled to notice that the monkey fiends in his camp had scattered in terror. He broke away and fled, his cudgel in his hand. Seeing him go, the True Lord Erlang hurried after him with long strides. "Where are you going?" he asked. "If you surrender at once, your life will be spared." The Great Sage, who had no heart left for the fight, was running as fast as he could.

The Great Sage arrived at Guanjiangkou, changed himself into the likeness of the god Erlang with a shake of his body, put away his cloud, and went into Lord Erlang's temple. The demon judges did not realize who he really was, so they all kowtowed to welcome him. He took his seat in the middle of the temple, and inspected the offerings. As he was looking round it was announced that another Lord Erlang had arrived. All the demon judges hurried to look, and they were all astonished. The True Lord Erlang asked, "Has a so-called Great Sage Equalling Heaven been here?" "We haven't seen any Great Sages," they replied, "only another god who's looking around inside." The True Lord rushed in through the gates, and as soon as the Great Sage saw him he reverted to his own appearance and said, "There's no point in shouting, sir. This temple's mine now." The True Lord raised his double-bladed trident and swung at the Monkey King's head, but the Monkey King dodged the blow by magic, took his embroidery needle, shook it till it was as thick as a bowl, and rushed forward to meet the attack. Shouting and yelling, they fought their way out through the gates, and went on fighting through the mists and clouds all the way back to the Mountain of Flowers and Fruit. The Four Heavenly Kings and all their soldiers were so alarmed that they kept an even tighter guard. Marshals Kang and Zhang and the others came to meet the True Lord, and combined their efforts to surround the Handsome Monkey King.

After the Strongarm Demon King had sent the True Lord Erlang and his six sworn brothers with their troops to capture the fiend, he had gone back to Heaven to report. He found the

Jade Emperor, the Bodhisattva Guanyin, the Queen Mother and all his immortal ministers in conference. "Although Erlang has joined the fight, we have had no reports on it all day," the Jade Emperor said. Guanyin put her hands together and replied, "May I suggest that Your Majesty go out through the Southern Gate of Heaven with Lord Lao Zi to see for youself what is happening." "A good idea," said the Emperor, and he went by chariot with Lao Zi, the Queen Mother, and all the immortal ministers to the Southern Gate of Heaven. The Bodhisattva addressed Lao Zi and asked, "What do you think of the god Erlang I recommended? He really does have divine powers. He's just got that Great Sage cornered, and all he has to do now is to catch him." Lao Zi said, "Just wait while I give him a little help." He pulled up his sleeve and took a bracelet off his right arm. "This weapon," he said, "is made of tempered steel to which I have added the magic elixir. It preserves my miraculous essence, can transform itself, is proof against fire and water, and can snare anything. One of its names is Diamond Jade and the other is Diamond Noose. When I went out through the Han Pass some years ago to turn into a foreigner and become a Buddha, I had a great deal to thank it for. It's the best protection at any time. Just watch while I throw it down and hit him."

As soon as he had finished speaking he threw it down from outside the heavenly gate, and it fell into the camp on the Mountain of Flowers and Fruit, hitting the Monkey King neatly on the head. The Monkey King was too preoccupied with fighting the seven sages to notice this weapon falling on him from heaven, and when it struck him on the forehead he lost his balance and stumbled, then picked himself up and started to run. The slim dog of the god Erlang caught him up and bit him in the calf, bringing him down again. He rolled over and tried unsuccessfully to get up, but the seven sages all held him down, roped him up, and put a sickle-shaped blade round his collarbone to prevent him from making any more transformations.

Lord Lao Zi then recovered his Diamond Jade and invited the Jade Emperor, Guanyin, the Queen Mother, and all the immortal ministers to return to the Hall of Miraculous Mist. Down below, Heavenly King Li and the four other Heavenly Kings assembled their troops and pulled up the stockade.

CHAPTER 9
Further Havoc in the Heaven Ends in Capture by Lord Buddha

The story goes on to tell how the Great Sage Equalling Heaven was escorted by the hosts of heavenly soldiers to the Demon-beheading Platform and tied to the Demon-subduing Pillar. They hacked at him with sabres, sliced at him with axes, lunged at him with spears and cut at him with swords, but they were unable to inflict a single wound on him. The Southern Dipper angrily ordered all the gods of the Department of Fire to set him alight and burn him up, but he would not ignite. He told the gods of the Department of Thunder to nail splinters of thunder into him, but however hard they tried they could not harm a hair of his body. The Strongarm Demon King and the rest of them then reported this to the throne. "Your Majesty," they said, "this Great Sage has learnt somewhere or other how to protect himself by magic. Although your subjects have hacked at him with sabres, sliced at him with axes, struck at him with thunder and tried to burn him with fire, we have not been able to harm a hair of his body. What are we to do?" "How can we deal with a wretch like this?" the Jade Emperor asked, and the Lord Lao Zi replied to this in a memorial: "That monkey has eaten the peaches of immortality, drunk the imperial liquor, and stolen the pills of elixir. He swallowed those five gourds of pills of mine, fresh ones and mature ones alike, which he tempered with the fire of samadhi into one lump and made his body a diamond one that cannot be harmed.

八卦爐中逃大聖

Escape from the Eight Trigrams Furnace

The best course would be to let me take him and put him in my Eight Trigrams Furnace, where I can refine out my elixir with slow fire and high heat and reduce him to ashes at the same time." The Jade Emperor then ordered the heavenly soldiers to untie him and hand him over to the Lord Lao Zi, who took him away in obedience to the imperial decree.

When he reached the Tushita Palace, Lord Lao Zi had the Great Sage untied, took the hook from his collar-bone, pushed him into the Eight Trigrams Furnace, and ordered the priests in charge of it and the fire-boys to fan the fire up to refine him.

Time soon passed, and without him realizing it the seven times seven, or forty-nine, days had passed, and Lord Lao Zi's fire had reached the required temperature and burned for long enough. One day the furnace was opened for the elixir to be taken out. The Great Sage, who was shielding his eyes with both hands and wiping away his tears, heard a noise at the top of the furnace. He looked hard and saw daylight; and, unable to stand being in there a moment longer, leapt out of the furnace, kicked it over with a crash, and was off. In the ensuing chaos the fire-boys, the keepers of the furnace and the heavenly soldiers all tried to grab him, but he knocked them all down. Lord Lao Zi rushed up to seize him, but was thrown head over heels as the Great Sage freed himself. He took the as-you-will cudgel from his ear, and shook it in the wind till it was thick as a bowl, and once more created total chaos in the Palace of Heaven, not caring in the least what he did. He laid about him to such effect that the Nine Bright Shiners shut their windows and doors, and not a sign was to be seen of the Four Heavenly Kings.

The Monkey King fought his way into the Hall of Universal Brightness outside the Hall of Miraculous Mist, where the Kingly Spirit Officer, the lieutenant of the Helpful Sage and True Lord, was on duty. When he saw the Great Sage charging around he took up his golden flail and went forward to resist him. "Where are you going, damned monkey?" he asked. "If you go wild you'll have me to deal with." The Great Sage was not in a position to argue with him, so he raised his cudgel to strike him. The Spirit Officer lifted his flail and advanced to meet him.

As they fought together without either of them emerging as victor, the True Lord sent an officer with a message to the Thunder Palace ordering the thirty-six thunder generals to surround the Great Sage. Although they all fought with the utmost ferocity, the Great Sage was not in the least frightened, he shook his as-you-will cudgel and changed it into three cudgels, and wielding the three cudgels in his six hands he flew round and round inside the encirclement like a spinning wheel. None of the thunder generals could get anywhere near him.

Although the gods had the Great Sage cornered, they were unable to get near him. The noise of the shouting and the fighting had already alarmed the Jade Emperor, who ordered the Miracle Official Youyi to go to the West with the Helpful Sage and True Lord and ask the Buddha to subdue him.

When these two sages received the order they went to the wonderful land of the Vulture Peak where they offered their greetings to the Four Vajrapanis and Eight Bodhisattvas before the Thunder Monastery and asked them to pass on their message. The gods went to the foot of the lotus seat to inform the Tathagata, who invited the two sages to his presence. When the sages had performed the threefold obeisance to the Buddha they stood in attendance below the throne. "Why has the Jade Emperor troubled you two sages to come here?" asked the Buddha. The Sages reported in detail on what had happened and said, "The Jade Emperor makes a special appeal to you, Tathagata, to save his throne." On hearing this the Tathagata said to the assembled Bodhisattvas, "You stay here quietly in this dharma hall and behave yourselves in your seats of meditation while I go to deal with the demon and save the throne."

Telling the Venerable Ananda and the Venerable Kasyapa to accompany him, the Tathagata left the Thunder Monastery and went straight to the gate of the Hall of Miraculous Mist, where his ears were shaken by the sound of shouting as the thirty-six thunder generals surrounded the Great Sage. The

Buddha issued a decree that ran: "Tell the thunder generals to stop fighting, open up their camp, and call on that Great Sage to come out, so that I may ask him what divine powers he has." The generals then withdrew, whereupon the Great Sage put away his magic appearance and came forward in his own body. He was in a raging temper as he asked, "Where are you from, man of religion? You've got a nerve, stopping the fighting and questioning me!" The Buddha replied with a smile, "I am the Venerable Sakyamuni from the Western Land of Perfect Bliss. You are only a monkey spirit and you have the effrontery to want to grab the throne of the Jade Emperor." The Great Sage said, "As the saying goes, 'Emperors are made by turn; next year it may be me.' If he can be persuaded to move out and make Heaven over to me, that'll be fine. But if he doesn't abdicate in my favour I'll most certainly make things hot for him, and he'll never know peace and quiet again." "What have you got, besides immortality and the ability to transform yourself, that gives you the nerve to try to seize the Heavenly Palace?" the Buddha asked. "I can do very many tricks indeed," the Great Sage replied. "I can do seventy-two transformations, and I can preserve my youth for ten thousand kalpas. I can ride a somersault cloud that takes me thirty-six thousand miles at a single jump. So why shouldn't I sit on the throne of Heaven?" "I'll have a wager with you then," said the Buddha. "If you're clever enough to get out of my right hand with a single somersault, you will be the winner, and there will be no more need for weapons or fighting: I shall invite the Jade Emperor to come and live in the west and abdicate the Heavenly Palace to you. But if you can't get out of the palm of my hand you will have to go down to the world below as a devil and train yourself for several more kalpas."

When he heard this offer the Great Sage smiled to himself and thought, "This Buddha is a complete idiot. I can cover thirty-six thousand miles with a somersault, so how could I fail to jump out of the palm of his hand, which is less than a foot across?" With this in his mind he asked eagerly, "Do you guarantee that yourself?" "Yes, yes," the Buddha replied, and he stretched out his right hand, which seemed to be about the size of a lotus leaf. Putting away his as-you-will cudgel, the Great Sage summoned up all his divine powers, jumped into the palm of the Buddha's hand, and said, "I'm off." Watch him as he goes like a streak of light and disappears completely. The Buddha, who was watching him with his wise eyes, saw the Monkey King whirling forward like a windmill and not stopping until he saw five flesh-pink pillars topped by dark vapours. "This is the end of the road," he said, "so now I'll go back. The Buddha will be witness, and the Hall of Miraculous Mist will be mine." Then he thought again, "Wait a moment. I'll leave my mark here to prove my case when I talk to the Buddha." He pulled out a hair, breathed on it with his magic breath, and shouted "Change". It turned into a writing brush dipped in ink, and with it he wrote THE GREAT SAGE EQUALLING HEAVEN WAS HERE in big letters on the middle pillar. When that was done he put the hair back on, and, not standing on his dignity, made a pool of monkey piss at the foot of the pillar. Then he turned his somersault round and went back to where he had started from. "I went, and now I'm back. Tell the Jade Emperor to hand the Heavenly Palace over to me," he said, standing in the Buddha's palm.

"I've got you, you piss-spirit of a monkey," roared the Buddha at him. "You never left the palm of my hand." "You're wrong there," the Great Sage replied. "I went to the farthest point of Heaven, where I saw five flesh-pink pillars topped by dark vapours. I left my mark there. Do you dare come and see it with me?" "There's no need to go. Just look down." The Great Sage looked down with his fire eyes with golden pupils to see the words "The Great Sage Equalling Heaven was here" written on the middle finger of the Buddha's right hand. The stink of monkey-piss rose from the fold at the bottom of the finger. "What a thing to happen," exclaimed the Great Sage in astonishment. "I wrote this on one of the pillars supporting the sky, so how can it be on his finger now? He must have used divination to know what I was going to do. I don't believe it. I refuse to believe it! I'll go there and come back again."

The splendid Great Sage hurriedly braced himself to jump, but the Buddha turned his hand over and pushed the Monkey King out through the Western Gate of Heaven. He turned his five fingers into a mountain chain belonging to the elements Metal, Wood, Water, Fire, and Earth, renamed them the Five Elements Mountain, and gently held him down. The Buddha produced from his sleeve a strip of paper on which were written the golden words *Om mani padme hum*. He gave this piece of paper to Ananda and told him to stick it on the summit of the mountains.

The Buddha then took his leave of the Jade Emperor and all the other deities. When he and his two disciples had gone out through the gates of Heaven his merciful heart moved him to chant a spell ordering a local tutelary god and the Protectors of the Five Regions to live on the mountain and keep guard over the Great Sage. When he was hungry they were to feed him iron pellets, and when he was thirsty they were to give him molten copper to drink. When the time of his punishment was over, someone would come and rescue him.

Monkey is Confined Under the Five Elements Mountain

CHAPTER 10
Buddha Prepares to Give the Scriptures; Guanyin Subdues the Four Monsters

Our story goes on to tell how our Buddha, the Tathagata, left the Jade Emperor and went back to the Thunder Monastery.

One day, as the Buddha dwelt in the Thunder Monastery on the Vulture Peak, he called together all the other Buddhas, Arhats, guardian deities, Bodhisattvas, Vajrapanis, monks and nuns and said, "As we are beyond time, I don't know how long it has been since the crafty ape was subdued and Heaven pacified, but by earthly reckoning it must be about five hundred years. As today is a fine early autumn day and I have a precious bowl filled with a hundred kinds of rare flowers and a thousand varieties of exotic fruit, what would you say to our having an Ullambana Feast?" They all put their hands together and performed the reverence of going round him three times in acceptance. The Buddha then ordered Ananda to hold the bowl of flowers and fruit while Kasyapa laid them out. The host were moved to gratitude, which they expressed in verse.

The Buddha said to the host, "I have observed that in the Southern Jambu Continent living creatures are greedy and lecherous and delight in the sufferings of others; they go in for a great deal of killing and quarrelling. That continent can with truth be called a vicious field of back-biting and calumny, an evil sea of disputation. I now have Three Stores of True Scriptures with which they can be persuaded to be good." On hearing this, all the Bodhisattvas put their hands together in

submission, then went forward to ask, "What Three Stores of
True Scriptures does the Tathagata have?" "I have one store of
the Vinaya, the law, which is about Heaven; one of Sastras,
expositions which are concerned with Earth; and one of Sutras,
or scriptures, which save ghosts. The Three Stores consist of
fifteen thousand one hundred and forty-four scrolls in thirty-five
classes. They are the scriptures for cultivating the truth, and the
gate to real goodness. I want to send them to the eastern lands
because it is intolerable that the beings of that quarter should
all be such stupid wretches who slander and defame the true
word, not understanding my Law. How am I to find one with
the magic powers to go to the East, choose a worthy believer and
bid him make the arduous crossing of a thousand mountains and
ten thousand rivers in search of the scriptures until he finally
comes to this abode of mine to receive them? When he does come
they will be sent to the East for ever to convert all living beings,
which will be a blessing as big as a mountain, a cause for
congratulation as deep as the sea. Is anyone willing to go and
find him?" The Bodhisattva Guanyin went up to the lotus
throne, and after going round the Buddha three times by way
of salutation she said, "Your untalented disciple wishes to go
to the East to find a man to come and fetch the scriptures."

The Buddha was very pleased to see her. "No one but the
venerable Guanyin, whose divine powers are so great, will do
for this mission," he said. "What instructions have you for
your disciple as she goes to the East?" Guanyin asked. "You
must watch the route all the way," said the Buddha. "You may
not go via the Milky Way, but if necessary you may have a little
cloud or mist. As you cross mountains and rivers you must
note the distances carefully to enable you to give full instructions to the man who will come to fetch the scriptures. But
that true believer will, I'm afraid, have a difficult journey, so
I shall give you five treasures for him." The Buddha ordered
Ananda and Kasyapa to bring out a brocade cassock and a nine-
ringed monk's staff. "Give this cassock and staff to him who
will come to fetch the scriptures: they are for him to use. If he
is determined to come here, he can avoid the Wheel of Rein-

carnation by wearing this cassock, and he will be free from evil if he carries this staff." The Bodhisattva bowed and took them. The Buddha then produced three bands. "These precious things are called 'tight bands'," he told the Bodhisattva as he handed them to her. "Although all three of them look the same, they have different uses. I also have three Band-tightening Spells. If you meet any devils with great magic powers on your journey you should persuade them to reform and become the disciples of the pilgrim who will come to fetch the scriptures. If they do not do as they are told these bands should be put on their heads, where they will of themselves take root in the flesh. If the appropriate spell for each one is recited the victim's eyes will bulge, his head will ache, and his forehead will split open. He will thus be certainly induced to adopt our religion."

When he finished speaking the Bodhisattva bowed eagerly and withdrew. She told Huian the Novice (Prince Moksa) to accompany her, and Huian took his iron staff weighing a thousand pounds with him so that he could act as a demon-quelling escort for the Bodhisattva. The Bodhisattva wrapped the cassock up in a bundle and gave it to him to carry. She then put the golden bands away safely and went down the Vulture Peak with the staff in her hand.

As the teacher and her disciple were on their journey they suddenly noticed a thousand miles of weak water, which was the River of Flowing Sands. "Disciple," said the Bodhisattva, "this will be hard to cross for the man who will come to fetch the scriptures, as he will be of impure bone and mortal flesh. How will he do it?" "Teacher, how wide does the river look to you?" asked Huian. The Bodhisattva stopped her cloud to investigate.

As the Bodhisattva was surveying the scene she heard a splash and saw a hideous ogre leap out of the waves. This ogre climbed up the bank with a pole in his hands to catch the Bodhisattva, but was stopped by Huian's staff. "Don't run away," Huian shouted as the ogre advanced towards him. The battle that ensued between them was quite terrifying.

The pair of them fought several dozen rounds without either gaining the upper hand. The ogre then realized who Huian was. "I remember," he said, "you used to cultivate your conduct with Guanyin of the Southern Sea in the Purple Bamboo Grove. Why have you come here?" "Can't you see my teacher standing there on the bank?"

When the ogre heard this he chanted "re-e-er" several times to show his respect, withdrew his pole and let Moksa seize it. Then he bowed to Guanyin and said, "Forgive me, Bodhisattva, and listen to what I have to tell you. I am not a demon, but the Curtain Raising General who used to stand in attendance by the imperial chariot in the Hall of Miraculous Mist. Just because I accidentally smashed a crystal dish at a Peach Banquet the Jade Emperor had me given eight hundred strokes of the rod, exiled me to the lower world, and made me look like this. It's agony. I get so unbearably cold and hungry that I have to emerge from the waves every two or three days to devour a traveller. I never thought that in my ignorance I would insult the merciful Bodhisattva today." "You were exiled here for a crime against Heaven, but now you are deepening your guilt by harming living beings. I am now going to the East on the Buddha's orders to find the man who will fetch the scriptures. Why don't you become one of us and ensure yourself good retribution in future by accompanying the pilgrim as a disciple and ascending to the Western Heaven to pay homage to the Buddha and seek the scriptures? I will see to it that the flying sword stops coming to pierce you, and when you are successful you will be forgiven your crimes and your old job will be given back to you. What do you think of that?" "I am willing to return to the truth," the ogre replied. The Bodhisattva then laid her hands on his head and administered the monastic rules to him, chose for him the surname Sha ("Sand") and gave him the Buddhist name of Wujing ("Awakened to Purity"). Then he entered monkish life and took the Bodhisattva across the river. He washed his heart, cleansed his thoughts, and stopped killing living creatures. All he did now was to wait for the pilgrim who would come to fetch the scriptures.

After leaving him the Bodhisattva and Huian hurried on towards the east. When they had been travelling for a long time they saw a high mountain veiled with an evil mist, and they were unable to climb it on foot. Just when they were intending to cross the mountain by cloud, a gale wind blew up and a monster suddenly appeared.

He rushed upon them, and without a second thought smote at the Bodhisattva with his rake. Moksa the Novice parried his blow, and shouted at the top of his voice, "Remember your manners, damned monster, and watch out for my staff." "Monk," the other replied, "you don't know how to keep yourself in one piece. Mind my rake!" At the foot of the mountain the pair of them rushed upon each other as they struggled for supremacy.

Just when the fight was getting really good, Guanyin threw down a lotus flower from mid-air to separate the two weapons. The monster, shocked at the sight of it, asked, "Where are you from, monk? How dare you try to fool me with a 'flower in front of the eyes'?" "I'll get you, you stinking, flesh-eyed mortal," replied Moksa. "I am a disciple of the Bodhisattva of the Southern Sea, and this lotus was thrown down by her. Don't you know that?" "By the Bodhisattva of the Southern Sea do you mean Guanyin Who Eliminates the Three Calamities and Saves from the Eight Disasters?" the monster asked. "Who else could I mean?" retorted Moksa. The monster threw down his rake, bowed to him, and asked, "Where is the Bodhisattva, elder brother? May I trouble you to introduce me?" Moksa looked up and pointed. "There she is," he said. The monster kowtowed to her and shouted in a shrill voice, "Forgive me, Bodhisattva, forgive me. I used to be Marshal Tian Peng in the Milky Way. Because I took some wine to seduce a moon maiden, the Jade Emperor sentenced me to two thousand hammer blows and exile in the mortal world. My spirit had to find a womb to occupy, but I lost my way and entered the womb of a sow. That's why I look like this. I ate up my sow mother, drove all the other pigs away, and seized this mountain, where I keep myself by eating people. I never meant to offend you, Bodhisattva. Save me, save me, I beg you." "'If a man wishes to be good, Heaven will certainly allow him to be'," said the Bodhisattva. "If you are prepared to submit to the truth, there are of course ways to feed yourself. There are the five kinds of food-grains, and they are sufficient to assuage hunger, so why eat people to keep alive?"

When the monster heard these words it was as if he awoke from a dream, and he said to the Bodhisattva, "I would love to reform, but isn't it true that 'a sinner against Heaven has nowhere to pray to'?" "I'm going to the East on the orders of the Buddha to find the man who will fetch the scriptures," she replied. "You can be a disciple of his and make this journey to the Western Heaven; thus you will gain merit and atone for your crimes, and I will see to it that you are freed from disaster." "I'll go with him, I'll go with him," the monster said over and over again. The Bodhisattva then laid her hands on his head and he accepted the monastic rules. She gave him the surname Zhu ("Pig") because of his appearance, and gave him the Buddhist name Zhu Wuneng ("Pig Awakened to Power"). She ordered him to adhere to the truth and eat only vegetarian food, cutting out the five pungent vegetables as well as the three forbidden meats — wild goose, dog and fish. He was now to wait single-mindedly for the pilgrim who would come to fetch the scriptures.

The Bodhisattva and Moksa then took their leave of the Pig Awakened to Power and continued on their way by low-altitude cloud. As they were travelling along they heard a jade dragon call to them in mid-air. "Which dragon are you?" the Bodhisattva asked as she went up to him. "And why are you undergoing punishment here?" "I am the son of Ao Run, the Dragon King of the Western Sea. Because I burnt up the bright pearls in the palace, my father reported me to the court of Heaven as a rebel. The Jade Emperor had me hung up in mid-air and given three hundred strokes, and I am to be executed any day now. I beg you to save me, Bodhisattva."

When she heard his plea the Bodhisattva went to the Jade Emperor and said, "I have come here especially to ask you to spare the Dragon's life and give him to me so that he can serve the pilgrim with his legs." On hearing this the Jade Emperor issued a decree pardoning him, and he sent a heavenly general to release him and give him to the Bodhisattva. The Bodhisattva took him to a deep ravine, where he was to wait until the pilgrim came. When that happened he was to turn into a white horse and achieve merit by going to the Western Heaven.

The Bodhisattva led Moksa the Novice across this mountain, and they hurried on towards the east. Before they had gone much further they suddenly saw ten thousand beams of golden light and a thousand wisps of propitious vapour. "Teacher," said Moksa, "the place where all the light is coming from is the Five Elements Mountain, where the Tathagata's restriction order is posted." "This must be because that Great Sage Equalling Heaven who wrecked the Peach Banquet and threw the Heavenly Palace into chaos is imprisoned there." "That's right," Moksa replied, and teacher and pupil climbed the mountain together.

At the foot of the mountainside the local gods, the mountain gods and the heavenly generals who were guarding the Great Sage all bowed to the Bodhisattva in greeting and took her to the Great Sage. She saw that he was pressed down inside a stone box, so that he could speak but could not move his body. "Monkey," the Bodhisattva said, "do you know who I am?" The Great Sage opened wide his fiery eyes with their golden pupils, nodded his head and shouted at the top of his voice, "Of course I recognize you. You, thank goodness, are the All-Compassionate, All-Merciful Deliverer from Suffering, the Bodhisattva Guanyin from Potaraka Island in the Southern Sea. You're a very welcome visitor. Every day here seems like a year, and nobody I know has ever come to see me. Where have you come from?" "I have received a mandate from the Buddha to go to the East and find the man who will fetch the scriptures," she replied, "and as I was passing this way I decided to come over and see you." "The Buddha fooled me and crushed me under this mountain — I haven't been able to stretch myself for five hundred years. I desperately hope that you will be obliging

enough to rescue me, Bodhisattva." "You wretch," she replied,
"you have such an appalling criminal record that I'm afraid
you'd only make more trouble if I got you out." "I have already
repented," he said, "and hope that you will show me the road
I should follow. I want to cultivate my conduct."

The Bodhisattva was delighted to hear what he said, and
replied, "If this is your state of mind, then wait while I go to
the East to find the man who will fetch the scriptures; I'll tell him
to rescue you. You can be his disciple, observe and uphold the
faith, enter our Buddha's religion, and cultivate good
retribution for yourself in the future. What do you say to that?"
"I'll go, I'll go," the Great Sage repeated over and over again.
"As you have reformed," she said, "I'll give you a Buddhist
name." "I've already got a name. It's Sun Wukong." The
Bodhisattva, very pleased, said, "I made two converts earlier,
and their names both contained Wu ('Awakened'). There's no
need to give you any further instructions, so I'll be off."

CHAPTER 11
In the Great Tang Empire
Sanzang Vows to Fetch the
Scriptures

After leaving that place the Bodhisattva and Huian carried straight on to the east, and before long they reached Chang'an, the capital of the Great Tang. Putting away their mists and clouds, teacher and pupil turned themselves into a pair of scabby itinerant monks and went inside the city of Chang'an. It was already dark, and beside the great market street they saw a shrine to a local tutelary god and went in. The local god was thrown into confusion at the sight of them, and the devil soldiers quaked with terror; they knew that she was a Bodhisattva, and kowtowed to her in greeting. The local god then scurried off to tell the City God, the Lord of the Altar, and the gods of all the other shrines in Chang'an. When they knew that the Bodhisattva had come they all went to report to her and said, "Bodhisattva, please forgive us for our crime in being late to welcome you." "You mustn't let a whisper of this get out," she said. "I have come here on a decree from the Buddha to find someone to fetch the scriptures. I shall be borrowing your temple for a few days while I find this true monk, and then I shall go back."

The Bodhisattva Guanyin spent a long time in Chang'an, looking on the Buddha's orders for the man to fetch the scriptures, but she could not find anyone really virtuous. Then she heard that the Tang emperor Taizong was propagating the True Achievement and had selected the Hierarch Xuanzang, who had been a monk from infancy and was the son of a Senior Graduate in the Palace Examination, to hold a Great Land and Water Mass and preach the Buddhist faith. Guanyin was very pleased. She took her disciple Moksa together with the cassock and the staff that the Buddha had given her and presented them to the Tang emperor.

Taizong arranged for a court to be held at midday and sent his minister Wei Zheng with a decree summoning Xuanzang to attend. The monastic official went with Wei Zheng to the imperial presence. "Up till now we have had nothing suitable with which to thank you, Your Grace, for your efforts in acquiring merit," the emperor said. "This morning Xiao Yu met two monks who have vowed to give you a precious brocade cassock and a nine-ringed monk's staff. We have therefore sent for you, Master, to come and receive them." Xuanzang kowtowed in thanks.

Time passed in the snap of a finger, and it was time for the special assembly on the seventh day, so Xuanzang wrote a memorial inviting the Tang Emperor to come and burn incense. His reputation for piety had now spread throughout the empire. Taizong therefore led a large number of civil and military officials and his empresses, consorts and their families to the monastery in a procession of carriages to the temple early that morning. Everyone in the city, whether young or old, humble or mighty, went to the temple to hear the preaching. The Bodhisattva said to Moksa, "Today is a special day of the Great Land and Water Mass, which will go on from this first seventh day to the seventh seventh day, as is proper. You and I are going to mingle with the crowds for three reasons: to see the service, to see the Golden Cicada enjoying the blessing of wearing our treasure, and to hear what branch of the scriptures he preaches on." The pair of them went to the temple.

On his dais the Master of the Law read through the *Sutra to Give Life and Deliver the Dead*, discussed the *Heavenly Charm to Protect the Country* and preached on the *Exhortation to Cultivate Merit*. The Bodhisattva went up to the dais, hit it, and shouted out at the top of her voice, "Why are you only talking about the doctrine of the Little Vehicle, monk? Can't you preach about the Great Vehicle?" On hearing these questions a delighted Xuanzang leapt down from the preaching dais, bowed to the Bodhisattva, and said, "Venerable teacher, your disciple has sinned grievously in failing to recognize you. We monks who stand before you only preach the Law of the Little Vehicle, and we know nothing of the doctrine of the Great Vehicle." "That doctrine of the Little Vehicle of yours will never bring the dead to rebirth; it's only good enough for a vulgar sort of enlightenment. Now I have the Three Stores of the Buddha's Law of the Great Vehicle that will raise the dead up to Heaven, deliver sufferers from their torments, and free souls from the eternal coming and going."

As the Bodhisattva was talking, the Master of Incense, an official who patrolled the temple, made an urgent report to the Tang Emperor that just when the Master of the Law was in the middle of preaching the wonderful Law a pair of scabby itinerant monks had dragged him down and were engaging him in wild argument. The emperor ordered them to be arrested and brought before him, and a crowd of men hustled the two of them into the rear hall of the monastery. When they saw Taizong they neither raised their hands in greeting nor bowed, but looked him in the eye and said, "What does Your Majesty want to ask us about?" Recognizing them, the Emperor asked, "Are you not the monk who gave us the cassock?" "That's right," replied the Bodhisattva. "If you came here to listen to the preaching you should be satisfied with getting something to eat," said Taizong. "Why did you start ranting at the Master of the Law, disturbing the scripture hall and interfering with our service to the Buddha?" "That master of yours was only teaching the doctrine of the Little Vehicle, which will never send the dead up to Heaven," replied the Bodhisattva. "I have the Three Stores of the Buddha's Law of the Great Vehicle, which can save the dead, deliver from suffering, and ensure that the body will live for ever without coming to harm." Showing no signs of anger, Taizong earnestly asked where the Buddha's Law of the Great Vehicle was. "It is in the Thunder Monastery in the land of India in the West, where our Buddha lives," the Bodhisattva replied, "and it can untie the knots of all injustice and save the innocent from disaster."

Taizong immediately issued an order to the assembly of monks: "Suspend this service until we have sent someone to fetch the scriptures of the Great Vehicle, and then you shall once more strive sincerely to achieve good retribution." The monks all obeyed his instructions. The Emperor then asked those present in the monastery, "Who is willing to accept our commission to go to the Western Heaven to visit the Buddha and fetch the scriptures?" Before he had finished his question, the Master of the Law came forward, bowed low in greeting, and said, "Although I am lacking in ability, I would like to offer my humble efforts to fetch the true scriptures for Your Majesty and thus ensure the eternal security of your empire." The Tang Emperor, who was overjoyed to hear this, went forward to raise him to his feet. "Master," he said, "if you are prepared to exert your loyalty and wisdom to the full, not fearing the length of the journey or the rivers and mountains you will have to cross, I shall make you my own sworn brother." Xuanzang kowtowed to thank him. As the Tang Emperor was indeed a man of wisdom and virtue he went to a place before the Buddha in the monastery where he bowed to Xuanzang four times, calling him "younger brother" and "holy monk". Xuanzang thanked him effusively. "Your Majesty," he said, "I have no virtue or talent that fits me for the sacred honour of being treated as your kinsman. On this journey I shall give my all and go straight to the Western Heaven. If I fail to reach there or to obtain the true scriptures, then I shall not return to this country even in death, and shall fall for eternity into Hell." He burned incense in front of the Buddha to mark this vow.

The next morning, the Tang Emperor and a host of officials went to accompany Xuanzang to the checkpoint and gave him the name "Sanzang" (meaning the "Three Stores of Scriptures" in the Western Heaven). Xuanzang thanked the Emperor and took his leave, accompanied by two servants appointed by the Emperor.

玄奘東誠建大會

Xuanzang at the Great Mass

CHAPTER 12
Sun Wukong Becomes a Disciple of the Master Sanzang

It has been told already how Sanzang was seen off at the checkpoint outside Chang'an by the Tang Emperor and a host of officials on the twelfth day of the ninth month in the thirteenth year of *Zhen Guan*. For two days his horse's hoofs were never still, and he soon reached the Fa Men Monastery.

Early in the morning, after a peaceful night's sleep, Sanzang put on his cassock and went to worship the Buddha in the main hall. "Your disciple Chen Sanzang," he said, "is going to the Western Heaven to fetch the scriptures, but my fleshly eye is too dim to see the true image of the living Buddha. I now vow that whenever I come across a temple on my journey I shall burn incense; whenever I see a Buddha's image I shall worship it; and whenever I pass a stupa I shall sweep it. My only wish is that Buddha in his mercy will soon appear to me in his golden body and give me the true scriptures to take back and propagate in the land of the East." When he had prayed he went back to the abbot's room for breakfast. After breakfast his two attendants saddled the horse and set off at a good pace. At the gate of the monastery Sanzang took his leave of the monks, who were so unwilling to be parted from him that they accompanied him for some three miles before turning back with tears in their eyes, while Sanzang carried on westwards.

When the master and his attendants had been travelling for several days they reached the city of Gongzhou, where all the local officials were waiting to greet them and take them into the city. After a night's rest they set out again the next morning. They ate when they were hungry and drank when they were thirsty, travelling by day and stopping at night. Two or three days later they reached the garrison city of Hezhou, which was on the frontier of the Great Tang Empire. The garrison commander and the local Buddhist monks and priests had all heard that the Master of the Law, the Imperial Younger Brother, was going to the West on His Majesty's orders to see the Buddha, so they were all very respectful. The Director of Monks took him into the city, provided him with all he needed, and invited him to spend the night in the Fuyuan Monastery. All the monks of the monastery came to pay their respects to him, and when he had finished the meal they prepared for him he told his attendants to give the horse a good feed as they would be setting out before dawn. As soon as the cocks started to crow he called for his attendants, thus disturbing the monks, who brought him tea and food. When he had eaten he crossed the frontier.

In his impatience Sanzang had got up too soon. As it was late autumn the cocks had crowed very early, and it was still only about two in the morning. The three of them — four, including the horse — covered about a dozen miles through the frost, finding their way by the light of the moon, until they saw a large mountain in front of them. They had to push the undergrowth aside as they looked for their way, and the going was indescribably rough and difficult. Just when they were wondering whether they were lost, all three of them and the horse stumbled and fell into a pit. Sanzang was thrown into a panic, and his attendants were trembling with fear, when to add their terror they heard roars coming from further inside and loud shouts of "Get 'em! Get 'em!" With a ferocious blast of wind a crowd of fifty or sixty fiends fell upon them and dragged them out. When the shivering and shaking Master of the Law took a stealthy look he saw a thoroughly evil demon king sitting above them.

The sight of him frightened Sanzang out of his wits and made his two attendants feel their bones turn to jelly and their muscles go numb. When the demon king roared out an order to tie them up the fiends bound them with rope. He was just on the point of devouring them when a great noise was heard outside and the arrival of Mountain Lord Bear and Hermit Ox was announced. Sanzang looked up and saw that one of them was a dark fellow. Behind him was a fat man. When these two came swaggering in, the demon king rushed out to greet them.

Sanzang's two attendants meanwhile were howling pitifully in their bonds. "How did those three get here?" asked the dark fellow. "They delivered themselves to the front door," the demon king replied. "Will you be serving them to your friends?" asked the Hermit with a smile. "I should be honoured to," answered the demon king. "We won't need them all," remarked the Mountain Lord. "We could eat two and keep the third." With a "re-e-er" of obedience the demon king told his servants to cut open the two attendants, scoop their hearts out, and chop their bodies into mince. He presented the heads, hearts, and livers to his two guests, eating the limbs himself and dividing the rest of the flesh and bones among the fiends. All that could be heard was a crunching and a munching that sounded just like tigers devouring lambs, and in a few moments it had all been eaten up. Sanzang was almost dead with fright, yet this was only his first tribulation, coming so soon after leaving Chang'an.

In his despair he noticed that the east was beginning to grow light, and when dawn broke the two monsters left, saying, "We have been handsomely entertained today, and we shall repay your hospitality in full another day." With that they both rushed out. A moment later the red sun rose high in the sky, but Sanzang was too befuddled to know where he was. Just when all seemed lost, an old man appeared, walking towards him with the help of a stick. He came up to Sanzang, broke all his bonds with a wave of his hand, and revived him by blowing into his face. Sanzang fell to his knees and bowed low to him, saying, "Thank you, venerable ancient, for saving my humble life." The old man returned his bow and said, "Get up. Have you lost anything?" "My attendants have been eaten by monsters, and I don't know where my baggage or my horse is," replied Sanzang. The old man pointed with his stick and asked, "Isn't that a horse with two baggage-rolls over there?" When Sanzang turned round he saw that his things had not been lost after all, which somewhat relieved his anxiety. "Venerable sir," he asked, "what is this place, and how did you get here?" "This is the Double Forked Mountain, where tigers and leopards make their dens. How did you fall in here?" "I crossed the frontier at the garrison city of Hezhou at cock-crow, not realizing that I had got up too early," replied Sanzang. "Just as we were making our way through frost and dew we suddenly fell into this pit. A dreadfully ferocious demon king appeared and had me and my attendants tied up. Then a dark fellow called Mountain Lord Bear and a fat one called Hermit Ox came in, and they addressed the demon king as General Yin. The three of them ate up my two attendants, and their party only ended at dawn. I cannot imagine why I should have been fated with the good fortune of you coming to rescue me, venerable sir." "The Hermit is a wild bull spirit, the Mountain Lord is a bear spirit, and General Yin is a tiger spirit," the old man replied. "The fiends who serve him are mountain spirits, tree devils, monsters, and wolves. The reason they did not eat you was because your fundamental nature is enlightened. Come with me and I'll show you the way." Overcome with gratitude, Sanzang put the packs on his horse and led it by the bridle as he followed the old man out of the pit and on to the main road. Tying the horse to a bush beside the road, he turned round to bow low to the old man and thank him, but the old man changed into a puff of wind and rose into the sky on the back of a red-crested white crane. All that could be seen was a piece of paper drifting down in the wind with four lines of verse written on it:

"I am the Great White Planet of the Western Heaven,
Who came to save your life.
In the journey ahead divine disciples will come to your
  aid:
Do not in your troubles blame the scriptures."

When he had read this Sanzang worshipped Heaven and
said, "Many thanks, Planet, for delivering me from this danger."
This done, he continued on his difficult journey, feeling very
lonely as he led his horse along.

Sanzang did not spare himself as he pressed ahead amid
the mountain peaks. He had been going for many hours without
seeing any sign of a human house; he was hungry and finding
the going heavy. Just at this critical moment he saw in front
of him a pair of ferocious tigers roaring, while two long snakes
were coiled up behind him. To his left were venomous reptiles,
and to his right were terrible monsters. Being by himself and
unable to think of a way out, Sanzang prepared to abandon
his mind and body and let Heaven do as it would. Besides,
the horse's back was now so tired and its legs so bent that
it fell to its knees on the ground and collapsed. Sanzang could
not move it, either by blows or by dragging at its bridle. The
poor Master of the Law, who had nowhere to shelter, was feeling thoroughly wretched, convinced that nothing could save him
from death. But when his troubles were at their worst someone
came to his rescue. Just when all seemed lost he saw the venomous reptiles and the evil monsters flee, while the tigers and
the snakes hid themselves. Sanzang looked up and saw a man
coming across the hillside with a steel trident in his hand and
bow and arrows at his waist.

Seeing him approach, Sanzang knelt down beside the path,
put his hands together, and shouted at the top of his voice,
"Spare me, bandit king, spare me." The man went over to
him, put down his trident, and raised him to his feet. "Don't
be frightened, venerable monk," he said, "I'm not a bad man;
I'm a hunter who lives in these mountains. My name is Liu

Boqin and I am known as the warden of the mountain. I came along here because I wanted a couple of animals for the pot. I never expected to meet you here — I must have offended you." "I am a monk sent by the Emperor of the Great Tang to visit the Buddha in the Western Heaven and ask for the scriptures," Sanzang replied. "I had just got here when I found myself completely surrounded by wolves, tigers, snakes and other creatures, which meant that I could go no further. Then suddenly you appeared, High Warden, and saved my life. Thank you very much indeed." "Those of us who live here," replied Liu Boqin, "can only support ourselves by killing tigers and wolves, and catching snakes and other reptiles, which is why all those animals fled in terror from me. As you are from the Tang Empire, we are compatriots. This is still the territory of the Great Tang, and I am a Tang citizen. Both of us depend on the emperor's lands and rivers for our food and drink, and we are fellow countrymen, so there is nothing to fear. You must come with me to my hut, and your horse can rest. I'll take you on your way tomorrow." Sanzang, who was delighted to hear this, thanked him and went along behind him, leading the horse.

Liu Boqin treated Sanzang with great hospitality for the night. Early the next morning, they continued the journey.

When they had been travelling for some time they saw a mountain in front of them, a high and precipitous one that towered right up to the azure sky. Before long they had reached its base. The high warden climbed it as if he were walking on level ground, and when they were half-way over it he turned round, stood beside the path and said, "Venerable monk, I must ask you to take yourself on from here. I have to go back." On hearing this Sanzang tumbled out of his saddle to say, "Please, please, take me another stage, High Warden." "You don't seem to know that this is called Double Boundary Mountain," said the high warden. The eastern part belongs to our Great Tang, but the western part is Tatar territory. The tigers and wolves on that side are not subject to my control, which is why I can't cross the boundary. You must go on by yourself." The monk was so alarmed to hear this that he waved his arms around and grabbed hold of the hunter's clothes and sleeves, weeping and refusing to let him go. When at last Sanzang was bowing repeatedly to the hunter to take his leave, a shout like thunder came from under the mountain: "My master's come, my master's come." Sanzang stood frozen with fear at the sound of it, and Boqin had to hold him up.

The terror-stricken Liu Boqin and Sanzang then heard another shout of "My master's come." "That must be the old monkey who lives in a stone cell under this mountain," said the high warden. Boqin then led Sanzang and his horse down the mountain. A mile or two later they saw that there really was a monkey poking out his head out of a stone cell, and making desperate gestures with his outstretched hands as he shouted, "Master, why didn't you come before? Thank goodness you're here, thank goodness. If you get me out of here I guarantee that you'll reach the Western Heaven."

High Warden Liu showed great courage in going up to him, pulling away the grass that was growing beside his temples and the sedge under his chin, and asking, "What have you got to say?" "I've got nothing to say," the monkey replied, "You just tell that monk to come over here while I ask him a question." "What question do you want to ask me?" said Sanzang. "Are you the fellow sent to the Western Heaven by the emperor of the East to fetch the scriptures?" asked the monkey. "Yes, I am," Sanzang replied. "Why do you ask?" "I am the Great Sage Equalling Heaven who wrecked the Heavenly Palace five hundred years ago. The Lord Buddha put me under this mountain for my criminal insubordination. Some time ago the Bodhisattva Guanyin went to the East on the Buddha's orders to find someone who could fetch the scriptures. When I asked her to save me she told me that I was to give up evil-doing, return to the Buddha's Law, and do all I could to protect the traveller when he went to the Western Paradise to worship Buddha and fetch the scriptures; she said that there'll be something in it for me when that's done. Ever since then I've been waiting day and night with eager anticipation for you to come and save me, Master. I swear to protect you on your way to fetch the scriptures and to be your disciple." Sanzang, delighted to hear this, said, "Although you now have these splendid intentions and wish to become a monk thanks to the teaching of the Bodhisattva, I've no axe or chisel, so how am I to get you out?" "There's no need for axes or chisels. As long as you're willing to save me, I can get myself out," the monkey replied. "I'm willing to save you," Sanzang said, "but how are you going to get out?" "On the top of this mountain there is a detention order by the Tathagata Buddha written in letters of gold. If you climb the mountain and tear it off, I'll be straight out." Accepting his suggestion, Sanzang and Liu Boqin climbed the high mountain again and gently removed the paper seal. Then they went down the mountain to the stone cell, where they said to the monkey, "The restriction order has been torn off, so you can come out." The delighted monkey said, "Master, please stand well clear so that I don't give you a fright when I come out."

On hearing this Liu Boqin took Sanzang and the rest of them to the east, and when they had covered some two or three miles they heard the monkey shout, "Further, further!" So Sanzang went much further until he was off the mountain. Then there was a great noise as the mountain split open. As they were all shaking with terror, the monkey appeared kneeling stark naked in front of Sanzang's horse and saying, "Master, I'm out." He bowed four times to Sanzang, then jumped up, addressed Liu Boqin with a respectful noise, and said, "Thank you, elder brother, for escorting my master, and thank you too for weeding the grass off my face." He then picked up the luggage and put it on the horse's back. At the sight of him the horse felt so weak and trembling that it could not stay on its feet. Because the monkey had once been the Protector of the Horses and looked after the dragon steeds of Heaven mortal horses were terrified at the very sight of him.

Seeing that his intentions were indeed good and that he really was now a Buddhist, Sanzang asked him what was his surname. "My surname's Sun," replied the Monkey King.

"I'll give you a Buddhist name that I can call you by," said Sanzang. "There's no need to trouble yourself," said the Monkey King, "I've already got one: Sun Wukong — Monkey Awakened to Emptiness." "That's just right for our sect," exclaimed the monk. "As you look so much like a young novice, I'll give you another name and call you Brother Monkey. Is that all right?" "Yes, yes, yes," said Sun Wukong, and from then on he was also called Brother Monkey, or Sun the Novice.

When he saw that Brother Monkey was determined to go, the high warden turned to Sanzang, chanted a noise of respect and said, "It's splendid that you have got so good a disciple, venerable sir. He'll certainly make the journey. I must now take my leave." Sanzang bowed to him in thanks, saying, "I have brought you a long way, and am deeply indebted to you." Liu Boqin returned his bow, and with that they parted.

Brother Monkey asked Sanzang to mount the horse while he ambled ahead, stark naked, carrying the luggage on his back. Before long they were over the Double Boundary Mountain. Suddenly a ferocious tiger rushed at them, roaring and lashing about with its tail. Sanzang on his horse was terrified. Brother Monkey, who was standing beside the path, put down the luggage and said happily, "Don't be scared, Master, it's just bringing me my clothes." He pulled a needle out of his ear and shook it in the wind, turning it into an iron cudgel as thick as a bowl. "I haven't used this little treasure in over five hundred years," he said, holding it in his hand. "Today I'm bringing it out to get myself some clothes to wear." Just watch as he rushes at the tiger, shouting, "Where d'you think you're going, wretch?" The tiger crouched in the dust, not daring to move, as the cudgel smashed into its head. Thousands of drops of red brain and many a pearly piece of tooth flew everywhere, so terrifying Sanzang that he fell out of the saddle, biting on his finger and crying, "Heavens, the high warden had to fight for ages before killing the striped tiger the other day, but this Sun Wukong has smashed a tiger to pulp with a single blow. He really is a tough's tough."

"Sit down for a moment, Master, while I strip the clothes

off him to wear on the journey," said Brother Monkey as he dragged the tiger over. "But he hasn't got any clothes," Sanzang protested. "Don't bother yourself about it, I know how to cope." The splendid Monkey King pulled a hair from his body, breathed some magic breath on it, and said "Change!", on which it turned into a pointed knife shaped like a cow's ear. Cutting into the skin on the tiger's belly, he took it all off in a single stroke, chopped off the head and claws, then held up the square hide to get an idea of its size. "It's on the big side," he said, "so I could make two kilts out of it," and with these words he took his knife and cut it in two. One piece he put away, and the other he wrapped round his waist to cover the lower half of his body and tied firmly with a creeper he pulled down from beside the path. "Let's go on, Master, let's go on," he said. "The sewing can wait till we reach a house where we can borrow a needle and thread." He pinched his iron cudgel to make it as small as a needle again, put it back in his ear, took the luggage on his back, and asked Sanzang to mount the horse.

Sanzang and Sun Wukong went along their way. They ate when hungry and drank when thirsty, travelling by day and resting by night, until it was early winter.

When master and disciple had been travelling for a long time they heard a whistle from beside the path, and six men rushed out with spears, swords, cutlasses, and strongbows. "Where do you think you're going, monk?" they roared. "If you give us your horse and luggage we'll spare your life." Sanzang fell from his horse, scared out of his wits and unable to utter a word.

The brave Brother Monkey did not stop to argue. Instead he stepped forward, folded his arms across his chest, bowed to the six bandits and said, "Why are you gentlemen obstructing our way?" "We are mighty robber kings, benevolent lords of the mountain. We have been very famous for a long time, although you don't seem to have heard of us. If you abandon your things at once, we'll let you go on your way; but if there's even a hint of a 'no' from you, we'll turn your flesh into mincemeat and your bones into powder." Sun Wukong laughed at them. "You're just a bunch of small-time crooks. You can't see that I'm your lord and master although I'm a monk, and you have the effrontery to get in our way. Bring out all the jewels you've stolen, and the seven of us can share them out equally. I'll let you off with that." At this the bandits brandished their spears and swords, and they rushed Brother Monkey, hacking wildly at his face. Seventy or eighty blows crashed down on him, but he simply stood in the middle of them, ignoring everything. "What a monk!" the bandits said. "He's a real tough nut." "I can get by reasonably well," said Brother Monkey with a smile. "Your hands must be tired after all that bashing. Now it's my turn to bring out my needle for a bit of fun." "This monk must have been an acupuncturist," said the bandits. "There's nothing wrong with us. Why is he talking about needles?"

Taking the embroidery needle from his ear, Brother Monkey shook it in the wind, at which it became an iron cudgel as thick as a ricebowl. With this in his hand he said, "Stick around while I try my cudgel out." The terrified bandits tried to flee in all directions, but Monkey raced after them, caught them all up, and killed every one of them. Then he stripped the clothes off them, took their money, and went back with his face wreathed in smiles. "Let's go, Master; I've wiped those bandits out," he said. "Even though they were highwaymen, you're really asking for trouble," Sanzang replied. "Even if they had been arrested and handed over to the authorities, they wouldn't have been sentenced to death. You may know a few tricks, but it would be better if you'd simply driven them away. Why did you have to kill them all? Even taking a man's life by accident is enough to stop someone from becoming a monk. A person who enters the religious life

Spares the ants when he sweeps the floor,
Covers the lamps to save the moth.

What business did you have to slaughter the lot of them, without caring which of them were guilty and which were innocent? You haven't a shred of compassion or goodness in you. This time it happened in the wilds, where nobody will be able to trace the crime. Say someone offended you in a city and you turned murderous there. Say you killed and wounded people when you went berserk with that club of yours. I myself would be involved even though I'm quite innocent." "But if I hadn't killed them, they'd have killed you, Master," protested Sun Wukong. "I am a man of religion, and I would rather die than commit murder," said Sanzang. "Had I died, there'd only have been me dead, but you killed six of them, which was an absolute outrage. If the case were taken to court, you couldn't talk your way out of this even if the judge were your own father." "To tell you the truth, Master, I don't know how many people I killed when I was the monster who ruled the Mountain of Flowers and Fruit," said Sun Wukong, "but if I'd acted your way I'd never have become the Great Sage Equalling Heaven." "It was precisely because you acted with such tyrannical cruelty among mortals and committed the most desperate crimes against Heaven that you got into trouble five hundred years ago," retorted Sanzang. "But now you have entered the faith, you'll never reach the Western Heaven and never become a monk if you don't give up your taste for murder. You're too evil, too evil."

Monkey, who had never let himself be put upon, flared up at Sanzang's endless nagging. "If you say that I'll never become a monk and won't ever reach the Western Heaven, then stop going on at me like that. I'm going back." Before Sanzang could reply, Monkey leapt up in a fury, shouting, "I'm off." Sanzang looked up quickly, but he was already out of sight. All that could be heard was a whistling sound coming from the east. Left on his own, the priest nodded and sighed to himself with great sadness and indignation. "The incorrigible wretch," he reflected. "Fancy disappearing and going back home like that just because I gave him a bit of a telling-off. So that's that. I must be fated to have no disciples or followers. I couldn't find him now even if I wanted to, and he wouldn't answer if I called him. I must be on my way."

Sanzang had no choice but to gather up the luggage and tie it on the horse. He did not ride now. Instead, holding his monastic staff in one hand and leading the horse by the reins with the other, he made his lonely way to the West. Before he had been travelling for long he saw an old woman on the mountain path in front of him. She was holding an embroidered robe, and a patterned hat was resting upon it. As she came towards him he hurriedly pulled the horse to the side of the path to make room for her to pass. "Where are you from, venerable monk," the old woman asked, "travelling all alone and by yourself?" "I have been sent by the great king of the East to go to the West to visit the Buddha and ask him for the True Scriptures," he replied. "The Buddha of the West lives in the Great Thunder Monastery in the land of India, thirty-six thousand miles away from here. You'll never get there, just you and your horse, without a companion or disciple." "I did have a disciple, but his nature was so evil that he would not accept a little reproof I administered to him and disappeared into the blue," said Sanzang. "I have here an embroidered tunic and a hat inset with golden patterns that used to be my son's," the woman said, "but he died after being a monk for only three days. I've just been to his monastery to mourn him and say farewell to his master, and I was taking this tunic and this hat home to remember the boy by. But as you have a disciple, venerable monk, I'll give them to you." "Thank you very much for your great generosity, but as my disciple has already gone, I couldn't accept them." "Where has he gone?" "All I heard was a whistling sound as he went back to the east." "My home isn't far to the east from here," she said, "so I expect he's gone there. I've also got a spell called *True Words to Fix the Mind*, or the Band-tightening Spell. You must learn it in secret, and be sure to keep it to yourself. Never leak it to anyone. I'll go and catch up with him and send him back to you, and you can give him that tunic and hat to wear. If he's disobedient again, all you have to do is recite the spell quietly. That will stop him committing any more murders or running away again."

Sanzang bowed low to thank her, at which she changed into a beam of golden light and returned to the east. He realized in his heart that it must have been the Bodhisattva Guanyin who had given him the spell, so he took a pinch of earth as if he were burning incense and bowed in worship to the east most reverently. Then he put the tunic and hat in his pack, sat down beside the path, and recited the *True Words to Calm the Mind* over and over again until he knew them thoroughly, and had committed them to his memory.

Let us turn to Sun Wukong, who after leaving his master went thirty-six thousand miles on his somersault cloud.

On his way he met the Bodhisattva Guanyin. "What are you doing here, Sun Wukong?" she asked. "Why did you reject the Tang Priest's teaching and stop protecting him?" Brother Monkey frantically bowed to her from his cloud and replied, "As you had predicted, Bodhisattva, a monk came from the Tang Empire who took off the seal, rescued me, and made me his disciple. I ran away from him because he thought I was wicked and incorrigible, but now I'm going back to protect him." "Hurry up then, and don't have any more wicked thoughts." With that they each went their separate ways.

A moment later Monkey saw the Tang Priest sitting gloomily beside the path. He went up to him and said, "Why aren't you travelling, Master? What are you still here for?" Sanzang looked up. "Where have you been?" he asked. "I couldn't move without you, so I had to sit here and wait till you came back. When I spoke to you a little severely you resented it and went off in a huff. I had to stay here and go hungry. You ought to be sorry for me," said Sanzang. "If you're hungry, Master, I'll go and beg you some food," suggested Monkey. "No need," his master replied, "there are still some dry provisions in my bundle. Take that bowl and fetch some water. When we have eaten we can be on our way."

Opening the bundle, Brother Monkey found some scones made of coarse flour, which he took out and gave to his master. He also noticed the dazzling brocade tunic and the hat with inlaid golden patterns. "Did you bring this tunic and hat with you from the east?" he asked. Sanzang had to make something up on the spot. "I used to wear them when I was young. With that hat on you can recite scriptures without ever having been taught them, and if you wear that tunic you can perform the rituals without any practice." "Dear Master, please let me wear them," Monkey pleaded. "I don't know whether they'll fit you, but if you can get them on, you can wear them." Monkey took off the old white tunic, put the brocade one on instead, and found that it was a perfect fit. Then he put the hat on his head. As soon as he had the hat on, Sanzang stopped eating and silently recited the Band-tightening Spell. "My head aches, my head aches," cried Brother Monkey, but his master went on and recited the spell several times more. Monkey, now rolling in agony, tore the hat to shreds, and Sanzang stopped reciting the spell for fear he would break the golden band. The moment the spell stopped the pain ended. Reaching up to feel his head, Monkey found something like a golden wire clamped so tightly around it that he could not wrench or snap it off. It had already taken root there. He took the needle out of his ear, forced it inside the band, and pulled wildly at it. Sanzang, again frightened that he would snap it, started to recite the spell once more. The pain was so bad this time that Monkey stood on his head, turned somersaults, and went red in the face and ears. His eyes were popping and his body went numb. Seeing the state he was in, Sanzang had to stop, and the pain stopped again too. "Master," said Monkey, "What a curse you put on me to give me a headache like that." "I didn't put a curse on you, I recited the Band-tightening Spell," Sanzang replied. "Say it again and see what happens," said Monkey, and when Sanzang did as he asked, Monkey's head ached again. "Stop, stop," he shouted, "the moment you started reciting it my head ached. Why did you do it?" "Will you accept my instruction now?" Sanzang asked. "Yes," Monkey replied. "Will you misbehave again in future?" "I certainly won't," said Monkey. "In that case you had better help me back on the horse," Sanzang replied. Monkey, who had been plunged into despair, summoned up his spirits, tightened the belt round his brocade tunic, got the horse ready, gathered up the luggage, and hurried off towards the West.

CHAPTER 13
The Dragon Subdued
Turns into a White Horse

Monkey looked after the Tang Priest as they headed west. They had been travelling for several days in the twelfth month of the year, with its freezing north winds and biting cold. Their path wound along overhanging precipices and steep cliffs, and they crossed range after range of dangerous mountains. One day Sanzang heard the sound of water as he rode along, and he turned around to shout, "Monkey, where's that sound of water coming from?" "As I remember, this place is called Eagle's Sorrow Gorge in the Coiled Snake Mountain. It must be the water in the gorge." Before he had finished speaking, the horse reached the edge of the gorge. Sanzang reined in and looked.

As master and disciple watched they heard a noise in the gorge as a dragon emerged from the waves, leapt up the cliff, and grabbed at Sanzang. Monkey dropped the luggage, lifted Sanzang off his horse, turned, and fled. The dragon, unable to catch him up, swallowed the white horse at a single gulp, then disappeared once more beneath the surface of the water. Monkey came back to swear and shout at it.

Now when the dragon had eaten Sanzang's white horse it lay low in the stream, hiding its miraculous powers and nourishing its vital nature. When it heard someone shouting and cursing it and demanding the horse back, it was unable to hold back its temper. Leaping up through the waves it asked, "How dare you make so free with your insults?" The moment he saw it, Monkey roared, "Don't go! Give us back our horse!" and swung his cudgel at the dragon's head. Baring its fangs and waving its claws, the dragon went for him. It was a noble battle that the pair of them fought beside the ravine.

Coming and going, fighting and resting, wheeling and turning, they battled on for a very long time until the dragon's strength was exhausted and his muscles numb. Unable to resist any longer, it turned around, dived into the water, and lay low at the bottom of the stream. It pretended to be deaf as the Monkey King cursed and railed at it, and did not emerge again.

Monkey could do nothing. Then he heard the voice of the Gold Headed Protector shouting from the sky, "Great Sage, there's no need for you to move. I'll go and ask the Bodhisattva to come here." Monkey, who was delighted, replied, "This is putting you to great trouble, but please be as quick as you can." The Protector then shot off on his cloud to the Southern Sea.

The Bodhisattva and the Protector reached the Coiled Snake Mountain before long, and stopping their cloud in mid-air they looked down and saw Brother Monkey cursing and shouting at the edge of the ravine. The Bodhisattva told the Protector to go to the edge of the ravine and shout, "Come out, Prince Jade Dragon, son of the Dragon King Ao Run, to see the Bodhisattva of the Southern Sea," at which he would emerge. The Protector went to the edge of the gorge and shouted this twice, at which the young dragon leapt up through the waves, took human form, stepped on a cloud, and greeted the Bodhisattva in mid-air. "In my gratitude to you, Bodhisattva, for saving my life, I have been waiting here for a long time, but I have had no news yet of the pilgrim who is going to fetch the scriptures." The Bodhisattva pointed to Brother Monkey and said, "Isn't he the pilgrim's great disciple?" "He's my enemy," the young dragon replied when he looked at him. "I ate his horse yesterday because I was starving, so he used some powers of his to fight me till I returned exhausted and terrified, then swore at me so that I had to shut myself in, too frightened to come out. He never said a word about anyone fetching scriptures." "You

never asked me my name, so how could I have told you?"
Monkey retorted. "I asked you 'Where are you from, you
bloody devil?' and you yelled, 'Never mind where I'm from, and
give me back that horse,'" said the dragon. "You never so
much as breathed the word 'Tang'." "You monkey, you are so
proud of your own strength that you never have a good word
for anyone else," said the Bodhisattva. "There will be others
who join you later on your journey, and when they ask you any
questions, the first thing you must mention is fetching the
scriptures. If you do that, you'll have their help without any
trouble at all."

Monkey was happy to accept instruction from her. The
Bodhisattva then went forward, broke off some of the pearls
from the dragon's head, soaked the end of her willow twig in
the sweet dew in her bottle, sprinkled it on the dragon's body,
breathed on it with magic breath and shouted. The dragon
turned into the exact likeness of the original horse. "You must
concentrate on wiping out your past sins," she told him, "and
when you have succeeded, you will rise above ordinary dragons
and be given back your golden body as a reward." The young
dragon took the bit between his teeth, and her words to heart.
The Bodhisattva told Sun Wukong to take him to see Sanzang
as she was returning to the Southern Sea. Monkey clung to her,
refusing to let her go. "I'm not going," he said, "I'm not going.
If the journey to the West is as tough as this, I can't possibly
keep this mortal priest safe, and if there are many more such
trials and tribulations, I'll have enough trouble keeping alive
myself. How can I ever achieve any reward? I'm not going,
I'm not going." "In the old days, before you had learnt to be a
human being," the Bodhisattva replied, "you were prepared to
work for your awakening with all your power. But now that
you have been delivered from a Heaven-sent calamity, you have
grown lazy. What's the matter with you? In our faith, to
achieve nirvana you must believe in good rewards. If you meet
with injury or suffering in future, you have only to call on
Heaven and Earth for them to respond; and if you get into a
really hopeless situation I shall come to rescue you myself. Come

over here as I have another power to give you." The Bodhisattva plucked three leaves from her willow twig, put them on
the back of Brother Monkey's head, and shouted "Change", on
which they turned into three life-saving hairs. "When the time
comes when nobody else will help you," she said, "they will
turn into whatever is needed to save you from disaster."

After hearing all these fine words, Monkey finally took his
leave of the All-merciful Bodhisattva, who went back to
Potaraka amidst scented breezes and coloured mists.

Monkey brought his cloud down to land, and led the dragon
horse by the mane to see Sanzang. "Master," he said, "we've
got our horse." Sanzang cheered up the moment he saw it.
"Why is it sturdier than it was before?" he asked. "Where did
you find it?" "Master, you must have been dreaming. The
Golden-headed Protector asked the Bodhisattva to come here,
and she turned the dragon in the gorge into our white horse.
The colouring is the same, but it hasn't got a saddle or a bridle,
which is why I had to drag it here." Sanzang was astounded.
"Where's the Bodhisattva? I must go and worship her," he
said. "She's back in the Southern Sea by now, so don't bother,"
Monkey replied. Sanzang took a pinch of earth as if he were
burning incense, knelt down, and bowed to the south. When
he had finished he got up and helped Monkey put their things
together for the journey ahead.

CHAPTER 14
At Gao Village Pig Becomes
Sanzang's Disciple

One evening, after they had been travelling along a desolate path for six or seven days, master and disciple saw a distant village. "Monkey," said Sanzang, "do you see the village not far over there? Let's go and ask them to put us up for the night; we can set off again tomorrow morning." "Wait till I've made sure it's all right before deciding," Monkey replied, gazing at the village as his master pulled on the silken rein.

When he had surveyed the scene, Brother Monkey said, "Go ahead, Master. It's definitely a good village. We can spend the night there." Sanzang urged his horse forward, and in a few moments they were at the beginning of the main street. A young man appeared wearing a silken turban, a blue jacket, a pair of trousers tied at the ankles, and a pair of straw sandals. He was carrying an umbrella in his hand and a pack on his back. He was a fine sight as he walked briskly down the street. Monkey grabbed him and asked, "Where are you going? I want to ask you something — where is this?" The fellow, who was trying to break loose, shouted, "Why ask me? I'm not the only person in the village." "Don't be angry, kind sir," replied Monkey, all smiles. "To help others is to help yourself. What harm can it do to tell me what the place is called? We might be able to bring your troubles to an end, you know." Struggle as he might, the fellow could not break loose. "This is Old Gao Village in the country of Stubet," he replied. "I'm Gao Cai from the family of Squire Gao. His youngest daughter is twenty and not yet married, but three years ago an evil spirit came and took her. He's been staying with us for three years, and the old man isn't at all pleased. He's always wanted to get rid of the evil spirit, but he refuses to go. Now he's shut the girl up in the back building for the best part of a year, and he won't let any of the family see her. My old man gave me two ounces of silver and sent me to find a priest to capture the monster. I've been on the go for ages now, and asked three or four of them, but they were all hopeless monks or pimples of Taoists — none of them could control him. The old man's just been swearing at me as an utter idiot, given me another half an ounce of silver as travelling expenses, and told me to find a good priest who'll deal with the monster. Then I was grabbed by you, you evil star, and that's made me later than ever. Let me go now — I've told you everything." "You're in luck," Monkey replied. "You needn't go any further or spend any of your money. We're not hopeless monks or pimples of Taoists. We've got some real magic powers, and we know how to deal with evil spirits. Go back and tell the head of your household that my master is a saintly monk, and the younger brother of the Emperor of the East, who has sent him to visit the Buddha in the Western Heaven and seek the scriptures. We are very good at controlling devils and capturing monsters." "Don't lie to me," the young man replied. "I've had enough of being pushed around. If you're tricking me, you haven't really got any special powers, and you can't capture that fiend, you'll only be getting me into more trouble than ever." "I swear I'm not fooling you," answered Monkey. "Show us the way to your front door." The young man saw that there was nothing for it but to pick up his bundle and umbrella, turn round, and take the two of them to his gate, where he said to them, "Reverend gentlemen, would you mind sitting here on the verandah for a moment while I go in and tell the master?" Only then did Monkey let go of him, put down the carrying-pole, take the horse's reins, and stand beside his master, who sat down by the gate.

The young man went in through the gate and straight to the main hall, where he happened to meet Squire Gao and told him everything.

The old man quickly put on his best clothes and went out with the youngster to greet the monks. He said with a smile, "Greetings, Venerable Elders," as he bowed, holding his hands together. Sanzang returned his bow, but Monkey stood there immobile. At the sight of Brother Monkey's ugly face the old man decided not to bow to him. "Why won't you pay your respects to me?" Monkey asked, at which the old man, somewhat frightened, said to the young man, "You'll be the death of me, you little wretch. We've already got one hideous monster at home as a son-in-law we can't get rid of, so why ever did you have to bring this thunder god here to ruin us?" "Gao, old chap, you've been living all these years for nothing — you've still got no sense. It's completely wrong to judge people by their faces. I may be no beauty, but I'm quite clever. I'll grab that evil spirit for you, catch that demon, seize your son-in-law, and give you back your daughter. I'll be doing you a good turn, so there's no need to fuss about my looks." The old man, now shaking with fear, pulled himself together and asked them in. Monkey took the horse's bridle, told the young man to carry the luggage, and went in with Sanzang. In his usual devil-may-care way he tethered the horse to one of the pillars of an open-air pavilion, pulled up a gleaming lacquered armchair, and told his master to sit down. Then he brought over a chair for himself and sat beside him.

When they were all seated the old man said, "The boy told me a moment ago that you were from the East." "That's right," Sanzang replied. "The court has sent me to worship the Buddha in the Western Heaven and ask for the scriptures. As we are passing this way on our journey, we would like to spend the night here before continuing on our way tomorrow morning." "If you two gentlemen just want to spend the night here, why all the talk about catching monsters?" "As we'll be spending the night here," Monkey put in, "we thought it would be fun to catch a few monsters while we're about it. May I ask how many there are in your residence?" "Good heavens," the old man exclaimed, "how ever many do you want? We've only got this monster of a son-in-law, and he's ruined our lives." "Tell me all about this monster from the beginning," Monkey said. "I must know about his magic powers if I'm to capture him for you." "This village has never had any trouble from ghosts, demons or evil spirits before. It was my misfortune to have no son, and three daughters, of whom the eldest is called Fragrant Orchid, the second Jade Orchid, and the third Blue Orchid. The other two were betrothed to men from the village when they were children and have been married off. I wanted the third to marry a man who would live here to support me in my old age, look after the household, and do jobs about the place. About three years ago a good-looking young fellow turned up who said that his name was Zhu and he came from the Mountain of Blessing. He told me that he had no parents or brothers, and wanted to marry and live with his in-laws. As he had no family commitments I offered him my daughter's hand, old fool that I am, and from the moment he became a member of our family he worked very hard. He ploughed and hoed without using oxen or tools; and he didn't need a scythe or a stick to harvest the crops. As day followed day, there was nothing wrong with him, except that he started to look different." "How?" Monkey asked. "At first he was a plump, dark chap, but later on he became a long-nosed, big-eared idiot with thick black hairs running down from the back of his head and a great, thick body. His face is just like a pig's. His appetite is enormous, too. He needs several bushels of grain at every main meal, and over a hundred griddle-cakes for breakfast. Luckily he is a vegetarian. If he ate meat and wine he would have ruined us in six months." "He has to eat so much because he works so hard," Sanzang commented. "But that's not the main thing," Squire Gao continued. "He can also summon up a wind, make clouds and mist come and go, and send pebbles and sand flying. He's terrified our neighbours, who don't feel safe living here any longer. He's shut my daughter away in the building at the back, and nobody's seen her for six months. We don't even know if she's still alive. That is how we know he's an evil monster, and why we want a priest to come and get rid of him." "No difficulty there," Monkey replied. "Don't worry, old chap, I guarantee that I'll get him tonight, make him write out a document divorcing your daughter, and bring her back to you. What do you say to that?" "Because I thought there'd be no harm in offering him my daughter, I've ruined my reputation and estranged all my relations," Squire Gao replied. "If you can catch him, why bother with a divorce document? Wipe him out for me, if you please." "Easy, easy," said Monkey. "I'll get him tonight."

Just watch Monkey as with his cudgel in his hand he takes hold of the old man and says, "Take me to the building at the back. I want to see where this evil spirit lives." Squire Gao led him to the door of the back building, and Monkey told him to bring the key at once. "Look here," the old man answered, "if a key would have done the trick, I wouldn't have had to ask for your services." "Can't you tell at your age when someone's joking?" Monkey asked. "I was only teasing. You shouldn't have taken me seriously." He felt the lock and found that molten copper had been poured into it, so he struck it a vicious blow with his cudgel and shattered it. Pushing the doors open, he saw that it was pitch-black inside. "Call your daughter's name, Old Gao, to see whether she's in here," he said. The old man summoned up his courage and called her name, and the daughter, recognizing her father's voice, answered feebly, "Dad, I'm in here."

When she came out and saw her father, she grabbed hold of him, put her hand round his head, and wept. "Don't cry," Monkey said, "don't cry. Where has the monster gone?" "I don't know. These days he's been setting out at dawn and only coming back in the middle of the night. There's always so much cloud and mist that I can't tell where he goes. He knows that my father wants to exorcise him, so he's always on the alert. That's why he comes back late and leaves at dawn." "Of course he would," Monkey remarked, adding, "old fellow, take the girl to the front building. You two can have a good long talk; I'm going to wait for the monster here. Don't be surprised if he doesn't turn up; but if he does, I'll wipe him out for you." The old man happily took his daughter to the front building.

Monkey then used some of his magic powers to turn himself into the likeness of the girl with a shake of his body. Then he sat down in the room to wait for the evil spirit. Before long there was a marvellous wind that sent stones and dust flying.

As this gale wind passed, an evil spirit appeared in midair. He was certainly ugly with his dark face, stubbly hair, long nose, and big ears. He wore a cotton tunic that was somewhere between black and blue, and round his waist was a patterned cotton cloth. "So that's what he's like," thought Monkey with a secret smile, and without greeting him or asking him anything he lay down on the bed, breathing heavily and pretending to be ill. Not knowing who this really was, the monster came straight in, put his arms around him and was going to kiss him. Monkey laughed to himself again as he thought, "So he really wants to do me." Then he thrust his hand up under the monster's long nose to throw him off balance. The monster fell off the bed. As the monster pulled himself up he leaned on the edge of the bed and said, "Darling, why are you so angry with me today? Is it because I'm late?" "I'm not angry," Monkey replied, "not angry at all." "If you're not angry with me, why did you make me fall over?" "You should have been more thoughtful and not tried hugging me and kissing me since I'm not feeling very well today. If I'd been my usual self I'd have been waiting for you at the door. Take your clothes off and come to bed." Not realizing what he was up to, the monster undressed. Monkey jumped out of bed and sat on the pot as the monster went back to bed and groped around without finding the girl. "Where've you gone, darling?" he asked. "Take your clothes off and come to bed." "Go to sleep," Monkey replied, "I'm doing a shit." The monster did as he was told. Monkey sighed and said, "What terrible luck." "What are you so fed up about?" the monster asked. "What do you mean by 'terrible luck'? I may have eaten some food and drunk some tea since marrying you, but I haven't been idle either. I've swept for your family and dug ditches, I've shifted bricks and tiles, I've built walls for you, I've ploughed and weeded your fields, I've sown your wheat, and I've transplanted your rice. I've made your family's fortune. These days you dress in brocade and have golden pins in your hair. You have fruit and flowers in all four seasons, and vegetables for the pot throughout the year. But despite this you're still not satisfied, groaning and moaning like that and complaining about your 'terrible luck'." "I didn't mean that," Monkey replied. "Today I could hear my parents through the wall. They were smashing up bricks and tiles and pretending to curse and beat me." "Why should they want to do that?" the monster asked. "They said that since we married and you became their resident son-in-law, all respectability has gone by the board. They were complaining about having such an ugly fellow as you around, and about never meeting any brother-in-law or other relations of yours. Besides, with all that wind and cloud whenever you come in or go out, they wonder who on earth you can be and what you are called. You're ruining their reputation, and disgracing the family. That's why they were so angry that they went through the motions of beating and cursing me." "I may be a bit of an eyesore," the monster said, "but if you want me to be a good-looker I can fix that without any difficulty. When I first came I had a word with your father, and he agreed to the marriage of his own free will. Why is he talking like this now? My home is the Cloud Pathway Cave on the Mount of Blessing. My surname, Zhu, is like my face — piggy — and my correct name is Zhu Ganglie, Iron-Haired Pig. You tell them all that if they ask you again."

"He's an honest monster," thought Monkey with delight. "He came out with all this without being tortured. Now I know who he is and where he's from, I'm sure I can catch him." "He's sent for a priest to come and catch you," Monkey said aloud. "Come to bed, come to bed, and forget about him," the monster said with a laugh. "I can do as many transformations as the Plough, and I have my nine-pronged rake too, so what have I to fear from priests, monks or Taoists?" "My father said that he'd asked that fellow by the name of Sun, the Great Sage

Equalling Heaven who made such trouble up in the Heavenly
Palace some five hundred years ago, to come and capture you."
The monster was somewhat taken aback on hearing this name,
and said, "In that case I'm off. We're through." "You can't just
go like that," said Monkey. "You wouldn't know," the monster
replied, "but that Protector of the Horses who made such
trouble in the Heavenly Palace is quite a fighter. I might not be
able to beat him, and my name would be mud." With these
words he pulled on his clothes, opened the door, and was just
going out when Monkey grabbed him, gave his own face a rub,
and changed back into his real form. "Where d'you think
you're going, my fine monster?" he roared, adding, "take a look
and see who I am." The monster turned round and saw
Monkey's protruding teeth, pinched face, fiery eyes with golden
pupils, bald head and hairy face. At the sight of this thunder
god incarnate his hands were numbed and his legs paralyzed;
then with a great tearing sound he broke free, ripping his
clothes, and escaped in the form of a hurricane. Monkey rushed
after him, grabbed his iron cudgel, and took a swipe at the
wind. The monster then changed into ten thousand sparks and
went straight back to his mountain. Monkey mounted his cloud
and went after him.

As he was racing along, Monkey saw a tall mountain appear
in front of them. Here the monster put himself together again
by reassembling the sparks, rushed into a cave, and came out
with a nine-pronged rake in his hand to do battle. Monkey was
in no mood to spare him after this, and he struck at the
monster's head with his cudgel.

They fought from the second watch of the night until the
sky began to grow light in the east. The monster, no longer able
to resist his enemy, broke away and fled, turning himself into a
hurricane again. He went straight back to his cave, shut the
gates behind him, and did not come out. Monkey saw a stone
tablet outside the cave on which was inscribed CLOUD PATH-
WAY CAVE. The monster did not come out again and it was
now broad daylight, so Monkey thought that as his master might
be waiting for him he had better go back to see him. He could

come back later to catch the monster. He gave his cloud a kick and was back in Old Gao Village in an instant.

Sanzang, meanwhile, had been talking all night with the elders about things ancient and modern, and had not slept a wink. Just as he was beginning to think that Brother Monkey would not come back, Monkey appeared in the courtyard, put away his iron club, straightened his clothes, and entered the main room. "Master, I'm here," he announced, giving the old men such a surprise that they all fell to their knees and thanked him for his efforts. "You've been out all night, Monkey," Sanzang said. "Where did you catch that evil spirit?" "He's no common or garden ghost, Master," Monkey replied, "and he isn't an ordinary wild animal turned monster. He is Marshal Tian Peng, who was exiled to the mortal world. As he was placed in the wrong womb he has a face like a wild boar, but he's still kept his original divine nature. He says that he takes his name from his looks and is called Zhu Ganglie, Iron-haired Pig. He fought with me all night. He broke off the engagement in terror as the dawn broke and shut himself in his cave. I was going to smash down the gates and have it out with him, but then it occurred to me that you might be worried after waiting for me so long, so I came back to put you in the picture first."

As soon as Monkey had made his report, he disappeared. He leapt up the mountain again and smashed the gates of the cave to splinters with a single blow of his cudgel, shouting, "Come out and fight Monkey, you chaff-guzzling moron." The monster, who had been snoring inside, heard the gates being smashed and the insulting "chaff-guzzling moron", and went wild with fury. Seizing his rake and summoning up his spirit, he rushed out and shrieked, "I remember you, you baboon! When you made trouble in Heaven, you lived in the Water Curtain Cave on the Mountain of Flowers and Fruit . I haven't heard of you for a very long time. What brings you here, and why are you bullying me in front of my own gates? Surely my father-in-law didn't go all that way to ask you to come here?" "No," said Monkey, "he didn't. I have turned away from evil and been converted to good. I have given up Taoism and become a

Buddhist. I am protecting the Patriarch Sanzang, the younger brother of the Great Tang Emperor, on his journey to the Western Heaven to visit the Buddha and ask for the scriptures. We happened to ask for a night's lodging when we came to Gao Village, and in the course of our conversation Old Gao asked me to rescue his daughter and capture you, you chaff-guzzling moron."

The monster dropped his rake to the ground, and said, "Where's this pilgrim? Please take me to meet him." "What do you want to see him for?" Monkey asked. "Guanyin converted me and told me to go with that pilgrim, the one who's going to the Western Heaven to worship the Buddha and ask for the scriptures. I'll be able to make up for my sins through this good deed, and win a good reward. I've been waiting for him for years, but there's been no news of him till now. If you're a disciple of his, why didn't you say something about fetching the scriptures before, instead of making this vicious attack on me in my own home?" "This had better not be a trick to make me let you get away," said Monkey. "If you really want to protect the Tang Priest and you aren't trying to kid me, then you'd better make a vow to Heaven, and I'll take you to meet my master." The monster fell to his knees with a thud, and kowtowed to the sky. He cried out, "If I'm not completely sincere, cut me up into ten thousand bits for breaking the laws of Heaven." After hearing him swear this oath, Monkey said, "Very well then, now light a brand and burn this place of yours out. If you do that, I'll take you." The monster piled up some reeds and brambles, lit a brand, and set the Cloud Pathway Cave on fire; it burned as well as a brick kiln that has got out of control. "I've no second thoughts," he said, "so please take me to see him."

The two of them went back through cloud and mist to Gao Village. In a moment they were back at the village. Holding the monster's rake in one hand and twisting his ear with the other, Monkey brought him before Sanzang. The monster went forward, fell to his knees, and kowtowed to Sanzang with his hands behind his back. "Master," he shouted, "Your disciple failed to welcome you. Had I known, Master, that you were staying in my father-in-law's house, I'd have come to greet you and do homage, and I'd have been saved all this agony." "How did you make him submit and come to pay homage?" Sanzang asked Monkey. Monkey then let the monster go, hit him with the handle of the rake, and yelled, "Tell him, fool." The monster then told Sanzang all about how he had been converted by the Bodhisattva.

Sanzang was so pleased that he asked Squire Gao for an incense table to be brought, which was done at once. Sanzang then washed his hands, burnt incense, bowed low to the south, and said, "Thanks be to the Bodhisattva for her divine grace." The elders also burnt incense and bowed low in worship. When this was done, Sanzang took the seat of honour in the hall and told Monkey to untie the monster. Monkey shook himself to take his hairs back, and the ropes untied themselves. The monster bowed to Sanzang once more and vowed to go to the West with him. Then he bowed to Monkey as his elder brother because he had joined first, addressing him as "elder brother" from then on. "If you wish to earn a good reward by going with me as my disciple, I'll give you a Buddhist name to call you by." "Master," he replied, "when the Bodhisattva laid her hands upon my head and told me to obey the prohibitions, she gave me a Buddhist name — Zhu Wuneng, Pig Awakened to Power." "Wonderful, wonderful," said Sanzang with a smile. "Your elder brother is called Wukong, Awakened to Emptiness, and you're called Awakened to Power. That makes us members of the same sect in the Buddhist faith." "Master," said Pig, "I have been instructed by the Bodhisattva and I never eat the five stinking foods and the three forbidden meats — wild goose, dog, and snake-fish. I've eaten vegetarian food in my father-in-law's house and never touched the stinking foods; but now that I have met you, Master, I'm freed from these restrictions." "You are not," Sanzang replied. "You are not to eat the five stinking foods and the three forbidden meats, and I'm giving you another name: Eight Prohibitions, or Bajie." "I shall obey my master's command," the idiot happily replied, and from then on he was known as Zhu Bajie, or Eight Prohibitions Pig.

高老莊大聖降魔

The Great Sage Subdues a Demon at Gao Village

Early next morning, Sanzang and his two disciples set out to continue their journey to the west.

CHAPTER 15
At the Flowing Sands River Friar Sand Becomes a Disciple

The Tang Priest and his two disciples were heading west across a plain. The time passed rapidly, and summer gave way to autumn. Cold cicadas sang in moulting willow trees, and the Great Fire Star sank below the western horizon. As they were travelling one day they saw the mighty waves of a great river, boiling and raging. Depressed and worried, Sanzang reined in his horse and noticed a stone tablet beside the river. The three of them went to look at it, and they saw the words FLOWING SANDS RIVER inscribed on it in the ancient curly style. On the base of the tablet were four lines in the standard script:

> "Three hundred miles of flowing sands,
> Three thousand fathoms of weak water,
> On which a goose feather will not float,
> And the flower of a reed will sink."

As the three of them were looking at this tablet they heard the waves make a roar like a collapsing mountain as a most hideous evil spirit emerged from the water. The ogre had an indigo face, neither black nor green, with a head of matted hair, as red as fire, and a pair of staring eyes, gleaming like lamps.

The monster came to the bank in a whirlwind and rushed straight at the Tang Priest. Monkey picked Sanzang up at once, turned, and made off up the high bank. Pig dropped his carrying-pole, grabbed his rake, and struck at the evil spirit, who parried the blow with his staff.

The pair of them battled on for twenty rounds, but neither emerged as the victor. The Great Sage, who was holding on to the horse and looking after the luggage after carrying the Tang Priest to safety, became worked up into such a fury at the sight of Pig and the monster fighting that he ground his teeth and clenched his fists. When he could hold himself back no longer, he pulled out his cudgel and said, "Master, you sit here and don't be afraid. I'm going to play with him." Ignoring Sanzang's pleas for him to stay, he whistled, jumped down to the side of the river, and found that the fight between Pig and the ogre was at its height. Brother Monkey swung his cudgel and aimed it at the ogre's head, but the ogre made a lightning turn and plunged straight into the river.

The two of them then clasped hands and went back talking and laughing to see Sanzang, who asked, "Did you catch the ogre?" "No," Monkey said, "he couldn't take any more and dived back into the water." "He has lived here for a long time, disciple," Sanzang said, "and must know the shallows and deeps here. We must have a water expert to lead us across this vast expanse of weak water that has no boats." "Yes," said Monkey, "as the saying goes, 'What's near cinnabar goes red, and what's next to ink turns black.' As that ogre lives here he must be a water expert, so if we catch him we shouldn't kill him — we should make him take you across, Master, before finishing him off." "There's no time to lose, brother," said Pig. "You go and catch him while I look after the master." "This is something I can't talk big about," said Monkey with a smile. "I'm not all that good at underwater stuff. Even to walk underwater I have to make a magic hand movement and recite a water-repelling spell before I can move. The only other way I can get about there is by turning myself into a fish, a shrimp, a crab or a turtle. I can manage any strange and wonderful magic on a mountain or in the clouds that you can do, but when

it comes to underwater business, I'm useless." "When I was
the commander of the Milky Way, the heavenly river, in the
old days," said Pig, "I had a force of eighty thousand sailors,
so I know a bit about water. But I'm afraid that he might have
generations of clansmen down there, and that would be too
much for me. And if they got me, we'd be in a real mess."
"You go into the water and start a fight with him there," said
Monkey. "Don't fight hard, and don't win. You must lose
and lure him out, then I can finish him off for you." "Very well
then, I'll be off," said Pig. After stripping off his brocade tunic
and removing his shoes he swung his rake in both hands and
made his way into the water, where the tricks he had learnt
years back enabled him to go through the waves to the river-bed,
across which he advanced.

The ogre had now recovered his breath after his earlier
defeat, and when he heard someone pushing the waters aside
he leapt to his feet to look. Seeing that it was Pig brandishing
his rake, the monster raised his staff and shouted at him,
"Where do you think you're going, monk? Watch out, and take
this." Pig warded off the blow with his rake and replied, "Who
are you, evil spirit, and why are you blocking the way?" "You
may not realize who I am," the monster replied, "but I'm no
fiend, demon, ghost or monster, and I don't lack a name either."
"If you're not a fiend, a demon, or a monster, then why do you
live here taking life? Tell me your name truthfully and I'll
spare your life." The monster replied, "I was the General who
Lifts the Curtain for the Great Jade Emperor. However, as I
carelessly smashed some jade and crystal, I was exiled to this
Flowing Sands River. Here, I make my meals on passers-by. As
you brought yourselves to my gates today, I'll turn you into salted
mince."

Pig was extremely angry to hear this, and he replied,
"You're completely blind, wretch. Damned cheek — take a
dose of this rake." When the monster saw the rake coming at
him he did a "phoenix nod" to avoid it. The two of them fought
their way up to the surface of the water, where each of them
trod on the waves. They battled on for four hours, but the issue

was still undecided.

The Great Sage, who was standing beside the Tang Priest to guard him, watched the fight on the water with longing, unable to do anything. Then Pig feinted with his rake, pretended to be beaten, and made for the eastern bank with the ogre rushing after him. When he had almost reached the bank, Monkey could hold himself back no longer. Abandoning his master, he sprang down to the river's edge with his cudgel in his hand and took a swing at the ogre's head. Not daring to face him, the monster went straight back into the river. "Protector of the Horses," Pig shouted, "you impatient ape. You should have taken it a bit more slowly and waited till I'd drawn him up to high ground, and then cut him off from the river-bank. Then he wouldn't have been able to go back and we'd have caught him. But now he's gone back in, he'll never come out again." "Don't shout, idiot," Monkey said with a smile, "don't shout. Let's go back and see our master."

Pig reached the top of the bank with Monkey and joined Sanzang. "So what are we going to do?" Sanzang asked. "Relax, Master," said Monkey, "there's no need to worry. It's getting late, so you'd better sit on the bank while I go and beg some food. When you've eaten that you can go to sleep, and we can decide what to do tomorrow morning." "Good idea," said Pig. "Be as quick as you can."

Monkey leapt up on his cloud, went due north to a house where he begged some food, and came back to give it to his master. Seeing him come back so soon, Sanzang said to him, "Monkey, let's go to the house where you begged this food and ask them how to cross this river. That would be better than having to fight this ogre." "But that house is a long way away," laughed Monkey. "It's about two thousand miles from here. What would be the point in asking them about this river? They wouldn't know anything about it." "You're telling tall stories again," Pig said. "If it's two thousand miles away, how did you get there and back so fast?" "You wouldn't know, of course," Brother Monkey replied, "that my somersault cloud can cover thirty-six thousand miles with a single bound. To do a mere two-thousand-mile return journey takes only a couple of nods and a bow — there's nothing to it." "If it's so easy, brother," said Pig, "you should carry the master on your back, take him across with just a couple of nods and a bow, and save us all the trouble of fighting the monster." "You can ride clouds, can't you?" said Monkey. "Why don't you carry the master across?" "The master's mortal flesh and bones are heavier than Mount Tai," said Pig, "so although I can ride clouds I could never lift him. Nothing but your somersault will do the trick." "My somersault is the same as cloud-riding," Monkey said, "except that it takes you further. I'm no more able to carry him than you are. Although our master cannot escape from the sea of suffering he wants to go to a foreign land, so he finds every inch of the way heavy going. All we can do is escort him and see that he comes to no harm. We can't undergo all that suffering on his behalf, nor can we fetch the scriptures for him. Even if we went ahead to see the Buddha, he wouldn't give the scriptures to you or me. After all, if we could get them that easily, we'd have nothing to do." Pig accepted everything Monkey said, then they ate some plain rice without any vegetables, after which the three of them went to sleep on the eastern bank of the Flowing Sands River.

The next morning, Pig rubbed his face, summoned up his energy, took his rake in both hands, went down to the river, and parted the waters as he went back to the monster's lair once more. The ogre, who had only just woken up, turned to see what was happening the moment he heard the waters being pushed apart. Observing that a rake-wielding Pig was upon him, he sprang to his feet to stop him, shouting, "Not so fast, not so fast. Take this." Pig blocked the blow from the staff with his rake and said, "What do you mean by telling your ancestor to 'take this' from that mourner's staff of yours?" "You know nothing, you wretch," the monster replied, and continued, "This staff of mine was given me by the Jade Emperor. It's no ordinary weapon. It is not like that rusty rake of yours, which is only any good for farming or vegetable-growing."

The ogre dropped his defensive posture and fought with Pig

from the river-bed to the surface of the water. The battle went on for thirty rounds, but neither emerged victorious. Pig feigned defeat once again, and fled trailing his rake behind him. The ogre charged through the waves after him as far as the bank, when Pig shouted at him, "I'll get you, you damned ogre. Come up on this higher ground where we can fight with dry land under our feet." "You're trying to lure me up there, damn you," the monster replied, "for your mate to come and get me. Come back and fight in the water." The fiend, who had more sense than to go up the bank again, stood at the river's edge, shouting it out with Pig.

When Monkey saw that the monster was not coming up on the bank he seethed with frustration at not being able to catch him. "Master," he said, "you sit here while I do a 'Hungry Eagle Falling on Its Prey' on him." He somersaulted into mid-air, then plummeted down to catch the ogre, who heard the noise of a wind as he was yelling at Pig, turned immediately, and saw Monkey descending from the clouds. He put his staff away, plunged into the water with a splash, and was seen no more. "Brother," said Monkey to Pig as he landed on the bank, "the monster's got a lot more clever. Whatever are we to do if he won't come on to the bank again?" "It's impossible," said Pig, "we'll never be able to beat him. Even if I put everything I've got into it, I can only hold my own against him." "Let's go and see the master," Monkey said.

The two of them climbed the bank and told the Tang Priest about the difficulty of capturing the ogre. "It's so hard," said Sanzang, tears streaming down his cheeks. "However are we going to cross?" "No need to worry, Master," said Monkey. "The monster is lurking deep down on the river-bed, where it's very hard to move around. You stay here and look after the master, Pig, and don't fight with the ogre again. I'm going to the Southern Sea." "What for?" Pig asked. "This whole business of fetching the scriptures was started by the Bodhisattva Guanyin, and it was she who converted us. Now we are stuck here at the Flowing Sands River nobody but she can sort this one out. It's better to ask for her help than to fight that monster." "Yes, yes," said Pig, "and when you're there, please thank her for converting me." "If you're going to ask the Bodhisattva to come," Sanzang said, "don't waste a moment, and be back as quickly as possible."

Monkey then somersaulted off on his cloud towards the Southern Sea, and before an hour was up he saw Potaraka Island. An instant later he landed outside the Purple Bamboo Grove, where the twenty-four devas came forward to greet him with the words, "Why have you come, Great Sage?" "Because my master is in trouble," Monkey replied, "I have come for an audience with the Bodhisattva." After hearing the news, the Bodhisattva opened the door and summoned Monkey to her presence. The Great Sage greeted her with grave reverence.

"Why aren't you looking after the Tang Priest," she asked. "and why have you come to see me?" "My master won a new disciple at Gao Village, Bodhisattva," Brother Monkey reported. "He's called Zhu Bajie and also has the Buddhist name Wuneng thanks to you. We have now reached the Flowing Sands River after crossing the Yellow Wind Ridge, but it's a thousand miles of Weak Water and my master cannot cross it. On top of this there's an evil monster in the river who's a great fighter, and although our Pig had three great battles with him on the surface of the water, he couldn't beat the ogre, who is still blocking our way and preventing my master from crossing. This is why I've come to see you and ask you in your mercy to help him across." "You have revealed your conceit once again, you ape," said the Bodhisattva. "Why didn't you tell the monster that you were protecting the Tang Priest?" "We wanted to catch him," Monkey replied, "and make him take our master across the river. As I'm not up to much in the water and Pig was the only one who could find the ogre's den and did all the talking, I expect he never mentioned fetching the scriptures." "The ogre of the Flowing Sands River is the mortal incarnation of the Great Curtain-lifting General," said Guanyin, "and is a believer whom I converted myself and instructed to protect those who would be coming to fetch the scriptures. If you had told him that you had come from the East to fetch the scriptures, far from fighting you, he would certainly have joined you." "But the craven monster is now skulking in the river, too frightened to come out," Monkey said, "so how are we to make him join us, and how is my master to cross the weak water?"

The Bodhisattva sent for her disciple Huian and produced a red bottle-gourd from her sleeve. "Take this gourd," she said, "and go with Sun Wukong to the Flowing Sands River. Shout 'Wujing' — 'Awakened to Purity' — and he'll come out. First take him to submit to the Tang Priest, and then make him thread his nine skulls on a string like the nine palaces of the Pole Star. If he puts this gourd in the middle of them, it will make a dharma boat to ferry the Tang Priest across the river." In obedience to the Bodhisattva's command, Huian and the Great Sage took the gourd with them from the Tide Cave and the Purple Bamboo Grove.

A little later the pair of them brought their clouds down to land on the bank of the Flowing Sands River. Moksa then went by cloud and stood over the river with the gourd in his hands. "Wujing, Wujing," he shouted at the top of his voice, "the pilgrims who are going to fetch the scriptures have been here for a long time. Why haven't you submitted to them?"

The ogre, who had gone back to the river-bed for fear of the Monkey King, was resting in his den when he heard his Buddhist name being called and realized that this was a message from the Bodhisattva Guanyin. On hearing that the pilgrims were there, his fears of being attacked melted away, and he pushed his head up through the waves to see that it was Moksa the Novice. Look at him as he bows to Moksa, his face wreathed in smiles. "I'm sorry I did not welcome you properly, Your Holiness," he said. "Where is the Bodhisattva?" "She didn't come," Moksa replied. "She sent me to tell you to be the Tang Priest's disciple. You are to take the nine skulls you wear round your neck, arrange them with this gourd in the pattern of the nine palaces of the Pole Star, and make a dharma boat to ferry him across this weak water." "Where is the pilgrim?" Wujing asked. "There he is, sitting on the bank," said Moksa, pointing at Sanzang. Wujing then noticed Pig and said, "I don't know where that bloody creature is from, but he fought with me for two whole days and never said a word about fetching scriptures. And as for this one," he added, noticing Monkey, "he's that one's accomplice and a real terror. I'm not going with them." "That one is Zhu Bajie, and this one is Brother Monkey. They are both disciples of the Tang Priest who have been converted by the Bodhisattva, so you have nothing to fear from them. Let me present you to the Tang Priest." Wujing put away his staff, straightened his yellow brocade tunic, jumped ashore, knelt before the Tang Priest, and said, "Master, your disciple's eyes have no pupils in them — I beg you to forgive me for attacking your followers instead of recognizing who they were." "You pustule," said Pig, "why did you fight me instead of submitting? What did you mean by it?" "You can't blame him, brother," said Monkey. "We didn't tell him our names or even mention fetching the scriptures." "Do you believe in our teachings with all your heart?" Sanzang asked. "I was converted by the Bodhisattva," Wujing replied, "and she gave me this river's name as a surname and called me by the Buddhist name of Sha Wujing, or Sand Awakened to Purity, so of course I must follow you, Master." "In that case," said Sanzang, "bring the razor over, Monkey, and cut his hair off." The Great Sage obediently shaved the monster's head, who then bowed to Sanzang, Monkey, and Pig with appropriate degrees of reverence. When Sanzang saw him do this just like a real monk he gave him another name — Friar Sand. "Now that you have entered the faith," said Moksa, "there's no need to waste time talking. Make that dharma boat at once."

Friar Sand took the skulls from round his neck without delay and tied them into the pattern of the nine palaces of the Pole Star with the Bodhisattva's gourd in the middle. Then he asked Sanzang to board it, and Sanzang found when he sat on it that it was as stable as a small dinghy. Pig and Friar Sand supported him to left and right, while Monkey led the dragon horse through the clouds behind him, and Moksa stood above him on guard. Sanzang thus made a calm and windless crossing of the weak water of the Flowing Sands River. He moved with the speed of an arrow, and it was not long before he climbed ashore on the other side. Moksa then landed his cloud, and took back the gourd. The nine skulls changed into nine gusts of wind and disappeared. Sanzang bowed to Moksa to thank him and worshipped the Bodhisattva. Moksa then returned to the Eastern Ocean, while Sanzang and his disciples set out again on their journey to the west.

八戒大戰流沙河

The Fight in the Flowing Sands River

CHAPTER 16
In Wuzhuang Temple Monkey Steals Manfruits

One day, after they had been going for a long time, they saw a high mountain blocking their way.

This mountain was called the Mountain of Infinite Longevity, and there was a Taoist temple on it called the Wuzhuang Temple. In this temple lived an immortal whose Taoist name was Zhen Yuan Zi. He was also known as Conjoint Lord of the Age. The temple had a rare treasure which was known as "Grass-returning Cinnabar" or "manfruit". It took three thousand years to blossom, three thousand years to form the fruit, and another three thousand years for the fruit to ripen, so that very nearly ten thousand years had to pass before the fruit could be eaten. Only thirty fruit were formed each ten thousand years, and they were shaped just like a newborn baby, complete with limbs and sense organs. Anyone whose destiny permitted him to smell one would live for three hundred and sixty years, and if you ate one you would live for forty-seven thousand years.

That day the Great Immortal Zhen Yuan had received an invitation from the Original Celestial Jade Pure One inviting him to the Miluo Palace in the Heaven of Supreme Purity to hear a lecture on the Product of Undifferentiated Unity. The immortals who had studied under this great immortal were too numerous to count, and he now had forty-eight disciples who had all attained to the full truth of the Way. That day, the

Great Immortal took forty-six of them with him to hear the lecture in the upper world, leaving the two youngest, Pure Wind and Bright Moon, to look after the temple. Pure Wind was 1,320 years old, and Bright Moon had just turned 1,200. The Great Immortal gave his instructions to the two boys: "You two will have to look after the temple carefully. An old friend of mine who is a holy monk sent by the Tang Emperor in the East will be coming this way before long. He is known as Sanzang and is going to ask for the scriptures in the Western Heaven. You can pick two manfruits for him but no more."

The Tang Priest and his three followers, meanwhile, were strolling on the mountain when they noticed some tall buildings rising above a bamboo grove. It did not take them long to reach the gate.

Sanzang dismounted and saw that there was a stone tablet outside the gate on which was inscribed in large letters:

BLESSED LAND OF THE MOUNTAIN
OF INFINITE LONGEVITY
CAVE HEAVEN OF THE WUZHUANG TEMPLE

"Good people must live in this temple," said Friar Sand, "set as it is in such fresh, light scenery. Let's go in and have a look round. When we go back to the East at the end of our journey, this will be one of the finest sights we'll have seen." "Well spoken," said Monkey, and they all went in.

As they went through the second gate they saw two boys come scurrying out.

The two boys bowed and greeted them. "We are sorry we did not welcome you properly, venerable master," they said. "Please sit down." Sanzang was delighted, and he accompanied the two boys up to the main hall of the temple, which faced south. There was a patterned lattice window that let through the light on top of the door that the boys pushed open. They asked the Tang Priest to come in, and he saw two huge words executed in many colours hanging on the wall — Heaven and Earth. There was an incense table of red carved lacquer on which stood a pair of golden censers and a supply of incense.

Bright Moon and Pure Wind went over to Sanzang and said, "May we ask you, venerable master, whether you are the Sanzang of the Great Tang who is going to the Western Heaven to fetch the scriptures?" "Yes, I am," said Sanzang, returning their bows. "How did you know who I was?" "Our master told us before he went," they replied, "to go out to meet you long before you got here, but as you came faster than we expected we failed to do so. Please sit down, teacher, while we fetch you some tea." "I am honoured," said Sanzang. Bright Moon hurried out and came back with a cup of fragrant tea for him. When Sanzang had drunk the tea, Pure Wind said to Bright Moon, "We must do as our teacher told us and fetch the fruit."

The two boys left Sanzang and went to their room, where one of them picked up a golden rod and the other a red dish, on which he put many a silk handkerchief as cushioning. They went into the manfruit orchard, where Pure Wind climbed the tree and tapped the fruit with the golden rod while Bright Moon waited below to catch them in the dish. They only took a few moments to knock down and catch a couple, which they took to the front hall to offer to Sanzang with the words, "This temple of ours is on a remote and desolate mountain, master Sanzang, and there is no local delicacy we can offer you except these two pieces of fruit. We hope they will quench your thirst." At the sight of the manfruit the monk recoiled some three feet, shaking with horror. "Goodness me!" he exclaimed. "How could you be so reduced to starvation in this year of plenty as to eat human flesh? And how could I possibly quench my thirst with a newborn baby?" "Venerable master," said Bright Moon, "this is what is called 'manfruit', and there is no reason why you should not eat one." "Nonsense, nonsense," said Sanzang. "They were conceived by their fathers and mothers and had to go through no end of suffering before they were born. How can you treat them as fruit when they haven't been alive for three days yet?" "They really and truly grew on a tree," said Pure Wind. "Stuff and rubbish," Sanzang replied. "Babies don't grow on trees."

As he refused absolutely to eat them, the two boys had to take the dish away and go back to their room. This fruit was rather difficult to handle, and did not keep for long without becoming hard and inedible, so the boys sat on their beds and ate one each.

They did not realize that as there was only a wall separating their room from the kitchen, their whispering could be clearly heard. Pig was in there cooking the rice when he heard them talk as they fetched the golden rod and the red dish. Later he heard them saying that the Tang Priest had not recognized the manfruit, which was why they took them back to their room to eat. "I'd love to try one, but I don't know how," thought Pig, unable to prevent his mouth from watering. Too stupid to do anything about it himself, he had to wait until he could talk it over with Brother Monkey. He had now lost all interest in stoking the stove as he stood in front of it, constantly poking his head outside the kitchen to look for Monkey. Before long Monkey appeared leading the horse, which he tethered to a locust tree. As he came round to the back, Pig waved frantically to him and said, "Come here, come here." Monkey turned round, came to the kitchen door, and said, "What are you yelling for, idiot? Not enough food for you? Let the old monk eat his fill, then we two can go to the next big house that lies ahead and beg for some more." "Have you seen manfruit then?" Pig asked. "No, I haven't," said Monkey with astonishment. "But I've heard that manfruit is Grass-returning Cinnabar, and that anyone who eats it lives to a great old age. Where can we get some?" "Here," said Pig. "Those boys gave two to our master, but master didn't know what they were. He thought they were newborn babies and wouldn't eat them. Those boys are disgraceful — instead of giving them to us as they should have done they sneaked off into their room and had one each — I was drooling. I wish I knew how I could try one. Surely you've got some dodge for getting into the orchard and pinching a few for us. You have, haven't you?" "Easy," said Monkey. "I'll go in and pick some." As he rushed out Pig grabbed him and said, "I heard them saying in their room that they needed a golden rod to knock them down with. You must do this very carefully — nobody must know about it." "I know, I know," replied Monkey.

The Great Sage made himself invisible and slipped into the boys' room, only to find that after eating the fruit they had gone to the front hall, where they were talking to Sanzang. Monkey looked all around the room for the golden rod until he saw a two-foot length of gold hanging from the window lattice. It was about as thick as a finger. At the bottom was a lump like a bulb of garlic, and at the top was a hole through which was fastened a green silk tassel. "So this must be what they call the golden rod," he thought as he took it down. He left the room and pushed open a pair of gates at the back.

Monkey saw a huge tree in front of him with fragrant branches and shade-giving green leaves shaped rather like those of plantains. The tree was about a thousand feet high, and its trunk was some seventy or eighty feet round. Monkey leant against it and looked up, and on a branch that was pointing south he saw a manfruit, which really did look just like a newborn child. The stem came from its bottom, and as it hung from the branch its hands and feet waved wildly around and it shook its head. Monkey was thoroughly delighted, and he thought in admiration, "What a splendid thing — a real rarity, a real rarity." And with that thought he went shooting up the tree.

With one blow from the golden rod Monkey sent the manfruit tumbling down. He jumped down to fetch it, but it was nowhere to be seen. He searched the grass all around, but could not find a trace of it. "It must be the case that if the manfruits meet earth they go into it," thought Monkey.

The Great Sage now had a plan. He climbed the tree and then held the rod in one hand while he undid the lapel of his cloth tunic and made it into a kind of pouch. He pushed the leaves and branches aside and knocked down three manfruits, which he caught in his tunic. He jumped out of the tree and went straight to the kitchen, where a smiling Pig asked him if he had got any. "This is the stuff, isn't it?" said Monkey.

"I was able to get some. We mustn't leave Friar Sand in the dark, so give him a shout." "Come here, Friar Sand," Pig called, waving his hand. Friar Sand put the luggage down, hurried into the kitchen, and asked, "Why did you call me?" "Do you know what these are?" Monkey asked, opening his tunic. "Manfruits," said Friar Sand as soon as he saw them. "No need to ask," said Monkey. "We're having one each."

So each of them had one manfruit to eat. Pig had both an enormous appetite and an enormous mouth, and had, moreover, been suffering pangs of hunger ever since hearing the Taoist boys eating. So the moment he saw the fruit he grabbed one, opened his mouth, and gulped it down whole; then he put on an innocent expression and shamelessly asked the other two what they were eating. "Manfruit," Friar Sand replied. "What does it taste like?" Pig asked. "Ignore him, Friar Sand," said Monkey. "He's already eaten his, and he's no business to ask you." "Brother," said Pig, "I ate mine too fast. I didn't nibble it delicately and taste the flavour like you two. I don't even know if it had a stone or not as I gulped it straight down. You should finish what you've started: you've whetted my appetite, so you ought to get me another to eat slowly." "You're never satisfied," Monkey replied. "These things aren't like rice or flour — you can't go stuffing yourself full of them. Only thirty grow in every ten thousand years, so we can think ourselves very lucky indeed to have a whole one each. Come off it, Pig, you've had enough." He got up and tossed the golden rod back into the Taoist boys' room through the window, paying no more attention to Pig, who went on grumbling.

Before long the Taoist boys were back in their room, and they heard Pig moaning, "I didn't enjoy my manfruit; I wish I could have another." Pure Wind's suspicion was aroused, and he said to Bright Moon, "Did you hear that long-snouted monk saying he wished he could have another manfruit? Our master told us when he went that we were to be careful of those gangsters and not let them steal our treasures." "This is terrible, terrible," said Bright Moon. "What's the golden rod doing on the floor? We'd better go into the garden and take a look around." The two of them rushed round the flower garden, found the vegetable garden gate open too, and charged into the manfruit garden. They leant on the tree and looked into it to count the fruit, but however often they added the number up, it always came to twenty-two. "Can you do arithmetic?" Bright Moon asked, and Pure Wind replied, "Yes. Tell me the figures." "There were originally thirty manfruits," said Bright Moon. "When our master opened the garden two were divided up and eaten, which left twenty-eight. Just now we knocked two down to give the Tang Priest, which left twenty-six. But there are only twenty-two now, which means that we're four short. It goes without saying that those evil men must have stolen them. Let's go and tell that Tang Priest what we think of him."

The two of them went from the garden to the front hall, where they pointed at Sanzang and poured the most filthy and stinking abuse on him. It was more than Sanzang could stand, so he said, "What are you making all this fuss about, immortal boys? Please stop. I wouldn't mind you being a bit offhand with me, but you can't talk in this outrageous way." "Are you deaf?" Pure Wind asked. "We're not talking a foreign language, and you can understand us perfectly well. You've stolen our manfruit, and you've no right to forbid us to mention it." "What does manfruit look like?" Sanzang asked. "It's what we offered you just now and you said looked like babies." "Amitabha Buddha!" Sanzang exclaimed. "I shook with terror at the very sight of them — I couldn't possibly steal one. What do you mean by making so unjust an accusation?" "Although you didn't eat any," said Pure Wind, "those underlings of yours stole and ate some." "Even if they did, you shouldn't shout like that. Wait till I've questioned them. If they stole some, I'll see that they make it up to you." "Make it up?" said Bright Moon. "They are things that money can't buy." "Well then," said Sanzang, "if money won't buy them, 'decent behaviour is worth a thousand pieces of gold,' as the saying goes. I'll make them apologize to you, and that will be that. Besides, we still don't know whether they did it." "Of course they did," retorted Bright Moon. "They're still quarrelling in there because they

were divided unfairly." "Come here, disciples," called Sanzang.
"We've had it," said Friar Sand when he heard Sanzang
calling. "The game's up. Our master is calling us and the young
Taoists are swearing and cursing. The cat must be out of the
bag." "How disgraceful," said Monkey, "all that fuss about
some food. But if we confess it, they'll say it was stealing food;
the best thing is not to admit it at all." "Quite right, quite right,
we'll cover it up," said Pig, and three of them went from the
kitchen to the hall.

"The meal is cooked," the three disciples said as they
entered the hall. "What did you call us for?" "I'm not asking
about the meal, disciples," said Sanzang. "'This temple has
things called manfruit or whatever that look like babies. Which
of you stole and ate some?" "I don't know anything about it,
honest I don't — I never saw any," said Pig. "That grinning one
did it," said Pure Wind, "that grinning one." "I've had a smile
on my face all my life," shouted Monkey. "Are you going to
stop me smiling just because you can't find some fruit or
other?" "Don't lose your temper, disciple," said Sanzang. "As
men of religion we should control our tongues and not eat
anything against our conscience. If you ate their fruit you
should apologize to them, instead of trying to brazen it out like
this."

Seeing that his master was talking sense, Brother Monkey
began to tell the truth. "I didn't start it, master," he said.
"Pig heard the Taoist boys eating something called manfruit
next door to him and wanted to try one himself. He made me
go and get three so that we three disciples could have one each.
But now they've been eaten, that's that. What about it?"
"How can these monks deny that they are criminals when
they've stolen four of our manfruits?" said Bright Moon.

Now that they knew that the fruit really had been stolen,
the two boys started to abuse them even more foully. The
Great Sage ground his teeth of steel in his fury, glaring with his
fiery eyes and tightening his grip on his iron cudgel. "Damn
those Taoist boys," he thought when he could restrain himself
no longer. "If they'd hit us we could have taken it, but now

they're insulting us to our faces like this, I'll finish their tree off, then none of them can have any more fruit." Splendid Monkey. He pulled a hair out from the back of his head, breathed a magic breath on it, said "Change", and turned it into an imitation Monkey who stayed with the Tang Priest, Pig and Friar Sand to endure the cursing and swearing of the Taoist boys, while the real Monkey used his divine powers to leap out of the hall by cloud. He went straight to the garden and struck the manfruit tree with his gold-banded cudgel. Then he used his supernatural strength that could move mountains to push the tree over with a single shove. After pushing the tree over Monkey searched through the branches for manfruit, but he could not find a single one. These treasures dropped at the touch of metal, and as Monkey's cudgel was ringed with gold, while being made of iron, another of the five metals, one tap from it brought them all tumbling down, and when they hit the ground they went straight in, leaving none on the tree. "Great, great, great," he said, "that'll make them all cool down." He put the iron cudgel away, went back to the front of the temple, shook the magic hair, and put it back on his head.

A long time later, when the two Taoist boys felt that they had railed at them for long enough, Pure Wind said to Bright Moon, "These monks will take anything we say. We've sworn at them as if we were swearing at chickens, but they haven't admitted anything. I don't think they can have stolen any, after all. The tree is so tall and the foliage is so dense that we may well have miscounted, and if we have, we shouldn't be cursing them so wildly. Let's go and check the number again." Bright Moon agreed, and the pair of them went back to the garden. When they saw that the tree was down with its branches splayed out, the leaves fallen, and the fruit gone, they were horror-struck. Pure Wind's knees turned soft and he collapsed, while Bright Moon trembled and shook. Both of them nearly passed out and mumbled, "What are we to do, what are we to do? Whatever are we going to say to the master when he comes back?" "Stop moaning, brother," said Bright Moon. "We must tidy ourselves up and not let those monks know anything's wrong. That hairy-faced sod who looks like a thunder god must have done it. He must have used magic to destroy our treasure. But it's useless to argue with him as he'll deny everything, and if we start a quarrel with him and fighting breaks out, we two haven't a chance against the four of them. We'll have to fool them and say that no fruit is missing. We'll pretend we counted wrong before, and apologize to them. Their rice is cooked, and we can give them a few side dishes to eat with it. The moment they've each got a bowl of food you and I will stand on either side of the door, slam it shut, and lock it. When our master comes back he can decide what to do with them."

The two of them pulled themselves together, forced themselves to look happy, and went back to the front hall. "Master," they said, bowing low to Sanzang, "we were extremely rude to you just now. Please forgive us." "What do you mean?" asked Sanzang. "The fruit is all there," they replied. "We couldn't see it all before as the tree is so tall and the foliage so thick but when we checked just now the number was right." "You're too young to know what you're doing," said Pig, taking the chance to put the boot in. "Why did you swear and curse at us, and try to frame us up? It's wicked." Monkey, who understood what the boys were up to, said nothing and thought, "Lies, lies. The fruit is all finished. Why ever are they saying this? Can it be that they know how to bring the tree back to life?" "Very well then," Sanzang was saying meanwhile, "bring our rice in and we'll be off after eating it."

Pig went off to fill their bowls and Friar Sand arranged a table and chairs. The two boys hurried out and fetched some side dishes — salted squash, salted eggplant, turnips in wine-lees, pickled bean, salted lettuce, and mustard plant, some seven or eight plates in all. These they gave to the pilgrims to eat with their rice, and then they waited on them with a pot of good tea and two cups. As soon as the four pilgrims had their ricebowls in their hands, the boys, who were on either side of the doorway, slammed the doors to and locked them with a double-sprung bronze lock. The two boys then locked the main and the inner gates of the temple, then came back to the main hall to

abuse them with filthy language and call them criminals and
bandits till evening, when they went off to eat. The two of them
returned to their rooms after supper.

"You're always causing trouble, you ape," grumbled Sanzang at Monkey. "You stole their fruit, so you should have let
them lose their temper and swear at you, then that would have
been the end of it. Why on earth did you push their tree over?
If they took this to court you wouldn't be able to get off even if
your own father were on the bench." "Don't make such a row,
Master," said Monkey. "Those boys have gone to bed, and
when they're asleep we can do a midnight flit." "But all the
gates have been locked," said Friar Sand, "and they've been
shut very firmly, so how can we possibly get away?" "Don't let
it bother you," said Monkey, "I have a way."

It was now dark, and the moon had risen in the east. "It's
quiet now," said Monkey, "and the moon is bright. This is the
time to go. Watch this trick," he said, and gripping his cudgel
in his hand he pointed at the doors and applied unlocking magic
to them. There was a clanking sound, and the locks fell from all
the doors and gates, which he pushed them open. Then he asked
his master to go out and mount the horse. Pig shouldered the
luggage, Friar Sand led the horse, and they headed west. "You
carry on," Monkey said, "while I go back to make sure that those
two boys will stay asleep for a month." "Mind you don't kill
them, disciple," said Sanzang, "or you'll be on a charge of
murder in the pursuit of theft as well." "I'm aware of that,"
replied Monkey and went back into the temple. Standing outside
the door of the room where the boys were sleeping, he took a
couple of sleep insects from his belt which he had won from the
Heavenly King Virudhaka at the Eastern Gate of Heaven in a
drinking game. Now he threw them in through a gap in the
window lattice. They landed straight on the boys' faces, and
made them fall into a deeper sleep from which they would not
wake up for a long time. Then he streaked back by cloud and
caught up with Sanzang. They headed west along the main road.

That night the horse never stopped, and they kept on till
dawn. "You'll be the death of me, you ape," said Sanzang.

"Because of your greed I've had to stay awake all night." "Stop grumbling," said Monkey. "Now that it's light you can rest in the forest beside the road and build your strength up before we move on." Sanzang obediently dismounted and sat down on the roots of a pine tree, using it as a makeshift meditation platform. Friar Sand put down the luggage and took a nap, while Pig pillowed his head on a rock and went to sleep. Monkey, the Great Sage, had his own ideas and amused himself leaping from tree to tree.

After the lecture in the palace of the Original Celestial Jade Pure One the Great Immortal Zhen Yuan led his junior Immortals down from the Tushita Heaven through the jade sky on auspicious clouds, and in a moment they were back at the gates of the Wuzhuang Temple. When they went into the hall of worship there was no incense burning and nobody to be seen. Where were Bright Moon and Pure Wind, they wondered. When the immortals went to look in their room they found the doors closed and heard the boys snoring. They hammered on the doors and shouted for all they were worth, but the boys did not wake up. They forced the doors open and pulled the boys from their beds: the boys still did not wake up. "Fine immortal boys you are," said the Great Immortal with a smile. "When you become an immortal your divine spirit should be so full that you do not want to sleep. They must have been bewitched. Fetch some water at once." A boy hastily handed him half a bowl of water. He intoned a spell, took a mouthful of the water, and spurted it on their faces. This broke the enchantment. The two of them work up, opened their eyes, rubbed their faces, looked around them, and saw the Great Immortal as well as all their immortal brothers. Pure Wind bowed and Bright Moon kowtowed in their confusion, saying, "Master, that old friend of yours, the priest from the East . . . a gang of bandits . . . murderous, murderous. . . ."

"Don't be afraid," said the Great Immortal with a smile. "Calm down and tell us all about it." The Great Immortal did not lose his temper when he heard their story, "Don't cry," he said, "don't cry. What you don't realize is that Monkey has vast magic powers. Could you recognize those monks?" "I could recognize all of them," replied Pure Wind. "In that case come with me," said the Great Immortal. "The rest of you are to prepare the instruments of torture and be ready to flog them when we come back."

The other immortals did as they were told while the Great Immortal, Bright Moon and Pure Wind pursued Sanzang on a beam of auspicious light. It took them but an instant to cover three hundred miles. The Great Immortal stood on the edge of the clouds and gazed to the west, but he did not see Sanzang; then he turned round to look east and saw that he had left Sanzang over two hundred and fifty miles behind. "Master," said one of the immortal boys, "there's the Tang Priest, sitting under a tree by the side of the road." The Great Immortal landed his cloud, shook himself, and turned into an itinerant Taoist.

"Greetings, venerable sir," he called, raising his hands. "Oh, I'm sorry I didn't notice you before," replied Sanzang hastily. "Where are you from?" the Great Immortal asked. "And why are you in meditation during your journey?" "I have been sent by the Great Tang in the East to fetch the scriptures from the Western Heaven," Sanzang said, "and I'm taking a rest along the way." "You must have crossed my desolate mountain if you have come from the East." "May I ask, immortal sir, which mountain is yours?" "My humble abode is the Wuzhuang Temple on the Mountain of Infinite Longevity."

"We didn't come that way," said Monkey, who realized what was happening. "We've only just started out." The Great Immortal pointed at him and laughed. "I'll show you, you damned ape. Who do you think you're fooling? I know that you knocked our manfruit tree down and came here during the night. You had better confess: you won't get away with concealing anything. Stay where you are, and give me back that tree at once." Monkey flared up at this, and with no further discussion he struck at the Great Immortal's head with his cudgel. The Great Immortal twisted away from the blow and went straight up into the sky on a beam of light, closely pursued by Monkey on a cloud. In mid-air the Great Immortal reverted to his true appearance, and this is what he looked like:

A golden crown on his head,
A No-worries cloak of crane's down on his body.
A pair of turned-up sandals on his feet,
And round his waist a belt of silk.
His body was like a child's;
His face was that of a beautiful woman.
A wispy beard floated down from his chin,
And the hair on his temples was crow-black.
He met Monkey unarmed
With only a jade-handled whisk in his hands.

Monkey struck wildly at him with his club, only to be parried to left and right by the Great Immortal's whisk. After two or three rounds the Great Immortal did a "Wrapping Heaven and Earth in His Sleeve" trick, waving his sleeve gently in the breeze as he stood amid the clouds, then sweeping it across the ground and gathering up the four pilgrims and their horse in it. "Hell," said Pig, "We're all caught in a bag." "It isn't a bag, you idiot," said Monkey, "he's caught us all in his sleeve." "It doesn't matter, anyhow," said Pig. "I can make a hole in it with a single blow of my rake that we can all get through. Then we'll be able to drop out when he relaxes his grip on us." But however desperately he struck at the fabric he could make no impression on it: although it was soft when held in the hand it was harder than iron when hit.

The Great Immortal turned his cloud round, went straight back to the Wuzhuang Temple, landed, sat down, and told his disciples to fetch rope. Then, with all the junior immortals in attendance, he took the Tang Priest out of his sleeve as if he were a puppet and had him tied to one of the pillars of the main hall. After that he took the other three out and tied each of them to a pillar. The horse was taken out, tethered, and fed in the courtyard, and their luggage he threw under the covered walk. "Disciples," he said, "these priests are men of religion, so we cannot use swords, spears or axes on them. You'd better fetch a leather whip and give them a flogging for me — that will make me feel better about the manfruit." The disciples immediately produced a whip — not an oxhide, sheepskin, deerskin or calfskin whip, but a seven-starred dragon-skin one — and were told to soak it in water. A brawny young immortal was told to take a firm grip on it. "Master," he said, "which of them shall I flog first?" "Sanzang is guilty of gross disrespect," the Great Immortal replied, "flog him first."

"That old priest of ours couldn't stand a flogging," thought Monkey when he heard this, "and if he died under the lash the fault would be mine." Finding the thought of this unbearable, he spoke up and said, "You're wrong, sir. I stole the fruit, I ate the fruit, and I pushed the tree over. Why flog him first when you ought to be flogging me?" "That damn monkey has a point," said the Great Immortal with a smile, "so you'd better flog him first." "How many strokes?" the junior immortal asked. "Give him thirty," the Great Immortal replied, "to match the number of fruits." The junior immortal whirled the lash and started to bring it down. Monkey, frightened that the immortal might have great magical powers, opened his eyes wide and looked carefully to see where he was going to be hit. It turned out to be on his legs. He twisted at the waist, shouted "Change!", turned them into a pair of wrought-iron legs, and watched the blows fall. The junior immortal gave him thirty lashes, one after the other, until it was almost noon. "Sanzang must be flogged too," the Great Immortal commanded, "for training his wicked disciple so slackly and letting him run wild." The junior immortal whirled the lash again and was going to strike Sanzang when Monkey said, "Sir, you're making another mistake. When I stole the fruit, my master knew nothing about it — he was talking to those two boys of yours in the main hall of the temple. This plot was hatched by us three disciples. Anyhow, even if he were guilty of slackness in training me, I'm his disciple and should take the flogging for him. Flog me again." "That damn monkey may be cunning and vicious, but he does have some sense of his obligations to his master. Very well then, flog him again." The junior immortal gave him another thirty strokes. Monkey looked down and watched his legs being flogged till they shone like mirrors but still he felt no pain. It was now drawing towards evening, and the Great Immortal said, "Put the lash to soak. We can continue the flogging tomorrow." The junior immortal took the lash away to be soaked while everyone retired to their quarters, and after supper they all went to bed.

"It was because you three got me into this trouble that I was brought here to be punished," moaned the venerable Sanzang to his three disciples as tears streamed down from his eyes. "What are you going to do about it?" "Don't grumble," Monkey replied. "I was the one to be flogged first, and you haven't felt the lash, so what have you got to groan about?" "I may not have been flogged," Sanzang replied, "but it's agony being tied up like this." "We're tied up too to keep you company," said Friar Sand. "Will you all stop shouting?" said Monkey. "Then we can be on our way again when we've taken a rest." "You're showing off again, elder brother," said Pig. "They've tied us up with hempen ropes and spurted water on them, so we're tightly bound. This isn't like the time we were shut in the hall of the temple and you unlocked the doors to let us out." "I'm not boasting," said Monkey. "I don't give a damn about their three hempen ropes sprayed with water. Even if they were coir cables as thick as a ricebowl they would only be an autumn breeze." Apart from him speaking, all was now silence. Splendid Monkey made himself smaller, slipped out of his bonds, and said, "Let's go, Master." He freed Sanzang, Pig and Friar Sand, straightened his tunic, tightened his belt, saddled the horse, collected their luggage from under the eaves, and went out through the temple gates with the others. "Go and cut down four of the willow-trees by that cliff," he told Pig.

Monkey stripped off their tops and branches and told his two fellow-disciples to take the trunks back in and tie them up with the ropes as they themselves had been tied up. Then Monkey recited a spell, bit the tip of his tongue open, and spat blood over the trees. At his shout of "Change!" one of the trees turned into Sanzang, one turned into Monkey, and the other two became Friar Sand and Pig. They were all perfect likenesses; when questioned they would reply, and when called by their names they responded. The three disciples then hurried back to their master, and once more they travelled all night without stopping as they fled from the Wuzhuang Temple.

By the time it was dawn the venerable Sanzang was swaying to and fro as he dozed in the saddle. "Master," called Monkey when he noticed, "you're hopeless. Take a rest in the hollow place under this hill where you can shelter from the wind before we go any further."

We shall leave them resting beside the path to tell how the Great Immortal got up at dawn, ate his meatless breakfast, and went to the hall. "Today Tang Sanzang is to be lashed," he announced as he sent for the lash. The junior whirled it around and said to the Tang Priest, "I'm going to flog you." "Flog away," the willow tree replied. When he had given it thirty resounding lashes he whirled the whip around once more and said to Pig, "Now I'm going to flog you." "Flog away," the willow tree replied. When he came to flog Friar Sand, he too told him to go ahead. But when he came to flog Monkey, the real Monkey on the road shuddered and said, "Oh, no!" "What do you mean?" Sanzang asked. "When I turned the four willow trees into the four of us I thought that as he had me flogged twice yesterday he wouldn't flog me again today, but now he's lashing the magic body, my real body is feeling the pain. I'm putting an end to this magic." With that he hastily recited an incantation to break the spell.

Look at the terror of the Taoist boys as they threw down their leather whips and reported, "Master, we started by flogging the Priest from the Great Tang, but all we are flogging now are willow trunks." The Great Immortal laughed bitterly on hearing this and was full of admiration. He sprang up on a cloud and looked west to see the monks carrying their bundles and spurring their horse as they went on their way. Bringing his cloud down he shouted, "Where are you going, Monkey? Give me back my manfruit tree." The three disciples rushed forward, Friar Sand wielding his staff, Pig with his rake held high, and the Great Sage Monkey brandishing his iron cudgel. The three of them went for him with their magic weapons, but the Great Immortal kept them at bay with his fly-whisk. After about an hour he opened wide his sleeve and caught up master, disciples, horse, and baggage in it once more. Then he turned his cloud around and went back to his temple, where all the immortals greeted him.

After taking his seat in the hall he took them out of his sleeve one by one. He had the Tang Priest tied to a stunted locust tree at the foot of the steps, with Pig and Friar Sand tied to trees next to him. Monkey was tied up upside down, which made him think that he was going to be tortured and interrogated. When Monkey was tightly bound, the junior immortals fetched home-woven cloth, and on being told by the Great Immortal to wrap up Pig and Friar Sand with it, they came forward to do so. "Excellent," said Monkey, "excellent — you're being encoffined alive." Within a few moments the three of them were wrapped up, and the immortals quickly fetched some lacquer that they had tapped and dried themselves, with which they painted the three bandaged bodies all over except for the heads. "Never mind about our heads, sir," said Pig, "but please leave us a hole at the bottom to shit through." The immortals carried out a large cauldron and put it under the steps, and the Great Immortal called for dry wood to be stacked up round it and set ablaze. "Ladle it full of pure oil," he commanded, "and when it is bubbling hot, deep-fry Monkey in it to pay me back for my manfruit."

Monkey was secretly delighted to hear this. "This is just what I want," he thought. "I haven't had a bath for ages, and my skin's getting rather itchy. I'd thoroughly appreciate a hot bath." Very soon the oil was bubbling and Monkey was having reservations. Hastily looking around him, he saw that there was a sundial to the east of the dais and a stone lion to the west. Monkey rolled towards it with a spring, bit off the end of his tongue, spurted blood all over the stone lion, and shouted "Change", at which it turned into his own image, tied up in a bundle like himself. Then he extracted his spirit and went up into the clouds, from where he looked down at the Taoists.

It was just at this moment that the junior immortals reported, "The oil's boiling hard." "Carry Monkey down to it," the Great Immortal ordered, but when four of them tried to pick him up they could not. Eight then tried and failed, and four more made no difference. Twelve junior immortals were then told to pick him up with the aid of carrying-poles, and when they threw him in there was a loud crash as drops of oil splashed about, raising blisters all over the junior immortals' faces. "There's a hole in the cauldron — it's started leaking," the scalded immortals cried, but before the words were out of their mouths the oil had all run out through the broken bottom of the cauldron. They realized that they had thrown a stone lion into it.

"Damn that ape for his insolence," said the Great Immortal in a terrible rage. "How dare he play his tricks in my presence! Untie Tang Sanzang instead and fetch another pot. We can fry him to avenge the destruction of the tree." The junior immortals set to and began to tear off Sanzang's lacquered bandages.

Monkey could hear all this clearly from mid-air. "The master will be done for," he thought. "I must go back down and save him." The splendid Great Sage brought his cloud down to land, clasped his hands in front of him, and said, "Don't spoil the lacquered bands, and don't fry my master. Put me in the cauldron of oil instead." The Great Immortal laughed coldly, came out of the hall, and seized him.

The Great Immortal Zhen Yuan held Monkey in his hand and said, "I've heard about your powers and your fame, but this time you have gone too far." "Would you agree to release my master if I gave you back the tree alive?" Monkey asked. "If your magic is strong enough to revive the tree," the Great Immortal replied, "I shall bow to you eight times and take you as my brother." "That's easy then," said Monkey. "Release them and I guarantee to give you back your tree alive." Trusting him not to escape, the Great Immortal ordered that Sanzang, Pig and Friar Sand be set free.

Monkey immediately straightened up his tiger-skin kilt, went out through the door, and said to the Great Immortal, "Don't worry, sir, I'll soon be back. Mind you look after my master well. Give him tea three times a day and six meals, and don't leave any out. If you do, I'll settle that score when I come back, and I'll start by holing the bottoms of all your pans. If his clothes get dirty, wash them for him. I won't stand for it if he looks sallow, and if he loses weight you'll never see the back of me." "Go away, go away," the Great Immortal replied. "I certainly won't let him go hungry."

The splendid Monkey King left the Wuzhuang Temple with

a bound of his somersault cloud and headed for the Eastern Sea. He went through the air as fast as a flash of lightning or a shooting star, and he was soon in the blessed land of Penglai.

As he was walking along, he noticed three old men sitting round a chess table under the shade of a pine tree outside a cloud-wreathed cave. The one watching the game was the Star of Longevity, and the players were the Star of Blessings and the Star of Office. "Greetings, respected younger brothers," Monkey called to them, and when they saw him they swept the pieces away, returned his salutation, and said, "Why have you come here, Great Sage?" "To see you," he replied, going on to explain his problem.

"If you have any cures that will bring a tree back to life, please tell me one so that I can get the Tang Priest out of trouble as quickly as possible."

"You ape," the Three Stars said gloomily when they heard this. "You don't know who you're up against. That Master Zhen Yuan is the Patriarch of the immortals of the earth, and we are the chiefs of the divine immortals. Although you have become a heavenly immortal, you are still only one of the irregulars of the Great Monad, not one of the elite. You'll never be able to escape his clutches. If you'd killed some animal, bird, insect or reptile, Great Sage, we could have given you some pills made from sticky millet to bring it back to life, but that manfruit tree is a magic one and can't possibly be revived. There's no cure, none at all." When he heard that there was no cure, Monkey's brows locked in a frown, and his forehead was creased in a thousand wrinkles. "Calm down, Great Sage," said the Star of Longevity, "there's no need to worry. Although that Great Immortal is senior to us, he is a friend of ours, and as we haven't visited him for a long time and would like to do you a favour, we'll go and see him. We'll explain things for you and tell that Tang monk not to recite the Band-tightening Spell. We won't go away until you come back, however long you take, even if it's a lot longer than three to five days." "Thank you very much," said Monkey. "May I ask you to set out now as I'm off?" With that he took his leave.

The Three Stars went off on beams of auspicious light to the

Wuzhuang Temple, where all present heard cranes calling in the sky as the three of them arrived. Sanzang quickly tidied himself up and bowed to the Three Stars. The Three Stars greeted the Great Immortal as befitted members of a younger generation, after which they all sat down. "We have not seen your illustrious countenance for a long time," the Star of Office said, "which shows our great lack of respect. The reason we come to see you now is because the Great Sage Monkey has made trouble in your immortal temple." "Has Monkey been to Penglai?" the Great Immortal asked. "Yes," replied the Star of Longevity. "He came to our place to ask for a formula to restore the elixir tree that he killed. As we have no cure for it, he has had to go elsewhere in search of it. We are afraid that if he exceeds the three-day time-limit the holy priest has imposed, the Band-tightening Spell may be said. We have come in the first place to pay our respects and in the second to ask for an extension of the limit." "I won't recite it, I promise," answered Sanzang as soon as he heard this.

Monkey meanwhile had bounded away from Penglai by auspicious cloud and come to the magic mountain Fangzhang. This was a really wonderful place, but as he brought his cloud down he was in no mood to enjoy the view. As he was walking along he smelt a fragrance in the wind, heard the cry of the black stork, and saw an immortal, the Lord Emperor of Eastern Glory.

When Brother Monkey saw him he hailed him with the words, "I salute you, Lord Emperor." The Lord Emperor hastened to return his greeting and say, "I should have welcomed you properly, Great Sage. May I ask you home for some tea?" He led Monkey by the hand to his palace of cowrie-shells, where there was no end of jasper pools and jade towers. Monkey asked him for a formula that would revive the manfruit tree. "You thoughtless ape," the Lord Emperor replied, "you make trouble wherever you go. Master Zhen Yuan of the Wuzhuang Temple has the sacred title Conjoint Lord of the Age, and he is the Patriarch of the immortals of the Earth. I have a nine-phased returning pill of the Great Monad, but it can only bring animate objects back to life, not trees. Trees are lives compounded of the Wood and Earth elements and nurtured by Heaven and Earth. If it were an ordinary mortal tree I could bring it back to life, but the Mountain of Infinite Longevity is a blessed land before Heaven, the Wuzhuang Temple is the Cave Paradise of the Western Continent of Cattle-gift, and the manfruit tree is the life-root from the time when Heaven and Earth were separated. How could it possibly be revived? I have no formula, none at all."

"In that case I must take my leave," replied Monkey, and when the Lord Emperor tried to detain him with a cup of jade nectar he said, "This is too urgent to allow me to stay." He rode his cloud back to the island of Yingzhou, another wonderful place.

On reaching Yingzhou he saw a number of white-haired immortals with the faces of children playing chess and drinking under a pearl tree at the foot of a cinnabar cliff.

"How about letting me play with you?" Monkey shouted at the top of his voice, and when the immortals saw him they hurried over to welcome him.

Monkey, who knew the Nine Ancients, said with a smile, "You nine brothers seem to be doing very nicely." "If you had stayed on the straight and narrow in the old days, Great Sage," they replied, "and not wrecked the Heavenly Palace you would be doing even better than we are. Now we hear that you have reformed and are going West to visit the Buddha. How did you manage the time off to come here?" Monkey told them how he was searching for a formula to cure the tree. "What a terrible thing to do," they exclaimed in horror, "what a terrible thing. We honestly have no cure at all." "In that case I must take my leave of you."

Monkey hurried away from Yingzhou and back to the Great Eastern Ocean. When he saw that Potaraka was not far away, he brought his cloud down to land on the Potara Crag, where he saw the Bodhisattva Guanyin expounding the scriptures and preaching the Buddha's Law to all the great gods of heaven, Moksa, and the dragon maiden in the Purple Bamboo Grove.

Monkey went into the Purple Bamboo Grove, did obeisance to the Bodhisattva and told her what had happened. "You wretched ape," said the Bodhisattva angrily now that she knew about it, "you have no conscience at all. That manfruit tree of his is the life-root from the time when Heaven and Earth were separated, and Master Zhen Yuan is the Patriarch of the Earth's immortals, which means even I have to show him a certain respect. Why didn't you come and see me earlier instead of searching the islands for a formula?"

"I'm in luck," thought Monkey with delight when he heard this, "I'm in luck. The Bodhisattva must have a formula." He went up to her and pleaded for it again. "The sweet dew in this pure vase of mine," she said, "is an excellent cure for magic trees and plants." "Has it ever been tried out?" Monkey asked. "Yes," she said. "How?" he asked. "Some years ago Lord Lao Zi beat me at gambling," she replied, "and took my willow sprig away with him. He put it in his elixir-refining furnace and burnt it to a cinder before sending it back to me. I put it back in the vase, and a day and a night later it was as green and leafy as ever." "I'm really in luck," said Monkey, "really in luck. If it can bring a cinder back to life, something that has only been pushed over should be easy." The Bodhisattva instructed her subjects to look after the grove as she was going away for a while. Then she took up her vase, and her white parrot went in front singing while Monkey followed behind.

The Great Immortal and the Three Stars were still in lofty conversation when they saw Monkey bring his cloud down and heard him shout, "The Bodhisattva's here. Come and welcome her at once." On bringing her cloud to a stop, she first talked with Master Zhen Yuan and then greeted the Three Stars, after which she climbed to her seat. Monkey then led the Tang Priest, Pig, and Friar Sand out to do obeisance before the steps, and all the immortals in the temple came to bow to her as well. "There's no need to dither about, Great Immortal," said Monkey. "Get an incense table ready at once and ask the Bodhisattva to cure that whatever-it-is tree of yours." The Great Immortal Zhen Yuan bowed to the Bodhisattva and thanked her: "How could I be so bold as to trouble the Bodhisattva with my affairs?" "The Tang Priest is my disciple, and Monkey has offended you, so it is only right that I should make up for the loss of your priceless tree." "In that case there is no need for you to refuse," said the Three Stars. "May we invite you, Bodhisattva, to come into our orchard and take a look?"

The Great Sage had an incense table set up and the orchard swept, then he asked the Bodhisattva to lead the way. The Three Stars followed behind. Sanzang, his disciples and all the immortals of the temple went into the orchard to look, and they saw the tree lying on the ground with the earth torn open, its roots laid bare, its leaves fallen and its branches withered. "Put your hand out, Monkey," said the Bodhisattva, and Brother Monkey stretched out his left hand. The Bodhisattva dipped her willow spray into the sweet dew in her vase, then used it to write a spell to revive the dead on the palm of Monkey's hand. She told him to place it on the roots of the tree until he saw water coming out. Monkey clenched his fist and tucked it under the roots; before long a spring of clear water began to form a pool. "That water must not be sullied by vessels made of any of the Five Elements, so you will have to scoop it out with a jade ladle. If you prop the tree up and pour the water on it from the very top, its bark and trunk will knit together, its leaves will sprout again, the branches will be green once more, and the fruit will reappear." "Fetch a jade ladle this moment, young Taoists," said Monkey. "We poor monks have no jade ladle in our destitute temple. We only have jade tea-bowls and wine-cups. Would they do?" "As long as they are jade and can scoop out water they will do," the Bodhisattva replied. "Bring them out and try." The Great Immortal then told some boys to fetch the twenty or thirty tea-bowls and the forty or fifty wine-cups and ladle the clear water out from under the roots. Monkey, Pig and Friar Sand put their shoulders under the tree, raised it upright, and banked it up with earth. Then they presented the sweet spring water cup by cup to the Bodhisattva, who sprinkled it lightly on the tree with her spray of willow and recited an incantation. When a little later the water had all been sprinkled on the tree the leaves really did become as dense and green as ever, and there were twenty-three manfruits growing there. Pure Wind and Bright Moon, the two immortal boys, said, "When the fruit disappeared the other day there were only twenty-two of them; so why is there an extra one now that it has come back to life?" "'Time shows the truth about a man'," Monkey replied. "I only stole three that day. The other one fell on the ground, and the local deity told me that this treasure always entered earth when it touched it. Pig accused me of taking it as a bit of extra for myself and blackened my reputation, but at long last the truth has come out."

"The reason why I did not use vessels made from the Five Elements was because I knew that this kind of fruit is allergic to them," said the Bodhisattva. The Great Immortal, now extremely happy, had the golden rod fetched at once and knocked down ten of the fruits. He invited the Bodhisattva and the Three Stars to come to the main hall of the temple to take part in a Manfruit Feast to thank them for their labour.

The Bodhisattva and the Three Stars ate one manfruit each, as did the Tang Priest, who realized at last that this was an immortal's treasure, and Monkey, Pig and Friar Sand. Master Zhen Yuan had one to keep them company and the immortals of the temple divided the last one between them. Monkey thanked the Bodhisattva, who went back to Potaraka, and saw the Three Stars off on their journey home to the island of Penglai. Master Zhen Yuan set out some non-alcoholic wine and made Monkey his sworn brother. This was a case of "if you don't fight you can't make friends", and their two households were now united. That night Sanzang and his disciples went to bed feeling very happy.

CHAPTER 17
Sun Wukong Kills the White Bone Demon Three Times

Soon after they had set out again, master and disciples saw a high mountain in front of them. "I'm afraid that the mountain ahead may be too steep for the horse," Sanzang said, "so we must think this over carefully." "Don't worry, master," said Monkey, "we know how to cope." "I've been hungry all day, so would you please go and beg some food for us," said Sanzang to him.

Monkey leapt up into the clouds with a single jump, and shading his eyes with his hand he looked around. Unfortunately he could see nothing in any direction except emptiness. There was no village or house or any other sign of human habitation among the countless trees. After looking for a long time he made out a high mountain away to the south. On its southern slopes was a bright red patch. Monkey brought his cloud down and said, "Master, there's something to eat." Sanzang asked him what it was. "There's no house around here where we could ask for food," Monkey replied, "but there's a patch of red on a mountain to the south that I'm sure must be ripe wild peaches. I'll go and pick some — they'll fill you up." "A monk who has peaches to eat is a lucky man," said Sanzang. Monkey picked up his bowl and leapt off on a beam of light with a somersault and a whistling gust of cold air. Within a moment he was picking peaches on the southern mountain.

There is a saying that goes, "If the mountain is high it's

bound to have fiends; if the ridge is steep spirits will live there."
This mountain did indeed have an evil spirit who was startled
by Monkey's appearance. It strode through the clouds on a negative wind, and on seeing the venerable Sanzang on the ground
below thought happily, "What luck, what luck. At home they've
been talking for years about a Tang monk from the East who's
going to fetch the Great Vehicle; he's a reincarnation of Golden
Cicada, and has an Original Body that has been purified
through ten lives. Anyone who eats a piece of his flesh will live
for ever. And today, at last, he's here." The evil spirit went
forward to seize Sanzang, but the sight of Pig and Friar Sand
to Sanzang's left and right made it too frightened to close in on
him. "I'll try a trick on them and see what happens," the spirit
said to itself.

The splendid evil spirit stopped its negative wind in a hollow and changed itself into a girl with a face as round as the
moon and as pretty as a flower. Her brow was clear and her
eyes beautiful; her teeth were white and her lips red. In her
left hand she held a blue earthenware pot and in her right a
green porcelain jar. She headed east towards the Tang Priest.

When Sanzang saw her he sprang to his feet, put his hands
together in front of his chest, and said, "Bodhisattva, where is
your home? Who are you?" At just this moment Brother
Monkey was somersaulting back with his bowl full of the
peaches he had picked on the southern mountain. When he saw
with the golden pupils in his fiery eyes that the girl was an evil
spirit, he put the bowl down, lifted his cudgel, and struck at the
evil spirit's face. The fiend, who knew a trick or two, used a
magic way of abandoning its body: when it saw Monkey's
cudgel coming it braced itself and fled, leaving a false corpse
lying dead on the ground. Sanzang shook with terror and said
to himself, "That monkey is utterly outrageous. Despite all my
good advice he will kill people for no reason at all." "Don't be
angry, Master," said Monkey. "Come and see what's in her
pot." Friar Sand helped Sanzang over to look, and he saw that
so far from containing tasty rice it was full of maggots with long
tails. The jar had held not gluten-balls but frogs and toads,

which were now jumping around on the ground. Sanzang was now beginning to believe Monkey. This was not enough, however, to prevent a furious Pig from deliberately making trouble by saying, "Master, that girl was a local countrywoman who happened to meet us while she was taking some food to the fields. There's no reason to think that she was an evil spirit. My elder brother was trying his club out on her, and he killed her by mistake. He's deliberately trying to trick us by magicking the food into those things because he's afraid you'll recite the Band-tightening Spell. He's fooled you into not saying it."

This brought the blindness back on Sanzang, who believed these trouble-making remarks and made the magic with his hand as he recited the spell. "My head's aching, my head's aching," Monkey said. "Stop, please stop. Tell me off if you like." "I've nothing to say to you," replied Sanzang. "A man of religion should always help others, and his thoughts should always be virtuous. When sweeping the floor you must be careful not to kill any ants, and to spare the moth you should put gauze round your lamp. Why do you keep murdering people? If you are going to kill innocent people like that there is no point in your going to fetch the scriptures. Go back!" "Where am I to go back to?" Monkey asked. "I won't have you as my disciple any longer," said Sanzang. "If you won't have me as your disciple," Monkey said, "I'm afraid you may never reach the Western Heaven." "My destiny is in Heaven's hands," replied Sanzang. "If some evil spirit is fated to cook me, he will; and there's no way of getting out of it. But if I'm not to be eaten, will you be able to extend my life? Be off with you at once." "I'll go if I must," said Monkey, "but I'll never have repaid your kindness to me." "What kindness have I ever done you?" Sanzang asked. Monkey knelt down and kowtowed. "When I wrecked the Heavenly Palace," he said, "I put myself in a very dangerous position, and the Buddha crushed me under the Double Boundary Mountain. Luckily the Bodhisattva Guanyin administered the vows to me, and you, Master, released me, so if I don't go with you to the Western Heaven I'll look like a 'scoundrel who doesn't return a kindness, with a name that will be cursed for ever'." As Sanzang was a compassionate and holy monk this desperate plea from Monkey persuaded him to relent. "In view of what you say I'll let you off this time, but don't behave so disgracefully again. If you are ever as wicked as that again I shall recite that spell twenty times over." "Make it thirty if you like," replied Monkey. "I shan't hit anyone else." With that he helped Sanzang mount the horse and offered him some of the peaches he had picked. After eating a few the Tang Priest felt less hungry for the time being.

The evil spirit rose up into the air when it had saved itself from being killed by Monkey's cudgel. Gnashing its teeth in the clouds, it thought of Monkey with silent hatred: "Now I know that those magical powers of Sun Wukong that I've been hearing about for years are real. I never thought that Monkey would turn up, wreck my plans, and almost kill me. If I spare that monk now I'll have gone to all that trouble for nothing, so I'll have another go at tricking him."

The splendid evil spirit landed its negative cloud, shook itself, and changed into an old woman in her eighties who was weeping as she hobbled along leaning on a bamboo stick with a crooked handle. "This is terrible, Master," exclaimed Pig with horror at the sight of her. "Her mother's come to look for her." "For whom?" asked the Tang Priest. "It must be her daughter that my elder brother killed," said Pig. "This must be the girl's mother looking for her." "Don't talk nonsense," said Monkey. "That girl was eighteen and this old woman is eighty. How could she possibly have had a child when she was over sixty? She must be a fake. Let me go and take a look." The splendid Monkey hurried over to examine her.

Realizing that she was an evil spirit, Monkey did not wait to argue about it, but raised his cudgel and struck at her head. Seeing the blow coming, the spirit braced itself again and extracted its true essence once more. The false corpse sprawled dead beside the path. Sanzang was so horrified that he fell off the horse and lay beside the path, reciting the Band-tightening Spell twenty times over. Poor Monkey's head was squeezed so hard that it looked like a narrow-waisted gourd. The pain was unbearable, and he rolled over towards his master to plead, "Stop, Master. Say whatever you like." "I have nothing to say," Sanzang replied. "If a monk does good he will not fall into hell. Despite all my preaching you still commit murder. How can you? No sooner have you killed one person than you kill another. It's an outrage." "She was an evil spirit," Monkey replied. "Nonsense, you ape," said the Tang Priest, "as if there could be so many monsters! You haven't the least intention of reforming, and you are a deliberate murderer. Be off with you." "Are you sending me away again, Master?" Monkey asked. "I'll go if I must, but there's one thing I won't agree to." "What," Sanzang asked, "would that be?" "To be quite honest with you, Master," he replied, "when I lived in the Water Curtain Cave on the Mountain of Flowers and Fruit and knew all the great heroes, I won the submission of seventy-two other demon kings and had forty-seven thousand minor demons under me. I used to wear a crown of purple gold and a yellow robe with a belt of the finest jade. I had cloud-treading shoes on my feet and held an as-you-will gold-banded cudgel in my hands. I really was somebody then. But when I attained enlightenment and repented, I shaved my head and took to the Buddhist faith as your disciple. I couldn't face my old friends if I went back with this golden band round my head. So if you don't want me any longer, Master, please say the band-loosening spell and I'll take it off and give it back to you. I'll gladly agree to you putting it round someone else's head. As I've been your disciple for so long, surely you can show me this kindness." Sanzang was deeply shocked. "Monkey," he said, "the Bodhisattva secretly taught me the Band-tightening Spell, but not a band-loosening one." "In that case you'll have to let me come with you," Monkey replied. "Get up then," said Sanzang, feeling that he had no option, "I'll let you off again just this once. But you must never commit another murder." "I never will," said Monkey, "never again." He helped his master mount the horse and led the way forward.

The evil spirit, who had not been killed when hit the second time by Monkey either, was full of admiration as it floated in mid-air. "What a splendid Monkey King," it thought, "and what sharp eyes. He saw who I was through both my transformations. Those monks are travelling fast, and once they're over the mountain and fifteen miles to the west they'll be out of my territory. Any other fiends and monsters who catch them will be laughing till their mouths split, and I'll be heartbroken with sorrow. I'll have to have another go at tricking them." The splendid evil spirit brought its negative wind down on the mountain-side and with one shake turned itself into an old man reciting Buddhist sutras.

When Sanzang saw him from the back of his horse he said with great delight, "Amitabha Buddha! The West is indeed a blessed land. That old man is forcing himself to recite scriptures although he can hardly walk." "Master," said Pig, "don't be so nice about him. He's going to give us trouble." "What do you mean?" Sanzang asked. "My elder brother has killed the daughter and the old woman, and this is the old man coming to look for them. If we fall into his hands you'll have to pay with your life. It'll be the death penalty for you, and I'll get a long sentence for being your accomplice. Friar Sand will be exiled for giving the orders. That elder brother will disappear by magic, and we three will have to carry the can." "Don't talk such nonsense, you moron," said Monkey. "You're terrifying the master. Wait while I go and have another look." Hiding the cudgel about his person he went up to the monster and said, "Where are you going, venerable sir? And why are you reciting scriptures as you walk along?" The monster, failing to recognize the key man, thought that the Great Sage Monkey was merely a passer-by and said, "Holy sir, my family has lived here for generations, and all my life I have done good deeds, fed monks, read the scriptures, and repeated the Buddha's name. As fate has it I have no son, only a daughter, and she lives at home with her husband. She went off to the fields with food early this morning, and I'm afraid she may have been eaten by a tiger. My wife went out to look for her, and she hasn't come back either. I've no idea what's happened to them, so I've come to search for them. If they have died, I shall just have to gather their bones and take them back for a decent burial." "I'm a master of disguise," replied Monkey with a grin, "so don't try to pull the wool over my eyes. You can't fool me. I know that you're an evil spirit." The monster was speechless with fright.

The splendid Great Sage uttered a spell and called out to the local deities and the gods of the mountain, "This evil spirit has tried to trick my master three times, and I'm now going to kill it. I want you to be witnesses in the air around me. Don't leave!" Hearing this command, the gods all had to obey and watch from the clouds. The Great Sage raised his cudgel and struck down the monster. Now, at last, it was dead.

The Tang Priest was shaking with terror on the back of his horse, unable to speak. Pig stood beside him and said with a laugh, "That Monkey's marvellous, isn't he! He's gone mad. He's killed three people in a few hours' journey." The Tang Priest was just going to say the spell when Monkey threw himself in front of his horse and called out, "Don't say it, Master, don't say it. Come and have a look at it." It was now just a pile of dusty bones. "He's only just been killed, Wukong," Sanzang said in astonishment, "so why has he turned into a skeleton?" "It was a demon corpse with magic powers that used to deceive people and destroy them. Now that I've killed it, it's reverted to its original form. The writing on her backbone says that she's called 'Lady White Bone'." Sanzang was convinced, but Pig had to make trouble again. "Master," he said, "he's afraid that you'll say those words because he killed him with a vicious blow from his cudgel, and so he's made him look like this to fool you." The Tang Priest, who really was gullible, now believed Pig, and he started to recite the spell. Monkey, unable to stop the pain, knelt beside the path and cried, "Stop, stop. Say whatever it is you have to say," "Baboon," said Sanzang, "I have nothing more to say to you. You have killed three people, one after the other, in this wild and desolate place, and there is nobody here to find you out or bring a case against you. But if you go to a city or some other crowded place and start laying about you with that murderous cudgel, we'll be in big trouble and there will be no escape for us. Go back!" "You're wrong to hold it against me, Master," Monkey replied, "as that wretch was obviously an evil monster set on murdering you. But so far from being grateful that I've saved you by killing it, you would have to believe that idiot's tittle-tattle and keep sending me away. I'd be a low and shameless creature if I didn't go now. I'll go, I'll go all right, but who will you have left to look after you?" "Damned ape," Sanzang replied, "you get ruder and ruder. You seem to think that you're the only one. What about Pig and Friar Sand? Aren't they people?"

On hearing him say that Pig and Friar Sand were suitable people too, Monkey was very hurt. "That's a terrible thing to hear, Master," he said. "When you left Chang'an Liu Boqin helped you on your way, and when you reached the Double Boundary Mountain you saved me and I took you as my master. I've gone into ancient caves and deep forests capturing monsters and demons. I won Pig and Friar Sand over, and I've had a very hard time of it. But today you've turned stupid and you're sending me back. When these birds have all been shot the bow is put away, and when the hares have all been killed the hounds are stewed.' Oh well! If only you hadn't got that Band-tightening Spell." "I won't recite it again," said Sanzang. "Don't be so sure," replied Monkey. "If you're ever beset by evil monsters from whom you can't escape, and if Pig and Friar Sand can't save you, then you'll think of me and you won't be able to stop yourself from saying the spell again. My head will ache even if I'm many tens of thousands of miles away. But if I do come back to you, never say it again."

The Tang Priest grew angrier and angrier as Monkey talked on, and tumbling off his horse he told Friar Sand to take paper and brush from the pack. Then he fetched some water from a stream, rubbed the inkstick on a stone, wrote out a letter of dismissal, and handed it to Monkey. "Here it is in writing," he said. "I don't want you as my disciple a moment longer. If I ever see you again may I fall into the Avichi Hell." Monkey quickly took the document and said, "There's no need to swear an oath, Master. I'm off." He folded the paper up and put it in his sleeve, then tried once more to mollify Sanzang. "Master," he said, "I've spent some time with you, and I've also been taught by the Bodhisattva. Now I'm being fired in the middle of the journey, when I've achieved nothing. Please sit down and accept my homage, then I won't feel so bad about going." The Tang Priest turned away and would not look at him, muttering, "I am a good monk, and I won't accept the respects of bad people like you." Seeing that Sanzang was refusing to face him, the Great Sage used magic to give himself extra bodies. He blew a magic breath on three hairs plucked from the back of his head and shouted, "Change!" They turned into three more Monkeys, making a total of four with the real one, and surrounding the master on all four sides they kowtowed to him. Unable to avoid them by dodging to left or right, Sanzang had to accept their respects.

The Great Sage jumped up, shook himself, put the hairs back, and gave Friar Sand these instructions: "You are a good man, my brother, so mind you stop Pig from talking nonsense and be very careful on the journey. If at any time evil spirits capture our master, you tell them that I'm his senior disciple. The hairy devils of the West have heard of my powers and won't dare to harm him." "I am a good monk," said the Tang Priest, "and I'd never mention the name of a person as bad as you. Go back." As his master refused over and over again to change his mind Monkey had nothing for it but to go back, angry and sad, to the Water Curtain Cave on the Mountain of Flowers and Fruit.

CHAPTER 18
The Yellow Robe Monster and the
Princess from Elephantia City

Let us return to the Tang Priest, who had trusted the word of the idiot and dismissed the Great Sage. He climbed into his saddle, and with Pig leading the way and Friar Sand carrying the luggage they carried on westwards. After crossing the White Tiger Ridge they saw a range of forested hills of which it could truthfully be said that creepers climbed and twisted among the bluish cypresses and green pines. "Disciples," said Sanzang, "this rough mountain path is very hard going, and we must be careful in the dense pine forests ahead as I'm afraid there may be evil spirits and monsters." At this the idiot Pig summoned up his spirits and, telling Friar Sand to guide the horse, cleared a path with his rake along which he led the Tang Priest into the forest. As they were going along, the venerable Sanzang reined in his horse and said to Pig, "I'm really starving today. Is there anywhere you could find some food for me?" "Please dismount, Master," Pig replied, "and wait here while I go and find some." Sanzang dismounted, while Friar Sand put down his load, took out his begging bowl, and handed it to Pig. "I'm off," said Pig. He was away for a very long time, sleeping in the grass.

Sanzang was left waiting in the forest. As he was feeling anxious and unsettled he said to Friar Sand, "It's late now. Why isn't Pig back from begging for food?" "Master," said Friar Sand, "you still don't understand him. He's found out that many of these westerners give food to monks, and with his big belly he won't be bothering about you. He won't be back till he's eaten his fill." "True," said Sanzang. "If he's greedily stuffing himself somewhere far away we need not concern ourselves with him. It's getting late and this is no place to spend the night. We must find somewhere to stay." "There's no rush, Master," said Friar Sand. "You sit and wait here while I go and find him." "Very well," said Sanzang, "very well. Never mind about the food. It's somewhere for the night that matters." Clasping his precious staff, Friar Sand went off through the pine forest in search of Pig.

Sanzang felt thoroughly tired and miserable as he sat alone in the forest, so he summoned up his spirits, leapt to his feet, hid all the luggage in a cache, tethered the horse to a tree, took off his reed hat, and drove his staff into the ground. Then he straightened out his black robes and took a leisurely stroll among the trees to cheer himself up. As he looked at all the wild flowers he did not hear the calls of the birds returning to their nests. The grass was deep and the forest paths were narrow, and in his distraction he lost his way. He had started out to cheer himself up and also to find Pig and Friar Sand; what he did not realize was that they had headed due west while he, after wandering in all directions, was going south. He came out of the forest and looked up to see a dazzling golden light. On closer examination he saw that it was the golden roof of a pagoda gleaming in the setting sun.

Sanzang stepped out and was soon at the gate of the pagoda. Seeing a curtain of speckled bamboo hanging inside, he lifted it up and went in. He raised his head and saw an evil monster with a blue face and white fangs, sleeping on a stone bed.

Sanzang was so terrified at the sight of him that he shrank back, his whole body numb with terror. No sooner had he turned to go than the monster, whose powers really were tremendous, opened a fiendish eye with a golden pupil and shouted, "Who is that outside the door, little ones?" A junior devil poked his head out to look, saw a shaven-headed priest, and ran in to report, "A monk, Your Majesty. He has a large face and a round head, and his ears hang down to his shoulders. His flesh looks most tender and his skin extremely delicate. He's a very promising monk." The monster cackled and said, "This is what they call 'a fly landing on a snake's head, or food and clothing presenting themselves to you'. Go and catch him for me, lads, and bring him back here. I'll reward you well." The junior demons rushed out after Sanzang like a swarm of bees; and Sanzang, in his alarm, started to run so fast he seemed to fly. But he was so terrified that his legs were soon like numb jelly, and on top of this the path was very uneven and it was twilight in the deep forest. He could not move fast enough, and the junior demons picked him up and carried him back.

The junior devils carried the Tang Priest in and announced with great delight, "We've brought the monk back, Your Majesty." "Where do you live, monk?" the monster asked. "Where have you come from, and where are you going? Tell me at once." "I am a priest from the Tang country, and I am going to the West on the command of His Majesty the Tang Emperor to ask for holy scriptures. As I was passing your distinguished mountain, I came over to visit the holy men of this pagoda. I did not realize that I would disturb Your Excellency, and I beg you to forgive me. When I return East with the scriptures from the West I shall see to it that your fame will be eternally celebrated." "I thought you must be someone from a superior country," said the fiend, bellowing with laughter, "and as that's who you are, I'm going to eat you up. It was splendid of you to come, splendid — otherwise we might have let you slip. You were fated to be the food in my mouth, so of course you came rushing here. We'll never let you go, and you'll never escape." Then he ordered the junior demons to tie him up. They rushed upon him and bound him tight to a soul-fixing stake.

Holding his sword in his hands, the old fiend asked, "How many of you are there altogether? You wouldn't have the guts to go to the Western Heaven all by yourself." Eyeing the sword in his hand, Sanzang had to answer truthfully. "I have two disciples, Your Majesty," he said, "called Pig and Friar Sand. They have both gone begging for food outside the pine forest.

Apart from them there is a load of baggage and a white horse that I left in the wood." "More luck," said the fiend. "Two disciples as well makes three of you, four counting the horse, which is enough for a meal." "We'll go and get 'em," the junior fiends said. "No," the old monster said, "don't go. Lock the front gate. As they've gone begging for food they'll have to find their master for him to eat it, and when they can't find him they're bound to come searching for him here. As the saying goes, 'it's easiest to do business at home.' Just wait and we'll catch them all in good time." The junior demons shut the front gate.

We will leave the unlucky Sanzang and return to Friar Sand, who was now three or four miles outside the forest in his search for Pig but had not yet seen any village. As he stood on a hillock looking around him, he heard a voice in the undergrowth; and sweeping the tall grass aside with his staff, he discovered the idiot talking in his sleep. Pig woke up when Friar Sand twisted his ear. "You idiot," said Friar Sand, "who said you could sleep here instead of begging for food as our master told you?" Pig, waking up with a start, asked, "What's the time, brother?" "Get up at once," replied Friar Sand. "The master told us two to find somewhere to stay whether we can beg any food or not."

Holding his begging bowl and his rake, the drowsy Pig headed straight back with Friar Sand, and when they looked for their master in the wood they could not see him. "It's all because you didn't come back from begging for food, you idiot," said Friar Sand indignantly. "Master must have been carried off by an evil spirit." "Don't talk nonsense, brother," replied a grinning Pig. "This forest is a very proper sort of place and couldn't possibly have any evil spirits in it. I expect our master got bored sitting here and went off somewhere to look around. Let's go and find him." They took the horse's bridle, picked up the shoulder-pole with the luggage, collected Sanzang's hat and staff, and left the pine wood in search of their master.

But Sanzang was not fated to die this time. When the two had been looking for him without success for a while, they saw a shimmering golden light due south of them. "Blessed indeed are the blessed, brother," said Pig. "Look where the master must be staying. . That light is coming from a pagoda, and they would be bound to look after him well. I expect they've laid on a meal and are making him stay to eat it. Let's get a move on and have some of it ourselves." "It certainly can't be anything sinister," replied Friar Sand. "We must go and have a look."

As the pair of them arrived at the gates they found them closed. Above the gates they saw a horizontal tablet of white jade on which were carved the words MOON WATERS CAVE, BOWL MOUNTAIN. "Brother," said Friar Sand, "this is no temple. It's an evil spirit's cave. If our master is in there we'll never see him." "Never fear," replied Pig. "Tether the horse and mind the luggage while I ask for news of him." With that the idiot raised his rake and shouted at the top of his voice, "Open up, open up." The junior devil who was on gate duty opened the gates, and at the sight of the pair of them he rushed inside to report, "Your Majesty, we're in business." "What sort of business?" the old monster asked. "There are two monks outside the gates," the junior demon replied. "One has a long snout and big ears and the other looks down on his luck, and they are shouting at us to open up." "That means Pig and Friar Sand have come looking for him," said the old monster. "Ha! They were bound to. What brought them here?" He called for his golden armour to be put on him, took his sword in his hand and marched straight out of the cave.

As the old monster Yellow Robe came out through the gates he asked, "Where are you monks from, and why are you yelling at my gates?" "Don't you recognize me, son?" said Pig. "I'm your father. I've been sent by the Great Tang on a mission to the Western Heaven. My master is Sanzang, the emperor's younger brother. If he's here, send him out at once and save me the trouble of having to smash my way in with this rake." "Yes indeed," laughed the monster, "there is a Tang Priest in my place. I haven't showed him any discourtesy, and I've laid on a meal of human-flesh dumplings for him. Why don't you two come in and have some?"

Pig struck at the evil monster's face with his rake. The monster sidestepped and parried with his steel sword. They both showed their magic powers as they leapt up on clouds to continue the fight in mid-air. Friar Sand abandoned the baggage and the white horse and rushed to Pig's aid. The three of them fought dozens of rounds in mid-air without issue. They were all fighting for their very lives, and nothing could have kept them apart.

We must leave the three of them locked in struggle and return to Sanzang sobbing his heart out in the cave and speculating about his disciples. "When will I be delivered from my troubles so that we can hurry to the Vulture Peak?" As he fretted and wailed he saw a woman come out from the innermost part of the cave. "Venerable father," she said, leaning on the soul-fixing stake, "where have you come from? Why has he tied you here?" When Sanzang heard this he sneaked a quick look at her through his tears and observed that she was about thirty. "Don't ask me that, Bodhisattva," he said, "I was fated to die: I walked into your home. Eat me if you must, but don't ask me why." "I don't eat people," she replied. "My home is over a hundred miles west of here in the city called Elephantia. I'm the third daughter of the king, and my childhood name was Prettier-than-a-flower. Thirteen years ago, on the fifteenth night of the eighth month, the Moon Festival, that evil monster came and snatched me away in a whirlwind while we were out enjoying the full moon. I have been his wife all these thirteen years and borne him sons and daughters, but I've never been able to send any message home. I miss my parents, and I can never see them. Where did you come from to be caught by him?" "I was sent to the Western Heaven to fetch the scriptures," replied Sanzang. "I never realized when I set out for a stroll that I would stumble into this. Now he's going to capture my two disciples and steam us all together, then eat us." "Don't worry, venerable sir," said the princess with a smile. "As you are going to fetch scriptures I can save you. Elephantia lies on the main route to the west, and if you will take a letter to my parents for me, I'll make him spare your life." "If you

save my wretched life, Bodhisattva," said Sanzang with a bow,
"I promise to be your messenger."

The princess hurried back inside, wrote a letter to her family, sealed it, released Sanzang from the stake, and handed him
the letter. "Bodhisattva," he said, taking the letter now that he
was free, "I am very grateful to you for saving my life. When
I reach your country I shall give this to the king. My only worry
is that after all these years your parents may not believe that
the letter is from you, and what would I do then? I could not
have them thinking that I was trying to deceive them." "That's
no problem. My father has only us three daughters and no sons.
If they see this letter they'll feel that they're seeing me." Sanzang
kowtowed and, as she had told him, left her, slipped out
through the back door, and hid among the thorns rather than
travel alone.

The princess, who had thought out a clever plan, hurried out
through the front gates and made her way through the hosts of
demons great and small to hear the furious clash of arms. Pig
and Friar Sand were still fighting with the monster in mid-air.
"Lord Yellow Robe," she shouted at the top of her voice, and
as soon as he heard her the demon king left Pig and Friar Sand,
landed his cloud, and, grasping his steel sword, took his wife
by the arm. "What is it, wife?" he asked. She replied, "I beg
you, lord and master, to respect me and spare that monk in
your mercy. Will you do this?" The monster then grasped his
sword once more and shouted, "Come here, Pig. I'm not afraid
of you, but I'm not fighting you any longer. For my wife's sake
I've spared your master, so hurry round and find him at the
back door and carry on west. If you set foot in my territory
again I won't let you off a second time."

This news made Pig and Friar Sand feel as if they had been
let out through the gates of Hell. They scurried away with the
horse and the baggage, and going round to the other end of the
Moon Waters Cave they called "Master" outside the back entrance. Sanzang recognized their voices and called back from
among the thorn bushes. Friar Sand made his way through the
undergrowth, helped his master out, and hurriedly helped him

mount the horse.

They covered stage after stage of their journey, sometimes longer and sometimes shorter, and before they realized it they had done ninety-nine miles. Suddenly they looked up and there was a fine city in front of them. This was Elephantia, and it was a splendid place.

Gazing at the view of Elephantia the master and his two disciples dealt with the luggage and the horse and settled down in a rest-house.

Next day, Sanzang and his disciples had a personal audience with the King, bringing the letter written by the third princess. Sanzang produced the letter from his sleeve and handed it to the king, who on seeing the words, "All is well" on the outside felt so weak in his hands that he could not open it. He ordered a Grand Scholar from the Academy of Letters to climb the steps of the throne and read it aloud.

When the Grand Scholar had read it through, the king wept aloud, the ladies of the palace were all in tears, and the officials were all saddened. Everyone was miserable.

After weeping for a long time the king asked the civil and military officials which of them would lead troops to capture the monster and rescue Princess Prettier-than-a-flower for him. He asked them all several times, but nobody would accept.

"If you have any supernatural skills, venerable sir," the king said, turning at once to Sanzang, "then use your dharma powers to capture this evil monster and bring my daughter back to the palace. If you do that there will be no need to travel to the West and visit the Buddha. You can let your hair grow and I will make you my brother. We shall sit together on the dragon throne and share my wealth and honour. What about it?" "My only humble skill," Sanzang hastened to reply, "lies in invoking the Buddha's name, and I really cannot subdue fiends." "If you can't subdue fiends," the king retorted, "how can you have the courage to go to visit the Buddha in the Western Heaven?" Sanzang then told him about the two disciples as he could not keep them a secret any longer. After hearing this, the King pleaded for their help and asked Sanzang and his disciples to rescue the princess. Out of pity for the King, Sanzang decided to go back with Pig and Friar Sand.

Before long they reached the mouth of the cave and landed their cloud. Pig brought his rake down with all his might on the door of the cave and made a hole the size of a bucket in it. The junior demons guarding it were so frightened that they opened up the gates. At the sight of the pair of them they rushed inside to report, "Bad news, Your Majesty. The long-snouted monk with big ears and the other one with a horrible face have come back and smashed down our doors." "Pig and Friar Sand again?" exclaimed the monster in astonishment. "How dare they come and break down my door after I've spared their master's life?" "Perhaps they've come to fetch something they left behind," suggested a junior demon. "Nonsense," snorted the monster. "Would they break the gate down if they'd just left something behind?" He hastily tied on his armour, took his steel sword, went outside and asked, "Monks, what do you mean by smashing down my door? I spared your master, didn't I?" "Will you do a decent thing, wretched ogre?" said Pig. "What?" asked the old monster. "You forced the Third Princess of the land of Elephantia to come to your cave," said Pig, "and you've made her stay here for thirteen years. You should send her back now. We've come here to capture you on the king's orders, so you'd better hurry in and tie yourself up if you don't want me to hit you." The old fiend was now furious. Just watch him as he gnashes his fangs of steel, glares so hard that his eyes become round with fury, raises his sword, and hacks at Pig's head. Pig avoided the blow and struck back at the monster's face with his rake, after which Friar Sand rushed forward to join in the fight with his staff.

When they had fought eight or nine bouts on the mountain side Pig was beginning to tire; his strength was flagging and he could only raise his rake with difficulty. "You come forward and fight him, Friar Sand," said the idiot, "while I go off for a shit." Then with no further thought for Friar Sand he streaked off into the undergrowth. Then he fell into a doze, too frightened to come out again.

Seeing Pig flee, the monster charged at Friar Sand, who could do nothing to stop the ogre from seizing him and carrying him into the cave.

CHAPTER 19
Pig Provokes Monkey to Come to the Rescue

Pig had been hiding in the undergrowth ever since he abandoned Friar Sand. He slept through to the middle of the night. When he woke up, he worked out from the position of the stars that it was around midnight, and thought, "I must go back and rescue Friar Sand. It's all too true that 'you cannot make thread with a single strand, or clap with a single hand.' No, no. I'd better go back to the city, see the master, and report on this to the king. He can give me some more brave soldiers to help me rescue Friar Sand."

The idiot went back to the city on his cloud as fast as he could, and in an instant he was back at the hostel. It was a still, moonlit night, and he could not find his master in either wing of the building. There was only the white horse asleep there, his body covered in sweat, and with a greenish wound the size of a dish on his hind leg. "This is double trouble," thought Pig in horror. "Why is this horse covered with sweat and injured on his leg? He hasn't been anywhere. Some crooks must have carried off the master and wounded the horse." Seeing Pig, the horse suddenly called out, "Elder brother." Pig collapsed from shock, got up again, and was about to flee when the horse took his clothes between his teeth and said, "Brother, don't be afraid of me." "Why ever have you started to talk today?" asked Pig, who was shaking all over. "Something terrible must have happened to make you do it." "Do you know that our master is in danger?" the horse asked. "No," Pig replied. "You wouldn't," said the horse, and explained, "The monster turned himself into a handsome scholar, came to the palace, and made the king accept him as his son-in-law. He changed our master into a tiger, who has been captured by the officials and put in a cage in the court waiting room. The news made me feel as if my heart were being sliced to pieces. It was already two days since you two went, and for all I knew you might have been killed, so I had to turn back into a dragon and try to rescue our master. When I reached the court I couldn't find him, though I saw the monster outside the Hall of Silvery Peace. He dodged my blow, picked up a giant candlestick in both hands, and soon had me on the run. I escaped with my life by hiding in the palace canal. The scar is where he hit me with the candlestick."

"Is this all true?" asked Pig. "Don't think I'm trying to fool you," said the dragon. "What are we to do?" said Pig.

The dragon thought for a moment before replying, still in tears, "All you need do to rescue the master is to ask someone to come here." "Who?" asked Pig. "Take a cloud back to the Mountain of Flowers and Fruit as fast as you can, and ask our eldest brother Monkey to come here. With his tremendous ability to beat demons he ought to be able to rescue the master and avenge our defeat." "Can't we ask someone else?" said Pig. "He hasn't been on the best of terms with me since he killed the White Bone Spirit on White Tiger Ridge. He's angry with me for encouraging the master to say the Band-tightening Spell. I only meant it as a joke — how was I to know the old monk would really say it and drive him away? Goodness knows how furious he is with me. He definitely won't come. I'm no match for him with my tongue, and if he's disrespectful enough to hit me a few times with that murderous great cudgel of his, it'll be the death of me." "Of course he won't hit you," said the dragon. "He's a kind and decent Monkey King. When you see him don't tell him that the master's in trouble. Just say, 'The master's missing you.' Once you've lured him here and he sees the situation he won't possibly be angry. He's bound to want to fight the monster. I guarantee that he'll capture the monster and save our master." "Oh well," said Pig, "oh well. As you're so determined I'll have to go, or else I'll look half-hearted. If Monkey's prepared to come, I'll come back with him; but if he isn't, then don't expect me — I won't be back." "Go," said the dragon. "I promise he'll come."

The idiot picked up his rake, straightened his tunic, leapt up on a cloud, and headed east. Soon he saw Monkey, who was once more lording it over his monkey hordes.

"Why have you come here instead of going to fetch the scriptures with the Tang Priest?" Monkey asked. "Have you offended the master and been sent back too? Show me your letter of dismissal."

"I'll tell you the truth," said Pig. "After you came back here Friar Sand and I escorted the master. But we met a Yellow Robe Monster who turned our master into a tiger, captured Friar Sand and wounded the white horse. It was the white horse who sent me here to fetch you. Please, please remember that 'if a man has been your teacher for a day, you should treat him as your father for the rest of his life'. I beg you to save the master."

"Idiot," said Monkey, "I told you over and over again before leaving that if any evil monsters captured the master you were to tell them I am his senior disciple. Why didn't you mention me?" Pig reflected that to a warrior a challenge was more effective than an invitation and said, "It would have been fine if we hadn't used your name. It was only when I mentioned you that he went wild." "What did you say?" asked Monkey. "I said, 'Behave yourself, kind monster, and don't harm our master. I have an elder brother called Brother Monkey who is an expert demon-subduer with tremendous magic powers. If he comes he'll kill you, and you won't even get a funeral.' This made the ogre angrier than ever, and he said, 'I'm not scared of Monkey. If he comes here I'll skin him, tear his sinews out, gnaw his bones, and eat his heart. Although monkeys are on the skinny side, I can mince his flesh up and deep-fry it.' " This so enraged Monkey that he leapt around in a fury, tugging at his ear and scratching his cheek. "Did he have the bloody cheek to say *that* about me?" he asked. "Calm down, brother," said Pig. "I specially remembered all his insults so as to tell you."

"Up you get," said Monkey, "I didn't have to go before, but now he's insulted me I've got to capture him. Let's be off. When I wrecked the Heavenly Palace five hundred years ago all the generals of Heaven bowed low at the sight of me and called me 'Great Sage'. How dare that fiend have the nerve to insult me behind my back! I'm going to catch him and tear his corpse to shreds to make him pay for it. When I've done that I'll come back here." "Quite right," said Pig. "When you've captured the monster and got your own back on him, it'll be up to you whether you come on with us."

Taking Pig's hand, Monkey mounted a cloud and left the Mountain of Flowers and Fruit, heading back westwards. When they had crossed the Eastern Sea he stooped at the western shore. When they saw the gleam of the golden pagoda Pig pointed at it and said, "That's where the Yellow Robe Monster lives. Friar Sand is still there." "You wait for me up here," said Monkey, "while I take a look around the entrance before fighting the evil spirit." "No need," said Pig, "as he's not at home." "I know," said Monkey.

The splendid Monkey King saw two boys hitting a feather-stuffed ball with curved sticks, grabbed them by the hair, and carried them up to the top of a cliff. "If you release my brother Friar Sand," he shouted when the princess ran out of the cave in alarm, "I'll give you your sons back. You'll be getting a good bargain — two for one." The princess hurried back into the cave and untied Friar Sand, who felt as though the oil of enlightenment had been poured on his head and the sweet dew had enriched his heart. "Come up here," said Monkey, and Friar Sand sprang up on the cliff. Monkey told him and Pig to take the boys to the city, drop them on the palace steps, and say that they were the sons of the Yellow Robe Monster. That would surely bring the ogre back to fight him. The Great Sage then persuaded the princess to go away and hide. The Monkey King turned himself with a shake of his body into the very image of the princess, and waited for the coming back of Yellow Robe Monster.

Meanwhile Pig and Friar Sand took the two boys to the city

of Elephantia and hurled them down on the palace steps, where they were smashed to mincemeat. The Yellow Robe Monster was not sure whether the dead boys really were his sons, so he decided to go home to find out.

When Monkey saw the monster coming back to the cave he blinked till the tears came down like rain, started to wail for the children, and jumped and beat his breasts as if in grief, filling the cave with the sound of his sobbing. The monster failed to recognize who Monkey really was and put his arms round him. "What makes you so miserable, wife?" he asked. He told the monster how the two boys had been abducted by Pig and Friar Sand, which made the monster furiously angry and determined to have his revenge. "Don't cry, wife," he said. "There's nothing wrong with me," said Monkey, "except that I've cried so much that my heart aches." "Never mind," the monster replied. "Come over here. I've got a treasure here that you just have to rub on your pain to stop it hurting. But be very careful with it and don't flick it with your thumb, because if you do you'll be able to see my real body." Monkey was secretly delighted. "What a well-behaved fiend," he thought, "giving that away without even being tortured. When he gives me the treasure I'll flick it to see what kind of monster he really is." The ogre then led him to a remote and secluded part of the cave and spat out a treasure about the size of a hen's egg. It was a magic pill skilfully fashioned from a piece of conglomeration of internal secretion. The ape took it, rubbed it over his pretended pain, and was just going to flick it with his thumb when the monster took fright and tried to grab it from him. The crafty Monkey popped it into his mouth and swallowed it. The monster clenched his fist, and hit at him, but Monkey parried the blow, rubbed his face, and reverted to his real form with a shout of, "Behave yourself, ogre. Take a look and see who I am."

The monster at once ordered all the fiends and ogres in and around the cave to muster with their weapons and put a close blockade on all the doors. Monkey was delighted to see them, and wielding his cudgel with both hands he shouted "Change!" and suddenly had six arms and three heads. Then he shook his gold-banded cudgel and turned it into three gold-banded cudgels. He went into action with his six arms and three cudgels. He was a tiger in a sheepfold, a hawk in a chicken run. The poor little demons had their heads smashed to pulp, while their blood flowed like water. He rushed to and fro as if there was nobody else there until only the old ogre was left. He followed Monkey outside and said, "Insolent ape. How dare you come here and bully us?" Monkey turned, beckoned to him and said, "Come here, come here. Let me win the credit for killing you."

The monster struck at the head with his sword, and Monkey riposted to the face with his cudgel.

They had fought fifty or sixty rounds without issue when Monkey thought, "That bloody monster's sword is as good as my cudgel. I'll pretend to give him an opening and see if he can tell it's a trick." The Monkey King raised his cudgel and did a "Reaching Up to a Tall Horse" movement. The monster, not realizing that this was a trick, and imagining that he saw a real opening, took a tremendous swipe at Monkey with his sword. Monkey at once did a high swing to avoid the blow, then struck at the monster's head with a "Stealing a Peach from under the Leaves" movement and knocked him so hard he vanished without a trace. Monkey put his cudgel away and looked for him but without success. "Wow," exclaimed Monkey in astonishment, "I didn't just hit him — I knocked him out of existence. But if I really killed him there ought at least to be some blood and pus, and there's no sign of any. Perhaps he got away." He leapt up on a cloud to look around, but nothing was moving. "My eyes can see anything at a glance," he thought, "so how can he have got away so mysteriously? Now I see. He said he seemed to recognize me, so he can't be an ordinary monster. He must be some spirit from Heaven."

This was too much for Monkey, who lost his temper and somersaulted up to the Southern Gate of Heaven with his cudgel in his hands. He rushed to the Hall of Universal Brightness, where the four great Heavenly Teachers asked, "What have you come for, Great Sage?" "As I was escorting the Tang Priest to

Elephantia an evil monster abducted a princess and harmed the master. I had to fight him, and in the middle of our battle he disappeared. I thought that he couldn't be an ordinary monster and was probably a spirit from Heaven, so I've come to check up if any wicked deities have left their posts." On hearing this the Heavenly Teachers went to make an investigation.

A moment later, the Heavenly Teachers reported to the throne, "Strider, the Wooden Wolf, has gone down to Earth." "How long has he been away from Heaven?" the Jade Emperor asked. "He has missed four roll-calls," they replied, "and with one roll-call every three days that makes thirteen days." "Thirteen days in Heaven would be thirteen years down on Earth," said the emperor, and he ordered the Strider's fellow stars to go down and bring him back to Heaven.

On receiving this edict the twenty-seven other constellations went out through the gates of Heaven and startled the Strider as each chanted his own spell. Do you know where he had been hiding? He had been one of the heavenly generals who was beaten when Monkey had sacked the Heavenly Palace, and he had lain low in a mountain stream that masked his demonic cloud and kept him out of sight. Only when he heard the other constellations shouting their spells did he dare to emerge from the water and go back to Heaven with them. The Great Sage was blocking the gates of Heaven and would have killed him but for the pleas of the other constellations, who saved him and escorted him to see the Jade Emperor. The monster now produced his golden tablet of office from his belt and kowtowed on the floor of the palace, admitting his guilt. The Jade Emperor withdrew his tablet of office and degraded him to be a menial helping Lord Lao Zi stoke his fires in the Tushita Palace while retaining his old pay. If he did well he would be restored to his previous post; if not, his sentence would be made heavier. Monkey, delighted to see how the Jade Emperor dealt with him, left Heaven.

The Great Sage brought his shining cloud straight down to the Moon Waters Cave on Bowl Mountain, found the princess, and joined Pig and Friar Sand.

The three disciples took the princess to the throne hall, where she bowed to her royal parents and met her sisters again. All the officials came to bow to greet her. Then she reported, "We are indebted to the infinite powers of the venerable Monkey for the defeat of the Yellow Robe Monster and my rescue."

The three disciples left the throne hall and went with all the courtiers to the antechamber, where the iron cage was carried in and the false tiger unchained. Monkey was the only one who could see that he was human; all the others thought he was really a tiger. As Sanzang was under the demon's spell he could not move, and although he was clear in his mind, he was unable to open his mouth or his eyes. "What a fine monk you are, Master," said Monkey, "getting yourself into this revolting shape. You accused me of being a murderer and sent me home for it, but you wouldn't be such an awful sight if your heart had been set on goodness." "Save him, brother, don't tell him off," said Pig. "It was you who put him up to it all," said Monkey. "You were his favourite disciple. Why didn't you save him instead of sending for me? Besides, I told you that I'd go back when I'd defeated the monster and avenged that insult." Friar Sand went over and knelt down before him. "As the old saying goes," he pleaded, " 'If you won't do it for the monk's sake, do it for the Buddha's sake.' I beg you to save him now that you're here. I wouldn't have gone all that way to ask you to come if we'd been able to save him ourselves." "I couldn't bear not to save him," replied Monkey, raising Friar Sand to his feet. "Bring me some water." Pig flew back to the hostel, fetched the horse and luggage, took the golden begging bowl from it, half-filled it with water, and handed it to Monkey. Monkey took the water in his hand, said the words of a spell, and spurted it at the tiger's head. The evil magic was dissolved, and the tiger-aura was dispersed.

Sanzang was seen in his true form once more. Once he had gathered himself together and opened his eyes he saw Monkey, took hold of him, and said, "Monkey, where have you come from?" Friar Sand, who was standing in attendance, told him

all about how Monkey had been asked back, defeated the
monster, rescued the princess, dispersed the tiger-aura, and come
back to the palace. "Worthy disciple," said Sanzang, full of
gratitude, "thank you, thank you. When we return to the East
from our journey to the West I shall report to the Tang Emperor
that you have won the greatest distinction." "Don't mention
it," said a smiling Monkey, "don't mention it. The best way
you can show your gratitude is by not saying that spell." When
the king heard about all this he thanked the four of them and
gave a great vegetarian banquet for them in the eastern wing.
After this expression of the king's kindness master and disciples
took their leave of him and set out for the West.

CHAPTER 20
In Lotus Flower Cave on Flat-top Mountain Pig Runs into Trouble

The story tells how after Monkey had rejoined the Tang Priest the four of them headed west, united in their shared determination. The king of Elephantia had escorted them beyond his capital to thank them for bringing back his daughter. From there they travelled on, eating when hungry and drinking when thirsty, moving by day and resting at night.

Master and disciples were enjoying their journey when they saw a mountain blocking their way. "Be careful, disciples," said the Tang Priest. "I'm worried that tigers and wolves may prevent us from crossing that high mountain ahead." "There's no need to be so glum," said Monkey. "Remember the Heart Sutra. Besides, with me here you'll come to no harm even if the sky falls down, so why be scared of wolves and tigers?" said Monkey. This cheered up Sanzang, who gave his dragon-horse the rein and urged it forward. As they climbed the mountain they found it truly craggy and precipitous.

As Sanzang reined in his horse to look at the mountain he saw that they had reached a most difficult spot. There was a wood-gatherer standing on the green, grassy slope.

"Stop here for a moment on your journey west," he shouted. "I must warn you that there is a pack of vicious ogres and fierce wolves on this mountain. They eat travellers from the east who are heading west."

The news terrified Sanzang out of his wits. Trembling

in the saddle, he turned round sharply and called for his disciples. "Did you hear what the woodman said?" he asked. "There are ogres and wolves on this mountain. Do any of you dare ask him for more details?" "Don't worry, Master," said Monkey, "I'll find out from him."

Brother Monkey hurried up the mountain, and addressing the woodman as "Elder Brother" he asked all about it. "Why have you come here, venerable sir?" asked the woodman, returning his greeting. "To tell you the truth, elder brother," said Monkey, "we have come from the east and are heading west to fetch the scriptures. That's my master on the horse. He's a bit timid, so when you told him about the ogres and wolves he sent me to ask you about them. How long have they been here? Are they experts or just beginners? Please tell me about them. Then I can make the gods of the mountain and the local deities march them off." At this the woodman threw back his head and roared with laughter. "You really are a mad monk," he said. "I'm not mad," replied Monkey, "I'm talking sense." "If you're talking sense," said the woodman, "then how can you say you'll have them marched off?"

"If they were sky monsters," replied Monkey, "I'd send them to the Jade Emperor, and if they were earth monsters I'd send them to the Earth Palace. Western ones would go to the Buddha and Eastern ones to the Sage. I'd send northerners to the True Martial God of the North and southerners to the Fire God. Dragon spirits would go to the Lord of the Seas and demons to King Yama. They all have somewhere to go. I know the people in all those places, so I'd only need to write out an order for the monsters to be sent there at the double the very same night."

"You mad monk," said the woodcutter with a mocking laugh, "you may have travelled in the clouds and learnt a little magic, but even if you can expel evil spirits and bind demons you've never come up against such vicious fiends." "What's so vicious about them?" asked Monkey. "This mountain is about two hundred miles across," said the woodcutter, "and it's called Flat-top Mountain. There is a cave in it called the Lotus

Flower Cave where two devil chieftains live. They are so determined to capture monks that they've drawn pictures of them and found out the name of the man they want to eat — the Tang Priest. "Those monsters have five treasures that they carry about with them, and their magic powers are enormous. Even if you're one of the jade pillars of the heavens or one of the golden beams that support the sea you may well have to pass out in order to get the Tang Priest through." "How often?" Monkey asked. "Three or four times," replied the woodcutter. "That's nothing," said Monkey, "nothing at all. We all pass out seven or eight hundred times a year, so it will be easy to pass out three or four times more and then we'll be able to get through."

The fearless Great Sage, whose one thought was to protect the Tang Priest, left the woodcutter and hurried back. When he reached the horse standing on the mountainside he said, "It's nothing much, Master. It's true that there are a few evil spirits here, but the local people only worry about them because they are timid. With me here there's no need for you to be afraid of them, so let's be on our way again." Sanzang was relieved to hear this, and he followed Monkey's lead.

As they travelled along they realized that woodcutter had disappeared some time back. "Why can't we see the woodcutter who gave us the message?" asked Sanzang. "What lousy luck," said Pig. "We would have to meet a ghost in broad daylight." "He must have gone into the forest to look for some more firewood," said Monkey. "I'll take a look." Opening wide his fiery eyes with their golden pupils, the splendid Great Sage searched the mountain, but no sign of the woodcutter was to be seen. Then he looked up into the clouds and saw the Duty God of the Day there. He sprang up there himself and cursed him for a hairy devil several times before saying, "Why didn't you tell me straight instead of transforming yourself and putting on that act for me?" The Duty God bowed to him anxiously and said, "Please forgive me for being so late with the warning. Those monsters really have enormous magic powers and can perform all kinds of transformations. You'll need all your skill and cunning to protect your master. You won't possibly reach the Western Heaven if you are at all slack."

Monkey dismissed the Duty God. He was feeling worried as he landed his cloud and went up the mountainside until he found Sanzang, Pig and Friar Sand pressing ahead. "If I tell the master straight what the Duty God said," he thought, "the master won't be able to face up to it and will start crying. But if I don't tell him and keep him in the dark he won't know how things stand, and it'll be a great nuisance for me if he gets captured by monsters. I'd better go and see Pig. I can send him ahead to fight the monster. If he wins, that will be something to his credit. If he can't do it and gets captured by the monster, I can go and rescue him."

The Great Sage resorted to a trick. He rubbed his eyes till they watered then went up to the master. "The person who gave us the message just now," said Monkey, "was the Duty God of the Day. He said that the evil spirits here are so ferocious that it will be hard to get through; besides, we'll never be able to make our way across these steep mountains. Let's go another day." Trembling with fear at this news, Sanzang tugged at Monkey's tigerskin kilt and said, "Why these thoughts of turning back when we've already done half the journey?" "It's not that I'm wavering," said Monkey, "but we'd be no match for so many monsters. 'A lump of iron in the furnace can only make a few nails.' " "You are right," said Sanzang, "it would be very difficult by yourself. As the military classic says, 'few are no match for many'. But I also have Pig and Friar Sand for you to deploy as your subordinates. Make a joint effort to clear the path and take me over the mountain. Then you will receive your just reward."

As Brother Monkey's little show had only wrung these words out of his master, he wiped away his tears and said, "Pig will have to do two things I tell him to if you're to have even one chance in three of crossing the mountain as you want to, Master. If he won't do these two things for me you'll have no hope at all." "Brother," Pig said, "if we can't cross the mountain, let's disband. Leave me out of this." "Disciple," said Sanzang, "ask your brother what he wants you to do." "What do you want me to do, brother?" Pig asked.

"You can patrol the mountains," said Brother Monkey. "What would that involve?" asked Pig. "You would have to go into these mountains," said Monkey, "to find out how many monsters there are, and all about the mountains, and what the monsters' caves are like, so that we can go across." "Nothing to it," replied Pig. "I'll patrol the mountains." The idiot hitched up his tunic, grasped his rake, and proudly struck deep into the mountains. His spirits were high as he hurried along the path.

In this Flat-top Mountain there was a Lotus Flower Cave where there dwelt two fiends, the Senior King Gold Horn and the Junior King Silver Horn. Gold Horn sat in his chair of office and said to Silver Horn, "It's a long time since we patrolled the mountain." "A fortnight," replied Silver Horn. "You should make a patrol today," said Gold Horn. "Why today?" asked Silver Horn. "You can't have heard the news," said Gold Horn, "that the Tang Priest, the younger brother of the Tang Emperor in the East, has been sent to worship the Buddha in the West. He has three followers called Sun the Novice, Pig and Friar Sand, so with their horse there are five of them in all. Find them and bring them to me." "If we want to eat some humans," said Silver Horn, "we can catch a few anywhere. Why not let this monk go wherever he's going?" "You don't realize," replied Gold Horn, "that when I left Heaven a few years back I heard that the Tang Priest was a mortal incarnation of the Venerable Golden Cicada, and a holy man who had pursued goodness for ten lives and lost not a drop of his original essence. Anyone who eats his flesh will live for ever." "If you can live for ever by eating his flesh," said Silver Horn, "we won't have to bother with meditation, winning merit, refining elixirs, or matching the male and female. All we need do is eat him. I'm off to fetch him." "You're too impatient, brother," said Gold Horn. "Don't be in such a hurry. It would be wrong to rush out and catch some monk who isn't the Tang Priest. I remember what he looks like and I once drew pictures of him and his disciples. Take them with you and check any monks you meet against them." He went on to tell him all their names, and when Silver Horn had their pictures and knew their names he went out of the cave, mustered thirty underlings, and left to patrol the mountain.

Pig's luck was out. He walked straight into the gang of monsters who blocked his way and said, "Who are you? Where are you from?" The idiot looked up, lifted his ears from over his eyes, and saw to his horror that they were evil ogres. "If I say I'm a pilgrim," he thought, "they'll catch me. I'll say I'm just a traveller." The junior demon reported to the king that he was a traveller. Among the thirty junior demons there were some who had recognized him and some who had not, and one of these who had recognized him remembered Silver Horn being given his instructions. He said, "This monk looks like Pig in the picture, Your Majesty." Silver Horn had the picture hung up, which made Pig think with horror, "No wonder, I'm in such low spirits these days — they've got my spirit here." As the junior devils held it up with their spears, Silver Horn pointed at it and said, "The one on the white horse is the Tang Priest, and the hairy-faced one is Sun the Novice." "City god," thought Pig, "you can leave me out. I'll offer you the triple sacrifice and 24 cups of pure wine." He muttered prayers as the devil continued, "The tall dark one is Friar Sand, and that's Pig with a long snout and big ears." At the mention of himself Pig tucked his snout into his clothes. "Bring your snout out, monk," said the monster. "I was born like this," said Pig, "so I can't bring it out." The monster ordered the junior devils to pull it out with hooks, at which Pig hastily thrust it out and said, "I just feel shy about it. Here it is. Look at it if you must, but don't hook it."

Recognizing Pig, the monster raised his sword and hacked at him. Pig parried him with his rake and said, "Behave yourself, my lad, and take this." "You took your vows quite late," said the monster with a smile. "Clever boy," replied Pig, "but how did you know?" "From the way you handle that rake," the monster said, "you used it to level up the ground in a vegetable garden. You must have stolen it." "You don't know this rake, my boy," said Pig. "It's not the sort used in ground-levelling."

Pig's reply made the monster even more determined. With his Seven-starred Sword he battled through twenty inconclusive rounds with Pig on the mountain. Pig fought back with deadly fury, and at the sight of him pricking up his ears, spewing out saliva, and waving his rake with grunts and shouts, the frightened demon turned round to bring all his underlings into the battle beside him. Had he been fighting only the one enemy, Pig would have done fine, but when all the little devils rushed him he lost control, could no longer put up any resistance, and fled in defeat. As he was not paying attention to the uneven path he tripped over a creeper and fell over. He was just picking himself up and starting off again when a junior demon who was lying there tugged at his ankle and brought him tumbling down like a dog eating muck. A crowd of demons seized him and carried him back to the cave, holding him by the bristles, ears, legs and tail.

Taking Pig into the cave the monster said, "Here's one, brother." "Let me have a look at him," said the older demon with delight. "Isn't this the one?" asked the younger demon. "No," the other replied, "you've caught the wrong one. He's useless." "Your Majesty," said Pig, taking his chance, "I'm just a useless monk, so let me go. I'm scarcely human." "No, don't let him go, brother," said the younger monster. "He may be no use himself, but he's with the Tang Priest. Pig's his name. We can soak him in the drinking-water pool at the back till his bristles come out, salt him and dry him to eat with our wine some rainy day." The junior demons carried Pig inside and threw him into the pool.

Sanzang meanwhile was sitting on the slope feeling uneasy. His ears were hot and his eyes twitched. "Wukong," he said, "Pig's been a long time patrolling the mountain. Why isn't he back?" "Don't you understand his mentality yet, Master?" said Monkey. "What mentality?" Sanzang asked. "If there were monsters in the mountains he'd be completely helpless," said Monkey. "He'd make a tremendous fuss and come rushing back to tell me. I don't think that there can be any monsters. I expect he found the path easy and went straight ahead." "If he has gone ahead," said Sanzang, "where shall we meet him? This is a vast wilderness. It won't be like finding him in a city or a market-place." "Mount your horse and stop worrying," said Monkey. "That lazy idiot won't be walking fast, so you only have to make your horse get a move on. We're bound to catch him up and continue our journey together." The Tang Priest mounted his horse as asked, and Monkey led the way into the mountains as Friar Sand carried the baggage.

"Brother," said Gold Horn the senior demon king to Silver Horn the junior demon king, "as you've captured Pig we can be sure that the Tang Priest is here. Make another search and don't get the wrong one this time." "Right away," said Silver Horn, who immediately mustered fifty junior demons and set out on patrol.

As they went along they saw an auspicious cloud drifting and circling around. "The Tang Priest is here," said the junior demon king. "Where?" the other demons asked. "An auspicious cloud always shines above a good man's head and an evil effluence rises over a bad man," said Silver Horn. "The Tang Priest is an incarnation of the Venerable Golden Cicada. He's a holy man who has cultivated his conduct for ten lives. That's why he has that auspicious cloud." When the others still could not see it the junior demon king pointed again and said, "There it is." Sanzang shuddered thrice in the saddle, once each time the demon pointed. "Why did I shudder, disciples?" he asked uneasily. "Probably it's indigestion," said Friar Sand. "Nonsense," said Monkey, "it must be because these steep mountains make the master feel nervous. Don't be frightened. You'll feel better when I've cleared the path with my cudgel." Monkey then ran through all the routines in the military manuals as he swung his cudgel up and down and all around in front of his master's horse. The Tang Priest watched as he displayed divine powers unmatched on earth.

At the sight of Monkey hacking his way forward the demon almost died of terror; his souls went flying as he watched from the mountain top. "Well," he found himself saying, "now I know that all I've been hearing about Sun the Novice for years is absolutely true." "Your Majesty," said the junior demons, coming up to him, "you're boosting your enemy and making yourself small. Why? Who is it who's so terrific?" "With Monkey's magic powers we'll never be able to eat the Tang Priest," said Silver Horn. "We were right to capture him and shouldn't let him go," said the junior king. "We may not be able to eat the Tang Priest yet but sooner or later we will." "How many years will that take?" the others asked. "It won't be a matter of years," replied the junior king. "In my opinion we must catch him by cunning, not by being vicious. Try to grab him by force and we won't get so much as a smell of him. But if we make friends with him by kindness we'll be able to get him by trickery." "Please find a place for us in your plan, Your Majesty," said the little demons, "Go back to the camp," the junior demon king told them, "but don't let on to His Senior Majesty. If he gets alarmed and gives the game away our plan will be ruined. I can catch the Tang Priest through magical transformations." As the other demons went away he leapt down the mountainside to the path, shook himself and changed into a aged Taoist.

There he was, beside the path, pretending to be a Taoist who had broken his leg. His feet were covered in blood. "Help, help," he shouted.

Just as Sanzang was happily walking along, supported by the Great Sage Monkey and Friar Sand, he heard a shout of "Help me, Father." "Well I never," said Sanzang. "Who could that be shouting in these wild and uninhabited mountains? It must be someone who's been frightened by tigers, leopards or wolves." Reining in his horse he called, "Who's that in trouble? Come out." The demon crawled out from the undergrowth and kowtowed noisily for all he was worth before the Tang Priest, who was most upset to see that he was a Taoist and of such advanced years at that. He dismounted rapidly and helped the old man to his feet, begging him to rise. "It's agony," said the demon, "agony."

When the Tang Priest released his hold and looked down he saw that blood was pouring from the old man's foot. "Where have you come from, sir," asked a shocked Sanzang, "and how did you injure your foot?" "West of this mountain, Father," lied the demon, "there is a pure and quiet Taoist temple. I am a priest there." "What were you doing, wandering around here instead of looking after the incense and reciting the scriptures and the law in your temple?" Sanzang asked. "The other day a benefactor of ours from south of the mountain invited all us priests to perform a service for his natal star and spread blessings for him. I was about half-way there with my disciple — we were late — when a ferocious and strongly patterned tiger carried my disciple off. As I staggered along shaking with terror and not knowing where to go I lost my balance on a scree and injured my foot. I can't find my way back. Thank heavens I have met you today, Father. I beg you in your great mercy to save me. If we find our way back to the temple, I'd even sell myself into slavery to repay your kindness." "Sir," replied Sanzang, completely taken in, "you and I share a common destiny. I am a Buddhist priest and you are a Taoist. Although we wear different robes, we cultivate our conduct according to the same principles. Were I to fail to save you I would not be a true monk. But help you though I would, you can't walk." "I can't even stand, let alone walk," replied the demon. "Never mind, never mind," said Sanzang. "I can walk, so you can ride my horse for a while and give it back when we reach your temple." "You are very generous and I am most grateful," said the demon, "but I have hurt my thigh and couldn't ride." "Indeed," said Sanzang, who then instructed Friar Sand to put the luggage on the horse and carry the Taoist over his shoulders. Friar Sand assented.

The monster turned round at once and looked closely at Friar Sand. "Father," he said, "I got such a scare from that tiger, but this terrible-looking Father frightens me even more. I'd be too afraid to let him carry me." "Wukong, you carry him," said Sanzang. "Certainly, certainly," replied Monkey. The demon recognized him and docilely allowed himself to be carried by him, saying no more.

As Monkey carried the demon on his shoulders he muttered to himself with some amusement, "Wretched demon, how dare

you try to provoke me? Do you think I'm a mere child? Your
devilish nonsense may be good enough to hoodwink the Tang
Priest but it won't fool me. I can see that you are a local mountain demon. I reckon you want to eat my master. He's no
ordinary person — he's not for you to eat. Besides, if you want
to eat him you'll have to give a good half to me." Hearing Monkey's mutterings the monster replied, "Father, I'm a Taoist monk
from a decent family who was unlucky enough to meet that tiger
today. I'm no evil spirit." "If you were afraid of the tiger why
didn't you recite the Great Bear Scripture?" Monkey asked.
Sanzang, hearing Monkey's grumbling just as he was mounting
the horse, told him off: "Insolent ape. 'Better to save a human
life than to build a seven-storeyed pagoda.' If you're carrying
him, just get on with it. Stop talking about 'Great Bear Scriptures' or 'Little Bear Scriptures'." "You're in luck, damn you,"
said Monkey. "Merciful and pious my master may be, but he's
a bit rough under his kindly manner. He'll be angry if I don't
carry you with me. I'll do it if I must, but there's something
I want to tell you first: warn me if you want a piss or a shit.
If you do it down my back the stench will be more than I can
stand. Besides, there's nobody to wash my clothes if they get
dirty." To which the demon replied, "Of course I'm old enough
to understand that." At last Monkey hauled the demon up on
his back and hastened westwards with the Tang Priest and Friar
Sand. When the going became very uneven in the mountains
Monkey walked slowly and carefully, letting the Tang Priest
get ahead.

Before they had gone a couple of miles the Master and Friar
Sand dropped out of Monkey's sight into a hollow on the mountainside. "The Master doesn't have any sense of how things
should be done despite his great age," he grumbled to himself.
"On this long journey I'd feel overloaded even if I were empty-
handed. I wish I'd smashed this evil monster. I would have to
carry him. Even he's not a monster but a good man he ought
to die at his age. Why should I carry him? I'll fling him down
and kill him." The demon realized that the Great Sage was
deciding to kill him so he used his power to shift mountains and

made mountain-moving sea-overturning magic on Monkey's back. He recited the words of the spell, bringing Mount Sumeru flying through the air to come crashing down on Monkey's head. The Great Sage twisted his head to one side in a flash, and the mountain landed on his left shoulder. "Tell me, son," said Monkey, "what magic have you used to make yourself so heavy? You're crushing me. I don't mind the weight, but 'a badly-balanced carrying-pole is much harder to manage than a well-balanced one'." "A mountain's not enough to crush him," thought the demon, and he recited another spell to bring Mount Emei hurtling down through the air on Monkey's head. Monkey turned aside again, so that the mountain landed on his right shoulder. Just watch him as, with the two mountains on his shoulders, he hurries like a shooting star after his master. The monster broke into a cold sweat all over when he saw that Monkey could carry mountains. Then he pulled himself together, recited another spell, and brought Mount Tai down from the sky on Monkey's head. By now the Great Sage was so weak with exhaustion that this mountain landing on his head pinned him down: his three corpse-spirits exploded, and blood spurted from his seven orifices.

When he had crushed Monkey with his magical powers the splendid evil spirit mounted a fast wind and caught up with Sanzang. The monster reached down from his cloud and made a grab for the Tang Priest as he rode his horse. Friar Sand threw down the luggage in horror and rushed forward wielding his demon-subduing staff to stop him.

The ferocious demon wielded his Seven-star Sword like a shooting star as he fought till Friar Sand was exhausted. Friar Sand turned to flee, but the monster parried his staff and brought a great hand wheeling round to grab him. Tucking the friar under his left arm, the demon pulled Sanzang from his horse with his right hand, hooked their luggage with his toes, opened his mouth to get his teeth into the horse's mane, and used his magic to levitate them and carry them in a puff of wind back to the Lotus Flower Cave. "Elder brother," he yelled, "I've got all the monks."

"You have great powers, my brother," said the older monster with a laugh. "You've caught the three monks twice. But even though you've crushed him under a mountain you'll need some magic to get that Sun into our cooking pot. That'll be the day." "Please sit down, elder brother," said the younger monster. "I can get Monkey without lifting a finger. I just need to send two little devils with a couple of treasures to bring him back in." "What treasures?" "My gold and red gourd and your vase of muttonfat jade." The older monster fetched the two treasures, handed them to him, and asked which two little devils were to be sent. "Send Dexterous Ghost and Skilful Beast," replied the younger monster. He then instructed them, "Take the two treasures straight to the top of a high mountain, put them there upside-down and call out to Sun. If he responds he'll go straight inside. You must immediately paste this label on: 'Supreme Lord Lao: to be dealt with urgently in accordance with the Statutes and Ordinances.' Within three and a half hours he'll just be pus." The two little devils kowtowed and went off with the treasures to catch Monkey.

As he lay crushed under the three mountains the Great Sage thought in his distress of the holy priest Sanzang.

All this had alarmed the mountain spirits, the local gods and the Protectors of the four quarters and the centre. "Whose mountains are these?" asked the Gold-headed Protector. "Ours," said the local gods. "And who is it pinned under your mountains?" "We don't know," said the local gods. "You lot wouldn't," said the Protector. "It's Sun Wukong, the Great Sage Equalling Heaven who made havoc in the palaces of Heaven five hundred years ago. Now he's found religion and become the Tang Priest's disciple. Why ever did you let that demon use your mountains to crush him? You've had it now. He'll not spare you if ever he gets free. Even if he decides to let you off lightly it'll be exile for the local gods and hard labour for the mountain spirits. And I'll get a severe reprimand."

"We didn't know, really we didn't," said the gods and spirits, now terrified. "When the chief demon recited the mountain-moving spell we just moved them here. We never knew it was the Great Sage Sun." "Don't be afraid," said the Protector "The Legal Code says that you cannot be punished for what you are unaware of. We'll have to work out a plan to let him out in such a way that he won't kill us all." "It would be very unfair of him to kill us if we set him free," said the local gods. "There's something else you don't know," said the Protector. "He has a truly lethal as-you-will gold-banded cudgel. If he hits you with that you're dead, and just a touch of it will wound. A tap will shatter your sinews, and a graze from it rip your skin to shreds."

The terrified local gods and mountain spirits then conferred with the Protectors, approached the gates of the three mountains, and called, "Great Sage, the mountain spirits, local gods and Protectors from the four quarters and the centre have come to see you." Splendid Monkey. He was like a tiger who though skinny was as always full of spirit. "So what?" he called in a loud, clear voice. "We have a communication for the Great Sage," replied the local gods. "If we remove the mountains and set you free, Great Sage, will you forgive us humble spirits for our discourtesy?" "Move these mountains," said Monkey, "and I won't hit you." Then he shouted, "Get up." It was just like the authorities giving an order: the deities all said the magic words and the mountains went back to where they had come from. Monkey was free. He jumped up, shook the dirt off him, tightened his kilt, pulled out his cudgel from behind his ear, and said to the local gods and mountain spirits, "All hold out your feet. I'm going to give you two strokes each to work off my bad temper." "But you promised just a moment ago, Great Sage," said the deities in horror, "to forgive us. How can you go back on your word and hit us?" "My dear local gods and mountain spirits," said Monkey, "you're more afraid of that monster than of me." "But that demon has great and powerful magic arts. When he says his true spells he forces us to take it in turns to be on duty in his cave every day."

Just as the Great Sage was complaining about the demon a rosy light began to shine in the mountain hollow. "Mountain spirits, local gods," asked Monkey, "you serve in the cave, so what is it that's shining?" "The monsters' treasures," replied the local gods. "Some of the demons must have brought them to catch you out with." "Just what I need to play a little trick on them," said Monkey. "Tell me, who comes to see them in the cave?" "What they're interested in is refining elixirs of immortality, and their best friends are Taoist masters of the Quanzhen School," replied the local gods. "No wonder he turned himself into an old Taoist priest to trick my master." said Monkey. "Very well then, I'll let you off for now. Back you go. I'll get them myself." The spirits all rose into the air and made off.

The Great Sage shook himself and turned himself into an old Taoist master.

It was not long before the two little devils arrived. Monkey thrust his gold-banded cudgel out and tripped up the two demons, who were taken right off guard. It was only as they picked themselves up that they saw Monkey. "You villain. If our Great King weren't such an admirer of the likes of you we'd soon sort you out." "What do you mean, sort me out?" asked Monkey with a forced smile. "We're all Taoists — one big happy family." "Why are you lying here, and why did you trip us up?" asked the devils. "A little fall is a way for you boys to show your respect on meeting a Taoist elder like me," said Monkey. "Our Great King only demands a few ounces of silver when people first meet him," said the little devils, "so why do you expect us to fall over for you? That's not the custom here. You must be from somewhere else." "Indeed I am," said Monkey. "I'm from Mount Penglai." "But that's an island in the sea where immortals live," said the devils. "If I'm not an immortal," said Monkey, "I don't know who is." By now the devils' anger had given way to delight. "Venerable immortal," they said, "venerable immortal, please don't take offence at our rudeness. It was only because our common mortal eyes failed to recognize you." "I don't hold it against you," said Monkey. "As the saying goes, 'An immortal body does not tread the common ground.' You couldn't be expected to know. I've come to your mountain today to bring over a virtuous man who has become an immortal and completed the Way. Anyone wants to come with me?" "I'll go with you, Master," said Dexterous Ghost. "Me too," said Skilful Beast.

"Where have you two gentlemen come from?" asked Monkey, as if he did not know already. "From the Lotus Flower Cave," they said. "Where are you going?" "We are under orders from our Great King to capture Sun the Novice," the devils replied. "Who?" Monkey asked. "Sun the Novice," they repeated. "The Sun the Novice who's going with the Tang Priest to fetch the scriptures?" asked Monkey. "Yes, that one," the devils replied. "Do you know him?" "That ape's outrageous," said Monkey. "I know him, and I'm very angry with him too. Let me come along with you and help you catch him." "Thank you, Master," they replied, "but we won't be needing your help. Our Junior King used his magic arts to bring three mountains here to crush him. Now he can't move an inch. We two have been sent here with treasures to pack him into." "What treasures?" asked Monkey. "I've got the red gourd," said Dexterous Ghost, "and he's got the jade vase." "How are you going to fit him into them?" asked Monkey. "We'll set them upside down," said the little devils, "and call to him. If he responds we'll put him inside and stick on a label saying: 'Supreme Lord Lao: to be dealt with urgently in accordance with the Statutes and Ordinances.' Three and a half hours later he'll be just so much pus." This news shocked Monkey, who remarked to himself what a deadly plot this was. "The Duty God of the Day told me that there were five treasures all together," he thought. "These are two of them. I wonder what the other three are." "Gentlemen," he said aloud, "would you let me have a look at your treasures?" Not realizing that this was a trick the two little devils produced them from their sleeves and offered them respectfully with both hands to Monkey. He was delighted, though he did not show it. "Splendid things," he thought, "splendid. I just have to flick my tail in the air and go whizzing off with a jump. They've given them to me." Then he had second thoughts: "No, that's no good. Stealing them would be easy enough, but it would destroy my reputation. It'd be daylight robbery." So he handed them back with the words, "But you haven't seen my treasure yet." "What is it?" the devils asked. "Would you let us common mortals see it? It'd bring us luck."

The splendid Monkey put his hand down, pulled a hair from his tail, made a spell, and called "Change!" It turned into a big gold and red gourd one foot seven inches long that he produced from his waist. "Would you like to see my gourd?" he asked. Skilful Beast took it, looked at it, and said, "It's a very big gourd, Master, shapely, and very fine to look at, but it's useless." "What do you mean, useless?" asked Monkey. "Each of our treasures can contain a thousand people," the devils replied. "What's so special about being able to contain people?" said Monkey. "Mine can hold the sky itself." "The sky?" asked the devils. "Yes, it really can," Monkey replied. "You must be lying," said the little devils. "We could only believe that if we saw you do it. There's no way we're going to believe you otherwise." "If the sky annoys me," said Monkey, "I pack it in here seven or eight times a month; but if it doesn't annoy me I might leave it alone for half a year." "Let's see if he'll swap his sky-holding treasure with us," said Skilful Beast to the other demon. "But he'd never swap his sky-holder for our gourd that can only hold people," replied Dexterous Ghost. "If he won't swap we can throw our vase in too," said Skilful Beast. Concealing his delight, Monkey thought, "A gourd for a gourd and the vase too is two for one: I'll certainly agree to that." So he went up to Skilful Beast, clutched him, and asked, "Will you swap them if it can hold the sky?" "Yes, we'll swap them as long as it can hold the sky," said the devil, "and I'll be your son if we don't." "Very well then," said Monkey, "I'll put the sky in it to show you."

The splendid Great Sage bowed his head to make the spell and say the words of it. He called on the Patroller of the Day, the Patroller of the Night together with the Protector of the Four Quarters and the Centre: "Report on my behalf to the Jade Emperor that I have now found the true faith and am escorting the Tang Priest to the Western Heaven to fetch the

Scriptures. We are now held up on a high mountain and my master is in dire distress. I want to trick the devils into swapping their treasures with me, so I most humbly beg that I be lent the sky to put away for an hour. This will enable me to succeed. If there's so much as a hint of a refusal then I'll be coming up to the Hall of Miraculous Mist to give battle."

The Patroller of the Day went straight in through the Southern Gate of Heaven to the Hall of Miraculous Mist, where he reported everything to the Jade Emperor. "Outrageous ape," said the Jade Emperor. "This is insolence. It can't be done." As soon as he had said that the sky could not be put away Prince Nezha stepped forward from the officials at court and submitted a memorial: "Your Majesty, it is possible to contain the sky." "How?" the Jade Emperor asked. Prince Nezha replied, "I beg for the issue of an Imperial Edict to the Northern Gate of Heaven asking the True Martial God to lend us his Black Vulture Banner to spread outside the Southern Gate and block out the sun, moon and stars. Down there they will be unable to see each other and not even able to tell black from white. That will fool the devils into thinking that the sky has been packed into the gourd, and enable Sun the Novice to succeed." The Jade Emperor ordered that this suggestion be implemented. Bearing the imperial command Prince Nezha went to see the True Martial God at the Northern Gate of Heaven and tell him what had happened. The True Martial God handed the prince the banner.

By now a patroller had hurried down to whisper in the Great Sage's ear, "Prince Nezha is coming to help you." Monkey looked up to see swirling clouds of good omen, a sure sign of the presence of a god, then turned to the little devils and said, "We'll put the sky away then." "Put it away if you like," said the little devils, "but why all this playing for time?" "I was just saying the spell and calling up the magic powers," said Monkey. The little devils gazed wide-eyed, wondering how he was going to put the sky away. Monkey threw his imitation gourd up into the air. It was only a hair really, so you can imagine how light it was. As the winds round the mountain peak caught it, it floated in the air for an hour before landing. Meanwhile Prince Nezha was noisily spreading the Black Vulture Banner out at the Southern Gate of Heaven, obscuring the sun, the moon and the stars.

The two little devils were terrified. "When we were talking a moment ago," they said, "it was midday. How could it be dusk now?" "When the sky is put away," said Monkey, "distinctions of time disappear. Of course it's murky." "But why's it so dark now?" "The sun and the moon and the stars have all been put inside, so there's no light outside. It's bound to be dark." "Master," said the little devils, "where is your voice coming from?" "I'm just in front of you, aren't I?" said Monkey. The little devils stretched their hands out and felt him. "We can hear you but we still can't see you. Where are we, Master?" "Don't fidget," said Monkey, hoodwinking them, "you're on the coast of the Bohai Sea. One slip and you'd fall for seven or eight days before hitting the bottom." The little devils were panic-struck. "Enough, enough. Let the sky out again. Now we know how it's put away. If you go on a moment too long and we fall into the sea we'll never get home."

Splendid Monkey. As they were both convinced he said another spell that had an impact on Prince Nezha, who rolled the banner up again, revealing the noonday sun once more. "Fantastic," exclaimed the little devils in delight, "fantastic. If we don't do a swap for this treasure we won't be looking after our family's interest." Dexterous Ghost handed over the gourd and Skilful Beast produced the vase. When they gave them both to, Monkey he gave them his imitation gourd. The exchange had now been made, but Monkey wanted it to be final, so he plucked a hair from under his navel, blew a magic breath on it, and turned it into a copper coin. "Boys," he said, "take this coin and buy a sheet of paper." "Why?" they asked. "We'll write a legal contract for the exchange of your two man-holding treasures for my sky-holder," said Monkey. "We each need a written agreement to prevent later regrets with the passage of time." "But there's no brush or ink here to write a contract with," said the two little devils. "Let's swear an oath instead." "What sort of oath?"

asked Monkey. "We exchange our two man-holding treasures for your sky-holder," said the devils, "and if we ever have any regrets may we be struck with pestilence in all four seasons." "I certainly won't have any regrets," chuckled Monkey. "If I do, may I too be struck with pestilence in all four seasons." Having sworn his oath he leapt up, his tail in the air, and landed in front of the Southern Gate of Heaven, where he thanked Prince Nezha for helping him with the banner. The prince reported back to the palace and returned the banner to the True Martial God, leaving Monkey standing amid the stars and clouds, gazing at the little devils.

CHAPTER 21
The Great Sage Wins Treasures
through Trickery

With the imitation gourd in their hands the two little devils were quarrelling over who should examine it when they looked up and saw that Monkey had disappeared. "Brother," said Skilful Beast, "even immortals tell lies sometimes. He said that when we'd swapped the treasures he would make us into immortals. How come he's vanished without a word?" "We got ourselves a very good bargain," said Dexterous Ghost, "and he would not dare disappear. Pass the gourd over—I want to put the sky in it and try it out." He tossed the gourd into the air, but it came crashing down again, to the distress of Skilful Beast, who asked, "Why won't it take in the sky? Could it be that it was Sun the Novice disguised as an immortal, and that he swapped an imitation gourd for our real one?" "Nonsense," said Dexterous Ghost. "Sun the Novice is crushed under those three mountains. How could he possibly have got out? Pass the gourd over. I'll say the words of the spell he made and we'll put the sky inside." He too then threw the gourd up into the air, saying, "If there's so much as a hint of a refusal I'll be coming up to the Hall of Miraculous Mist to give battle." The gourd hit the ground before he could even finish saying the spell. "The sky hasn't gone in," they both said. "It must surely be a fake."

Up in the sky the Great Sage Sun Wukong could hear every word they said and see all that was happening while they made this commotion. For fear that they would go on too long and let the news out where it mattered he shook himself and put the hair that had been turned into a gourd back on his body, leaving both the little devils completely empty-handed. "Give me the gourd, brother," said Dexterous Ghost. "You give it me," said Skilful Beast. "Heavens! It's disappeared!" They both started to search wildly on the ground and in the grass, putting their hands in their sleeves and in their tunics, but it was nowhere to be found. "Whatever shall we do," said the two horror-struck little devils, "whatever shall we do? His Supreme Majesty gave them to us to catch Sun the Novice with. Now we haven't caught him and the treasures have disappeared. We can't report this to him or he'll have us beaten to death. Whatever are we going to do?" "Let's run away," said Skilful Beast. "Where to?" asked Dexterous Ghost. "Anywhere," said Skilful Beast, "because if we go back and say that we've lost the treasures that'll obviously be the end of us." "No," said Dexterous Ghost, "don't let's run away. Let's go back. Both their majesties are usually very fond of you, and I'll put in a word for you. If they are prepared to make allowances they'll spare your life. Even if we can't talk them out of having us beaten to death, at least they'll do it there, and we won't be caught between two stools. Let's go back." Having made their minds up the two little demons set out back to their own mountain.

Monkey, watching them heading back from where he was up in the sky, shook himself and turned into a fly that flew down and followed them. Where, you may wonder, did he put his treasures now that he was a fly? Had he left them on the path or hidden them in the grass someone might have found them and taken them, and all his efforts would have been for nothing. So he kept them on his person. But a fly is only the size of a bean: how could he find room for them? Because those two treasures of his, like his gold-banded cudgel, were as-you-will Buddha treasures that grow or shrink with you, that was why he could keep them on. He went buzzing along after the devils. Before long he was inside the cave, where the two demon kings were sitting and drinking.

The two little devils went up to them and knelt down.

Monkey perched on the doorframe, listening. "Your Majesties," said the little devils. "So you're back," said the Junior Demon King, putting down his cup. "Yes," said the little devils. "Have you got Sun the Novice?" was the next question. The two little devils banged their heads on the ground, not daring to reply. The old devils asked again, and still they dared not answer, but just kept banging their heads on the ground. Only when they had been asked this several more times did they prostrate themselves and tell the old devils about the loss of the treasures because of the tricks of Sun the Novice. At this the Senior Demon King thundered, "Damn it, damn it. It was Sun the Novice disguised as an immortal to trick them out of you. That monkey has enormous magic powers and knows people everywhere. What hairy little god let him out to con our treasures out of us?"

"Please calm yourself, brother," said the Junior Demon King. "That ape is the bloody limit. With all those powers it should have been enough for him to escape. Why did he have to trick us out of our treasures? If I don't have the powers to catch him then I'll never be a monster on the road west again." "How are you going to get him?" asked the Senior King. "We had five treasures," said the Junior King, "so even after losing two we have three left with which we can and must capture him." "What three treasures?" asked the Senior King. "The Seven-star Sword and the Plantain Fan that I carry with me," the Junior King replied, "and the Dazzling Golden Cord that's kept at our old mother's place in the Crushed Dragon Cave in Crushed Dragon Mountain. We should now send a couple of little devils to invite our mother to a meal of the Tang Priest's flesh and ask her to bring the Dazzling Golden Cord to catch Sun the Novice with." "Which ones should we send?" asked the Senior King. "Not rubbish like those two," replied the Junior King, who then shouted at Dexterous Ghost and Skilful Beast to get up.

"Send for my regular attendants Mountain Tiger and Ocean Dragon," ordered the Junior King. The two of them knelt before him while he gave them his instructions. "You must be very cautious." "We'll be cautious," they replied. "And careful." "We'll be careful," they replied. "Do you know the way to our mother's home?" he asked. "We do," they replied. "In that case go as soon as you can. When you get to the old lady's place bow to her very respectfully, then invite her to a meal of the Tang Priest's flesh and ask her to bring the Dazzling Golden Cord with her to catch Sun the Novice."

The two demons obediently hurried off, unaware that Monkey had heard every single word. He spread his wings and flew till he caught up with Mountain Tiger and settled on him. After about a mile he was going to kill the pair of them when he reflected, "Killing them would be no problem, but I don't know where the old lady keeps her Dazzling Golden Cord. I'd better question them before killing them." Splendid Monkey! He flew buzzing away from the two little devils and let them get a good hundred paces ahead. He then changed himself with a shake into another little devil with a fox-skin cap and a tigerskin kilt worn upside-down, who hurried after them and called, "Wait a moment, travellers." Ocean Dragon looked back and asked, "Where are you from?" "My dear brother," Monkey replied, "don't you even recognize members of your own household?" "You're not one of us," said the little devils. "What do you mean?" said Monkey. "Take another look and see if you can recognize me." "You're a stranger," they replied, "and we've never met." "That's right," Monkey said, "you've never met me. I'm one of the outside staff." "Well then," the little devils replied, "we would never have met you, sir. Where are you going?" "His Majesty told me," Monkey said, "that he'd sent you two gentlemen to invite the old lady to a meal of the Tang Priest's flesh. You were to ask her to bring the Dazzling Golden Cord along to catch Sun the Novice. He's worried that you two would dawdle and misbehave yourselves and mess things up, so he sent me along too to hurry you up." As he knew all the details the two little devils were not at all suspicious: they believed that Monkey really was one of them. They rushed along in a great hurry for about three miles. "This is too fast," said Monkey. "How far have we gone?" "About five miles," said the little devils. "And how much further is there to go?" "Just to the black wood over there," said Ocean Dragon, pointing it out. Monkey looked up to see a dark stretch of woodland not far away. The old demon must live somewhere nearby, he thought; so he stopped to let the little devils get ahead of him, pulled out his cudgel, rushed after them, and took a swipe at their legs. Unfortunately he hit them so hard that he turned the two little devils into mincemeat. He hid himself deep in the undergrowth beside the path, pulled out one of his hairs, blew on it, said "Change!" and turned it into Mountain Tiger. He turned himself into Ocean Dragon. Then the two imitation devils headed for the Crushed Dragon Cave to deliver the invitation to the old lady.

With four or five bounds both of him was in the wood. He searched until he saw a pair of stone doors standing ajar. Not daring to charge in, he shouted, "Open the doors."

The little she-devil on the doors was so startled that she opened one of them wide. "Where are you from?" she asked. "We've been sent from the Lotus Flower Cave on Flat-top Mountain with an invitation for the old lady," said Monkey, and the little she-devil invited both of him in. When he reached the inner doors he peeped round them and saw an old woman sitting in the middle of the cave.

When Sun the Great Sage saw her he did not go in, but covered his face with his hands and started to sob outside the inner doors. He thought, "I've used my powers to turn into a little demon and come with an invitation for this she-devil. It wouldn't do for me to stay upright when I talk to her: I'll have to kowtow to her. In my life I've been a real tough guy and only kowtowed to three people: Lord Buddha in the Western Heaven, Bodhisattva Guanyin in the Southern Ocean, and the Master—I kowtowed to him four times when he delivered me from the Double Boundary Mountain, and for him I'd wear out the six blades of my lungs and liver and the three hairs and seven apertures of my heart. But is it really worth banging my head on the ground before this she-devil for a roll of scripture?

If I don't, I'll give the game away. This is terrible. I suppose it's only because the master is in trouble that I'll humiliate myself like this." As he had no choice he rushed in, knelt down, and announced that he was kowtowing to the old lady.

"Get up, my child," said the she-devil. Monkey was delighted that his announcement had worked. "Where are you from?" the old devil asked. "I have been sent at the command of the two kings of the Lotus Flower Cave in Flat-top Mountain to invite you, Ma'am, to a meal of the Tang Priest's flesh. They also ask you to bring your Dazzling Golden Cord to capture Sun the Novice with." The old devil was very pleased indeed. "What good, dutiful boys," she said, sending for her carrying-chair. "Good lord," said Monkey to himself, "fancy a demon being carried in a chair." Two she-devils came up from behind with a chair made of fragrant rattan. They set it down outside the doors, then lifted the green gauze curtain. The old devil left the cave and got into the chair. "What are you two messengers called?" asked the old she-devil. "He's called Mountain Tiger," Monkey quickly replied, "and I'm Ocean Dragon." "You two take the lead and clear the way for me," said the old she-devil. "Stinking luck," thought Monkey. "No scriptures yet, on top of which I've got to be her slave." As there could be no question of refusing he had to lead the way, chanting loudly, "Lift the chair!"

When he had covered a couple of miles or thereabouts he sat down on the edge of a precipice. When the chair-porters caught him up he suggested, "What about a little rest? Your shoulders must be aching under the weight." Not realizing that this was a trick the little devils put the chair down. Standing behind it Monkey pulled a hair from his chest and turned it into a sesame bun that he ate as he held it. "What are you eating, sir?" the chair-porters asked. "It's a bit awkward to explain," replied Monkey. "We came a very long way to invite Her Highness, but as I've been given no food I'm hungry. When I've eaten some of these dry rations I brought with me we can be on our way." "Give us a bit," the porters pleaded. "Come over here, then," said Monkey. "There's no need to be too careful within the family." Unaware of what was up, the little devils crowded round Monkey for a share of his dry rations, whereupon he produced his cudgel. The one he hit on the head was smashed to pulp when trying to ward the blow off; the other, who was only grazed, survived to groan aloud. Hearing these groans the old demon poked her head out from the chair to take a look. Monkey leapt round to the front of the chair and brought his cudgel down on her head, denting her skull and making blood and brains spurt out. Dragging her out of the chair for a good look he found she was really a nine-tailed vixen. "Vicious brute," he said, "fancy you having yourself called 'Your Highness'. If you're a 'your highness' then you ought to address me as Supreme Ancestral Lord." The splendid Monkey King then found her Dazzling Golden Cord, and gloated as he tucked it up his sleeve, "Those lousy demons may have their magical powers, but three of their treasures are mine now." He then pulled out two more hairs that he turned into doubles of Mountain Tiger and Ocean Dragon, as well as two more that he turned into the chair-porters. He then made himself look like the old lady, sat in the chair, and had it carried straight back the way he had come.

It was not long before they were at the entrance to the Lotus Flower Cave and the two hairs turned chair-porters were clamouring for the doors to be opened. The little devil on the doors asked whether Mountain Tiger and Ocean Dragon were back. "Yes," replied the hairs. "Did you persuade Her Highness to come?" "Can't you see her in the chair?" asked the hairs, pointing. "Wait a moment while I report inside," said the little devil, who went in to announce, "Your Majesties, Her Highness is here." At this the two demon kings had a table of incense-sticks set out to greet her. Monkey was quietly delighted to hear all this. "What luck," he thought. "It's my turn to do it in style now. I had to kowtow with the invitation to the old she-devil when I turned myself into a little devil. Now that I've turned myself into her I'm their mother, and they'll have to kowtow four times to me. It may not mean much, but at least I'll be a couple of kowtows up." The splendid Great

Sage got out of the carrying chair, straightened his clothes, and put the four hairs back on his body. The little devil on the doors carried the empty chair inside, and Monkey walked slowly in behind him, imitating the old she-devil's affected wiggles. As he went straight in devils big and small knelt in greeting. A drum and fife band started to play, and clouds of incense rose from the Boshan burners. On reaching the main hall he sat down, facing regally south, while the two demon kings kow-towed to him with the words, "Mother, your children kowtow to you." "Get up, my children," said Monkey.

Pig, still hanging from a roof-beam, began to roar with laughter. "You're a fine one, brother," said Friar Sand, "laugh-ing while hung up." "I know what I'm doing," said Pig. "And what are you doing?" asked Friar Sand. "I was afraid that when the old woman came we'd be cooked and eaten. But it's not her: it's the old story." "What old story?" asked Friar Sand. "The Protector of the Horses is here," said Pig. "How can you tell?" asked Friar Sand. "When she leant forward and said, 'Get up, my children,' a monkey's tail stuck out behind her. I can see better than you because I'm hung up higher." "Stop talking," said Friar Sand. "Let's listen to what they say." "Yes, yes," said Pig.

"Well, boys, why have you asked me here?" asked Monkey as he sat between the two demon kings. "Mother," they replied, "we've been most discourteous to you for many days and not done our duty by you. But this morning we captured the Tang Priest from the East, and we wouldn't dream of eating him by ourselves. So we invited you over to present him to you live. We'll cook him and offer him to you to eat: he'll prolong your life." "I won't eat the Tang Priest's flesh, dear boys," Monkey replied, "but they do say that Pig's ears are delicious. Could you cut them off and have them prepared? They'd go down well with a drink." "A pox on you," exclaimed Pig in panic when he heard. "So you're here to cut my ears off. What I'll have to say won't make pleasant listening."

Oh dear! Because the idiot's remarks gave the game away the Monkey King's cover was blown. In burst a crowd of little demons, mountain rangers and doorkeepers to report, "Disaster, Your Majesties. Sun the Novice has killed the old lady and disguised himself as her." The moment the demon kings heard this there was no time for arguments: the Seven-star Sword was brought out, and it cut straight at Monkey's face. The splendid Great Sage moved in a flash: the cave was full of red light, and he was gone. A trick like that really was fun: he could concentrate himself into solid form, or disperse into vapour. The Senior Demon King was out of his wits with terror, while all the other devils hit their fingers and shook their heads. "Brother," said the senior king, "let's give the Tang Priest, Friar Sand, Pig, the white horse and all their baggage back to Sun the Novice and end the quarrel between us." "What a thing to say," replied the Junior King. "Goodness only knows how much trouble we went to in our plan to capture all those monks. But now you're so intimidated by Sun the Novice's amazing transformations that you want to give everything back to him. You really are a coward. No man would act like that. You sit down and stop being so terrified. I've heard you tell of his tremendous magical powers, but I've never tried my skill against his although we did meet. Bring me my armour. I'm going to find him and fight three rounds with him. If he can't beat me in those three rounds then the Tang Priest will be ours to eat; and if I can't beat him we'll give him back the Tang Priest." "You're right, brother," said the older demon, who then ordered that the armour be brought out. This was done.

When the Junior Demon King was fully accoutred he took his sword in his hand and went outside calling, "Sun the Novice, where have you gone?" The Great Sage, who was now up in the clouds, turned round to look as soon as he heard his name called and saw that it was the Junior Demon King.

"Sun the Novice," roared the Junior King, "give back our treasures and our mother and we will free your Tang Priest to go to fetch the scriptures." The Great Sage could not restrain himself from abusing him: "You revolting demon, you don't know what you're up against in me. Give me back my master, my brothers, the white horse and our baggage, and throw in some travelling expenses for our journey west too. If so much as the hint of a 'no' slips out between your teeth you'd better start making your own rope to save me the trouble of doing it myself." On hearing this the Junior Demon King sent a cloud shooting up and sprang into mid-air, swinging his sword round to cut through Monkey, who struck at his face with his iron cudgel.

The two of them fought thirty rounds, but neither came out on top. Monkey was delighted, though without showing it. "So this vicious devil is a match for my iron cudgel. As I've already got his three treasures I'm only wasting my time slogging it out with him like this. It'd be much better to pop him into the gourd or the vase. But that's no good," he reflected further. "As the saying goes, 'a possession is at its owner's disposal.' If they don't do what I tell them, everything will be ruined. I'll have to lasso him with the Dazzling Golden Cord."

Using one hand to parry the magic sword with his cudgel, the splendid Great Sage raised the rope in the other and sent it whistling through the air to lasso the demon king. Now the king had a Rope-tightening Spell and a Rope-loosening Spell. When he lassoed others he would say the tightening spell, and nobody would be able to get free; and if he lassoed his own people he would say the loosening spell and no one would be hurt. Recognizing this rope as one of his own family's treasures he said the loosening spell, at which the noose slid open. He got free and threw the rope back at Monkey, catching him. Before the Great Sage could apply some slimming magic to escape the demon had recited the tightening spell. Monkey was held fast, unable to free himself; he was locked tight by a gold ring at his neck. The demon jerked at the rope and pulled him over, then struck seven or eight blows at his head with the magic sword. This did not even redden Monkey's scalp. "If your head's that hard, you ape, I'll not hack at you any more," the demon said. "I'll take you back to kill later. Give me my two treasures back at once." "I haven't got any treasures of yours," Monkey replied, "so why ask me?" The demon king searched him very carefully, found the gourd and the vase, and dragged him back into the cave by the rope. "Brother, I've got him," he announced. "Who?" the Senior King asked. "Sun the Novice," replied the Junior King. "Come and see." When the Senior King saw that it was Monkey his face was wreathed in smiles. "It's him," he said, "it's him. Tie him to a pillar with a very long rope and we'll have some fun with him." And indeed Monkey was tied up while the two demon kings went into the back hall for a drink.

Monkey fidgeted at the foot of the pillar. Seeing that there was nobody in front of him Monkey used his magic powers to slide his cudgel out. He blew on it and said "Change!", turning it into a pure steel file. Tugging at the ring at his neck he filed it apart with four or five strokes of the file, then removed the file, freed himself, plucked out a hair, turned it into a replica of himself, and left it tied up there. Then in a flash he changed into a little devil and stood beside it. Up by the roof-beam Pig started to shout, "This is terrible, terrible. The one tied up is a fake. The genuine article is hanging up here." The Senior Demon King put his wine cup down to ask, "Why is Pig yelling?" Monkey, now in the guise of a little devil, came forward to report, "Pig was inciting Sun the Novice to transform himself and escape. Sun refused to do so, and so Pig is yelling." "Who said that Pig was well-behaved?" asked the Junior King. "Now we know just how cunning he is. He must be hit twenty times on the snout."

When Monkey fetched a rod to hit him with, Pig said, "Don't hit me hard, because if you do I'll start shouting again. I know who you are." "It's only for your sake that I'm making all these transformations," replied Monkey. "Why ever did you have to give the game away? None of the demons in the cave knew who I was. It would have to be you who found out." "You may have altered your face," Pig replied, "but you can't change your backside. You have a patch of red on either cheek down there, don't you? That's how I know it's you." Monkey went through to the inner quarters, slipped into the kitchens, rubbed the underneath of a pan, smeared the soot on both his buttocks, and went back to the front part of the cave. "Where's that monkey been messing around?" mocked Pig when he saw him. "His bum's all black."

Monkey was still standing in front of them, trying to steal their treasures. Being extremely wise he entered the main hall, tugged at the old demon's leg, and said, "Your Majesty, Sun the Novice is fidgeting around where he's tied to the pillar, trying to wear his way through the golden rope. It would be best to change it for a thicker one." "You're right," said the Senior Demon King, taking off the belt of lion-hide he wore at his waist and handing it to Monkey, who used it to tie up the imitation Monkey. The golden rope he tucked loop by loop into his sleeve before plucking out a hair, blowing on it with magic breath, and turning it into a copy of the Dazzling Golden Cord, which he respectfully returned to the demon with both hands. The demon was too preoccupied with his drinking to look at it carefully as he accepted it.

Now that he had this treasure he bounded out of the cave as fast as he could, turned back into himself, and shouted, "You devils." "Who are you, yelling like that?" the devils on the doors asked. "Go inside at once and announce to your lousy demon kings that the Novice Sun is here." When the little devils passed on the message the Senior King was greatly shocked. "We've captured Sun the Novice, so how can there be another Novice Sun?" "He's nothing to be frightened of," said the Junior King. "We have all our treasures back. I'll fetch the gourd and put him inside it." "Do be careful, brother," said the Senior King.

The Junior King went outside carrying the gourd to see someone just like Sun the Novice except that he was a little shorter. "Where are you from?" he asked. "I'm Sun the Novice's brother," Monkey replied. "I've heard that you've captured him, which is why I'm here to have it out with you." "Yes, I have got him," said the Junior Demon King. "He's tied up in the cave. As you're here you must want a fight, and I'm willing to cross swords with you. But do you have the guts to answer if I call your name?" "If you call my name a thousand times," said Monkey, "I'll answer ten thousand times." The demon leapt into mid-air with his treasure, which he held upside-down as he called out, "Novice Sun." Monkey did not dare reply. "If I reply," he thought, "he'll have me inside." "Why don't you answer me?" the demon asked. "I can't hear you," replied Monkey, "I'm a bit deaf. Shout louder." "Novice Sun," the demon shouted again. Down below Monkey pinched his own fingers as he thought things out: "My real name is Sun the Novice. Novice Sun is only a false name I've made up. With my real name I could be put in the gourd, but I reckon that with a false name I can't be." Unable to restrain himself any longer he replied this time. With a roaring of wind he was sucked into the gourd and the label was put on it. As it happened it made no difference to that treasure whether a name was real or false: any response was enough to get you put inside.

The Great Sage found it pitch-black inside the gourd. When he tried to raise his head he could not move it at all, so tightly was he squeezed in it. He now began to feel very anxious. "The two little devils I met on the mountain," he thought, "told me that anyone put in the gourd or the vase turns to pus in three and a half hours. Perhaps that's going to happen to me." Then he started on another line of thought: "No problem. I won't turn into pus. When I made havoc in the Palace of Heaven five hundred years ago Lord Lao Zi put me in his Eight Trigrams Furnace and fired me for forty-nine days, and this gave me a heart and liver of gold, lungs of silver, a brazen head, an iron back, eyes of fire and golden pupils. I couldn't possibly be turned to pus in three and a half hours. I'll let him take me inside and see what he does."

Taking Monkey inside, the Junior Demon King said, "I've got him, brother." "Who?" the Senior King asked. "I've got the Novice Sun packed in my gourd," the Junior King replied. "Do sit down, dear brother," said the Senior King, "and don't move. We must shake the gourd till we hear him sloshing around inside before taking the label off." Hearing this, Monkey wondered, "How could they shake my body till they heard it sloshing around? They wouldn't hear anything unless I'd turned runny. I'll take a piss, then if they shake me and hear it sloshing around they're bound to take the label and the lid off, and I'll be able to get the hell out of here. No, that won't do. Piss would sound right but it would get my tunic filthy. When he shakes the gourd I'll have my mouth full of saliva that I can swish around noisily to fool him into opening up. Then I'll be off." The Great Sage got ready, but the demons were too thirsty for their wine to shake the gourd. So he thought of a way to trick them into shaking it. "Heavens," he shouted, "my knuckles have turned to pus." But the demons still did not shake it. Then he shouted, "Mother, my waist has gone now." At this the Senior Demon King said, "If he's turned to pus as far as the waist he's finished. Take the label off and let's have a look."

When the Great Sage heard this he plucked out another hair, told it to change, and turned it into half of his own body, which he left in the bottom of the gourd. He turned himself into a tiny insect that perched near the mouth of the gourd. As soon as the Junior Demon King took the paper cover off he flew out, did a roll, and turned into Ocean Dragon, the little devil who had gone with the invitation to the old lady. In this guise he stood beside the path while the Senior King removed the stopper from the gourd, craned his neck, and saw the half body still moving. Not realizing that it was a fake he called out in panic, "Shut it again, brother, shut it. He hasn't rotted down yet." The Junior King put the cover back on. The Great Sage was discreetly delighted that they did not realize where he actually was.

The Senior Demon King took the gourd, filled a cup to the brim with liquor, and offered it with both hands to the Junior King, saying, "Please accept this drink from me." "Elder brother," replied the Junior King, "I've drunk a great deal. I can't accept another." To this the Senior King said, "Your capture of the Tang Priest, Pig and Friar Sand was nothing special;

but I insist on offering you some drinks to congratulate you on your achievement in tying up Sun the Novice and putting the Novice Sun into your gourd." As his elder brother was showing him so much honour and respect the Junior King would have to accept the cup. But he was still holding the magic gourd, and it would have been rude to accept the cup in one hand. So he passed the gourd to Ocean Dragon to allow himself to receive the cup with both hands, unaware that Ocean Dragon was Monkey in disguise. Just watch Monkey respectfully holding the gourd as he stands in attendance. When the Junior King had drunk the liquor he wanted to return the courtesy. "No need," said the Senior King, "I'll drink one with you." They were both being very modest. Monkey held the gourd and fixed his gaze on the two of them as they lost count of how many drinks they were giving each other. He slipped the gourd up his sleeve, pulled out a hair, and turned it into an exact facsimile of the gourd that he offered to the kings. After giving each other so many drinks the two kings did not check its authenticity but simply took their treasure, went to their places, sat down, and carried on drinking. The Great Sage got away. He was very pleased at having captured the treasures.

Concealing the gourd about him he slipped outside, reverted to his own form, and shouted at the top of his voice, "Open up, you devils." "Who do you think you are, shouting like that?" asked the devils who were there. "Tell your damned demon kings at once that Novice the Sun is here," he replied.

The demons rushed in to report, "Your Majesties, there's a Novice the Sun or something at the doors." The Senior King was shocked. "This is terrible, brother," he said. "We've stirred up a whole nest of them. Sun the Novice is tied up with the Dazzling Golden Cord, and the Novice Sun is inside the gourd, so how can there be a Novice the Sun as well? They must all be brothers and all have come." "Don't worry, brother," the Junior King replied. "I can put a thousand people into my gourd, and at present I've only got the Novice Sun inside. No need to be afraid of Novice the Sun or whoever. I'm going out to take a look and put him inside too." "Do be careful," said the Senior Demon King.

Watch as the Junior King goes out through the doors with his gourd, as heroic and impressive as the previous time. "Where are you from?" he shouted at the top of his voice, "and how dare you rant and roar here?" "Don't you know who I am?" Monkey said.

"Come here," said the demon. "I won't hit you. I'll just call your name. Will you answer?" "If you call my name," said Monkey, "I'll reply. But will you answer if I call your name?" "If I call you," said the demon, "I have a miraculous gourd that people can be packed into. But if you call me, what have you got?" "I've got a gourd too," Monkey replied. "If you have, then show me," said the demon. Monkey then produced the gourd from his sleeve and said, "Look, damned demon." He flourished it then put it back in his sleeve in case the demon tried to snatch it.

Monkey then said, "Mine is the male one, and yours is the female one." "Never mind about the sex," said the demon. "It's only a real treasure if it can hold people inside." "Quite right," said Monkey. "You try to put me inside first."

The overjoyed demon sprang into mid-air with a bound, held out his gourd, and called, "Novice the Sun." Without hesitation the Great Sage replied eight or nine times, but he was not sucked inside. The monster came down, stamping his feet, pounding his chest, and exclaiming, "Heavens! Who said that the world never changes? This treasure's scared of its old man! The female one hasn't the nerve to pack the male inside." "Put your gourd away now," said Monkey. "It's my turn to call your name." With a fast somersault he leapt up, turned his gourd upside-down with its mouth facing the demon, and called, "Great King Silver Horn." The demon could not keep quiet; he had to answer, and he went whistling into the gourd. Monkey then attached a label reading:

> To the Great Lord Lao: to be dealt with urgently in accordance with the Statutes and Ordinances.

"Well, my boy," he thought with pleasure, "today you've tried something new."

He landed his cloud, still carrying the gourd. His only thought was to rescue his master as he headed for the Lotus Flower Cave. The mountain path was most uneven, and he was besides bow-legged, so as he lurched along the gourd was shaken, making a continuous sloshing sound. The monster putrefied as soon as he went into the gourd. Monkey was back at the doors of the cave with the gourd before he realized it. He shook the gourd, and it kept making that noise.

When they saw him the little devils in the cave said, "Disaster, Your Majesty. Novice the Sun has put his Junior Majesty in the gourd and is shaking it." The news sent all the Senior King's souls flying and turned his bones and sinews soft. He collapsed, howling aloud, "You and I sneaked out of the world above to be reborn among mortals, brother. Our hope was to share glory for ever as rulers of this cave. We never dreamt that this monk would kill you and part us." All the devils in the cave wept and wailed.

Before long a little devil came in from outside to report that Novice the Sun was there again and being very abusive. "Damn him. He thinks we're completely useless," exclaimed the Senior Demon King with horror. "Hang Pig up again," he told the little demons, "and check what treasures we have left." "We still have three in the cave," reported the steward devil. "Which three?" the demon king asked. "The Seven-star Sword, the Plantain Fan, and the Pure Vase," replied the steward. "The vase is useless," said the demon king. "All you used to need to do was to call someone's name and get a reply for them to be put inside. But now Sun the Novice has learnt the words of the spell and put my brother in it. We won't need that — leave it here. Fetch me the sword and the fan at once." The steward immediately fetched them for the old demon, who tucked the fan inside the back of his collar and took the sword in his hand. Then he mustered all three hundred or more of his devils and drilled them in the use of spear, staff, rope and sword. The Senior Demon King then put on his helmet and breastplate, over which he threw a cloak of fiery red silk. The demons fell into battle formation, ready to capture the Great Sage Sun. The Great Sage meanwhile, now aware that the Junior Demon King had rotted down inside the gourd, tied it up very tight and fastened it to his belt, then prepared to fight, his gold-banded cudgel in his hand. With no more ado the demon lifted his sword and struck at Monkey's head, while Monkey raised his iron cudgel to meet him.

When the old demon had fought twenty rounds with Monkey and neither had emerged the victor he waved the scabbard of his sword and called all his little devils forward. Over three hundred of them all rushed up and surrounded Monkey. The splendid Great Sage, quite unperturbed, used his cudgel to strike and parry to either side, before and behind. The little devils all had great skill, and they fought their way ever closer to him, tying him up as if in a tangle of silk floss as they tugged at his waist and legs. They would not retreat. The Great Sage was so alarmed by this that he used extracorporeal magic. Plucking a bunch of hairs from under his left ribs he chewed them to pieces that he blew out with the shout, "Change!" Every piece turned into another Monkey. Just watch as the biggest ones wield cudgels, the short ones use their fists, and the tiniest ones, with no other way of attacking, grabbed knuckles and sank their teeth into muscles. The little devils were put to rout. The demon king was hard-pressed; rush around as he might, there was no escape for him.

In his alarm the demon took his precious sword in his left hand and reached behind his neck with right hand to bring out the Plantain Fan. Then he turned towards the fire-gods of the southeast and the Constellation Ligong, and waved the fan. At once flames shot out of the ground, for such was the power of that treasure. The monster was truly ruthless. He waved the fan seven or eight times, setting great fires burning heaven and earth.

The Great Sage trembled with fear at the sight of this evil fire. "This is terrible," he said. "It may do me no harm, but

I can't save those hairs of mine. If they are caught by the fire they'll burn the way hair does." So he shook himself and took the hairs back on his body, leaving just one behind as a facsimile of himself. Then, to avoid disaster by fire, his real self somersaulted upwards, reciting a spell to ward off the fire, and escaped from the inferno. He went straight back to the Lotus Flower Cave in the hope of rescuing his master. He rushed to the cave doors, brought his cloud down to land, and found over a hundred little devils there with smashed heads, broken legs, and open wounds. They had all been wounded by his magical other selves and were now standing there howling in agony. At the sight of them the Great Sage could not restrain his evil and murderous nature; he laid into them, swinging his iron cudgel.

Having wiped out all the little devils the Great Sage stormed into the cave to free his master. Seeing more dazzling flames inside he was struck by a thought that filled him with panic: "That's done it. The fire's come in through the back door. There's no way I'll be able to rescue the Master." Terrified though he was, he looked more carefully and saw that it was not flames but a golden glow. Pulling himself together he looked inside and saw that the light came from a vase in "muttonfat" jade. "What a beauty," he thought with glee. "That's the vase that shone on the mountain when those two little devils were carrying it. I took it off them, then the demon king found it when he searched me later. Now I see that it shines when they keep it here too." Watch him as he takes such pleasure in stealing the vase that instead of rescuing his master he gets out of the cave as fast as he can. He was just outside when the demon king appeared from the south, brandishing his magic sword and the fan. Before the Great Sage could take evasive action the demon raised the sword and hacked at his face. But the Great Sage immediately soared into the air on a somersault cloud and disappeared without trace.

Back at the cave mouth the demon king was so distressed by the sight of the corpses of his devils all over the place that he threw back his head and groaned, and could not help wailing loudly at the pain of it.

Overcome with remorse, the Senior Demon King sobbed at every step as he went into the cave. Although all the objects and furniture were still in the cave it was silent and deserted. It made him even more lonely and depressed. He sat alone in the cave, slumped on the stone table, the sword leaning against it, and the fan behind his neck again. Thus he drifted into sleep.

The story goes on to tell how the Great Sage Sun turned his somersault cloud round and brought it to a stop in front of the mountain. As he wanted to rescue his master he fastened the vase securely at his waist and went back to the cave to reconnoitre. The doors were wide open, and the silence was unbroken, so he crept stealthily inside to find the old demon slumped against the stone table, fast asleep. The Plantain Fan stuck out from his clothes at his shoulder, half covering the back of his head, and the Seven-star Sword was still leaning against the table. Monkey made his way forward very quietly, pulled the fan out, then turned and whooshed out. This was because the fan had rubbed against the monster's hair, waking him up. As soon as he looked up and saw that Monkey had stolen the fan he grabbed for his sword and went after him. By now Monkey was already outside the doors, the fan safely tucked in his belt and his iron cudgel in his hands as he met the monster's onslaught.

After thirty or forty rounds of fighting against Monkey, by when the day was almost over, the demon king could hold out no longer and he broke away, defeated. He made off to the south-west, heading for the Crushed Dragon Cave.

Monkey then brought his cloud down to land and rushed straight back into the Lotus Flower Cave, where he freed the Tang Priest, Pig, and Friar Sand. The three of them thanked Monkey for delivering them from dire peril, then asked where the demons had gone. To this Monkey replied, "The Junior Demon King is inside the gourd, and I reckon he must have dissolved by now. I've just beaten the Senior King, and he's gone back to the Crushed Dragon Cave. As for the little devils from the cave, I killed half of them with my magical extra bodies, then wiped out the wounded survivors of the rout who came back here. That's how I was able to get in here to rescue you." The Tang Priest thanked him no end: "I'm so grateful to you for your great efforts, disciple." "You're telling me it was a great effort," laughed Monkey. "You lot only had to put up with the pain of being hung up, but I wasn't allowed to stand still for a moment. I was more rushed than a postal courier with an urgent message, having to charge around all over the place without stopping. I was only able to put the demons down because I stole their treasures."

In their happiness master and disciples found the rice, noodles and vegetables in the cave, cleaned up the stove and cooking pots, and made themselves a vegetarian meal. When they were full they went to sleep in the cave. Nothing worth recounting happened that night, and before long the new day dawned.

The Senior Demon King meanwhile had gone straight to the Crushed Dragon Mountain, where he called together all the she-devils and told them how his mother had been murdered, his brother put in the gourd, the devil soldiers all killed and the treasures stolen. At this the she-devils all wept. A little devil from outside the doors reported, "Your Majesty, your lord uncle from the other side of the mountains is here with soldiers." At this news the Senior Demon King quickly put on white mourning garments and went out to greet him in person. This lord uncle was King Septimus Fox, the younger brother of the demon king's mother, and he had heard from devils of his who were out patrolling the mountains how Monkey had killed his sister then impersonated her to steal his nephew's treasures and was fighting him in the battle of Flat-top Mountain that same day. Septimus Fox was bringing over two hundred of his own devil troops to help in the battle when he called for news at his sister's place on the way. As soon as he stepped inside and saw the demon king in mourning for his mother the two of them started to weep aloud. After weeping for some time the demon king bowed to him and told him what had happened. In his anger Septimus told the demon king to change out of his mourning clothes, pick up his sword, call the roll of women soldiers and join forces with him. They then set off on winds and clouds towards the north-east.

The Great Sage had just told Friar Sand to get the breakfast ready as they would set off straight after eating it when he heard the sound of a wind. Going outside to look he saw a host of demon soldiers approaching from the south-west. This alarmed him, so he ran back in a hurry and shouted to Pig, "Brother, that evil spirit is back again with reinforcements." Sanzang went pale with fright at the news. "Disciple," he asked, "what can this mean?" "Don't worry," chuckled Monkey, "don't worry. Fetch me all their treasures." The Great Sage then tucked the gourd and the vase in his belt, put the Dazzling Golden Cord in his sleeve, stuck the Plantain Fan behind his shoulder, and whirled the iron cudgel around with both his hands. Friar Sand he ordered to stay put inside the cave guarding the master, while he asked Pig to come outside with his rake to meet the enemy.

When the demons' line of battle was drawn up King Septimus Fox took command. He had a jade face and long whiskers, a brow of steel and ears like swords. His helmet was of refined gold, he wore chainmail armour and he held a heaven-square halberd. "I'll get you, you bold and impudent ape," he shouted. "How dare you treat people so badly? You've stolen the treasures, wounded my relations, killed the demon soldiers, and to top it all occupied their cave palace. All of you stretch your heads out to be executed while I avenge my sister's family." "You hairy crowd, you misery-makers," replied Monkey, "you can't realize what powers I have. Don't go — take this from my cudgel." The monster twisted round to avoid the blow, then struck back at his head with the heaven-square halberd. The two of them fought three or four rounds on the mountain-top until the monster was too weak to continue. He fled from the field, followed by Monkey until he was blocked by the Senior Demon King. When these two had fought three more rounds Septimus Fox came back into the attack. Seeing this from where he was at the edge of the battle Pig brandished his nine-toothed rake to stop him. The battle went on undecided for a long time with each fighter blocked by another until the demon king called up all the demon troops to surround Pig.

Sanzang meanwhile was sitting in the cave hearing the shouts and the shaking of the ground. He told Friar Sand to go outside and see whether or not his brothers were winning. Friar Sand raised his demon-quelling staff and charged out with a roar, putting the devilish horde to flight. Seeing that things were going badly, Septimus turned to flee, only to be caught a blow on the back from Pig's rake as Pig came after him. At this nine jets of blood gushed out of him, and the poor spirit's true being carried on ahead of him. When Pig grabbed him and tore off his clothes he saw that Septimus was in fact a fox spirit.

At the sight of his uncle being wounded the demon king broke away from Monkey and raised his sword to strike at Pig, who parried with his rake. While the two of them were fighting it out Friar Sand came up and struck at the demon king with his staff. This was more than the demon could cope with, so he set off on his wind and cloud, fleeing south with Pig and Friar Sand close on his heels. Seeing this the Great Sage at once went soaring up into the sky on his cloud. He brought out the vase to catch the old demon in. "King Golden Horn," he shouted, and the old demon, imagining that one of his defeated little devils was calling, turned to reply. Into the vase he whistled, and Monkey put on a label reading:

To the Great Lord Lao: to be dealt with urgently
in accordance with the Statutes and Ordinances.

The Seven-star Sword fell to the ground, and it too was now Monkey's. "You've got the sword, brother," said Pig as he came towards him, "but where's the evil spirit?" "He's done for," laughed Monkey. "I've got him in this vase." Like Pig, Friar Sand was delighted when he heard it.

Now that all the evil spirits had been wiped out the disciples went back into the cave to tell the good news to Sanzang: "The mountain has been cleaned up and the demons no longer exist.

Please mount, Master, and we'll be on our way." Sanzang was beside himself with joy. Master and disciples ate their breakfast, got their baggage and horse ready, and hurried on their way west.

As they were walking along a blind man suddenly appeared beside the path, went up to them, and seized Sanzang's horse. "Where are you going, monk?" he asked. "Give me back my treasures." "That's done it," said Pig with horror. "It's the old demon here to demand his treasures back." When Monkey looked carefully and saw that it was the Supreme Lord Lao Zi he rushed up to him, greeted him and asked, "Where are you going, old fellow?" The venerable elder at once rose up to his throne in the realm of jade, drew himself upright amid the nine mists and called, "Sun the Novice, give me back my treasures." The Great Sage rose into the air and asked. "What treasures?"

"I use the gourd to keep cinnabar and the vase to hold water," replied the Lord Lao. "The precious sword I use for refining demons, the fan for fanning my fire, and the cord for tying round my gown. One of those two demons was a servant boy who looked after my golden furnace, and the other a servant who looked after my silver furnace. They stole my treasures and came down to the mortal world. I could not find them anywhere. You have done a very good deed in capturing them." "You're very rude indeed, old fellow," said the Great Sage. "You deserve to be charged with laxity for allowing members of your household to become evil spirits." "Don't blame the wrong person," said Lord Lao. "It was nothing to do with me. It was the Bodhisattva from the sea who asked me for the loan of them three times, and sent them here to be turned into monsters to test whether your master and his disciples truly wanted to go to the west." On hearing this the Great Sage thought, "That Bodhisattva is a terrible old liar. When she delivered me and told me to protect the Tang Priest on his journey to the west to fetch the scriptures I said that the journey would be tough and difficult. She promised to come and help me whenever things were really desperate. But so far from helping she's sent evil spirits to play me up and give me a hard time. The liar. She deserves to be an old maid all her life. If you old fellow hadn't come here yourself I most certainly would not have given them back to you. But now that you've told me all this you'd better have them." When the Lord Lao had his five treasures back he took the stoppers out of the gourd and the vase and tipped out two wisps of immortal vapour. As he pointed at them they turned into his two servants of the gold and silver furnace who waited on him on either side.

CHAPTER 22
Sanzang in Danger by Withered Pine Ravine

The story tells how Sun the Novice brought his cloud down to land and told the master and his fellow-disciples all about the Bodhisattva borrowing the two servant lads and Lord Lao recovering his treasures. Sanzang expressed his thanks at great length. Master and the disciples continued to head west.

They travelled on for a long time, resting at night and travelling by day, until they saw a mountain in front of them that touched the sky and blotted out the sun. Sanzang was alarmed. Reining in the horse he called urgently for Monkey, who asked, "What are your orders, Master?" "Do you see that big mountain in front of us?" said Sanzang. "It's so sheer that I'm sure there must be evil creatures lurking on it to catch us, so be on your guard." "Just keep going and don't worry," said Monkey with a laugh. "I'll protect you." With that the venerable elder relaxed and spurred his horse on. When they reached the craggy mountain they saw that it was indeed precipitous.

Master and disciples were already frightened enough when a red cloud emerged from a fold in the mountain and rose straight up into the sky, where it formed a ball of fire. Monkey was horrified. As he went to take a closer look he pushed the master's leg to get him off the horse and said, "Brothers, stay here. An evil spirit's coming." In their alarm Pig grabbed his iron rake and Friar Sand his staff as they stood guard on either side of the Tang Priest.

The red light was indeed from an evil spirit who had heard tell some years earlier that a Tang Priest from the East, a reincarnation of the Venerable Golden Cicada and a holy man who had cultivated his conduct through ten successive lives, was going to the Western Heaven to fetch the scriptures. Anyone who ate a piece of his flesh would live as long as heaven and earth. The evil spirit had been longing day in and day out for him to arrive, and now he was here. As the evil spirit looked at them from mid-air he saw the three disciples ready for action as they guarded the Tang Priest on his horse.

The splendid evil monster then dispersed his red light and brought his cloud down to land on the mountainside, where he turned himself with a shake of his body into a naughty boy of six, stark naked, tied hand and foot to the top of a pine tree, and shouting, "Help, help!"

"Disciple, what's that crying in the middle of these mountains?" Sanzang asked. "I know," said Monkey, "but it's no concern of yours. You just keep going."

The story switches back to the evil spirit, whose three or four shouts had found no response. "I've been waiting for the Tang Priest here," he thought, "and I saw that he was only about a mile away. I wonder why he's still not here after all this time. He must have taken a short cut." He then braced himself, slipped out of his bonds, and went up into the air again in his red light to take another look. He did not notice when the Great Sage looked up at him, recognized him as an evil spirit, and pushed the Tang Priest by his foot off the horse once more. "Brothers," said Monkey, "be very careful. The evil spirit's coming back." Again Pig and Friar Sand placed themselves on either side of the Tang Priest to protect him with their rake and staff.

He was not even settled in the saddle when he heard another call of "Help, master!" He looked up to see a little boy hanging naked in a tree. The Tang Priest asked, "Who are your parents? Why are you hanging up there? Tell me and I will save you."

The evil spirit put on even more of an act on hearing these questions. "Master," he called, tears pouring down, "I live in the village by Withered Pine Ravine to the west of the mountain. My grandfather was known as Millionaire Hong because he had such a huge fortune. He died a long time ago and left everything to my father. Nowadays we throw our money around and we're not nearly as rich any more. That's why my father's called Hundred Thousand Hong. All he likes doing is making friends with all the big shots around and lending his gold and silver out at interest. But they were crooks who swindled him out of the lot, and he lost both capital and interest. My father swore never to lend out another penny. Then the people who borrowed from him became so desperate with poverty that they formed a gang. They attacked us in broad daylight with fire and weapons, stole all our goods, and killed my father. Because my mother is so beautiful they carried her off to be the bandit chief's woman. She couldn't bear to leave me behind, so she hid me in her clothes and went weeping and trembling with the bandits. When they got to this mountain the bandits wanted to kill me. They only spared me from the sword because of my mother's desperate pleas. Instead they tied me to this tree to die of cold and hunger. I don't know where the bandits have taken my mother. I've been hanging up here for three days and nights, and you're the first people to come past. I must have earned merit in a previous life to have met you in this one, Master. If in your great compassion you can rescue me and take me home I'd gladly sell myself into slavery in order to repay you. I won't forget what you've done for me even when I'm buried."

Taking all this for the truth, Sanzang told Pig to undo the ropes and bring the boy down. The idiot, not realizing who he was, was just about to start doing it. This was more than Monkey could bear. "Damned beast," he shouted, "there's someone here who can see what you are. Cut out all that nonsense, and stop trying to fool us. If all your family's goods have been stolen, your father has been murdered and your mother kidnapped, then who are we going to hand you to after

we rescue you? What sort of reward will you give us? It doesn't
hang together. It's a pack of lies." This frightened the evil
spirit, who realized now that Monkey was an able opponent
and was keeping an eye on him. So he trembled and wept as
he continued, "Although I've lost both my parents and all my
family's goods I've still got all our land and my other relations."
"What relations?" Monkey asked. "My other grandfather lives
to the south of the mountain," the evil spirit replied, "and
my aunt's home is north of the ridge. Li the Fourth from the
head of the ravine is married to my aunt, and Hong the Third
in the woods is a distant uncle. I've also got cousins living
around the village. If the venerable master will save me and
take me back to the village and my relations I'll tell them all
about the venerable master's kindness in rescuing me. I'll
mortgage or sell some land, and reward you richly."

As all Pig could think about was his stomach he did not
care at all whether he was acting wisely as he cut through the
ropes with his monk's knife and let the demon down from the
tree. The demon then kept kowtowing and weeping copiously
in front of the Tang Priest's horse. The tender-hearted priest
then told Monkey to carry the boy, to which Monkey agreed
with a chuckle.

The monster concealed his delight as he docilely let Monkey
carry him.

As the Great Sage Monkey carried the evil spirit he felt very
resentful of the Tang Priest for not realizing how hard the
going was for him. "It would be bad enough to cross these
high mountains empty-handed, but he has to make me carry
someone else too. Even if this wretch is a good boy and not an
evil spirit, he's lost his parents and I don't know who I should
take him to. Best thing would be to dash him to the ground
and finish him off." The demon knew what Monkey was thinking, so he drew in four deep breaths from all around then blew
them out again on Monkey's back, which made Monkey feel he
weighed a thousand pounds. "You're using extra-weight magic
to weigh me down, my lad," laughed Monkey. This made the
monster afraid that Monkey was going to kill him, so he got his

spirit out of his body and sprang up into the ninth layer of cloud. Now that Monkey was finding the load on his back even heavier he grabbed the boy and smashed him so hard against a rock by the path that the boy's body looked like minced pork. Then, just to make sure that the boy would give no more trouble, Monkey tore off all four of his limbs and ripped them into little pieces that he scattered on both sides of the path.

At this the demon, who was watching from mid-air, could hold back his fiery temper no longer. "This ape of a monk is thoroughly vicious," he said. "Evil spirit wanting to kill your master I may be, but I've not yet laid my hands on him. How could you butcher me so atrociously? If I hadn't anticipated and got my spirit out you'd have slaughtered me in cold blood. I'm going to catch the Tang Priest here and now. If I delay any longer, he will become too clever."

The splendid evil spirit then conjured up a whirlwind in mid-air. It was a terrible one that sent stones and dust flying. It blew so hard that Sanzang could barely stay on his horse, Pig could not look straight ahead, and Friar Sand had to bend and cover his face. Realizing that this was a devil's wind, the Great Sage rushed forward to catch them up, but the demon had already scooped the Tang Priest up in his wind. Sanzang had disappeared without a trace. Nobody could tell where he had been taken or where to start looking for him.

Before long the wind fell and the sun was shining again. Monkey went up and saw that the white dragon horse was trembling and neighing. The luggage had been thrown into the path, Pig was hiding under a crag and whimpering, and Friar Sand was squatting howling on the mountainside. "Pig!" shouted Monkey, and recognizing his voice the idiot looked up to see that the storm was over. He climbed to his feet, grabbed hold of Monkey, and said, "What a wind." Friar Sand came forward too and said, "That was a twister, brother. But where's the master?" "The wind blew so hard," said Pig, "that we all had to hide our heads, close our eyes and take cover. The master lay down on the horse's back." "But where's he gone now?" Monkey asked. "He must have been blown away by the wind as if he were made of rushes," replied Friar Sand.

The three of them went up the mountain. Monkey found out from the local deities and mountain gods that the demon was Red Boy, son of the Bull Demon King and Raksasi.

Without caring whether it was day or night they had covered some forty miles when they saw a pine woods through which a stream flowed in a twisting ravine. The water was green and pure, and at the head of the ravine was a stone bridge leading to a cave. "Brothers," said Monkey, "I'm sure the evil spirit must live in that rockface over there. Let's have a council of war to decide who looks after the luggage and the horse and who comes with me to subdue the demon." "Brother," said Pig, "I'm no good at hanging around. I'll come with you." "Fine," said Monkey, continuing, "Friar Sand, hide the horse and the luggage deep in the woods and guard them carefully while we two go there to look for the master." Friar Sand did as he was told, while Monkey and Pig went fully armed to the cave.

The Great Sage Monkey and Pig sprang across the Withered Pine Ravine and headed straight for the demon's crag. They saw a stone tablet on which was carved in big letters, FIRE-WIND CAVE, WITHERED PINE RAVINE, MOUNT HAO. To the other side a crowd of little demons were sparring with sword and spear, leaping through the air, and generally enjoying themselves. "Little ones," shouted Monkey at the top of his voice, "tell your ruler at once that if he brings my master the Tang Priest out I'll spare all your lives, but that if so much as a hint of a 'no' comes out between his teeth I'll turn your mountain upside-down and trample your cave flat." Hearing this, the little demons all scurried back into the cave, shut the doors, and went in to report, "Trouble, Your Majesty."

The monster had carried Sanzang into the cave, stripped him, tied his hands and feet together, and sent little devils to fetch clean water to wash him with. He was going to put Sanzang into a steaming tray to cook, but when the alarm was raised he forgot about washing Sanzang, rushed into the main hall, and asked, "What trouble?" "There's a monk with a hairy face as ugly as a thunder-god. He's got another monk with a long snout and big ears. He's demanding their master, who's called the Tang Priest or something, and he says that if there's so much as a hint of a 'no' he'll turn the mountain upside-down and trample the cave flat." "They must be Sun the Novice and Pig," said the demon king with a cruel laugh. "They were bound to come looking for their master. But I carried their master fifty miles from the middle of the mountains to here. How did they find their way here?" The monster then told his carters to push the carts out, and the little devils responsible did so, opening up the front gates. "Brother," said Pig when he saw them, "I think they're so scared of us that they've brought their carts out and are going to move away." "No," said Monkey. "Look — they're leaving them there." The little devils set the carts out in the order of the Five Elements — metal, wood, water, fire and earth — checked them over, and went back inside to report. "Ready?" the demon king asked. "Ready," they replied. "Fetch my spear," said the demon king, and two of the little devils from the armoury carried in an eighteen-foot long fire-tipped spear that they handed to their king. The king tried out a few swings and thrusts with the spear. He wore no helmet or armour, just a battle-kilt of embroidered brocade around his waist, as he went out barefoot through the gates. When Monkey and Pig looked up at him they saw that the monster had a pale face and red lips, with a charming outlook. He was the son of the Bull Demon King and Raksasi, and was called the Red Boy.

The Red Boy came out shouting, "Who's making that row?" Monkey went closer, smiled and said, "Don't put on such an act, dear nephew. At the top of that pine tree this morning you were a skinny, jaundiced little baby, and you fooled my master. I carried you in all kindness, but you made a whirlwind and took my master off. Now you're putting on this big show, but I know who you are. Bring my master out at once if you don't want me to forget our kinship and turn nasty. I wouldn't like your respected father to think of me as a disgraceful bully."

These words threw the demon into a fury. "Vicious ape," he roared, "you're no relation of mine. You're talking a load of nonsense. You've got no reason to claim that I'm your nephew." "You wouldn't know about it, lad," said Monkey. "When your respected father and I were sworn brothers you hadn't even been thought of." "Rubbish, you baboon," said the demon. "Think where you come from and where I come from. How could you ever have been my father's sworn brother?" "You'd know nothing about it," said Monkey. "I'm Sun Wukong, the Great Sage Equalling Heaven who made havoc in Heaven five hundred years ago. Before that I roamed all over the seas and the sky and visited all of the four continents. In those days I was a great admirer of true heroes. Your respected father, the Bull Demon King, had the title of Great Sage Matching Heaven. He took me as his brother, and I let him be the eldest brother. When we brothers were having a fine old time back in those days you hadn't even been born."

The demon, refusing to believe a word of this, raised his fire-tipped spear to thrust at Monkey. With the unhurried ease of a true expert Monkey avoided the spear-thrust, swung his iron cudgel, and insulted him: "You don't know when you're out-classed, you little demon. Take this!" The evil spirit also moved out of the way and said, "Times have changed and you've been left behind, vicious ape. Take this!" There was no more talk of their kinship as the pair of them showed their magic powers in great anger.

While the evil spirit fought twenty rounds with Monkey without result Pig could see clearly from the sidelines that although the demon had not been defeated he was only holding Monkey at bay and had no hope of making an attack on him. And although Monkey had not yet beaten the demon, he was wielding his cudgel with such consummate skill that he kept striking at the demon's head without ever missing his aim. "This is no good," thought Pig. "Monkey's a slippery customer, and if he shows the monster an opening and gets the demon to charge, Monkey'll finish him off with one blow of his cudgel and there'll be no glory for me." Watch Pig as he summons up his spirit, raises the nine-pronged rake, and brings it down from mid-air towards the demon's head. This gave the demon so bad a fright that he fled in defeat. "After him," shouted Monkey, "after him."

The pair of them chased him to the mouth of the cave, where the demon stood on the middle one of the five little carts, brandishing his fire-tipped spear with one hand, and clenching the other into a fist with which he punched himself twice on the nose. "Shameless thing," laughed Pig, "punching yourself on the nose to make it bleed, then wiping the blood all over your face. Are you going to bring a lawsuit against us?" But when the demon hit his nose twice he also said a spell and breathed out fire, while he snorted thick clouds of smoke from his nose. In the wink of an eye flames were everywhere. Fire poured from the fire carts. After the demon had blown a few more times a great fire was leaping up to the sky, blotting out the Fire-cloud Cave. Heaven and earth were both engulfed in the blaze. "Brother," said Pig in horror, "this is terrible. Once in that fire that would be the end of you. I'd be baked, and he'd only need to add a few spices to make a meal of me. Let's get out of here." At that he fled back across the ravine, ignoring Monkey.

Monkey's magical powers really were very great. Making a fire avoidance spell with his fingers he plunged into the flames in pursuit of the demon. Seeing Monkey coming after him the demon breathed out yet more fire, which was even worse than ever.

Monkey could not find the monster amid the raging flames, or even see the way to the mouth of the cave, so he sprang back out of the fire. The demon, who could see all this clearly from the entrance to the cave, put his fire-making equipment away when he knew Monkey had gone, led his devilish horde back inside the cave, and shut the stone doors. He felt he had won a victory, so he told his underlings to lay on a banquet. There was music and much rejoicing, of which we will not speak.

Instead we return to Monkey, who had leapt back across

the Withered Pine Ravine and ridden his cloud far away. In a moment he was in the Eastern Ocean, parting the waves with water-repelling magic. As he was going through the water he met a patrolling yaksha, who hurried back into the water-crystal palace to report to the Senior Dragon King Ao Guang. Ao Guang came out to welcome Monkey at the head of his dragon sons and grandsons and his shrimp and crab soldiers. The dragon king invited Monkey to come in and sit down. When the courtesies were over the king offered Monkey some tea. "Please don't bother," said Monkey. "But there is something else I've come to trouble you with. My master the Tang Priest has been captured on his way to the Western Heaven to worship the Buddha and fetch the scriptures. He's been caught by an evil spirit called the Red Boy, from the Fire-cloud Cave by Withered Pine Ravine on Mount Hao. I went into the cave to look for my master and fight the demon, but the demon started a great fire. It was too much for me. I thought that as water overcomes fire I'd come here to ask you for some water. Could you make a torrential downpour for me that would put the fire out and save the Tang Priest?"

"You've come to the wrong place," said the dragon king. "I'm not the person to ask for rain." "But you're the dragon king of the four oceans," said Monkey, "the lord of rain. If I don't ask you who else should I ask?" "I am in charge of rain," replied the dragon king, "but I can't do anything without authorization. I must have permission from the Jade Emperor as to where and when and how many inches of rain I should pour down, and I've to get a lot of official signatures before I can ask the help of Grandpa Thunder, Mother Lightning, Uncle Wind and the Cloud Boys. As the saying goes, dragons can't travel without cloud." "But I don't need wind, clouds, thunder or lightning," said Monkey. "All I want is some rain to put the fire out." "You may not need wind, clouds, thunder or lightning, Great Sage," said the dragon king, "but I can't help you alone. What would you say if I asked my younger brothers too?" "Where are they?" Monkey asked. "Ao Qin is Dragon King of the Southern Sea, Ao Run is Dragon King of the

Northern Sea, and Ao Shun is Dragon King of the Western Sea."
"It'd be easier to go up to Heaven and ask the Jade Emperor
for an edict than to trek round all three seas," replied Monkey
with a laugh. "No need for you to go, Great Sage," said the
dragon king. "If I beat my iron drum and bronze bell they'll be
here this instant." "Please sound them at once, Senior Dragon
King," said Monkey.

A moment later the three other dragon kings came crowding
in. "Elder brother," they asked, "what orders do you have for
us?" "The Great Sage Monkey is here to borrow some rain to
help him subdue a demon," said the Senior Dragon King. After
the greetings were over Monkey explained why he needed
water. The dragons were all delighted to muster their forces.

Monkey was soon back at the Withered Pine Ravine on
Mount Hao with his dragon army.

Monkey then brought his cloud down to land in the pine
wood, saw Pig and Friar Sand, and called to them. "You were
quick," said Pig. "Did you get the dragon king to come?"
"They're all here," Brother Monkey replied. "You'd both better
be very careful not to let the baggage get wet if it rains hard.
I'm off to fight the demon." "Off you go, and don't worry,"
said Friar Sand. "We can cope."

Monkey leapt across the ravine to the cave entrance and
shouted, "Open up!" The little devils ran back in to report,
"Sun the Novice is here again." The Red Boy looked up with
a smile and said, "The monkey thinks no fire can burn him,
because none ever has. That's why he's here again. But this
time we won't let him off: we'll burn him to cinders." He
sprang up, grasped his spear, and ordered the little demons to
wheel the fire carts out. Then he went out in front of the gates
and asked Monkey, "Why are you here again?" "Give me back
my master," Monkey replied. "Keep up with the times, ape,"
said the demon. "He may be a master to you, but to me he's
something to eat with my drinks. You might as well forget about
him." These words threw Monkey into a fury. He raised his
gold-banded cudgel and struck at the monster's head. The de-

mon quickly parried the blow with his fire-tipped spear.

When the demon king had fought twenty rounds with Monkey and could see that neither of them was going to win he feinted, pulled back, clenched his fist, punched himself twice on the nose, and started breathing out fire again. Flames roared from the carts in front of the entrance, and his mouth and eyes were full of the blaze. Monkey looked back to shout, "Where are you, dragon kings?" The dragon king brothers then led their watery hosts in spurting rain on the demon's fire.

But heavy though it was, the downpour could not stop the demon's fire. Dragon kings' private rain can only put out ordinary fires, not this demon's Samadhi Fire. The rain was like oil poured on the flames: the more there was, the fiercer the blaze. "I'll make a hand-spell and plunge into the fire," said Monkey, who went after the demon, swinging his cudgel. Seeing Monkey coming, the demon blew a cloud of smoke straight into his face. Turn away though he did, Monkey's eyes smarted terribly, and he could not stop the tears from pouring down. Although not bothered by fire, the Great Sage was vulnerable to smoke. Back at the time when he had made havoc in Heaven and been refined by Lord Lao Zi in the Eight Trigrams Furnace he had saved himself from being burnt up by staying in the part of the furnace controlled by the Wind Trigram Xun. But the wind had blown smoke at him, and he had been so thoroughly cooked that his eyes turned fiery and his pupils golden. That was why he was still vulnerable to smoke. When the demon blew another cloud of smoke at him it was more than he could bear, and so he made off on his cloud. The demon king then had the fire-raising equipment put away and went back into the cave.

Friar Sand helped Monkey back into the woods, where they both sat down. Before long Monkey had recovered and was breathing normally as the tears poured down his cheeks. "Don't upset yourself so, brother," said Friar Sand. "We'll work out a plan to get reinforcements and rescue the master." "Where from?" Monkey asked. "Long ago, when the Bodhisattva ordered us to protect the Tang Priest, she promised us that if we called on Heaven or earth for help there would always be a response," replied Friar Sand. "Where shall we turn now?" "I remember that when I made havoc in Heaven," said Monkey, "the Heavenly soldiers were no match for me. That evil spirit has tremendous magic. Only someone with more powers than I have will be able to subdue him. As the gods of Heaven and earth are useless the only way to catch the monster will be by going to ask the Bodhisattva Guanyin for her help. But I can't ride my somersault cloud: my skin is much too sore and my body is aching. How are we going to get her help?" "Tell me what to say," said Pig, "and I'll go to ask her." "All right," said Monkey with a laugh, "you go. If the Bodhisattva receives you, you mustn't look her in the face. Keep your head down and bow to her respectfully. When she asks you, tell her what this place and the demon are called, then ask her to save the master. If she agrees to come she'll certainly capture the demon." Pig set off south on his cloud.

Back in the cave the demon was saying with delight, "Sun the Novice is beaten, my little ones. I may not have killed him this time, but at any rate he passed out for a long time." He sighed, then added, "The only thing is that he might send for reinforcements. Open up, and I'll go out to see who he's sending for."

The demons opened the gates for the evil spirit to spring out and look around from mid-air. Seeing Pig heading south the spirit reckoned that he must definitely be going to ask the Bodhisattva Guanyin to come as there was nowhere else to the south where he might be going. The demon brought his cloud down quickly and said to his followers, "Little ones, fetch my leather bag. The string at the mouth may not be any good now as I haven't used it for ages, so please put a new string in it and leave it outside the inner gates. I'll lure Pig back here and pop him in the bag. Then we can steam him nice and tender as a reward for all of you." The little demons fetched their king's as-you-will leather bag, replaced the string in it, and put it inside the main gates.

As the demon king knew which ways to the Southern Sea were quicker and which were longer, he rode his cloud by the quick route, overtook Pig and turned himself into an imitation Guanyin to sit on a crag and wait for him.

When the idiot suddenly saw Guanyin as he was hurtling along on his cloud he had no way of telling that this was a false one: it was a case of seeing the image and taking it for a Buddha. The idiot stopped his cloud, bowed down, and said, "Bodhisattva, your disciple Zhu Wuneng kowtows to you." "Why have you come to see me instead of escorting the Tang Priest to fetch the scriptures?' the Bodhisattva asked. "I was travelling with Master," Pig replied, "when an evil spirit called the Red Boy carried my master off to the Fire-cloud Cave by Withered Pine Ravine on Mount Hao. Monkey and us two went to find the demon and fight him. Because he can make fire we couldn't beat him the first time. The second time we asked the dragon kings to help out with rain, but even that couldn't put it out. The flames have hurt Monkey so badly that he can't move, which is why he's sent me to ask for your help, Bodhisattva. I beg you in your mercy to save the master." "Get up," said the evil spirit, "and come with me to the cave to see its lord. I shall ask him to be kind to you. You will just have to kowtow as an apology and ask for your master back." "Bodhisattva," said Pig, "I'll kowtow to him if I can get the master back that way."

"Come with me," said the demon king. Knowing no better, the idiot followed the demon back to the Fire-cloud Cave by the way he had come instead of going on to the Southern Sea. They were back at the entrance in an instant. "Do not worry," said the evil spirit as he went in, "he is an old acquaintance of mine. Come in." As soon as the idiot raised his foot to go inside the demons all captured him with a great shout, knocked him over, and pushed him into the bag. Then the cord at the mouth was drawn tight and Pig was hung up from a rafter. The evil spirit resumed his true form, took his seat in the midst of the demons, and said, "Pig, what powers do you think you have? How do you have the nerve to promise to protect the Tang

Priest on his way to fetch the scriptures, or to ask the Bodhisattva here to subdue me? Take a good look. Can't you see I'm the Red Boy? Now I've got you I'm going to hang you up for four or five days, steam you, and give you as a treat to the little devils to nibble with their drinks." Hearing this, Pig started cursing inside the bag: "Damn you, monster. It's disgraceful behaviour. You may have used all your tricks and devices to be able to eat me, but I guarantee I'll give every one of you the head-swelling plague." The idiot kept on cursing and yelling, but we will say no more of him.

Monkey meanwhile had felt a stinking wind rush past him as he sat with Friar Sand. "That's bad," he said with a sneeze. "That's a thoroughly ill wind. I'm afraid Pig's got lost." "But wouldn't he ask the way if he got lost?" asked Friar Sand. "He must have run into the demon," said Monkey. "But wouldn't he have come rushing back here if he'd met a demon?" said Friar Sand. "Can't be sure," said Monkey. "You sit here and look after the things while I go over the ravine and see what's going on." "Let me go," said Friar Sand. "Your back is still aching and he might fight you again." "You'd be useless," said Monkey. "It'll have to be me."

Splendid Monkey gritted his teeth against the pain, took his cudgel in his hand, crossed the ravine, and shouted "Vicious monster!" at the mouth of the cave. The little devil at the gate rushed inside to report that Sun the Novice was yelling at the gates again. The demon king ordered Monkey's capture. With a great battle-cry a crowd of demons armed with swords and spears opened the gates and shouted, "Get him." Monkey was indeed too exhausted to fight them. He squeezed himself against the side of the path, shouted, "Change," and turned himself into a bundle wrapped in a gold-embroidered cloth. As soon as they saw it the little devils picked it up and took it inside. "Your Majesty," they reported, "Monkey's a coward. As soon as we shouted 'Get him' he was so scared he dropped his bundle and ran." "There won't be anything in there that's worth anything," smirked the demon king. "Probably just some worn-out monks' habits and old hats. Get them in, and wash and tear them up to use as rags." One of the little demons took the bundle right inside the cave, not realizing it was really Monkey. The evil spirit dropped it inside the doors without paying any attention to it.

Splendid Monkey could work transformations within transformations and deceits within deceits. Pulling out one of his hairs he blew on it with magic breath and made it look just like the first bundle. He then turned himself into a fly that perched on the pivot of the door. He could hear Pig grumbling away rather indistinctly, like a hog with swine-fever. When Monkey buzzed over to look for him he found Pig hanging up in the leather sack. Monkey landed on the sack, where he could hear Pig cursing and swearing at the demon. "How dare you pretend to be the Bodhisattva Guanyin and trick me into coming here! Then you hang me up and say you're going to eat me. One day soon my elder brother will catch you all and let me out."

Monkey was delighted to hear this. "The idiot may be a bit stuffy in there, but he's not running down his colours. I'll get that demon and have my revenge on him."

Just as Monkey was working out how to rescue Pig he heard the demon king shouting, "Where are the six warriors?" Six of the little devils who were his friends had been given the title of Warrior. Each one had his own name. They were Mist in the Clouds, Clouds in the Mist, Fire-fast, Wind-speedy, Heater and Cooker. The six warriors stepped forward and knelt down. "Do you know where the Old King lives?" the demon asked. "Yes," the warriors replied. "Go tonight to invite His Majesty the Old King here. Tell him that I've caught a Tang Priest who I'm going to cook for him, and that this will make him live for another thousand ages." The six monsters slouched around as they went out with their orders. Monkey flew down from the bag with a buzz and followed the six demons as they left the cave.

CHAPTER 23
The Bodhisattva in Her Mercy Binds the Red Boy

The story tells how the six warriors left the cave and headed southwest. Monkey thought, "They are going to invite the Old King to eat our master. I'm sure he must be the Bull Demon King. In the old days we got on very well and were the best of friends, but now I've gone straight and he's still an evil monster. Although it's a long time since I last saw him, I remember what he looks like. I think I'll turn myself into a Bull Demon King, try to fool them, and see how it goes." Splendid Monkey gave the six little demons the slip, spread his wings, flew about a dozen miles ahead of them, shook himself, and turned into a Bull Demon King. He pulled out some hairs, shouted, "Change," and turned them into little devils with dogs, falcons, bows and crossbows as if they were a hunting party in the mountain valley. He then waited for the six warriors.

As the six warriors were making their way sloppily along they suddenly noticed that the Bull Demon King was sitting in their midst. Heater and Cooker fell to their knees in a panic and said, "Your Majesty, you're here already." Mist in the Clouds, Clouds in the Mist, Fire-fast and Wind-speedy were also all common mortals with fleshly eyes, unable to tell the true from the false, and they too fell to their knees, kowtowed and said, "Your Majesty, we've been sent by the Red Boy of the Fire-cloud Cave to invite Your Senior Majesty to a meal of Tang Priest meat that will lengthen your life by a thousand ages."

"Get up, children," said Monkey, "and come back to my cave with me while I change." "There will be no need for all that trouble, Your Majesty," said the little devils, still kowtowing. "You needn't go back. It's a long way, and I'm sure that our king would be angry with us if you did. Please come with us." "What good children," said Monkey. "Very well then, lead the way. I'm coming with you." The six little devils pulled themselves together and shouted to clear the way for the Great Sage, who was following them.

They were soon back at the cave. Wind-fast and Fire-speedy rushed in to report, "Your Majesty, His Senior Majesty is here." "You're capable lads to be back so soon," said the demon king with delight. He then ordered all his commanders to parade his forces with their banners and drums to greet the Old King. All the demons in the cave obediently went out on parade. Monkey threw-out his chest and acted very haughtily, braced himself, took back all the hairs he had turned into falconers and huntsmen, then strode straight in through the gates and took the central seat facing south as a monarch. The Red Boy knelt and kowtowed to him, saying, "Your Majesty, your son pays obeisance." "No need for that," said Monkey. After making four sets of kowtows the demon king stood below his father. "What have you asked me here for, boy?" Monkey asked.

"Your stupid son," said the demon with a bow, "caught someone yesterday —a priest from the Great Tang in the East. I've often heard tell that he is someone who has cultivated his conduct for ten lives, and that if you eat a piece of his flesh you'll live as long as an immortal from Penglai or Yingzhou. I did not dare to eat him by myself, which is why I asked Your Majesty to share the Tang Priest's flesh and extend your life by a thousand ages." At this Monkey looked shocked and asked, "Which Tang Priest, my boy?" "The one going to fetch scriptures in the Western Heaven," the demon king replied. "But isn't he the master of Sun the Novice?" Monkey asked. "Yes," said the demon king. Monkey waved his hand, shook his head and said, "Don't start trouble with him. Pick a fight with anyone else you like, but not with him. My dear boy, don't you know what sort of person he is? That ape has vast magic powers and can do all sorts of transformations. When he made havoc in Heaven the Jade Emperor sent a hundred thousand Heavenly soldiers to spread out Heaven-and-earth nets, but they could not catch him. How could you have the nerve to eat his master? Send the priest out this moment, and don't start trouble with that monkey. If he heard that you'd eaten his master he wouldn't even need to fight you. He'd just have to poke a hole in the mountainside with that gold-banded cudgel of his to bring the whole mountain tumbling down. Then where would you be able to live, my boy, and who would there be to support me in my old age?"

"What things to say, Your Majesty," said the demon king. "You're bolstering him and making me look small. That Monkey and a couple of his fellow disciples were crossing my mountains when I did a transformation and carried his master off. He and Pig traced me to the gates here and talked some nonsense about kinship. I got into such a raging fury that we fought a few rounds. That was all there was to it. He wasn't anything very special."

"My dear boy," laughed Monkey, "you're only aware of how you beat him with your True Samadhi Fire. What you forget is that he can do seventy-two transformations." "No matter what he turns himself into I can always spot him," said the demon king, "and I'm sure he won't dare try another attack here." "My son," said Monkey, "you may be able to recognize him sometimes, but he won't turn into something big like a wolf, an orang-utan or an elephant. If he did he wouldn't be able to get inside the cave. You'd find it hard to recognize him if he turned into something small." "No matter how small he made himself we have four or five little devils on every door. He'd never be able to get in." "You don't realize that he can turn himself into a fly, or a mosquito, or a flea, or a bee, or a butterfly, or the tiniest of insects. He could even make himself look just like me. You wouldn't possibly be able to tell." "Don't worry," said the demon king. "Even if he had guts of iron and a bronze heart he'd never dare come anywhere near here."

心猿遭火敗

Monkey Defeated by the Red Boy's Fire

"In that case, dear son," said Monkey, "what powers do you have that make you more than a match for him, so that you could invite me here today to eat the flesh of the Tang Priest? All the same, I don't think I'll have any today." "Why not?" the demon king said. "I'm getting old," said Monkey, "and your mother keeps nagging at me to do some good works. The only good deed I'm interested in is eating vegetarian food." "Your Majesty," said the demon king, "is this permanent or just for a month?" "Neither," said Monkey. "It's called 'thunder vegetarianism'. You do it for four days each month." "Which four?" the demon asked. "The three days each month with *Xin* in their names, and the sixth day too. Today is the day *Xin You*, so that means I ought to be on vegetarian food. Besides, *You* days are not good for having visitors. But tomorrow I could be back to scrub, wash and steam him myself, and enjoy him with you, my boy."

This all made the demon king think, "My father usually lives on human flesh, and he's already lived to be over a thousand. How come he's now thinking about a vegetarian diet? When you consider all the evil things he's done, three or four days of vegetarian food a month could never make up for them. There's something wrong here. It's very suspicious." He withdrew and went out through the inner gates, sent for the six warriors, and asked them, "Where was His Senior Majesty when you gave him the invitation?" "Halfway here," the little devils replied. "I thought you were quick," said the demon king. "Didn't you go to his place?" "No," said the little devils, "we didn't." "This is bad," said the demon king. "I've been fooled. It's not His Senior Majesty." The little devils all knelt before him and asked, "Your Majesty, can't you recognize your own father?" "He looks and moves just like my father," said the demon king, "but what he says doesn't fit. I'm afraid I've been taken in and beaten by one of his transformations. I want you all to be very careful. The swordsmen among you must draw your swords, the spearmen sharpen your spears, and those of you who can use staves and ropes get ready to do so. I'm going to question him again and watch what he says. If he really is His

Senior Majesty then it doesn't matter whether we have the feast today, tomorrow or in a month's time. But if what he says is wrong, then the moment I give a hum you're all to attack at once."

When the little devils had all been given their orders the demon king turned on his heels, went back inside and bowed to Monkey, who said, "No need for all that formality within the family, my boy. Don't bow. Just say whatever it is you have to say." The demon king prostrated himself before Monkey and replied, "Your foolish son actually invited you for two reasons. One was to present you with Tang Priest meat, and the other was to ask you something. When I was out for a spin on my auspicious light the other day I went right up to the ninth level of clouds and bumped into the Taoist Master Zhang Daoling." "Do you mean Zhang Daoling the Taoist pope?" Monkey asked. "Yes," the demon king replied. "What did he say to you?" Monkey asked. "Seeing that your son is complete in all his organs and that the spacing between my forehead, nose and chin is auspiciously even," the demon king replied, "he asked me the hour, day, month and year of my birth. Your child is too young to remember all that properly. Master Zhang is a brilliant astrologer, and he offered to cast my horoscope. That is what I wanted to inquire about, Your Majesty, so that I can ask him to cast my horoscope next time I meet him."

This made Monkey chuckle to himself: "What a magnificent demon. I've captured quite a few since I became a Buddhist and started escorting the Tang Priest on this journey, but none of them was as sharp as this one. He's asking me all trivial family details, and I'll just have to fake up my answers. How could I possibly know when he was born?" The splendid Monkey King was extremely crafty. He continued to sit in majesty in the central position, showing not a trace of fear as he replied with his face wreathed in smiles, "Please get up, dear boy. I'm getting so old now that nothing goes the way I want it to any more. I can't remember just now exactly when you were born. I'll ask your mother when I go home tomorrow."

"But Your Majesty is always reeling off the details of my

birth-time," the demon king said, "and telling me I'll live as long as Heaven. You can't have forgotten now. It's outrageous. You're a fake." He then hummed the signal and all the demons rushed on Monkey and stabbed at him with their swords and spears. The Great Sage parried their thrusts with his cudgel, went back to looking like himself again, and said to the evil spirit, "You're the outrageous one, dear boy. It can't possibly be right for a son to attack his own father." The demon king was so overwhelmed with shame that he dared not return Monkey's look. Brother Monkey then turned into a golden glow and left the cave. "Your Majesty, Sun the Novice has gone," the little devils reported. "Oh well, that's that," said the demon king, "Good riddance. He beat me this time. Shut the gates and say nothing to him. Let's clean, cook and eat the Tang Priest."

The Great Sage left the cave and set off immediately on the somersault cloud that took him straight towards the Southern Ocean. He had been flying for less than an hour when Potaraka Island came into view. He landed his cloud in an instant and went straight to Raka Crag, where the twenty-four devas asked him as he walked solemnly towards them, "Great Sage, where are you going?" After Monkey had exchanged courtesies with them he replied, "I would like to see the Bodhisattva." "Please wait for a moment while we report to her," the devas said. Hariti and the other devas went to the entrance of the Tide Cave to report, "Bodhisattva, Sun Wukong has come for an audience." The Bodhisattva asked for him to be brought in.

The Great Sage tidied his clothes and obediently walked inside at a respectful pace. When he saw the Bodhisattva he prostrated himself before her. "Wukong," she said, "why are you here instead of taking The Tang Priest to the West to fetch the scriptures?" "Bodhisattva," Monkey replied, "your disciple humbly reports that while escorting the Tang Priest on his journey he has reached the Fire-cloud Cave in the Withered Pine Ravine on Mount Hao. An evil spirit called the Red Boy has snatched my master. I and Pig found our way to his gates and fought him, but he started a True Samadhi Fire. This makes it impossible for us to beat him and rescue the master. I hurried to the Eastern Sea and asked the dragon kings of the four seas to make rain, but it couldn't control the flames, and I was badly hurt by the smoke, which all but killed me." "Why did you send for the dragon kings and not for me," the Bodhisattva asked, "if he has True Samadhi Fire and such great powers?" "I wanted to come," Monkey replied, "but I'd been so badly affected by the smoke that I couldn't ride a cloud. I sent Pig to come and ask you for help instead." "But he has not been here," the Bodhisattva replied. "That's just it," said Monkey. "Before Pig reached this island the evil spirit turned himself into your double, Bodhisattva, lured him into the cave, and has now hung him up in a leather bag ready to be steamed and eaten."

When the Bodhisattva heard this she said in a furious rage, "How dare that vicious demon turn himself into my double!" With a roar of anger she flung her precious pure vase into the sea. Monkey was so horrified that his hair stood on end. He rose to his feet, stood below the Bodhisattva's throne, and said, "If the Bodhisattva does not control her temper I'll be blamed for talking out of turn and ruining her conduct. This is terrible. You've thrown your vase away. Had I known you could have done me a big favour and given it to me."

Before the words were all out of his mouth the waves of the sea started to dance and the vase emerged from them, supported on the back of a tortoise.

Carrying the vase on his back, the tortoise crawled ashore, and made twenty-four nods to the Bodhisattva that counted as twenty-four kowtows. Seeing this Monkey laughed to himself as he said, "He must be the vase-keeper. I suppose they ask him for the vase whenever it's lost." "What is that you are saying, Wukong?" "Nothing," Monkey replied. "Fetch the vase," the Bodhisattva ordered. Monkey went over to pick it up, but he had no more chance of moving it than a dragonfly has of shifting a stone pillar by even a fraction of an inch. Monkey went back to the Bodhisattva, knelt before her, and said,

"Bodhisattva, your disciple cannot move it." "All you can do, you ape, is talk," said the Bodhisattva. "If you can't even move a vase how can you hope to subdue demons?" "To be honest, Bodhisattva, I would normally be able to move it, but today I just can't. I think that being beaten by the evil spirit must have weakened me." "It is usually an empty vase," said the Bodhisattva, "but when I threw it into the sea it went round the Three Rivers, the Five Lakes, the Eight Seas, the Four Streams, and all the brooks, springs, pools and caves to borrow a whole seaful of water. You are nowhere near strong enough to lift a sea up. That is why you can't move it." "Indeed," said Brother Monkey, his hands clasped before him, "your disciple didn't know that."

The Bodhisattva then stepped forward, gently lifted the vase with her right hand, and placed it on the palm of her left hand. The tortoise nodded to the Bodhisattva again and slipped back into the sea. "Wukong," said the Bodhisattva, seating herself, "the sweet dew in this flask of mine, unlike the dragon kings' private rain, can extinguish Samadhi Fire." "Bodhisattva," pleaded Monkey, "please, please save my master in your mercy." The Bodhisattva promised to help. Monkey was absolutely delighted. He invited the Bodhisattva to leave the Tide Cave.

Instructing all the devas to guard her immortal realm, the Bodhisattva left the Pota Cliff by auspicious cloud and went over to call, "Where are you, Huian?" Huian was Moksa, the second son of Heavenly King Li, the Pagoda-carrier; he was the disciple whom the Bodhisattva personally taught, and he never left her side. His full title was Huian the Novice, Protector of the Dharma. Huian placed his hands together and stood awaiting the Bodhisattva's orders. "Go straight up to Heaven," she said, "call on His Majesty your father, and ask him to lend me his Pole Star swords." "How many will you need, Mistress?" Huian asked. "The whole set," she replied.

Huian then went obediently straight up on his cloud, in through the Southern Gate of Heaven, and into the Cloud-tower Palace, where he kowtowed to his father. "Where have you come from?" Heavenly King Li asked after greeting him. "My

mistress has been asked by Sun Wukong to subdue a demon,"
Huian — or Moksa — replied. "She has sent me to visit you
and ask for the loan of your set of Pole Star swords." The Heavenly King then sent Nezha to fetch the thirty-six swords,
which he gave to Moksa. Taking his leave in a great hurry he
brought his auspicious light straight down to the Southern Sea,
where he presented the swords to the Bodhisattva.

The Bodhisattva took the swords, threw them into the air,
said a spell, and turned them into a thousand-petal lotus throne,
on which she took her seat. All of them left the coast by cloud.
The white parrot flew ahead, while the Great Sage and Huian
stood behind her.

Within moments they saw a mountain-top. "That's Mount
Hao," said Monkey. "It's about a hundred and fifty miles from
here to the demon's place." The Bodhisattva then ordered him
to lower the auspicious cloud. She said the magic word "*Om*"
above the summit, whereupon many a god and ghost — all the
local spirits of the mountain — emerged from all around the
mountain and gathered to kòwtow to the Bodhisattva's lotus
throne. "Do not be afraid," she said. "I am here to capture
this demon king. I want this whole area swept completely clean,
with not a living creature left behind within a hundred miles of
here. All the baby animals in their dens and fledglings in holes
in the trees must be put on the top of this high crag for safety."
Obediently the demons withdrew, and soon they were all back.
"Now that the place is clean, you may all return to your shrines,"
said the Bodhisattva. She then turned her vase of purity upside-
down, letting the water roar out with a noise like thunder.

The Great Sage Monkey was full of silent admiration:
"What great mercy and compassion. If I had that magic power
I'd just have tipped the vase over, and to hell with the birds,
beasts, reptiles and insects." "Stretch your hand out, Wukong,"
said the Bodhisattva. Monkey at once neatened his clothes and
put out his left hand. The Bodhisattva drew out her sprig of
willow, moistened it in the sweet dew, and wrote "Confusion"
on his palm. "Make a fist," she told him, "and go to challenge
the demon to battle. Let him beat you, then draw him back here.

I have a Dharma power with which to subdue him."

Monkey obediently took his cloud straight back to the cave entrance. Brandishing his cudgel with one hand and clenching the other into a fist, he shouted, "Open up, evil spirits." The little devils scampered back inside to report, "Sun the Novice is here again." The demon king leapt up and sprang outside, brandishing his spear and flinging insults back at Monkey: "You ape, you have no sense at all. I let you off lightly, but you don't know when enough is enough. You're trying to bully me again." "What about your crime in driving your own father away?" retorted Monkey.

In his humiliation and anger the demon king thrust his spear at Brother Monkey's chest. Monkey parried this with his cudgel and hit back. Once they started they fought four or five rounds in which Monkey, one hand holding the cudgel and the other clenched in a fist, gave ground. Not realizing that this was a trick, the evil spirit raised his spear and ran after him. Monkey trailed his cudgel and opened his other hand. The demon king then fell into confusion and chased Monkey for all he was worth. The quarry moved like a shooting star, and the pursuer like a bolt that had just been shot from a crossbow.

Before long Monkey saw the Bodhisattva. "Evil spirit," he said to the demon, "I'm scared of you. Please spare me. I'm going to where the Bodhisattva Guanyin of the Southern Sea lives. You go home now." The demon king was not going to believe this, so he gritted his teeth and continued the pursuit. With a shake of his body Monkey hid himself in the Bodhisattva's divine radiance. Seeing that Monkey had disappeared, the evil spirit went up to the Bodhisattva, glared at her, and asked, "Are you reinforcements sent for by Monkey?" The Bodhisattva did not answer. The demon king then twirled his spear and roared, "Hey! Are you reinforcements sent for by Monkey?" The Bodhisattva again did not answer. The demon king then thrust his spear straight at the Bodhisattva's heart, at which she turned into a beam of golden light and rose straight up to the highest heavens. Monkey went up with her and complained, "Bodhisattva, you've tricked me again. Why did you act deaf and dumb and say nothing when that demon kept asking you? One thrust from his spear and you ran away. You've even ditched your lotus throne." "Keep quiet," the Bodhisattva said, "and see what he does next."

Monkey and Moksa stood next to each other up there watching while the demon said with a derisive jeer, "Insolent ape, you didn't know who you were up against. You didn't realize what sort of person I am. You fought me and lost several times, and then you sent for that putrid Bodhisattva. One thrust from my spear and she's disappeared. She's even left her lotus throne behind. Well, I'm going to sit on it now." The evil spirit then sat cross-legged in the middle of the throne, imitating the Bodhisattva. "That's just marvellous," said Monkey. "Now you've given your lotus throne away." "What are you saying now, Wukong?" the Bodhisattva asked. "What am I saying?" Monkey replied. "I'm saying you've given your lotus throne away. That fiend has just sat himself down on it. Would you care to get it back?" "But I want him to sit on it," the Bodhisattva said. "He's so small he'll sit on it much more safely than you did," Monkey replied. "Stop talking," said the Bodhisattva, "and watch the power of the Dharma."

She pointed downwards with her sprig of willow and called, "Turn back." The colours and auspicious glow of the lotus seat all disappeared, leaving the demon king sitting on the points of swords. "Drive the swords in by hitting their handles with the demon-quelling pestle," she ordered Moksa. Moksa then took his cloud straight down and struck over a thousand times with the demon-quelling pestle as if he were ramming down earth to build a wall. The demon was now pouring with blood from his open wounds as the points of two swords both came out through his thighs. Watch the demon as he gritted his teeth against the agony. Throwing his spear down he pulled furiously at the swords. "Bodhisattva," exclaimed Monkey, "that monster's not afraid of pain. He's trying to pull the swords out." Seeing this she called to Moksa, "Don't kill him." She then pointed her sprig of willow down once more, said the magic word "Om", and turned the Pole Star swords into halberds with inverted barbs like wolf's teeth that could not be pulled out. This finally made the demon desperate. Trying to bend the sword-points he pleaded in his agony, "Bodhisattva, your disciple was blind. I failed to recognize your great Dharma powers. I beg you in your mercy to spare my life. I shall never do evil again, and I vow to become a Buddhist and observe the rules of conduct."

On hearing this the Bodhisattva went down on her golden light with Moksa, Monkey and the white parrot till she was in front of the evil spirit. "Will you really accept my rules of conduct?" The demon king nodded and said amid tears, "I will accept the rules if you spare my life." "Will you join my faith?" the Bodhisattva asked. "If you spare my life I swear I will." said the demon king. "In that case," said the Bodhisattva, "I shall lay my hands on your head and administer the vows." From her sleeve she produced a golden razor, with a few strokes of which she shaved the demon's head into a Mount Tai tonsure, leaving him with a topknot and with three little tufts. "Poor evil spirit," laughed Monkey. "Now you can't tell whether he's a boy or a girl. Goodness knows what he's meant to be." "As you have accepted my rules of conduct," said the Bodhisattva to the demon, "I will not mistreat you. I shall call you Page Sudhana. Do you accept?" The demon bowed in assent, wanting only to have his life spared. The Bodhisattva then pointed at him and called, "Withdraw!" With a crashing sound the Pole Star swords all fell into the dust. The boy was now unharmed.

"Huian," said the Bodhisattva, "will you take the swords back to the Heavenly Palace and return them to His Majesty your father? You need not come back to meet me: wait with all the devas on the Pota Crag." As instructed, Moksa took the swords back to Heaven and returned to the Southern Sea.

Now the boy's savage nature had not yet been tamed. When he realized that the pain in his legs had gone, that his backside was no longer wounded, and that he had three little tufts of hair on his head he ran over to grab his spear and said to the Bodhisattva, "You don't have any real Dharma powers that can put me down. It was all just an illusion. I refuse to accept your rules. Take this!" He jabbed at her face with his spear, making

Monkey so angry that he struck at the boy with his cudgel. "Don't hit him," the Bodhisattva called out. "I have a way of punishing him." From her sleeve she produced a gold band and continued, "This treasure is one of the three bands — a golden one, a tightening one, and a prohibition one — that the Tathagata Buddha gave me when I went to the East to find the pilgrim who would fetch the scriptures. You are wearing the tightening band. The prohibition band was used to subdue the great god guarding the mountain. I have not been able to bring myself to give the golden one away before, but as this demon is being so outrageous he shall have it." The splendid Bodhisattva then waved the band in the wind, shouted "Change!" and turned it into five bands that she threw at the boy with the command "Fix!" One went over his head, two on his hands, and two on his feet. "Stand clear, Wukong," the Bodhisattva ordered, "while I say the Gold-band Spell." "Bodhisattva," pleaded Monkey in panic, "I asked you here to subdue the demon, so why ever are you putting a curse on me?" "But this will not be the Band-tightening Spell that affects you," the Bodhisattva explained. "It will be the Gold-band Spell that works on the boy." Monkey felt easier in his mind as he stood beside the Bodhisattva and listened to her saying the spell. She made magic with her hands and recited the words silently several times over. The evil spirit twisted and tugged at his ears and cheeks, stamped his feet and rolled around.

The Bodhisattva recited the spell several times before stopping. Only then did the evil spirit's agony cease. When he recovered, stood up and looked at himself he found that he had gold bands round his neck, hands and feet. They were painfully tight, and try as he would he could not move them at all. The treasures had already taken root in his flesh, and the more he rubbed them the more they hurt. "There, there, little darling," mocked Monkey. "The Bodhisattva's put a lucky amulet ring round your neck to make sure you grow up safely." This jibe infuriated the boy, who grabbed his spear once more and started lunging wildly at Monkey. Monkey nimbly avoided it and went behind the Bodhisattva, yelling, "Say the spell, say the spell."

The Bodhisattva moistened her willow sprig with sweet dew, and flicked the ambrosial liquid at him with a call of "Together!" The boy dropped his spear and put his hands together in front of his chest, unable to pull them apart. Only when he could not pick up his spear because his hands were inseparably joined did the boy appreciate the deep mystery of the power of the Dharma. He could do no other than lower his head in a kowtow.

The Bodhisattva then recited another true spell and turned her vase over to take back the whole seaful of water. Not half a drop was left behind. "Wukong," she said to Monkey, "this demon has now surrendered. The only thing is that he still has some wild ideas. He will only accept the Dharma after he has gone from here to Potaraka Island making a kowtow at every step of the journey. You must go straight back to the cave to rescue your master." "As your disciple has put you to the trouble of this long journey," said Monkey with a kowtow, "I should see you some of your way back." "No need," said the Bodhisattva. "I am worried for your master's life." Brother Monkey then kowtowed to take his leave of her joyfully.

The story now turns to Friar Sand, who had long been sitting in the woods waiting for Monkey. When Monkey did not come back he tied the luggage on the back of the horse, and leading it by its bridle with one hand and holding his demon-quelling staff in the other he went out of the pine woods to take a look to the south. Seeing Monkey returning in a very good mood, Friar Sand went up to him and said, "Brother, why has it taken you so long to get back from asking the Bodhisattva to come? I've been half dead from worry." "You must have been asleep and dreaming," said Monkey. "I've already brought her here and she has subdued the demon." Monkey then told him all about the Bodhisattva's Dharma power. "Let's go and rescue the master," said Friar Sand with delight.

The two of them then leapt across the ravine and rushed to the doors, where they tethered the horse. Then they charged in together, their weapons at the ready, and wiped out the devils.

They let the leather bag down to release Pig, who thanked Monkey and asked, "Where's that evil spirit, brother? Just let me have a go at him with my rake; I want to get my own back." "Let's find the master," said Monkey.

The three of them went right to the back of the cave, where they found their master tied up stark naked and weeping in the rear courtyard. Friar Sand untied him while Monkey fetched his clothes to dress him. The three of them then knelt before him and said, "Master, you have suffered terribly." Sanzang thanked them and said, "Dear disciples, I have put you to great trouble. How was the demon subdued?" Monkey then told him how the Bodhisattva had been asked to come and had taken the boy as her page. Master and disciples then left the cave. The horse was saddled up, and once they found the main trail they headed west with whole-hearted determination.

CHAPTER 24
The Dragon Prince of the West Catches the Alligator Demon

One day when they had been travelling for over a month they came to a great black river. "Disciples," asked Sanzang as he dismounted, "why is this river so dark and turbid?" "Someone's washed out an indigo dyeing-vat in it," said Pig. "No," said Friar Sand, "somebody's been cleaning their inkstone in it." "Stop making silly guesses, you two," said Monkey, and let's work out how we're going to get the master across."

As they were talking on the bank a man appeared upstream rowing a little boat. "Disciples," said Sanzang with delight, "here's a boat. Let's ask the boatman to take us across." "Boatman," shouted Friar Sand, "ferry us over." "This isn't a ferry," replied the man on the boat, "and I couldn't possibly ferry you over." " 'Helpfulness first, in Heaven and earth,' " said Friar Sand. "You may not be a ferryman, but we don't keep coming to pester you. We are Buddhists from the East sent by the emperor to fetch the scriptures. If you could have a little consideration and ferry us over we'd show you our gratitude." At this the boatman brought his craft over to the bank and said as he rested on his oars, "Masters, this boat's too small to take all of you over." When Sanzang took a closer look he saw that the boat was carved from a single log with only enough room for two hollowed out in the middle. "What shall we do?" Sanzang asked. "This boat can take us over in two trips," said

Friar Sand. At this Pig tried what he thought would be a clever way of saving himself some trouble and getting himself well in with the master. "Friar Sand," he said, "you and Brother Monkey look after the luggage and the horse while I take the master over first. Then the man can come back for the horse. Brother Monkey can jump over the river." "Good idea," nodded Monkey.

While the idiot supported the Tang Priest, the boatman pushed off and rowed straight into the main stream. Once they reached the middle there was a great roar as huge waves blotted out the heavens, and a terrible storm blew up.

This wind was the work of the boatman, who was in fact a monster from the Black River. Watch as the Tang Priest and Pig plunge into the waters, boat and all. They disappeared without a trace, and nobody knew where they had been carried off to.

On the river bank Friar Sand and Monkey were desperate. "What are we to do?" they said. "The master keeps running into disaster. Now he's in trouble here at the Black River after escaping from the last demon and having a peaceful stretch of his journey."

The splendid Friar Sand took off his tunic, tied strips of cloth round his wrists and feet, and plunged into the waves with a great splash as he whirled his demon-quelling staff. As he strode through the waters he heard voices, so he drew aside to steal a look. He saw a pavilion, over the doors of which was written large PALACE OF THE GOD OF THE BLACK RIVER IN THE HENGYANG VALLEY. He could hear a monster saying to himself as he sat there, "It's been hard work getting him, but this priest is a holy man who has cultivated his conduct for ten lives. One piece of his flesh is enough to make you immortal. I've waited for him long enough, and now my ambition has been fulfilled." Then he issued his orders: "Little ones, fetch the metal steamer at once, cook those two monks whole, then write an invitation and deliver it to my second uncle asking him over to eat them as a birthday feast." This was too much for Friar Sand's temper. He beat on the doors with his staff, yelling abusively, "Damned monsters, give me back my master the Tang Priest and my brother Pig this minute!" This gave the demons inside the doors such a fright that they ran in to report, "Disaster!" "What disaster?" the old monster asked. "There's a very sinister-looking monk outside beating at the outer doors and yelling for them."

At this the monster went outside, holding his flail of steel pieces joined together by bamboo-shaped links.

"Who's that beating at my doors?" the demon roared. "I'll get you, you ignorant damned devil," said Friar Sand. "Deceitful monster, disguising yourself as a boatman and rowing over to snatch my master. Give him back at once and I'll spare your life." The demon roared with laughter at this. "Monk, you're throwing your life away, said the monster. "Your master's mine now, and I'm going to steam him for a feast. Come here and see if you can beat me. If you can hold out for three rounds I'll give you your master back; but if you can't I'll cook you with him and you can forget all about going to the Western Heaven." Friar Sand was now in a towering rage, and he swung at the monster's head with his staff, which the monster parried with his flail.

When they had fought thirty rounds without result Friar Sand thought, "This monster is as good a fighter as I am. I'm not going to be able to beat him. I'll have to lure him out for Monkey to kill." Friar Sand then pretended to drop his guard and took to his heels trailing his staff behind him. But instead of chasing him the evil monster said, "Off you go then. I won't fight you any more. I'm going to write invitations for my guests."

Friar Sand emerged from the waves snorting with fury. When he saw Monkey, he told him what had happened.

Before the words were out of his mouth an old man emerged from a bend in the river, knelt at a great distance from them, and said, "The God of the Black River kowtows to the Great Sage." "Weren't you the evil spirit who rowed the boat?" said Monkey. "Trying to fool us again, are you?" The old man wept and kowtowed as he replied, "I'm no monster, Great Sage.

I'm the real god of this river. The evil spirit came here from the Western Ocean on a flood tide during the fifth month last year. He fought me, and as I'm so old I was no match for him, so he seized my Palace of the God of the Black River in the Hengyang Valley, and killed many of my watery tribe. I had to go to the sea to bring a case against him. But the Dragon King of the Western Sea is his uncle, so of course he threw my case out and told me to turn my palace over to the monster. I tried submitting a protest to Heaven, but I was too humble a river god to obtain an audience with the Jade Emperor. Now that you are here, Great Sage, I've come to pay my respects and submit to you. I beg you to avenge me." "From what you say the Dragon King of the Western Sea is in the wrong too," said Brother Monkey. "Very well then, river god, you keep an eye on things with Friar Sand here while I go to the sea to arrest that dragon and make him capture the monster." "I'm very grateful, Great Sage," said the river god.

Monkey went by somersault cloud straight to the Western Ocean, where he landed, made water-repelling magic with his hands, and parted the waves. He saw a black fish spirit who was carrying a golden invitation box shoot upstream like an arrow. Monkey met him head-on and smashed his skull open with a single blow of his iron cudgel, sending the poor spirit's brains flying and splitting his cheeks apart, and with a loud noise it emerged from the water. In the box Monkey found an invitation from the monster to his uncle the Dragon King.

"That fellow has given me all the evidence I need for my case," chuckled Monkey, tucking the invitation in his sleeve and carrying on his way. By then a yaksha patrolling the sea had noticed Monkey and rushed straight back to the crystal palace to report to the Dragon King, "Lord Monkey, the Great Sage Equalling Heaven, is here." The Dragon King Ao Shun led his watery tribe from the palace to welcome Monkey: "Great sage, won't you come into my humble palace for a while and take a cup of tea?" "I've never had a single cup of your tea," said Monkey, "but you've drunk my wine before now." To this the Dragon King replied with a smile, "Great Sage, you have always been a faithful follower of the Buddha and have never touched meat or alcohol. You've never invited me to drinks." "You may never have been over for drinks, but you're already in trouble for being a boozer," said Monkey. "How am I in trouble?" asked Ao Shun with horror. Monkey produced the invitation and handed it to the dragon king.

At the sight of this the Dragon King was scared out of his wits. He fell to his knees in panic, kowtowed and said, "Forgive me, Great Sage. That awful boy is my younger sister's ninth son. I sent him to nourish his nature and cultivate the truth in the Black River. I never imagined he'd commit such terrible sins, and now I'll send people to arrest him." Ao Shun then told his son Mo'ang, "Take five hundred of our strongest prawn and fish soldiers to arrest and charge Alligator immediately."

Monkey bade farewell to the old dragon and left the Western Sea with Mo'ang and his troops. Soon they were back at the Black River, where Monkey said, "Catch the demon, Your Royal Highness, while I wait on the bank." "Don't worry, Great Sage," said Mo'ang. "I'll arrest him show him to you, Great Sage, to sentence and punish, and return your master to you. Only then will I take him back to the ocean and see my father." Monkey took leave of him cheerfully, recited the water-repelling spell and made it with his hands, sprang out of the waves, and made straight for the east bank, where Friar Sand and the river god said, "When you went it was by air, so why have you come back from under the water?" Monkey told them all about how he had killed the fish spirit, taken the invitation, charged the Dragon King, and brought soldiers back with the dragon prince. Friar Sand was very pleased, and they all stood on the bank waiting.

Prince Mo'ang sent a herald to the gates of the underwater palace to announce to the evil spirit, "Prince Mo'ang, son of the Old Dragon King of the Western Sea, is here." This news aroused the suspicions of the evil spirit as he sat inside. "I sent a black fish spirit with an invitation to my uncle some time ago," he thought, "and I haven't had any answer yet. Why is my cousin here instead?" As he was thinking, a little demon came in from a river patrol to report, "Your Majesty, there's a detachment of troops camped in the river west of the palace. Their banner says 'Young Marshal Mo'ang, Crown Prince and Son of the Dragon King of the Western Sea'." "That cousin of mine is outrageous," said the monster. "Presumably my uncle couldn't come and sent him to the feast instead, but he didn't have to bring an army with him. Hmm. There must be something up." "Little ones," he said a little later, "get my armour and my steel flail ready in case things turn rough while I go out to greet him and see what's happening." On hearing the orders all the devils rubbed their hands and got ready.

When the alligator came out he observed a whole force of sea soldiers camped there on the right.

When the alligator demon saw them he went straight to the gates of their camp and shouted at the top of his voice, "Cousin, I'm waiting for you here with an invitation." A conch patrolling the camp went straight to the commander's tent to report, "Your Royal Highness, Alligator Dragon is outside with an invitation." The prince picked up a three-edged mace, and hurried out of the camp. "What invitation do you have for me?" he asked. Alligator Dragon bowed and replied, "This morning I sent your father an invitation. No doubt he did not think it worth coming and sent you instead. But why did you have to bring an army with you? Why have you encamped here armed to the teeth?" "What did you invite my father to?" the crown prince asked.

"Yesterday," the alligator replied, "I caught a priest from the East who has, they say, cultivated his conduct for ten lives in succession. If you eat his body you can live much longer. I wanted to invite uncle to have a look at the priest before I cook him in the steamer as a birthday treat." "Complete and utter fool," yelled the crown prince. "Do you know who that priest is?" "He's a priest from the Tang who's going to fetch scriptures from the Western Heaven," the demon replied. "All you know is that he's a Tang priest," said the crown prince. "What you don't realize is what powerful disciples he has."

"He's got one long-snouted one called Pig who I've captured already and I'm going to steam with the Tang Priest," the alligator demon replied. "There's another disciple called Friar Sand, a dusky fellow with a sinister face who fights with the quarterstaff. He came to my gates yesterday demanding his master. I came out at the head of my river troops and it didn't take me long to see him off with my steel flail. I don't see what's so poweful about him."

"You still haven't got the message," the dragon prince replied. "His senior disciple is the Golden Immortal of the Supreme Ultimate, the Great Sage Equalling Heaven who made havoc in Heaven five hundred years ago. He's now escorting the Tang Priest on his way to worship the Buddha and fetch the scriptures in the Western Heaven. You'd better bring the Tang Priest and Pig straight to the bank, hand them back to the Great Sage Monkey, and join me in making apologies to him if you want to keep alive. If you even hint at a 'no' you can forget about remaining here in one piece." This threw the alligator monster into a terrible rage. "My own cousin taking their side!" he exclaimed. "Just because you're scared of him it doesn't mean that I am."

"Damned devil," the crown prince swore back at him, "you're a disgrace." The two of them were now glaring at each other and each wanted to play the hero. The orders were given and the drums rolled. A terrible fight ensued.

The prince pretended to drop his guard with his three-bladed mace. Not realizing that this was a trick, the evil spirit rushed him, whereupon the crown prince skilfully first struck him a blow with the mace on the right arm that made him stumble, caught up with him, then struck at his feet and sent him sprawling. The ocean soldiers rushed up, seized Alligator, tied both hands behind his back, put an iron chain through his collar bone, and hauled him up on the bank.

The river god and Friar Sand leapt into the river and went straight to the doors of the water palace, which were wide open and not guarded by a single soldier. Inside the pavilion they saw the Tang Priest and Pig tied up stark naked. Friar Sand quickly

251

untied the master while the river god released Pig. Next they each carried one up to the surface of the water and then to the bank. Seeing the evil spirit roped and in chains there Pig raised his rake to strike him and said abusively, "Evil beast, take this from me." Monkey held him back, saying, "Spare his life, brother, out of consideration for Ao Shun and his son." The prince then plunged into the water with his prisoner and took his ocean troops straight back to the Western Sea.

The God of the Black River then thanked Brother Monkey for the recovery of his water palace. "Disciple," said the Tang Priest, "we're still on the eastern bank. How are we going to get across this river?" "Don't worry about that, my lord," said the river god. "Please mount your horse and I will lead you across the river." The master then rode his horse while Pig led it, Friar Sand carried the luggage, and Monkey supported San-zang. The river god did water-stopping magic to hold the waters back. In an instant a broad road opened up where the waters had withdrawn; master and disciples crossed to the west bank, climbed it, thanked the river god, and continued on their way.

CHAPTER 25
In the Kingdom of Tarrycart
Monkey Shows His Powers

The story tells how master and disciples crossed the Black River and took the main trail west. They faced wind and snow, and travelled under the moon and the stars. After they had been going for a long time it was early spring again.

Master and disciples were ambling along enjoying the view when all of a sudden they heard a mighty shout like a warcry from a thousand throats. Sanzang was terrified. He reined in his horse, unable to take another step forward. "Wukong," he said, looking back at him, "where is that noise from?" "Just wait a moment while I go and take a look," said Monkey.

Splendid Monkey. With one bound he was on a cloud and up in the air looking all around. In the distance he could make out a walled city, and when he went closer he could see that it had a haze of auspicious light over it with no sign of any evil emanations. "It's a good place," he sighed to himself, "but why was there that terrible noise?"

Just as he was wondering about all this he noticed a big crowd of Buddhist monks on a sandbank outside the city gates, pulling a cart. The noise that had startled Sanzang was them all shouting, "King Powerful Bodhisattva."

When he slowly lowered his cloud for a better look he saw that the cart was loaded with kiln bricks, tiles, wood and adobe bricks. Above the sandbank was a high ridge, along the top of which ran a narrow track between two great gates. Below the gates the paths all went straight down the steep sides of the ridge: the cart could not possibly be pulled up there. Although the weather was so mild and pleasant the monks were all dressed in rags and looked thoroughly poverty-stricken. "I suppose they must be building a monastery," thought Monkey, "and are having to do the work themselves because it's harvest-time here and they can't hire any labour." He was still not sure when he saw two young Taoist priests arrive. They both had crowns on their heads, were wearing brocade and embroidered clothes, and had handsome and clever faces round as the moon.

The approach of the Taoists made the Buddhist monks all shake with fear as they redoubled their efforts and pulled harder than ever at the cart. "Ah!" thought Monkey as he realized what was up. "The monks must be scared of the Taoists. Why else would they be pulling so hard? I've heard people tell of a place on the way to the West where they believe in Taoism and persecute Buddhist monks. This must be it."

The splendid Great Sage shook himself and turned into the likeness of a wandering Quanzhen Taoist with a food basket over his left arm as he beat on a bamboo drum and sang Taoist songs. Monkey walked towards the city gates and bowed in greeting to the two Taoists, saying, "Could you two elders tell me which streets and which alleys in this city love the Way and its followers? I would like to beg for some food." The Taoist priest laughed and replied, "You're a stranger here and you don't know about our city. Here it's not just the civil and military officials, the rich and the elderly who love the Way and its followers. Young and old, men and women alike, everyone offers us food when they see us. But all that is hardly worth mentioning. By far the most important thing is that His Majesty the king is a devout lover of the Way and its followers." "I'm young," said Monkey, "and I'm a stranger from far away. I didn't know that. Could I trouble you two elders to do a fellow-believer a favour? Tell me more about what this place is called and how the king shows his love for the Way and its worthies." "This country is called Tarrycart," the Taoist priest replied, "and His Majesty is close to us."

When Monkey heard this he said with a chuckle, "Can it be that a Taoist priest is monarch?" "No," he replied. "For twenty years there was a drought here, and not a drop of rain fell. Nothing could grow. Everyone — king, ministers, commoners, the high and the humble — all bathed, burnt incense and prayed to Heaven for rain. When they were in really desperate straits three immortals were sent from Heaven to save all living beings." "Which three?" Monkey asked. "Our masters," the Taoist priest replied. "May I ask their titles?" Monkey asked. "Our senior master is the Great Immortal Tiger Power," the Taoist replied, "our second master is the Great Immortal Deer Power, and the third master is the Great Immortal Antelope Power." "What sort of magic can your three masters perform?" Monkey asked. "They can summon up wind and rain with a flick of the hand," the Taoist said, "and change water into oil or stone into gold as easily as turning around. Our king and his ministers treat them with great respect and they are now relations of ours."

Monkey went on to ask, "Why are the monks working on the sandbank?" "You wouldn't know that when we were all praying for rain that year the Buddhists were on one side praying to Buddha while we were on the other side praying to the Great Bear. We both asked the court for grain, but the Buddhists turned out to be useless. They got no results by reciting their sutras and didn't help in the least. It was our masters who came along, called up wind and rain, and saved the people from their distress. The king was so angry with those useless Buddhists that he had their monasteries torn down and their Buddha statues smashed. He revoked their ordination licences and refused to let them go home. Instead he gave them to us to work for us as slaves."

On the pretext of looking for an uncle among the monks Monkey headed straight for the sandbank, where the monks told him of their sufferings.

The Great Sage used magic to make the cart go through the two gates and along the ridge then lift itself right up and smash itself to smithereens. The bricks, tiles and timber all went tumbling down the slope. "Scatter," he told the monks, "and keep away from me until I've seen the king and wiped out those Taoists tomorrow." "But, my lord," a Buddhist monk said, "we dare not go far. We're frightened of being arrested by officials and brought back here to be flogged and punished in other ways. It would only make things worse for us." "In that case I'll give you some magical protection," said Monkey. The splendid Great Sage then pulled out a handful of hairs and chewed them into little pieces, one of which he gave to each of the monks. "Keep it inside the nail of your third finger, bunch your fingers together, and just keep walking," he told them. "Nothing will happen unless somebody tries to arrest you. If anyone does, clench your fist and shout, 'Great Sage Equalling Heaven.' Then I'll come and protect you." "But, my lord," the monk said, "what if you're far away and out of sight? What if you don't come when we call? Whatever shall we do?" "Don't worry yourselves," said Monkey. "I'll keep you completely safe even if I'm thousands of miles away."

The story switches back to Sanzang, who gave up waiting beside the track for Monkey to report back and told Pig to lead the horse westward. They met monks hurrying away, and when they were close to the city wall they found Monkey with a dozen or so monks who had not yet gone. "Wukong," said Sanzang, reining in his horse, "why did it take you so long to get back from investigating that noise?" Monkey led the dozen or so monks in performing obeisances before Sanzang's horse and then told him everything that happened. Sanzang was horrified: "What are we to do if that's the way it is?" "Please don't worry, my lord," said the dozen or so monks. "His Honour the Great Sage Monkey is a god down from Heaven whose divine powers are tremendous. He will most certainly be able to protect you. We are monks from the Deep Wisdom Monastery, a royal foundation in the city. Because our monastery was founded by the great-grandfather of the present king and there is a statue of him there, the monastery has not been demolished, although all the others in the city, big and small alike, have been torn down.

We would like to invite you to come straight into town to stay in our humble monastery. The Great Sage Monkey is bound to find some way of coping at court tomorrow morning." "You are right," said Monkey. "Very well then, let us go into the city without further delay."

The venerable elder then dismounted and went on foot to the city gate. The sun was setting in the west as they crossed the drawbridge and went in through the triple gates. People in the streets turned away when they saw the monks of the Deep Wisdom Monastery leading a horse and carrying luggage. When they reached the monastery gates the travellers saw a large sign over them reading DEEP WISDOM MONASTERY: FOUND- ED BY ROYAL COMMAND. The monks pushed the gates open and led them through the Hall of the Vajrapanis before opening the doors of the main hall of the monastery. Sanzang covered himself with his cassock and worshipped the Buddha before entering. "Steward!" the monks called, and an old monk came out who kowtowed to Monkey the moment he saw him. "My lord, are you really here?" he said. "Do you know which lord I am, bowing like that?" Monkey asked. "I can see that you are Lord Sun, the Great Sage Equalling Heaven," the old monk replied. "We see you in our dreams every night; the Great White Planet is always coming in them to tell us that we will only be saved when you arrive. Now that I have beheld your distinguished countenance I know that it is the same as in our dreams. I am glad you are here so soon, my lord. Had you been a day or two later we would all have become ghosts by then." "Please get up," said Monkey. "Things will be sorted out tomorrow." The monks then laid on a vegetarian meal for the master and his disciples and tidied up the abbot's lodgings for them to stay in. They settled down for the night.

A little before midnight Monkey, who had too much on his mind to go to sleep, heard music outside, got up quietly, dressed, and sprang into the air to look around. To the south he saw lamps and candles burning bright, and when he brought his cloud lower for a closer look he saw that in the Temple of the Three Pure Ones the Taoists were performing a star ritual.

Monkey saw three old Taoists wearing their religious robes; he took them to be the Great Immortals Tiger Power, Deer Power and Antelope Power. Standing below them to either side were a crowd of seven or eight hundred Taoists holding drums, bells, incense and divine petitions. Monkey was delighted. "I had meant to go down and fool around with them by myself," he thought, "but one strand of silk can't make a thread, and one hand can't clap. I think I'll go back and do Friar Sand and Pig a good turn by letting them join in the game with me."

Monkey then landed his auspicious cloud and went straight into the abbot's lodgings, where he found Pig and Friar Sand sleeping top to toe. Monkey first called Friar Sand, who woke up and said, "Aren't you asleep yet, brother?" "Get up," said Monkey. "We're going to have a good feed." "Whatever sort of good feed can I have in the middle of the night when my throat's dried out and my eyes are all bleary?" Friar Sand asked. "There's a Temple of the Three Pure Ones in this city where the Taoist priests are holding a service," Brother Monkey replied. "The Hall of the Three Pure Ones is full of offerings: steamed buns as big as a bucket, cakes that must weigh fifty or sixty pounds apiece, any amount of rice, and fresh fruit too. Let's go and have some." The talk of all this good food was enough to wake Pig up. "Won't you take me too, brother?" he asked. "If you want a feed," said Monkey, "keep your voice down and don't wake the master. Come with me."

The two of them dressed, slipped outside, and leapt up by cloud with Monkey. As soon as the idiot saw the lights he wanted to attack, but Monkey held him back and said, "Steady on. We'll go down when they've all gone." "But their recitations are only just warming up," said Pig. "They won't want to go." "I'll do some magic that will send them packing," said Monkey.

The splendid Great Sage said the words and made the hand movements of a spell, drew in a breath from the quarter of the wind, and blew a gale so terrible that as it tore into the Hall of the Three Pure Ones it knocked down all the vases, candlesticks, and offerings on the walls and put out all the lamps. The

Taoists all shook with terror. "You had better go, disciples," said the Great Immortal Tiger Power. "This divine wind has blown out all the lamps and the incense, so you should all go back to bed. Get up early tomorrow morning and recite some more scriptures to make the numbers up." The Taoists then did indeed all withdraw.

Monkey then led Pig and Friar Sand to land their clouds, and they charged straight into the Hall of the Three Pure Ones. The idiot grabbed some food, not caring whether it was cooked or raw, and was just about to eat it when Monkey raised his iron cudgel to hit him. Pig pulled back his hand and said, "You're going to hit me before I've even tasted anything." "Don't act so low," said Monkey. "You must pay your respects and sit down before eating." "You're shameless," said Pig. "You steal food and expect me to pay my respects too. What would I have had to do if we'd been properly invited?" "Do you know who the three Bodhisattvas sitting up there are?" Monkey asked. "Can't you recognize the Three Pure Ones themselves?" asked Pig. "How could you possibly think they are Bodhisattvas?" "What about those Three Pure Ones?" Monkey asked. "Oh well," said Pig, "the one in the middle is the Original Celestial Pure One, the one on the left is the Precious Pure One, and the one on the right is the Supreme Lord Lao Zi." "We've got to make ourselves look like them before we can eat in safety," said Monkey. The delicious smells of the offerings were making the idiot desperate with hunger, so he climbed on the pedestal of the statue and knocked Lord Lao Zi off it with one shove of his snout. "You've sat here for long enough, old man," he said. "It's my turn now." Pig turned himself into the Supreme Lord Lao Zi, Monkey turned himself into the Original Celestial Pure One, and Friar Sand into the Precious Pure One. When the statues had all been pushed over and the three of them were sitting up there Pig grabbed a big steamed bun. "Not so fast," said Monkey. "But brother," protested Pig, "we've already made ourselves look like them. What are we waiting for?"

"Brother," said Monkey, "eating is much less important than not giving ourselves away. If one of the Taoists got up early to hit the bell or sweep the floor and tripped over a piece of one of the statues we've knocked over the news would be out. You'd better hide them." "But where?" asked Pig. "I'm a stranger here and I don't know my way around." "When we came in," said Monkey, "there was a little pair of double doors to the right with an awful stench coming out of them. It must be the place where the five kinds of grain prepare for reincarnation. Put them in there."

The idiot really did have some brute strength. When he leapt down he put the three statues over his shoulders and carried them out. On kicking those doors open he found that it was in fact a big lavatory. "That Protector of the Horses certainly knows how to talk," he said with a laugh. "He even made up a fancy Taoist name for the shithouse — 'the place where the five kinds of grain are prepared for reincarnation'." Pig mumbled a prayer and threw the three statues in with a great splash that covered half his tunic with evil-smelling liquid. When he went back into the hall Monkey asked him, "Did you hide them properly?" "I hid them well enough," the idiot replied, "but I splashed some of that filthy water on my clothes. I hope the stench doesn't make you feel sick." Never mind," laughed Monkey, "come and eat now. But you'll have to clean up before we go outside." The idiot turned himself back into Lord Lao Zi and the three of them sat down to eat their fill.

What a thing to have done! There was a young Taoist priest who had just gone to bed in his dormitory by the eastern cloister when he suddenly got up. "I left my handbell in the hall," he thought, "and if I lose it my master will be angry with me tomorrow. You go to sleep," he said to other priest who shared his bed, "while I go to look for it." He was in such a hurry that he did not put his underclothes back on but just pulled on his tunic and went straight to the main hall to look for his bell. He groped all around till he found it and was about to turn and leave when to his consternation he heard the sound of breathing. As he fled in alarm he tripped on a lichee stone and crashed to the ground, smashing his bell to pieces with a tremendous clang. Pig could not help roaring with laughter at this, which terrified the young Taoist out of his wits. He staggered to the abbots' lodgings, knocked on the doors and said, "Masters, disaster."

The three senior Taoists were not yet in bed, so they opened the doors and asked, "What disaster?" "I'd lost my bell," said the young Taoist, shivering and shaking, "and was looking for it in the hall when I heard a loud laugh that all but scared me to death." "Fetch lanterns," said the senior Taoists on hearing this, "and see what evil creature it is." This order was passed on to the priests, young and old, in both cloisters, who all got up, lit lamps, and went to the main hall to look.

The story tells how the Great Sage Monkey pinched Friar Sand with his left hand and Pig with his right. The two of them realized what was happening and sat there on high, their heads bowed in silence, while the Taoists lit their lamps and shone them all around as they searched. The three of them looked just as if they really were made of clay covered with gold leaf. "If no evildoers have been here," said the Great Immortal Tiger Power, "how have the offerings all been eaten?" "It looks as though people have eaten them," said the Great Immortal Deer Power. "The fruit with skins has all been peeled and the stones have all been spat out of the stone fruit. But why can't we see anybody?" "There is no need to be so suspicious, brother," said the Great Immortal Antelope Power. "I think that the Heavenly Honoured Ones must have been moved by our reverence and respect in reciting scriptures and making readings day and night, and by the name of His Majesty. Evidently the Three Pure Lords came down to the mortal world to enjoy these offerings. I suggest that we should worship the Heavenly Honoured Ones before they fly away on their cranes. We should beg them for some holy water and golden elixir pills that we can present to His Majesty and thereby win credit for giving him immortality." "A good idea," said Tiger Power. "Let there be music and recitation, my disciples," he ordered, "and bring me my ceremonial robes so that I may pace out the Dipper dance and pray for immortality for His Majesty."

The young Taoists did as they were told and were soon neatly drawn up in two groups. At the sound of a stone chime they all began to recite in unison the *True Classic of the Way and Its Power of the Yellow Court.* Throwing his religious cloak over his shoulders, Tiger Power took his jade tablet in his hands, performed the ritual dance, raising the dust before the statues, then prostrated himself to pray to the Taoist deities.

Pig felt most uncomfortable at all this, and he murmured under his breath to Monkey, "We shouldn't have stayed to be prayed to after eating the stuff. How are we going to answer their prayers?" Monkey gave him another pinch, opened his mouth, and called out, "Cease your worship, young immortals. We have just come from a Peach Banquet, so we did not bring any golden elixir or holy water today. We will present you with some another day." When the priests young and old heard the statue speaking they all twitched at their clothes and trembled as they said, "My lord, a living Heavenly Honoured One has come down to earth. Don't let him go. Whatever you do get him to give us a recipe for eternal life." Tiger Power then stepped forward, bowed again and asked for some holy water.

"They must be desperate to get it, praying for it again," muttered Friar Sand under his breath to Monkey, giving him a pinch. "Then let's give them some," said Monkey. "But where will we get it?" mumbled Pig. "Watch me," said Monkey. "When I get some, you'll have some too." The Taoists had by now finished playing their music. "Young immortals," said Brother Monkey, "there is no need to prostrate yourselves. I did not originally want to leave any holy water with you in case it destroyed your offspring of immortality, but there would be no difficulty at all about giving you some." When the Taoists heard this they all prostrated themselves, kowtowed and said, "We beg and implore the Heavenly Honoured One to grant your disciples some in recognition of the respectful devotion. We have widely taught the Way and its power and won the respect of the king for our sect of mystery." "Very well then," said Monkey, "fetch a vessel." The Taoists all once again kowtowed in thanks. Tiger Power, who liked to show off, carried in a great earthen jar that he placed in the hall. Deer Power put an earthenware dish on the table for offerings, and Antelope Power took the flowers out of a vase and put it between the other two containers. "Withdraw from the hall, all of you," ordered Monkey, "and screen us off. The secrets of Heaven must not be revealed. Then we can give you some holy water." The priests then all prostrated themselves below the steps outside the hall and shut the doors.

Monkey then stood up, lifted his tiger-skin kilt, and filled the vase with stinking piss, to the delight of Pig, who said, "In all the years we've been brothers we've never done this before. I've just eaten, and you ask me to do such a thing." The idiot then lifted his clothes and noisily filled the earthenware dish. The sound was like that of a torrent pouring down a mountainside. Friar Sand half filled the earthen jar. Then they all straightened their clothes, sat down again, and said, "Come and receive the holy water, young immortals."

The Taoist elders then pushed the screens aside and kowtowed in worship and gratitude. When the jar was carried out and put together with the vase and the dish they called, "Disciples, fetch me a cup to try some." The younger Taoists fetched a teacup and handed it to the elders. The elder filled the cup, drained it, and made a show of wiping his mouth and smacking his lips. "Is it good, brother?" asked Deer Power. Pursing his lips together, the most senior of the elders said, "Not very. Tastes a bit off." "Let me have a taste," said Antelope Power. When he had drunk a mouthful he said, "Tastes rather like pig's urine." When Monkey heard this from where he was sitting up there he realized that they had been rumbled. "We're not the Three Pure Ones," he shouted, "we're Buddhist monks from the East. What you've been drinking there isn't holy water — it's our piss."

Hearing this the Taoist priests shut the doors and started throwing rakes, brooms, tiles and stones wildly into the hall. Splendid Brother Monkey tucked Friar Sand under his left arm and Pig under his right, rushed out through the doors and rode his cloud straight back to the abbot's lodgings in the Deep Wisdom Monastery. The three of them went back to bed without disturbing their master.

It was soon the third quarter of the fifth watch. The Tang
Priest woke up and called, "Disciples, come with me when I go
to show my passport and obtain an exit permit." Monkey, Pig
and Friar Sand got out of bed and into their clothes quickly,
then stood waiting in attendance on the master. "Master,"
Monkey reported, "the king here trusts those Taoist priests. He
promotes the Way and persecutes Buddhist monks. I'm afraid
that if you say the wrong thing he'll refuse you an exit permit.
We had better escort you to the palace."

The Tang Priest was delighted with this suggestion. He
put on his brocade cassock, Monkey took the passport, Pig
carried the begging bowl and Friar Sand the monastic staff.
The luggage and the horse were entrusted to the care of the
monks of the Deep Wisdom Monastery. They went straight
to the Tower of Five Phoenixes at the palace gate, where they
bowed to the eunuch on duty and told him their names. They
said that they were monks from Great Tang in the east on
their way to fetch the scriptures who had come to show their
papers and obtain an exit permit, and they asked him to pass
the message on. The officer of the gate went straight to the
throne hall where he prostrated himself by the steps and reported, "There are four monks outside awaiting Your
Majesty's command by the Tower of Five Phoenixes. They
say they are from the Great Tang in the east and going to
fetch scriptures." To this the king replied, "Do they have to
come looking for their deaths here? Can't they do it anywhere
else? Why didn't the police capture them and bring them here
under arrest?" The king's tutor slipped forward to submit this
memorial: "Great Tang in the east is known as the great land
of China. It is over three thousand miles from here, and the way
is beset with many a demon. These monks must have some
magic powers if they dared to travel west. I beg Your Majesty
to receive these monks who have come from the far country of
China, inspect their travel papers, and let them proceed. Then
you will be preserving good relations with China." The king
approved this suggestion. The Tang Priest and his disciples
were summoned to the throne hall, where they stood in a row

before the steps and submitted their travel document to the king.

The king had just opened the document and started reading it when the eunuch gate officer came in to report again, "The three Teachers of the Nation are here." This threw the king into such a fluster that he put the paper away, hurried down from the throne, told his attendants to fetch embroidered stools, and went out to meet the Taoist masters. Sanzang and his disciples turned round to look and saw the three Great Immortals come majestically in, followed by a pair of page boys with their hair in bunches. They walked straight in while the civil and military officers all bowed low, not daring to look up. As they entered the throne hall they did not deign to bow to the king, who asked them, "Teachers of the Nation, why have you honoured us with your presence although we have not yet invited you?" "I have something to report," the most senior of the Taoists replied. "Where are those four Buddhist monks from?" "They have been sent from Great Tang in the east to fetch the scriptures from the Western Heaven," the king replied, "and they are here to obtain an exit permit." The three Taoists clapped their hands with delight at this news. "We thought they had already gone, but they are still here." "What do you mean, Teachers?" the king asked in astonishment. "They have only just come to report their names. I was on the point of handing them over to you to use as you will when my tutor made a very sensible suggestion. Out of consideration for the great distance they have come and also to preserve good relations with the land of China I sent for them a moment ago and was just examining their papers when you three Teachers raised this question. Have they offended or harmed you?"

To this the Taoist replied with a smile, "What Your Majesty does not yet know is that they arrived yesterday, killed two of our disciples outside the East Gate, released the five hundred captive Buddhist monks, smashed our cart, broke into our temple at night, destroyed the statues of the Three Pure Ones, and stole their offerings. We were so deceived by them that we thought they were Heavenly Honoured Ones come down to earth and asked them for holy water and elixir pills to present to Your Majesty in the hope of securing eternal life for you. We never expected them to make fools of us by giving us urine. We each drank a mouthful to taste, but when we tried to capture them they escaped. If they are still here now it's a case of meeting your enemy on a narrow road." All this made the king so angry that he ordered the execution of the four monks.

Just at that moment the eunuch gate officer came in once more to report, "Your Majesty, there is a crowd of village elders outside the gates awaiting your summons." "What do they want?" the king asked, and ordered them to be sent in. Thirty or forty of them were brought before the throne hall, where they kowtowed to the king and said, "Your Majesty, there has been no rain this spring and we fear a drought this summer. We have come here to submit a request to Your Majesty that you invite the Teachers of the Nation to pray for timely rain that will save the common people."

"You may withdraw," said the king. "There will be rain." The elders thanked him for his mercy and withdrew. "Tang monks," said the king, "do you know why we honour the Way and persecute Buddhist monks? When the Buddhist monks of this country prayed for rain some years ago they did not get a single drop. It was fortunate that Heaven sent down to us the Teachers of the Nation to bring help and deliverance. You have come from afar and offended the Teachers of the Nation, and you thoroughly deserve to be punished for it. If I spare you for the time being, will you enter a rain-making competition with the Teachers of the Nation? If you can bring about a good fall of rain that saves the common people we shall pardon your crimes, return your papers and let you go. If you fail you will all be taken to the place of execution and publicly executed." "We humble monks know how to pray for things," said Monkey with a smile.

Hearing this, the king ordered that the altars be swept clean and sent for his carriage as he was going to watch the ritual from the Tower of Five Phoenixes. The officials then moved him in his carriage to the tower, where he was soon seated. The Tang Priest stood at the foot of the tower with Monkey, Friar Sand and Pig, while the three Taoist masters sat with the king in the tower. Before long an official galloped in to report, "Everything is ready at the altar. Will the Teacher of the Nation please come to the altar?"

The Great Immortal Tiger Power bowed to take his leave of the king and descended from the tower. Brother Monkey blocked his way and said, "Where are you going, sir?" "To the altar to pray for rain," the immortal replied. "You're being too arrogant," said Monkey. "Why don't you show some courtesy to us monks from far away? Oh well, 'a mighty dragon can't crush a snake in its lair.' You go first, but you'll have to explain to His Majesty." "Explain what?" the Great Immortal asked. "If we both pray for rain at the altar," Monkey replied, "how will we know whether it's your rain or mine? It'll be hard to tell who should get the credit. If later on both sides made false claims that would be terrible. We must have it all sorted out before we start." "When I go to the altar," said the Great Immortal, "this magic wand of mine will give the signal. When it first sounds, the wind will come. The second time the clouds will rise. The third time will bring thunder and lightning. The fourth time it will rain. The fifth time the clouds will break up and the rain will finish." "Splendid," said Monkey with a laugh. "I've never seen anything like that. Please go ahead."

The Great Immortal then strode straight to the gates of the altar compound, followed by Sanzang and his disciples. They looked up to see a raised terrace over thirty feet high. Behind the terrace many Taoist priests were writing things out, and in the middle of them was a stove for burning paper and some model figures representing the messengers who carried the charms and the local gods who supported the Taoist teachings.

The Great Immortal walked straight into the altar enclosure and without any show of modesty went straight up the altar mound and took his place. A young Taoist at his side handed him several yellow pieces of paper that had spells written on them and a precious sword. Holding the sword the Great Immortal recited a spell and burnt a spell on a candle. Two or three of the young Taoists standing below the altar mound passed him a model figure holding a spell and a written document, both of which he also lit and burnt. Then there was a loud report from the wand, and up in the sky the signs of a wind blowing up could be seen. "This is bad," muttered Pig. "The Taoist really has got some powers. He just had to sound his wand once to make the wind blow." "Keep quiet, brothers," said Monkey, "and don't say anything else to me. Look after the master while I get busy."

The splendid Great Sage then plucked out one of his hairs, blew on it with magic breath, called "Change!" and turned it into an imitation Monkey who stood by the Tang Priest while his true self escaped, rose up into the air and shouted, "Who's in charge of the wind?" This threw Granny Wind into such a fluster that she held her cloth bag closed while Young Master Xun tied the string round the mouth. They both came forward and bowed to him. "I'm protecting the holy priest from Tang on his journey to the Western Heaven to fetch the scriptures," Monkey said. "We're now having a rain-making competition with an evil Taoist in the country of Tarrycart. Why are you helping him instead of me? If you put your wind away I'll let you off, but if there's even enough wind to move a whisker in that Taoist's beard I'll give you twenty whacks each with my iron cudgel." "We wouldn't dare help him," said Granny Wind, and the wind then stopped. In his impatience Pig started to yell wildly, "Give up, give up. You've sounded your wand and there's not a breath of wind. Come down now and let us go up."

Once again the Taoist took his magic wand, burnt spells, and made a report with the wand. The sky filled with clouds. "Who's spreading the clouds out?" the Great Sage asked up overhead. Boy Cloudpusher and Young Lord Mistspreader bowed to him. Once again Monkey explained what had happened; Cloudpusher and Mistspreader put the clouds away, and the sun shone brightly once more in a clear sky. "This teacher has been fooling the king and hoodwinking the common people," laughed Pig. "He doesn't really have any powers at all. His wand has sounded for the second time, and there's not a cloud to be seen."

By now the Taoist was getting anxious. Leaning on his sword he let down his hair, said the words of a spell, and cracked his magic wand for the third time. From the Southern Gate of Heaven the Heavenly Lord Deng led Grandfather Thunder and Mother Lightning to bow to Monkey in mid-air. Monkey told them what had happened. As a result the thunder did not sound, nor did the lightning flash.

The Taoist was becoming more anxious than ever. He lit more incense-sticks, burnt charms, said incantations, and sounded his wand once more. The dragon kings of the four seas all gathered in mid-air. "Where are you going, Ao Guang?" Monkey asked. The four dragon kings Ao Guang, Ao Shun, Ao Qin and Ao Run came up and bowed to him. He told them what had happened and said, "When I troubled you the other day you didn't succeed. I hope you will help me again today." "We hear and obey," replied the dragon kings. "Now I would like you to do me a good turn," said Monkey. "That Taoist has now sounded his wand four times, so it's my turn to perform now. As I don't know how to use charms, burn talismans, or sound a magic wand I'll have to ask you gentlemen to help me out."

"We would not dare disobey a command from the Great Sage," Heavenly Lord Deng replied. "But we can only act when proper orders are given. Otherwise the thunder and the rain will happen at the wrong times, and the Great Sage will lose his credibility." "I'll give the signs with my cudgel," said Monkey, to the horror of Grandfather Thunder, who protested, "But my lord, none of us can take your cudgel." "No," said Monkey, "I won't be hitting you with it. When I point up with it the first time I want wind." "We'll let the wind out," promised Granny Wind and Young Master Xun. "The second time I point up I want clouds." "We'll spread out the clouds," said Cloudpusher and Mistspreader. "The third time I point up with the cudgel I want thunder and lightning." "We shall obey, we shall obey," said Grandfather Thunder and Mother Lightning. "The fourth time I point up with the cudgel I want rain." "Your orders will be carried out," the dragon kings replied. "And the fifth time I point up with the cudgel I want the sun shining in a clear sky. I won't have any disobedience or mistakes."

Having given his orders Monkey brought his cloud down, shook his hair, and put it back on his body. None of those with mortal, fleshly eyes could see what had happened. Monkey then called out in a loud voice, "Please finish now, teacher. You have sounded your magic wand four times without producing any wind, clouds, thunder or rain. It's my turn now." The Taoist could stay at the altar no longer; he had to come down and allow Monkey to take his place.

Brother Monkey hurried to the altar compound, tugged at the Tang Priest's clothes, and said, "Master, please climb the altar mound." "But I do not know how to pray for rain, disciple," said Sanzang. "You may not know how to pray for rain," said Monkey, "but you're good at reciting scriptures. I'll help you." Only then did the venerable elder start to climb to the altar. When he reached the top he sat down with great dignity, settled his nature, brought his spirit under control, and quietly recited the *Prajnaparamita Heart Sutra*. As he sat there an official messenger galloped up to him to ask, "Monk, why aren't you sounding a magic wand or burning charms and summonses?" "He doesn't need to," Monkey shouted back. "We pray in stillness and silence."

When Monkey heard that his master had finished reciting the sutra he produced his cudgel from his ear, waved it in the breeze to make it about twelve feet long and as thick as a ricebowl, and pointed it towards the sky. As soon as Granny Wind saw it she opened her leather bag while Young Master Xun untied the rope round its mouth. There was then the howling of a wind that tore off tiles and sent bricks flying throughout the city.

Just as this gale was at its height Brother Monkey gave

another display of his divine powers as he pointed his gold-banded cudgel up into the sky for the second time. In an instant there were dense fog and thick clouds everywhere. Monkey then pointed his gold-banded cudgel into the air a third time.

The thunder roared with the noise of an earthquake or a landslide, so frightening the people in the city that they all burnt incense and imitation money. "Deng," shouted Monkey familiarly, "make sure that you kill me a few more corrupt officials who twist the laws and disobedient sons who do not do their duty to their parents as an example to the people." The thunder became louder than ever, and Monkey pointed his cudgel upwards for the fourth time. The dragons gave their orders and rain filled heaven and earth.

> It pattered on the roof of the tower,
> Splashed against the windows.
> Now that the river in the sky had flooded,
> White waves rolled along the streets.

The rain started at about eight in the morning and lasted till around noon, by when all the streets inside and outside the capital of Tarrycart were running with water. The king then issued a command: "Enough rain has fallen now. If there is any more the growing crops will be drowned and it will be a disaster." The officer on duty at the foot of the Tower of Five Phoenixes whipped his horse and rode through the rain to say, "Holy monk, that is enough rain." Hearing this, Monkey pointed his gold-banded cudgel towards the sky again, and at once the thunder stopped, the wind fell, the rain ceased and the clouds scattered. The king was delighted, and all the civil and military officials said in admiration, "What a marvellous monk. How true it is that however good you are at something there's always somebody better. Our Teachers of the Nation are very effective at making rain, but when they ask for fine weather the drizzle goes on for hours before clearing up. How ever can this monk make the skies clear the moment he gives the word, so that the sun shines bright on the instant and there isn't a cloud to be seen for miles around?"

The king ordered that his carriage be taken back to the court, where he would return the Tang Priest's passport with an exit permit and allow him to go. Just when he was placing the royal seal on the document the three Taoists came in to stop him, saying, "Your Majesty, that rain was caused not by the monk but by our efforts." "But you told me earlier that it did not rain because the dragon kings were not at home," said the king. "When the Buddhist monk went up to the altar and prayed in stillness and silence the rain came. How can you possibly try to take the credit from him?" "When I went to the altar, burnt the charms and summonses and sounded my magic wand," the Great Immortal Tiger Power said, "the dragon kings would not have dared stay away. No doubt they had been called elsewhere, which was why the authorities in charge of wind, cloud, thunder and rain were all out. When they heard my order they hurried here, which happened to be just when I was coming down from the altar and he was going up to it. It was a coincidence that it rained then. Essentially it was I who summoned the dragons and made it rain. The credit can't possibly go to him." In his confusion the king took this suggestion seriously and was once again unable to make up his mind.

Monkey took a step forward, put his hands together in front of his chest, and said, "Your Majesty, these heterodox magic tricks achieved nothing; the credit is neither his nor mine. But the dragon kings of the four seas are still in the sky here. I haven't sent them away, and they wouldn't dare leave on their own initiative. If the Teacher of the Nation can make the dragon kings appear he can take the credit." This delighted the king, who said, "In the twenty-three years we have been on the throne we have never seen what a live dragon looks like. You must both display your magic powers. Whoever can make them come, be he Taoist or Buddhist, will have the credit; and whoever fails will be punished." Of course the Taoists did not have the power. In the presence of the Great Sage the dragon kings would not have dared show their faces in response to a call from the Taoists. "We cannot do it," said the Taoists. "You summon them."

The Great Sage looked up to the sky and yelled at the top of his voice, "Where are you, Ao Guang? You and your brothers must show yourselves to me in your true forms." On hearing this summons the dragon kings soon appeared in their true forms; writhing through the mist and clouds in the sky they danced through the air to the throne hall.

The king burnt incense in his palace hall and the ministers bowed low in worship before the steps. "Now that your noble selves have granted us your presence we need detain you no longer," said the king. "We shall have a thanksgiving mass said another day." "All you gods may now go too," said Monkey. "The king will have a thanksgiving mass said another day." The dragon kings went straight back to their oceans, and the gods all returned to Heaven.

The story tells how when the king saw that Monkey had the power to summon dragons and order gods about he put his seal on the passports and handed them to the Tang Priest, whom he allowed to continue on his journey west. The three Taoist masters were so terrified that they prostrated themselves in the Hall of Golden Bells and submitted a memorial to the king, who came down from his dragon throne, helped them to their feet with his own hand, and said, "Why are you performing this obeisance to me today?" "Your Majesty," the Taoists replied, "we came here to help the country, protect the state and look after the people. We have toiled here for twenty years but now these Buddhist monks have put themselves ahead of us and ruined our reputation with a magic trick. Are you not insulting us by letting them off their death sentences just because of some rain? We implore you to keep their papers and allow us three brothers to challenge them to another competition. What do you think?"

The king of Tarrycart really was muddle-headed: when he heard advice from the east he inclined to the east, and when he was advised from the west he inclined to the west. "What sort of competition with them do you propose, Teachers of the Nation?" he asked. "We would like to compete with them in sitting in meditation," said the Great Immortal Tiger Power. "The Teacher of the Nation must have made a mistake," the king replied. "That monk comes from a sect that practises *dhyana* meditation. He must have mastered the art of meditation before his emperor sent him to fetch the scriptures. Why would you want to compete with him at that?" "The way we sit in meditation," the Great Immortal replied, "is not the ordinary way. It has a special name: 'revealing one's holiness on a cloud ladder'." "What does that mean?" the king asked. "A hundred tables are needed," said the Great Immortal. "Fifty of them are piled one on top of each other to make the meditation platform. One must mount it not by using one's hands or a ladder, but by riding a cloud to take one's seat on it and sit motionless for the agreed number of hours."

Realizing that this was rather difficult he asked this question: "Monks, the Teacher of the Nation would like to compete with you in a way of sitting in meditation called 'revealing one's holiness on a cloud ladder'. Can any of you do that?" When Monkey heard this he kept silent and did not reply. "Brother," asked Pig, "why aren't you saying anything?" "I'll be honest with you," Monkey replied. "When it comes to sitting in meditation I'm beaten. I'm not a sitter by nature. Even if you chained me to an iron column I'd want to wriggle up and down. I'd never want to sit still." Then Sanzang cut in with, "I can sit in meditation." "That's splendid," said Monkey with delight, "splendid. But how long can you do it for?" "When I was young," Sanzang replied, "a monk of the Chan sect who came to my monastery taught the way of fastening one's being to the root, settling the nature, and fixing the spirit while on the boundary of life and death. I can sit for two or three years." "If you're going to sit there for two or three years, Master," said Monkey, "we can give up the idea of going to fetch the scriptures. You won't need to sit there for more than a few hours before coming down." "But I can't get up there, disciple," Sanzang protested. "Go forward and accept the challenge," said Monkey. "I'll get you up there." The venerable elder put his hands together in front of his chest and said, "This humble monk can sit in meditation." The king then ordered that the meditation platforms be built. The state had the resources to tear down mountains, and in less than an hour the two meditation platforms had been built, one to each side of the throne hall.

The Great Immortal Tiger Power then went down from the hall, stood in the middle of the steps, sprang into the air and went straight up on a cloud to the western platform and sat down. Monkey plucked out one of his hairs and turned it into a double of himself that stood below with Pig and Friar Sand while he made his real self into a coloured auspicious cloud that lifted the Tang Priest up through the air to take his seat on the eastern platform. Then he put the cloud away, turned into the tiniest of insects, flow into Pig's ear, and said, "Brother, keep a very close eye on the master and don't talk to my double." "I understand, I understand," replied the idiot with a grin.

The Great Immortal Deer Power had been sitting on his embroidered cushion for a very long time watching the two of them sitting on their high platforms without either emerging as the winner. He decided to help his elder brother, so he plucked a hair from the back of his head, rolled it into a ball, and flicked it straight at the Tang Priest's head, where it turned into a huge bedbug that started biting the venerable elder. Sanzang first itched and then was in pain. When sitting in meditation movements of the hand are forbidden; if he moved his hand he would lose. The agony was soon unbearable, and he pulled his head down to scratch it against his collar. "This is bad," said Monkey. "The master's being driven mad by epilepsy." "No," said Friar Sand, "it's a migraine." When Monkey heard this he said, "Our master is sincere and a gentleman. If he says he can sit in meditation he most certainly can. Gentlemen don't lie. You two shut up while I go up there for a look." The splendid Monkey then flew with a buzz straight up to the Tang Priest's head, where he saw a bedbug the size of a bean biting the master. He immediately picked it off him then scratched and rubbed his head for him, so that the venerable elder did not itch or ache any more and sat up straight again. "Monks have bald heads," thought Brother Monkey, "and not even a louse could settle on one, let alone a bedbug. I think it must have been a trick by those Taoists to get the master killed. Hunh! Well, they haven't won yet, despite their cheating. I'll try a trick on them." Monkey then flew up and landed on the head of one of the ceramic animals on the roof of the palace hall. He shook himself and turned into a poisonous centipede seven inches long that went straight for the Taoist and stung him in the nose. The Taoist could sit still no longer, and tumbling head over heels he fell off the platform and would probably have died had not the senior and junior officials saved him. The horrified king sent the royal tutor to take the Taoist to the Hall of Literary Splendour to comb his hair and clean himself up. Meanwhile Monkey went up on his auspicious cloud to carry his victorious master down to before the steps of the throne hall.

The king ordered that Sanzang be allowed to leave the country, but the Great Immortal Deer Power made this submission: "Your Majesty, my elder brother has long suffered from rheumatism. The heavenly wind in that high place brought on a new attack of his illness, which was why the Buddhist monk won. Please keep him here so that I can compete with him at guessing objects through wooden boards." "What is guessing objects through wooden boards?" the king asked. "This humble Taoist has the power of knowing what is on the other side of a board," Deer Power replied, "and I would like to see whether that Buddhist monk can too. If he is better at guessing than I am, let him go. But if he is not then I hope Your Majesty will decide what crime he is guilty of, avenge us brothers, and not allow our twenty years of protecting the country to be sullied."

The king was so utterly muddle-headed that he accepted this malicious suggestion and ordered that a red lacquered chest be carried by the eunuchs of the royal household into the harem, where his queen was told to put one of her treasures inside. The chest was carried out and set in front of the steps of the throne hall a few moments later. "You two faiths must each compete with your magical powers in guessing what treasure is in the chest," he told the Buddhist and the Taoist. "Disciple," asked Sanzang, "how can I tell what is inside?" Monkey put his cloud away, turned himself back into the smallest of insects, landed on Sanzang's face and said, "Don't worry, master. I'll go and take a look." The splendid Great Sage flew over to the chest, crawled under its legs, and saw a crack between the boards through which he squeezed inside. Here he saw a red lacquer tray in which was placed a set of court robes: a mountain, river and state jacket and a heaven, earth and land skirt. He picked them up, shook and crumpled them, bit the tip of his tongue, sprayed a mouthful of blood over them, called "Change!" and turned them into a worn-out cloak into which he pissed before crawling out through the crack between the boards. He then flew back to the Tang Priest's ear and said, "Master, say that it's a worn-out cloak." "But he told me to guess what treasure is inside," said the Tang Priest. "What sort of treasure is an old cloak?" "Never mind about that," said Monkey. "Just make that guess."

The Tang Priest stepped forward and was just about to state his guess when Deer Power said, "I shall make the first guess. The chest contains a mountain, river and state jacket and a heaven, earth and land skirt." "No," said the Tang Priest, "it does not. The chest contains a rotten cloak." "That monk is being outrageous," said the king. "He has the effrontery to suggest that our country has no treasures by guessing that it contains a tattered old cloak. Execute him!" The two groups of guards officers were just about to fall upon the Tang Priest when he called out desperately, "Your Majesty, spare me for a moment while the chest is opened for you to look inside. If there really is a treasure there I shall accept my punishment; but if there is not you would be doing me an injustice." The king then ordered that the chest be opened, and when the officials in attendance on him opened it and lifted out the red tray he saw that there really was a putrid old cloak on it. "Who put that there?" asked the king in a great fury. The queen then slipped forward from behind the dragon throne to say, "My lord, I put the mountain, river and state jacket and the heaven, earth and land skirt inside myself. I don't know how they can have turned into that." "You may retire, good wife," said the king. "I believe you. All the things used in the harem are of the finest silks and gauzes. We would never have anything like that." He then ordered that the chest be carried up to him so that he could put a treasure inside it himself for another test.

The king then went into the harem, picked a peach as big as a bowl from the magic peach tree in the palace gardens, placed it in the chest and had it carried down for the two of them to guess what it was. "Disciple," said the Tang Priest, "I have to guess again." "Don't worry," said Monkey, "I'll take another look." Once more he buzzed over, went in through the same crack, and saw a peach that was just to his liking. He turned back into himself and ate the peach clean up as he sat in the chest, nibbling every single piece of it, including the damaged parts of the skin, and leaving the stone there when he turned back into the tiniest of insects and flew back to land on Sanzang's ear. "Master," he said, "guess that it's a peach stone." "Don't make a fool of me, disciple," said Sanzang. "If I hadn't spoken up fast just now I would have been executed. This time I must guess that it is something precious, and there is nothing precious about a peach stone." "Don't be afraid," said Monkey. "All that matters is winning."

Before Sanzang could speak the Great Immortal Antelope Power said, "I shall make the first guess. It is a magic peach." "It is not a peach, only a peach stone," said Sanzang. "But we put the peach in there ourself," said the king. "It could not possibly be only a stone. The Third Teacher of the Nation is right." "Your Majesty," put in Sanzang, "open the chest up and look." Once more the officials in attendance carried the chest up to be opened, lifted out the dish, and revealed only a stone with no skin or flesh, a sight that shocked the king. "Teachers of the Nation," he said, "stop competing with him and let him go. We put the magic peach in there with our own hands. If there is only a stone there now, who can have eaten it? He must have gods or demons helping him in secret." As he was saying this the Great Immortal Tiger Power came back into the throne hall after combing his hair and washing himself in the Hall of Literary Splendour. "Your Majesty," he said, "this monk has the art of shifting and changing things. Have the chest brought up here. I will break his magic and have another divination contest with him." "What do you want to guess now?" the king asked. "Magic can change only things, not people," said Tiger Power. "Hide this boy Taoist in the chest, and I guarantee that the monk will not be able to change him." The boy got inside, the lid was put on, and the chest carried down. "Guess what treasure is inside it this third time, monk," the king said. "Again!" exclaimed Sanzang, to which Monkey replied, "Wait while I take another look." Once more he buzzed over and squeezed inside, this time to find a little boy inside.

Monkey shook himself, turned into the exact image of the old Taoist, went into the chest and said, "Disciple." "Where have you come from, master?" the boy asked him. "I came by disappearing magic," Monkey replied. "What instructions do you have for me?" the boy asked. "The Buddhist monk saw you getting into the chest," said Monkey, "and if he says that there's a young Taoist in here we'll have lost. I've come here to work out a plan with you. We'll shave your head and guess that you're a Buddhist monk." "Do whatever you decide, master," said the boy, "as long as we win. If we lose to him again our reputation will be ruined and the king will have no more respect for us." "You are right," said Monkey. "Come here, my boy, and if we win I'll reward you richly." He then turned his gold-banded cudgel into a razor, put his arms firmly round the boy, and said, "Put up with the pain, there's a good boy, and don't make a sound while I shave your head." In an instant he had shaved off the boy's hair, which he stuffed into a ball and hid in a corner of the chest. Then he put the razor away and stroked the boy's shaven pate saying, "Your head looks like a Buddhist monk's now, my boy, but your clothes are wrong. Take them off and I'll transform them for you." The boy took off his greenish-white cloud-patterned crane cloak with embroidered brocade hems. Monkey blew on it with a magic breath, called "Change!" and turned it into a brown Buddhist monk's habit for the boy to put on. Monkey pulled out two more hairs and turned them into a wooden fish that he gave to the boy saying, "Listen carefully, disciple. Whatever happens don't come out when you hear a call of 'Taoist boy'. But when you hear someone say 'Buddhist monk', lift the lid of the chest with your head, strike the wooden fish, and come out reciting a Buddhist sutra. Do that and we will win." "But I can only recite the *Classic of the Three Officials*, the *Classic of the Dipper*, and the *Classic of Elimination of Disaster*," said the boy, "I don't know any Buddhist scriptures." "Can you recite the name of a Buddha?" asked Monkey. "Anyone can recite 'Amitabha Buddha'," the boy replied. "That'll have to do then," said Monkey. "Recite the Buddha's name and save me the trouble of having to teach you a sutra. Remember what I've told you as I'm going now." Monkey then turned back into the tiniest of insects, squeezed out, flew back to beside the Tang Priest's ear, and said, "Master, say that there's a Buddhist monk inside."

As Monkey was saying this the Great Immortal Tiger Power said, "Your Majesty, this third time there is a Taoist boy inside." Tiger Power called and called but the boy would not come out. Sanzang then put his hands together and said, "There is a monk inside." "There's a monk inside the chest," shouted Pig at the top of his voice, at which the boy raised the lid of the chest with his head and stepped out, beating his wooden fish and repeating the name of the Buddha. The civil and military officials were so delighted that they all cheered; while the terrified Taoists were at a loss for words. "This monk is being helped by gods and demons," said the king. "How else could he have got into the chest as a Taoist boy and stepped out as a Buddhist monk? Even if a barber had got in with him he could only have shaved his head; but he's wearing a well-fitting habit and repeating the Buddha's name too. Teachers of the Nation, you must let those monks go."

To this the Great Immortal Tiger Power replied, "Your Majesty, this is a case of a chess-player meeting his match, or a general coming up against a master strategist. We would like to try the martial arts we learned as boys in the Zhongnan Mountains against him." "What martial arts?" the king asked. "We three brothers all have some divine powers," Tiger Power replied. "We can put our heads back on when they have been cut off; open up our chests, cut out our hearts, and make ourselves whole again; and take a bath in boiling oil." "But those are all certain death," exclaimed the king in horror. "We have these powers," said Tiger Power, "which is why I can give you a clear undertaking that we will not give up until we have been allowed a tournament with him."

Monkey had just turned himself back into the tiniest of insects and gone over to investigate when he heard all this. Reverting to his real form he roared with laughter and said, "What luck, what marvellous luck. Business has brought itself to my front door." "But those are all ways of getting yourself killed," said Pig. "How can you talk about business coming to your front door?" "You still don't know my powers," said Monkey.

Monkey then stepped forward and said, "Your Majesty, this humble monk can be beheaded." "What do you mean, you can be beheaded?" the king asked. "When I was cultivating my conduct in the monastery many years ago," Monkey replied, "a dhyana monk who came there taught me a method of being beheaded. I don't know if it's any good, and I'd like to try it out today." "That monk is too young to have any sense," said the king with a smile. "Having your head cut off isn't something that you can try out for fun. Your head is the chief of the Six Positives, and when it's cut off you're dead." "Your Majesty," said the Great Immortal Tiger Power, "this is just the way I want him to act so that we can get our revenge on him." Believing him, the foolish monarch ordered that a place for public execution be prepared.

As soon as the order was given, three thousand men of the

royal guard were drawn up outside the palace gates. "The monk shall be beheaded first," said the king. Monkey cheerfully agreed: "I'll go first, I'll go first." Then he put his hands together and shouted, "Teacher of the Nation, I hope you'll forgive my effrontery in going first." Monkey then turned round and went outside. "Be careful, disciple," said Sanzang, catching hold of him as he passed, "this is no place for fooling about." "What's there to be afraid of?" said Monkey. "Stop holding me; let me go."

The Great Sage went straight to the execution ground, where the executioners grabbed him and tied him up so that he was like a ball. When he was placed high on the earthen mound a shout of "Behead him!" was heard, and his head was cut off as the sword whistled down. The executioners then kicked it and sent it rolling thirty or forty paces away like a ripe watermelon. No blood came from Monkey's throat as a shout of "Come here, head" rose from his stomach. The Great Immortal Tiger Power was so appalled by this display of magical skill that he said a spell and ordered the local deity, "Hold on to that head. When I've beaten this monk I shall request His Majesty to rebuild your little shrine as a big temple and replace your clay statue with a gold one." Now the local deity was under Tiger Power's control because Tiger Power had the five-thunder magic, so he held Monkey's head down. "Come here, head," Monkey called again, but his head was no more able to move than if it had taken root there. Monkey was now feeling anxious, so he made a spell with his hands, burst out of the ropes that were binding him, and shouted, "Grow!" In a flash another head grew on his neck, so terrifying the executioners and the soldiers of the guard army that they all shivered and shook. The officer supervising the executions rushed into the palace to report, "Your Majesty, when the little monk's head was cut off he grew another one." "So that's another trick our brother can do," said Pig to Friar Sand with a mocking laugh. "As he can do seventy-two transformations," said Friar Sand, "he has seventy-two heads."

Before he had finished saying this Monkey came back and

282

called, "Master!" "Was it painful, disciple?" asked a greatly relieved Sanzang. "No, it wasn't painful," said Monkey, "it was fun."

While the brother-disciples were congratulating each other they heard the king calling on them to take their passport and saying, "We grant you a full pardon. Go at once." "We accept the passport, but we insist that the Teacher of the Nation must be beheaded too to see what happens," said Monkey. "Senior Teacher of the Nation," said the king, "that monk's not going to let you off. You promised to beat him, and don't give me another fright this time." Tiger Power then had to take his turn to go to be tied up like a ball by the executioners and have his head cut off with a flash of the blade and sent rolling over thirty paces when it was kicked away. No blood came from his throat either, and he too called out, "Come here, head." Monkey instantly pulled out a hair, blew a magic breath on it, said, "Change!" and turned it into a brown dog that ran across the execution ground, picking the Taoist's head up with its teeth and dropping it into the palace moat.

The Taoist shouted three times but did not get his head to come back. As he did not have Monkey's art of growing a new one the red blood started to gush noisily from his neck.

No use were his powers to call up wind and rain;
He could not compete with the true immortal again.

A moment later his body collapsed into the dust, and everyone could see that he was really a headless yellow-haired tiger.

Deer Power then rose to his feet and said, "My elder brother's life is now over, but he was no tiger. That monk in his wickedness must have used some deception magic to turn my elder brother into a beast. I will never forgive him for this, and am resolved to compete with him in opening the stomach and cutting out the heart."

When the king heard this he pulled himself together and said, "Little monk, the Second Teacher of the Nation wants another competition with you." "I hadn't had a cooked meal for ages," said Monkey, "until the other day I was given a meal at a vegetarian's house on our journey west. I ate rather a lot of steamed bread, and my stomach has been aching recently. I think I must have worms, so I'd be glad to borrow Your Majesty's sword, cut my stomach open, take out my innards, and give my spleen and my stomach a good clean-out before going to the Western Heaven." When the king heard this he said, "Take him to the place of execution." A whole crowd of people fell upon Monkey, took hold of him, and began dragging him there. Monkey pulled his hands free and said, "No need to grab hold of me. I can walk there myself. There's just one condition: my hands mustn't be tied up as I will need them to wash my innards." The king then ordered that his hands be left free.

Monkey walked with a swagger straight to the execution ground, where he leant against the stake, undid his clothes, and exposed his stomach. The executioners tied ropes round his neck and his legs, then made a quick cut in his stomach with a knife shaped like a cow's ear. This made a hole into which Monkey thrust both his hands to open it further as he brought out his entrails. He spent a long time checking them over carefully before putting them all back inside. Then he bent over again, pinched the skin of his stomach together, breathed a magic breath on it, called out, "Grow!" and made it join up again. The king was so shocked that he gave Monkey the passport with his own hands, saying, "Here is your passport. Please don't let me delay you holy monks on your journey west any longer." "Never mind the passport," said Monkey, "but what about asking the Second Teacher of the Nation to be cut open?" "This is nothing to do with me," the king said to Deer Power. "You wanted a match with him, and now you must go ahead." "Don't worry," said Deer Power. "I cannot possibly lose to him."

Watch him as he swaggers like the Great Sage Monkey to the execution ground to be tied up by the executioners and have his stomach cut open with a whistle of the cow's-ear knife. He too took out his entrails and sorted them out with his own hands. Monkey meanwhile pulled out one of his hairs, blew on it with a magic breath, shouted, "Change!" and turned it into a hungry eagle that spread its wings, stretched out its claws, swooped down, grabbed the Taoist's internal organs, heart, liver and all, and flew off nobody knew where to devour them. The Taoist was

> Left as an empty, eviscerated ghost,
> With no entrails or stomach as he wanders around lost.

The executioners kicked the wooden stake down and dragged the body over to look at it. To their surprise they found it was that of a white-haired deer.

To this the Great Immortal Antelope Power submitted the following reply: "How could my elder brother possibly look like an animal after his death? This is all the result of that monk using magic to ruin us. Let me avenge my elder brother." "What magic arts do you have at which you might beat him?" the king asked. "I will compete with him at bathing in boiling oil," Antelope Power replied. The king then ordered that a great cauldron be brought out and filled with sesame oil for the two of them to have their competition. "I'm most grateful for your consideration," said Monkey. "I haven't had a bath for a very long time, and these last couple of days my skin has begun to itch. I need a good, hot soak."

The officials in attendance on the king then set the cauldron of oil in position, built up a pile of dry firewood, set it burning fiercely, and heated the oil till it boiled and bubbled. Monkey was told to go in first. He put his hands together in front of his chest and said, "Is it to be a gentle bath or a rough one?" When the king asked him what they were, Monkey replied, "For a gentle bath you keep your clothes on, stretch your hands wide out, do a roll and come up again without getting your clothes at all dirty. If there is even a spot of oil on them you have lost. For a rough bath you need a clothes rack and a wash towel. You take your clothes off, jump in and somersault or do dragonfly-stands as you play around and wash yourself." "Do you want to compete with him at gentle baths or rough ones?" the king asked Antelope Power. "If it is gentle baths," said Antelope Power, "he might have treated his clothes with some drug that will keep the oil off. Let it be rough baths then." Monkey then stepped forward and said, "Excuse my impertinence in always going first." Watch him while he takes off his tunic and tigerskin kilt, jumps into the cauldron, and dives through the waves, enjoying himself as much as if he were swimming in water.

At the sight of this Pig bit his finger and said to Friar Sand, "We've underestimated that Monkey. I usually say nasty things about him as if he just liked fooling about. I never realized he had powers like this." When Monkey saw the two of them whispering his praises to each other, he thought suspiciously, "The idiot's mocking me again. How true it is that the clever have to do all the work and the clumsy stay idle. Here's me leaping around like this while he's standing there at his ease. Right, then. I'll get him tied up in knots and give him a real scare." In the middle of washing himself he made a great splash and plunged down to the bottom of the cauldron where he turned himself into a jujube stone. He did not come up again.

The officer supervising the executions went up to the king and reported, "Your Majesty, the little monk has been fried to death in the boiling oil." The king in his delight ordered that the bones be fished out for him to see. The executioners fetched an iron strainer on a long handle with which they fished around in the cauldron, but its mesh was so coarse that Monkey, who was now as small as a nail, kept slipping through the holes in it and they could not fish him out. They then reported that the monk was so small and his bones so soft that they had been fried right away.

"Arrest the three monks," the king ordered. The guard officers in attendance grabbed Pig first as he looked dangerous, pushed him down, and tied him up with his hands behind his back. They dragged Pig by his ears to the cauldron. Then the idiot said, snorting with anger as he lay tied up on the ground,

> "*Trouble-making monkey,*
> *Ignorant Protector of the Horses.*
> *The monkey deserved to die,*
> *The Protector had to fry.*
> *The Monkey found it too hot,*
> *The Protector's had his lot.*"

When Monkey at the bottom of the cauldron heard the idiot abusing him like that he could not restrain himself from turning back into himself, standing up in the cauldron, and saying, "Dreg-guzzling moron! Who do you think you're swearing at?" "Disciple," said Sanzang on seeing him, "you gave me a terrible fright." "Big Brother's used to shamming dead," said Friar Sand. The civil and military officials were thrown into such a panic that they went forward to report to the king, "Your Majesty, the monk did not die. He has just stood up in the cauldron." The officer supervising the executions was afraid that he would be in trouble for having earlier made a false report to the king, so he submitted a new one: "The monk did die, but as this is an ill-omened day he has come back as a ghost to haunt us."

This made Monkey so angry that he sprang out of the cauldron, wiped the oil off himself, put on his clothes, pulled out his cudgel, and hit the supervisor of the executions so hard that his head turned to a meatball. "A ghost, indeed," he said, giving the officers such a fright that they untied Pig, fell to their knees, and pleaded, "Forgive us, forgive us." As the king came down from his dragon throne Monkey went into the hall, seized hold of him, and said, "Don't go, Your Majesty. Make the Third Teacher of the Nation get into the cauldron of oil now." "Third Teacher of the Nation," said the king with much trembling, "you must get into the cauldron at once to save my life. Don't let the monk hit me." Antelope Power then went down from the throne hall and like Monkey took off his clothes, jumped into the oil, and went through the motions of washing himself.

Monkey let the king go, went up to the cauldron, and told those tending the fire to add more fuel. Then he put out his hand to feel and found to his astonishment that the bubbling oil was icy cold. "It was boiling hot when I had my bath," he thought, "but it's cold for his. I'm sure that one of the dragon kings must be protecting him." He leapt straight up into mid-air, said the magic word "*Om*", and summoned the Dragon King of the Northern Ocean. "I'll get you, you horned worm, you loach with scales on," said Monkey. "How dare you help the Taoist by protecting the bottom of the cauldron as a cold dragon and letting him beat me in this display of divine powers!" The dragon king was so frightened that he kept making respectful noises as he replied, "I'd never have dared help him. There is more to this than you realize, Great Sage. That evil beast has strenuously cultivated his conduct, shaken off his original shell, and has only really kept his five-thunder magic. In all other respects he has taken the path of heresy and could never return to the true Way. This is the 'Great Opening-up' that he learned on Lesser Mount Mao. The other two have already had their powers defeated by you, Great Sage, and reverted to their true appearances. The cold dragon this one uses is one that he created for himself, but it is only a trick with which to fool common mortals: it could not deceive you, Great Sage. I shall now take that cold dragon under my control, and guarantee that his skin and bones will now be fried to a crisp." "Hurry up about it if you don't want a beating," said Monkey, at which the dragon king changed into a fierce gust of wind that seized the cold dragon and carried it off to the sea.

Monkey now came down to earth and stood beside Sanzang, Pig and Friar Sand in front of the throne hall watching the Taoist struggling without success to climb out of the boiling oil. Then the Taoist slipped back into the cauldron, and in an instant his bones came apart as his skin was fried crisp and his flesh cooked tender.

The official supervising the executions came in again to report, "Your Majesty, the Third Teacher of the Nation has been deep-fried to death." Tears gushed from the king's eyes as he struck the table by the throne and cried aloud. He wept till nightfall.

Then Monkey stepped forward and called out, "Don't be so silly. Look at those Taoists' bodies. One was a tiger and the other was a deer. Antelope Power was an antelope. If you don't believe me, have his bones fished out and take a look at them. Is that a human skeleton? They were all mountain beasts who became spirits and came here to destroy you. The only reason they had not struck yet was because your life force is still strong; but in another couple of years when your life force was weaker they would have murdered you and your whole kingdom would have been theirs. You are very lucky that we came here in time to destroy their evil and save your life. What are you crying for? Give us our passport at once and let us go." This finally brought the king to his senses. He expressed his gratitude to Sanzang and his disciples by preparing a vegetarian banquet for them. The king also agreed to stop persecuting the Buddhist monks in his realm, and recalled them all. Monkey urged him to ensure the security of his kingdom by honouring the Buddhist clergy and the Way of Taoism, and educating men of talent in the Confucian tradition. Next day, the king and his officials accompanied the Tang Priest out of the city. They then said farewell to each other.

CHAPTER 26
At the River of Heaven Guanyin
Subdues the Goldfish

Setting out at dawn and not stopping till nightfall, they
drank when thirsty and ate when hungry. Before they realized
it spring and summer were over and it was autumn again. One
night, when they were looking for somewhere to stay, they heard
the sound of waves. "That's done it," said Pig. "We've come
to the end of the road." "There's a river in our way," said Friar
Sand. "How are we going to get across?" asked the Tang Priest.
"Let me test it for depth," said Pig. The idiot then picked up
a stone and threw it into the water; they heard the bubbles rising
as the stone sunk. "It's deep, too deep," he said, "we'll never
get across." "You have tested for depth," said the Tang Priest,
"but we don't know how wide it is." "I can't tell that," said Pig.
"Let me have a look," said Monkey. The splendid Great Sage
sprang up into mid-air on his cloud and took a good look. He
saw that there was no end to its waters in sight.

Monkey brought his cloud quickly down, put it away, and
reported, "It's wide, Master, very wide. We'll never get across
it. My fiery eyes with their golden pupils can see three hundred
miles by day and distinguish good from evil too. By night they
can see a hundred to a hundred and fifty miles. If even I can't
see the other bank goodness only knows how wide it is."

Sanzang was speechless with shock, then he sobbed, "What
are we to do, disciples?" "Don't cry, Master," said Friar Sand.
"There's someone standing by the river over there."   "I expect

it's a fisherman working his nets," said Monkey. "I'll go and ask him." Monkey took his iron cudgel in his hand and was before the man in two or three bounds, only to discover that it was in fact a stone tablet on which was inscribed in an ancient script three words in large letters and nine words in two rows of little ones underneath. The three words written large were RIVER OF HEAVEN, and the words in small writing were "250 miles across; few travellers have ever been here." "Master," called Monkey, "come and take a look." When Sanzang read this he said through his tears, "Disciple, when I left Chang'an all those years ago I thought that the Western Heaven would be easy to get to. I never knew that so many evil monsters would block my way, or that there would be such enormous mountains and rivers to cross."

"Listen, Master," said Pig. "Where is that sound of drums and cymbals coming from? It must be people holding a religious feast. Let's go and get some of the food to eat and find out where there is a boat that will ferry us across tomorrow." When Sanzang listened as he sat on the horse he could hear that it really was the sound of drums and cymbals. "Those aren't Taoist instruments," he said. "It must be some Buddhist monks performing a ceremony. Let's go there." Monkey led the horse as they headed towards the music. There was no track to follow as they climbed and then lost height again and crossed sandbanks until a village of some four or five hundred households came into sight.

When Sanzang dismounted he saw a house at the end of the road. He then took off his rain hat, straightened his habit, took his monastic staff in his hand and went bareheaded to the gates, which were ajar. Not venturing to walk in uninvited, Sanzang stood there for a while until a very old man with prayer-beads round his neck who was repeating the name of Amitabha Buddha came out to shut the gate. Sanzang at once put his hands together before his chest and said, "I salute you, benefactor." The old man returned his greeting then said, "You're too late, monk." "What do you mean?" Sanzang asked. "You're too late to get anything," the old man said. "If you had been here earlier we were giving each monk a good meal, three pints of polished rice, a piece of white cloth, and ten copper cash. Why have you only come now?" "Benefactor," Sanzang replied, "I am not here to collect offerings." "If you're not here for offerings, what are you here for then?" the old man asked. "I have been sent by the Emperor of the Great Tang in the east to fetch the scriptures from the Western Heaven," Sanzang replied. "It was already late when I reached this village, and I have come here to beg for a night's shelter because I heard the drums and cymbals. I will be on my way at dawn." The old man shook his hand at him as he replied, "Monk, men of religion should not tell lies. Great Tang in the east is 18,000 miles from here. How could you have come from there by yourself?" "You are quite right, benefactor," said Sanzang. "I have only been able to reach here because I have three disciples who protect me. They clear paths across mountains and build bridges across rivers." "If you have these disciples," the old man said, "why aren't they with you? But do come in. We have room for you to stay here." Sanzang then looked back and called, "Come here, disciples."

As Monkey was impatient by nature, Pig coarse, and Friar Sand impetuous, the moment they heard their master calling they grabbed the horse's bridle and the luggage and ran there hell for leather. The sight of them gave the old man such a shock that he collapsed, muttering, "Demons, demons." "Please don't be afraid, benefactor," said Sanzang. "They're not demons, they are my disciples." "But how could so handsome a master have such hideous disciples?" asked the old man, still shivering and shaking. "They may not be much to look at;" said Sanzang, "but they certainly know how to subdue dragons and tigers and capture monsters and demons." The old man was not entirely convinced as he helped the Tang Priest inside.

Monkey picked up a torch, lit some lamps and candles, and pulled up an armchair for the Tang Priest to sit in while the disciples sat on either side of him. As they were sitting there talking they heard a door leading from the inner part of the house being opened. Another old man came in leaning on a stick and asking, "What evil spirits are you, coming to this pious household in the middle of the night?" The first old man, who was sitting in front of them, rose and went to meet him behind the screen saying, "Stop shouting, elder brother. These aren't demons. This is an arhat sent from Great Tang in the east to fetch the scriptures. His disciples may look evil but really they are very good." Only then did the old man put his stick down and bow in greeting to the four of them, after which he too sat down in front of them and called for tea and vegetarian food.

Sanzang bowed to his hosts to thank them for the meal, then asked them their surname. "We are called Chen," they replied. "Then you are kinsmen of mine," said Sanzang, putting his hands together in front of his chest. "Is your surname Chen as well?" the old men asked. "Yes," Sanzang replied, "Chen was my surname before I became a monk. May I ask why you were holding that religious feast just now?" "It was a feast to prepare for death," the old men replied. "You don't know who you're talking to," said Pig, falling about with laughter. "As monks we know all about maigre-feasts. There are only preparatory maigre-feasts for transferring money to the underworld and for fulfilling vows. Nobody's died here, so why have a funeral feast?"

"Old man," Monkey said to him, "what you said must be wrong. How can you have a feast to prepare for death?" At this the two old men bowed and replied, "And if you were going to fetch the scriptures why did you come here instead of taking the main route?" "We were on the main route," replied Monkey, "but a river was in our way and we weren't able to cross it. We came to your distinguished residence to ask for a night's shelter because we heard the drums and cymbals." "What did you see by the side of the river?" one of the old men asked. "Nothing but a stone tablet on which was written 'River of Heaven' above and '250 miles across; few travellers have ever been here' underneath," Monkey replied. "Less than half a mile along the bank from the stone tablet is the Temple of the Great King of Miraculous Response," the old man said. "Did you not see it?" "No," Monkey replied. "Would you old gentlemen tell me why he's called 'Miraculous Response'?" The two old men burst into tears as they replied, "The Great King of Miraculous Response sends timely rain to the farms, which is a great favour to the villagers. However, he requires us to provide boys and girls for him to eat."

"He likes eating boys and girls?" Brother Monkey exclaimed. "Yes," replied the old man. "I suppose it's your family's turn now," said Monkey. "Yes, this year it is our turn," the old man said. "There are a hundred households living here. There is a sacrifice to the Great King every year at which a boy, a girl, pigs, sheep, oxen and wine have to be offered. If he gets his meal he gives us wind and rain at the right time; but if there is no sacrifice he sends disaster." "How many sons are there in your household?" Monkey asked. The old man beat his breast and said, "Alas, alas, we die of shame when you speak of sons. This is my brother, Chen Qing, who is fifty-seven. I am Chen Cheng and am sixty-two. As I had no son my friends and relations persuaded me to take a concubine when I was nearly fifty. I had no option but to find one and we had a daughter. She is just seven this year, and we call her Pan of Gold."

"What about sons?" Monkey asked. "My brother has a son who was also by a concubine. He is six this year, and we call him Chen Guan-given. My brother and I are 120 between us if you add our ages together, and these are our only two offspring. We never imagined that it would fall to us to provide the sacrificial offerings this year, and this is a duty we cannot escape. It is because as fathers we cannot bear to part from our children that we held this service to bring about rebirth, this maigre-feast to prepare for death."

"So it's like that," said Monkey. "Very well then, bring your son out for me to take a look at him." Chen Qing hurried to the inner part of the house, brought Guan-given back with him into the hall, and set the boy down in front of the lamp. Not realizing the mortal danger he was in the little boy leapt about, filled his sleeves with fruit, ate and played around. Monkey looked at him, said a spell silently, shook himself, and made himself look just like Guan-given. Then the two boys started to jump and dance in front of the lamp, giving the two old men such a shock that they fell to their knees. "Would I do for the sacrifice like that?" asked Monkey. "Perfect," said the old man, "just perfect. You would be accepted."

"I shall take the child's place and keep him alive for your family to have descendants to burn incense to you," said Monkey. "I shall be offered to the Great King instead." At this Chen Qing kowtowed as he knelt there, saying, "My lord, if in your mercy you were to take his place I will give His Reverence the Tang Priest a thousand ounces of silver towards the cost of his journey to the Western Heaven." "Aren't you going to reward me?" asked Monkey. "But if you are sacrificed in the boy's place it will be the end of you," said the old man. "What do you mean?" Monkey asked. "The Great King will eat you," the old man replied. "He'd dare to eat me?" said Monkey. "The only reason he might not eat you would be if he thought you would taste too high," the old man said. "Let Heaven do as it will," said Monkey. "If I'm eaten up it'll be because I'm fated to have a short life; and if I'm not eaten it'll be because I'm lucky. Take me to the sacrifice."

While Chen Qing kowtowed, expressed his thanks, and presented them with five hundred ounces of silver, Chen Cheng neither kowtowed nor thanked Monkey, but leant against the doorway sobbing. As soon as Brother Monkey noticed this he went up to him, took hold of his clothes, and said, "Old man, is it because you can't bear to lose your daughter that you're not giving me anything or thanking me?" Only then did Chen Cheng fall to his knees and reply, "Yes, I cannot bear to lose her. It is enough that in your great kindness you are saving my nephew by taking his place. But I have no son. She is my only child and she would weep for me bitterly after my death. I cannot bear to lose her." "Then you'd better go along at once and cook five bushels of rice and some good vegetarian dishes for that long-snouted venerable gentleman to eat. Then I'll make him turn into the likeness of your daughter and the two of us will be able to take part in the sacrifice. We'll see if we can do a meritorious deed and save your children's lives."

魔弄寒風飄雪大

The Monster Makes a Snowstorm

Chen Cheng then hurried inside and came back into the hall with Pan of Gold in his arms. "There's the girl," said Monkey. "Make yourself like her at once. We're off to the sacrifice." "But she's much too small and delicate for me to turn into, brother," said Pig. "Hurry up if you don't want me to hit you," said Monkey. "Don't hit me," pleaded Pig in desperation. "I'll see if I can make the change."

The idiot then said the words of a spell, shook his head several times, called "Change!" and really did make his head look like the little girl's. The only trouble was that his belly was still much too fat and disproportionately big. "Change some more," said Monkey with a laugh. "Hit me then," said Pig. "I can't change any more, and that's that." "But you can't have a little girl's head on a monk's body," said Monkey. "You won't do at all like that — you're neither a man nor a girl. Do the Dipper star-steps." Monkey then blew on him with magic breath and in fact did change his body to make it look like the little girl's. "Will you two old gentlemen please take the young master and the young lady inside and make no mistake about who they are," said Monkey. "My brother and I will be trying to dodge the monster and fooling around, and we may come in here, so that it will be hard to tell us from the real children. Have some fruit ready for them to eat and don't let them cry, in case the Great King notices and our secret gets out. Now we're off to see if we can fool him."

When Monkey and Pig were each sitting on a red lacquer dish they heard gongs and drums as the villagers opened the front gates and poured in, shouting, "Bring out the boy and the girl." The four young men then carried Monkey and Pig out to the sobs and wails of the old men.

The story tells how the believers in Chen Village noisily carried Monkey and Pig with pork, mutton, beef and wine straight to the Temple of Miraculous Response, where they set them all out with the young boy and girl in the most prominent place. Monkey looked around and saw that the offertory tables were covered with fragrant flowers and wax candles. In front of him was a tablet on which were inscribed in letters of gold,

GREAT KING OF MIRACULOUS RESPONSE. There were no statues of any other gods. When the believers had set everything out properly they all kowtowed and made this prayer:

'Great King, our lord, at this hour of this day of this month of this year Chen Cheng, the master of the sacrifice, and all the other faithful of different ages beg to offer in accordance with annual custom the little boy Chen Guan-given, the little girl Pan of Gold, pork, mutton, beef and wine for the delectation of the Great King. We beg you to give us the right amounts of wind and rain and to grant a good harvest for all our crops." After praying they burnt paper horses and all went home.

After a while they heard the howling of a wind outside. A moment later an evil creature came in through the temple doors. He had a golden helmet on his head and wore a gold armour with a jade belt at his waist. His teeth resembled those on a pair of saws.

The monster stood blocking the entrance to the temple and asked, "Who is making the sacrifice this year?" "Thank you for asking," Monkey replied. "This year the village heads are the family of Chen Cheng and Chen Qing." This reply struck the monster as very odd. "That boy has a lot of courage," he thought, "and he's a good talker too. Usually the children who are offered say nothing the first time I ask them a question and are frightened out of their wits the second time. Before I've even grabbed them in my hand they are already dead. So why's this boy today so good at answering?" Instead of seizing him the monster asked another question: "What is your name, boy?" "My name is Chen Guan-given, and the girl is called Pan of Gold." "According to the old custom of this sacrifice I should eat you first," said the monster. "I have no objection," said Brother Monkey. "Enjoy your meal." Hearing this the monster was once more afraid to grab Monkey, so instead he blocked the doorway and shouted, "I'll have none of your answering back. Usually I eat the boy first, but this year I shall start with the girl." "Better to follow the old custom," said Pig in a panic.

"Don't break with tradition."

Without any more discussion the monster made a grab for Pig, who leapt down, turned back into himself, and struck at the monster's hand with his rake. The monster pulled his hand back and fled. All that could be heard was a mighty clang. "I've smashed his armour," exclaimed Pig. Monkey, who had resumed his own true form as well, looked, saw two fish scales the size of an ice dish, and gave a shout of "After him!" The two of them sprang up into the air, where the monster, who had come unarmed to his feast, asked them from a cloud, "Where are you from, monks, and why have you come here to bully me, spoil my offerings, and ruin my reputation?" "What you don't realize, damned monster," Monkey replied, "is that we are disciples of the holy priest Sanzang from Great Tang in the east who has been sent by his emperor to fetch the scriptures from the Western Heaven. We were spending last night at the Chen household when we were told that an evil spirit pretending to be Miraculous Response demands the sacrifice of a boy and a girl every year. In our mercy we decided to save life and capture you, damned monster. You'd better make a full and true confession at once. How long have you been here calling yourself 'Great King', and at two a year how many little boys and girls have you eaten? Given me a full account and return them to me if you want your life spared." At that the monster fled, avoiding another blow that Pig struck at him with his rake. He turned into a wild wind and went straight into the River of Heaven.

"No need to chase him," said Monkey. "I'm sure the monster's a river creature. We'll have to work out a way of catching him and getting the master across the river tomorrow." Pig accepted this suggestion and went straight back to the temple, from where he carried the offerings of pork, mutton and wine, tables and all, back to the Chen house. Monkey reported how he had told the monster who he was and chased him into the river, to the immense delight of the two old gentlemen, who ordered that the side rooms were to be swept out and furnished with beds. Here the master and his disciples were invited to spend the night.

The Tang Priest and his three disciples slept in the Chen house. Shortly before dawn they all began to feel very cold in their bedding. As neither master nor disciples could sleep they rose and dressed. When they opened the door to look outside they saw to their astonishment a vast expanse of white. They spent the day enjoying the snowy scenery with their hosts.

Pig rose next day and said, "Brother, it was even colder last night. I think the river really must have frozen solid." Sanzang went to the door, bowed low to Heaven, and prayed, "All you gods who protect the teachings, on my journey west I have faithfully worshipped the Buddha and crossed many a river and mountain with great suffering and never a word of complaint. I am deeply grateful for Heaven's help in bringing me this far, and I also give most humble thanks that the river has now frozen. When I bring the scriptures back I shall report all this to the Tang Emperor and reward you sincerely." When he had finished his prayer he and his disciples prepared to leave so that they could cross the river while it was frozen.

When Sanzang and his party reached the bank of the river they reined in their horses to have a look. Pig jumped down from his horse. "I'm going to find out how thick the ice is." The idiot hitched up his clothes, strode to the edge of the river, raised his rake with both hands, and brought it down with all his might. There was a hollow thump as nine white scars appeared on the ice. His hand had been painfully jarred. "We can go," said the idiot with a grin, "we can go. It's frozen solid right down to the bottom." Only then did they start to cross.

As they were walking they heard a loud creaking noise from under the ice which so frightened the white horse that it almost fell over. "Disciples," asked Sanzang with horror, "what was that noise?" "The river has frozen so solid that it's made the earth rumble," said Pig. "Or perhaps the river's frozen right to the bottom here in the middle." Half reassured but still half terrified, Sanzang whipped the horse forward and they carried on.

300

Fighting for Sanzang in the Underwater Palace

Since coming back to his watery palace the evil monster had been waiting under the ice with all his spirits for a long time. As soon as he heard the horse's hoofs he used his magic to make the ice burst noisily open, giving Monkey such a fright that he sprang up into mid-air. The other three and the white horse sank into the water, where the evil monster captured Sanzang and took him back to his underwater palace with all his spirits. The monster had Sanzang stored away in a six-foot-long stone chest behind the palace.

Pig and Friar Sand meanwhile recovered the luggage in the river, loaded it on the back of the white horse, and swam up through the waves as they parted the waters. When Monkey saw them from up in the air he asked, "Where's the master?" "We can't find him anywhere, so let's go back ashore and decide what to do," Pig replied.

The three brothers returned to the Chen house, ate their fill, handed the horse and the luggage over to the care of the Chen houschold, got their weapons ready, and hurried off to the bank of the river to find their master.

Monkey explained that his magical powers did not work very well in the water as he had to be making hand spells all the time or else turn himself into something like a fish or crab. Pig then took Monkey on his back.

Friar Sand parted a way through the waters of the River of Heaven for the brother-disciples. They had covered many miles on the riverbed. When they looked up to see a tall building on which was written in large letters RESIDENCE OF THE RIVER TURTLE. "This must be where the monster lives," said Friar Sand. "We two can't go up to the doors and challenge him to battle without finding out how things stand." "Wujing," said Brother Monkey to Friar Sand, "is there water inside and outside the door?" "No," said Friar Sand. "In that case you two hide near here while I take a look round," said Monkey. He climbed out of where he had been hiding in Pig's ear, shook himself, turned into a female shrimp with long legs, and reached the doors with two or three jumps. When he took a good look around he saw the monster sitting up above the door with all his watery tribe drawn up around him and the female mandarin fish sitting at his side. They were all discussing how to eat the Tang Priest. Monkey looked carefully around but could see the master nowhere. Then he noticed another female shrimp coming over and standing in the portico to the west. Monkey leapt forward and called, "Sister-in-law, where is this Tang Priest that His Majesty and everyone else are talking about eating?" "His Majesty caught him yesterday when he made all that snow and ice," the female shrimp replied. "He's now in a stone chest behind the palace. If his disciples don't come here to make trouble we'll have music and feast on him tomorrow."

When Monkey heard this he kept up his act for a little longer then went straight round to the back of the palace where he found a stone chest just like a stone pig-trough in a sty or a stone coffin. He measured it, found that it was six feet long, lay on it and listened. He could hear Sanzang sobbing inside.

Monkey could not restrain himself from calling to him, "Master, I'm here." "Save me, disciple," said Sanzang, hearing Monkey's voice. "Don't worry," said Monkey, "I promise we'll save you when we've captured the monster." "Act fast," said Sanzang. "If I'm here for another day I'll die of suffocation." "No problem," said Monkey, "no problem. I'm off." He turned, sprang out through the main doors, turned back into himself, and called for Pig. "What's happening?" asked the idiot and Friar Sand as they came up to him. "The monster caught the master with that trick," Monkey replied. "He's unhurt, but the monster has put him inside a stone chest. You two challenge the monster to battle at once while I get out of the water. Capture him if you can, and if you can't then pretend to be beaten and lure him out of the water for me to kill." "Out you go, brother, and don't worry," said Friar Sand. "We'll find out what the monster's really like." Monkey then made a water-averting spell with his hands, shot up through the waves, and stood on the bank to wait.

Pig charged at the doors in a murderous mood, yelling, "Damned monster, give us our master back." The little devils inside the doors rushed back in panic to report, "Your Majesty, there are people outside asking for their master." "It must be those bloody monks here," said the monster. The monster put on his armour. Holding his weapons in his hand he ordered that the doors be opened. As he came out Pig and Friar Sand were standing one to each side.

The evil spirit came outside accompanied by a hundred or more of his little devils, who brandished their swords and spears as they formed themselves up into two companies. "Where are you from, monk," he asked Pig, "and why are you making this horrible noise here?" "You got away before, but I'll get you now, damned monster," Pig shouted back. He then raised his rake and hit the monster.

Friar Sand shouted also, "Wait there and see how you like my staff." The evil spirit allowed no more arguments and hit back with his mace.

When the three of them had been fighting under the water for four full hours without either side emerging as victor Pig realized that they were not going to beat the monster and gave Friar Sand a nod. Pretending that they were beaten, the two of them turned and fled, trailing their weapons behind them.

Monkey meanwhile had been standing on the bank watching the water with unwavering eyes. Suddenly he saw the waves thrown into turmoil as with a great roar Pig leapt ashore. "He's coming," he said, "he's coming." Next Friar Sand reached the bank saying, "He's coming, he's coming." Then came the monster after them shouting, "Where've you gone?" No sooner had his head come into view than Monkey struck with his cudgel, shouting, "Take that!" The evil spirit swerved to avoid it then parried with his copper mace. While the one stirred up the waves in the river the other showed his prowess on the shore. Before three rounds of the fight had been fought the monster, unable to keep up his resistance, did a feint and plunged back into the water, whereupon the wind fell and the waves subsided.

The evil monster fled to his palace in defeat. The little devils guarding the door soon came to report, "Your Majesty, those two monks are back here challenging you to battle again." The evil monster sent this urgent order: "Little ones, barricade the doors. They can hang around for a couple of days, and when they can't take any more and go away we'll feast on the Tang Priest at our ease." The little demons piled up rocks and made a clay cement to seal the doors firmly shut. When the repeated shouts of Pig and Friar Sand failed to bring the monster out the idiot lost his patience and started to smash the doors with his rake, but they were so firmly barricaded that even though he broke up the doors themselves with seven or eight blows there were still so many layers of clay and rocks behind them that he had no hope of getting through. "Brother," said Friar Sand when he saw this, "that demon is so scared that he's barricaded his doors and won't come out. We'd better go back to the shore and discuss it with Monkey." Pig agreed and they returned to the eastern bank.

When Monkey, who was waiting up in the mist and clouds with his cudgel in his hand, saw the two of them emerge with no demon after them he landed his cloud on the bank to meet them. "Brothers," he asked, "why haven't you brought him up with you?" "The monster has barricaded his doors and won't show himself," said Friar Sand. "We can't fight him." "It sounds hopeless," said Monkey. "I'm going to Potaraka to call on the Bodhisattva," Monkey replied, "and find out about the monster's name and background. When I've found his ancestral home and captured his relations and neighbours I'll come back to get him and rescue the master." "But doing all that will be too much trouble and take far too long," laughed Pig. "I assure you it won't take any time or trouble," replied Brother Monkey. "I'll soon be back."

The splendid Great Sage set off from the river bank at high speed on his auspicious cloud and headed for the Southern Sea. Within an hour Potaraka Island was in view, and he landed the cloud on Pota Cliff, where the twenty-four devas, the guardian god of the island, Moksa the Novice, the boy Sudhana, and the Naga Maiden Pengzhu all came forward to bow in greeting and ask, "Why have you come, Great Sage?" "There is something about which I would like to see the Bodhisattva," Monkey replied. "Be patient, Great Sage," the devas said, "the Bodhisattva told us to receive you here. It must be something to do with you." Monkey could do nothing but wait.

Before long the Bodhisattva emerged from her grove carrying a basket made from purple bamboo. "Wukong," she said, "you and I are going to rescue the Tang Priest." Monkey fell to his knees and replied, "Your disciple has the temerity to suggest that you should dress and take your seat on your lotus throne." "There will be no need to dress; I shall go as I am," the Bodhisattva replied, after which she dismissed the devas and set off on an auspicious cloud. Monkey could only follow.

In a moment they were on the banks of the River of Heaven. The Bodhisattva undid the silken sash around her tunic, tied one end to the basket, and rose on a coloured cloud. Holding the other end of the sash she threw the basket into the river then pulled it up through the current, reciting, "Die if you go, live if you stay, die if you go, live if you stay." When she had said this seven times she raised the basket again, and this time it contained a glistening goldfish, blinking its eyes and moving its scales. "Wukong," said the Bodhisattva, "go down into the water and rescue your master."

"How can I?" Monkey said. "The monster hasn't been caught yet." "Isn't that him in the basket?" the Bodhisattva asked. Pig and Friar Sand then bowed low and asked, "How could that fish have had such great powers?" "It originally was a goldfish that I raised in my lotus pool," the Bodhisattva replied. "Every day it would swim up to listen to sutras, and it trained itself to have magic powers. It escaped on a high tide."

Pig and Friar Sand cleared a way through the water straight to the River Turtle's Residence, where they searched for their master. All the water monsters and fish spirits there were now dead and rotten. They went round to the back of the palace, opened the stone chest, carried the Tang Priest up out of the water, and showed him to the crowds.

Amid all the noisy yelling on the bank a great shout came from the river, "I shall carry you all, master and disciples, across the river." A moment later an ancient soft-shelled turtle emerged from the water.

"Come ashore, come ashore," said Monkey with a smile. Only then did the Ancient Soft-shelled Turtle approach the shore, give a jump, and climb up the bank. When they all went closer they saw that he had a huge white shell about forty feet around. "Master," said Monkey, "let's climb on his back and cross over." "But, disciple," said Sanzang, "we could not get across that ice even though it was frozen so thick. I'm afraid that we would be even less safe on a turtle's back." "Do not be afraid, Master," said the Ancient Soft-shelled Turtle. "I'm much safer than those thick layers of ice. I'll only fail in my spiritual endeavours if I roll to the side." "Master," said Monkey, "no creature that can speak human language will tell a lie." He then told Pig and Friar Sand to lead the horse forward.

When they reached the bank everyone in the village came to see them off with deep bows. Monkey led the animal on to the turtle's white shell and asked the Tang Priest to stand to the horse's right, Pig to its left, and Friar Sand behind it while he stood in front. Just in case the Soft-shelled Turtle tried to misbehave, Monkey undid his belt of tiger sinew, threaded it through the turtle's nose, and held it like a halter. Then with one foot on the turtle's shell and one on its head, and with his iron cudgel in one hand and the halter in the other, he shouted, "Take it easy, Ancient Soft-shelled Turtle. One roll from you and I'll hit you on the head." "I'd never dare, I'd never dare," the turtle said, and he started to walk across the water on his four feet as if going across dry land.

In less than a day the master rode the White Soft-shelled Turtle across the 250 miles of the River of Heaven and landed on the other side with hands and feet still dry. When he had climbed ashore Sanzang put his hands together in thanks. The Ancient Soft-shelled Turtle plunged back into the water and Monkey helped Sanzang to mount the horse. With Pig shouldering the luggage and Friar Sand walking alongside, master and disciples took the main trail west.

CHAPTER 27
The Great Sage Twice Tries to Borrow the Plantain Fan

As master and disciples pressed westward they began to feel hotter and hotter in the warm air. "It is autumn now, so why is it getting hotter again?" Sanzang asked, reining in his horse. They saw a farm by the side of the road. It had a red tiled roof, red brick walls, and red painted doors, windows and furniture. It was red everywhere. "Wukong," said Sanzang, dismounting, "go to that house and find out why it's so burning hot."

The Great Sage put his gold-banded cudgel away, neatened his clothes, and swaggered along the road like a fine gentleman. When he reached the gate to have a look an old man suddenly appeared from inside.

The old man had a shock when he looked up to see Monkey. "Where are you from, you freak?" he asked, steadying himself on his stick. "What are you doing at my gate?" "Venerable patron," replied Monkey with a bow, "don't be afraid. I'm no freak. My master and we three disciples have been sent by the Great Tang emperor in the east to fetch the scriptures from the west. As we've now reached your residence I have come to ask you why it's so boiling hot here and what this place is called." Only then did the old man stop feeling worried and reply with a smile, "Please don't take offence, reverend sir. My old eyes are rather dim and I failed to recognize your distinguished self." "There's no need to be so polite," said Monkey. "Which road is your master on?" the old man asked. "That's him, standing on the main road due south," Monkey replied. "Ask him over, ask him over," the old man replied, to Monkey's pleasure. Monkey waved to them, and Sanzang came over with Pig and Friar Sand leading the white horse and carrying the luggage. They all bowed to the old man.

The old man was at the same time delighted by Sanzang's fine appearance and alarmed by Pig's and Friar Sand's remarkable ugliness. Inviting them in, he told the younger members of the family to bring tea and cook a meal. Hearing all this Sanzang rose to his feet to thank the old man and ask, "Could you tell me, sir, why it has turned so hot again although it is autumn now?" "These are the Fiery Mountains," the old man replied. "We don't have springs or autumns here. It's hot all the year round." "Where are the mountains?" Sanzang asked. "Do they block the way to the west?" "It's impossible to get to the west," the old man replied. "The mountains are about twenty miles from here. You have to cross them to get to the west, but they're over 250 miles of flame. Not a blade of grass can grow anywhere around. Even if you had a skull of bronze and a body of iron you would melt trying to cross them." This answer made Sanzang turn pale with horror; he dared not to ask any more questions.

Just then a young man pushing a red barrow stopped by the gate, shouting, "Cakes! Cakes!" The Great Sage pulled out one of his hairs and turned it into a copper coin with which he bought a cake off the young man. The man accepted the money and without a worry he lifted the cover off his barrow to release a cloud of hot steam, took out a cake and passed it to Monkey. When Monkey took it in his hand it was as hot as a burning coal or a red-hot nail in a furnace. Just look at him as he keeps tossing the cake from one hand to another shouting, "It's hot, it's hot, I can't eat it." "If you can't stand heat don't come here," the young man replied. "It's always this hot here." "You don't understand at all, my lad," said Monkey. "As the saying goes,

If it's never too cold and it's never too hot
The five kinds of grain will be harvested not.

If it's so hot here how do you get the flour to make your cakes?"
To this the young man said,

"You ask me where we can obtain the flour for the pan:
Politely we request it from Immortal Iron Fan."

"What can you tell me about this immortal?" Monkey asked.
"The immortal has a plantain fan," the young man replied. "If
you ask it to, the fan puts out the fire at the first wave, makes a
wind blow at the second wave, and brings rain at the third wave.
That is how we can sow and reap the crops to support ourselves.
Without it nothing would be able to grow."

On hearing this Monkey rushed back inside, gave the cakes
to Sanzang, and said, "Don't worry, Master. Don't get upset
about what's going to happen the year after next. Eat these cakes
up and I'll tell you all about it." Sanzang took the cakes
and said to the old man, "Please have a cake, sir." "I could not
possibly eat one of your cakes before we've offered you any of
our tea and food," the old man replied. "Sir," Monkey replied,
"there's no need to give us food or tea. But could you tell me
where the Iron Fan Immortal lives?" "What do you want to
know about the immortal for?" the old man asked. "The cake-
seller told me just now that the immortal has a plantain fan,"
said Monkey. "If you borrow it the first wave puts the fire out,
the second raises a wind and the third brings rain. That's why
you're able to sow and reap the crops to support yourselves. I
want to go to ask the immortal to come so we can put out the
flames on the Fiery Mountains and cross them. And you'll be
able to sow, reap and live in peace." "It's a nice idea," said the
old man, "but as you have no presents the immortal wouldn't
come." "What sort of presents would be wanted?" Sanzang
asked.

"Every ten years," the old man replied, "we go to visit the
immortal. We take four pigs and four sheep, all decorated with
flowers and red ribbons, delicious fruit in season, chickens, geese
and the best wine. We bathe ourselves and go very reverently
to pay a respectful visit to the mountain and ask the immortal to

leave the cave and come here to perform magic." "Where is this mountain?" Monkey asked. "What's it called? How far is it from here? I'm going there to ask for the fan." "It lies south-west of here," the old man said, "and it's called Mount Turquoise Cloud. When we believers go to worship at the magic mountain the journey takes us a month as it's about 485 miles altogether." "No problem," said Monkey. "I can be there and back in no time." "Wait a minute," said the old man. "Have something to eat and drink first, and we'll get some provisions ready for the journey. You'll need two people to go with you. Nobody lives along the way and there are many wolves and tigers. It'll take you many a day to get there. You must be serious about it." "No need," said Monkey with a laugh, "no need. I'm off." As soon as he had said that he disappeared. "My lord!" the old man said in astonishment. "He's a god who can ride clouds."

We shall say no more of how the family redoubled their offerings to the Tang Priest, but tell of Monkey, who arrived at Mount Turquoise Cloud in an instant, brought his auspicious light to a stop and started looking for the entrance to the cave. He heard the sound of an axe and saw a woodcutter felling a tree in the forest on the mountainside.

Going closer to the woodman Monkey said, "Greetings, woodman." Putting down his axe the woodcutter returned his courtesy and asked him where he was going. "May I ask if this is Mount Turquoise Cloud?" said Monkey. "Yes," the woodcutter replied. "Where is the Iron Fan Immortal's Plantain Cave?" Monkey asked. "There's a Plantain Cave here," the woodcutter replied, "but no Iron Fan Immortal, only a Princess Iron Fan. She's also called Raksasi." "They say the immortal has a plantain fan that can put out the flames of the Fiery Mountains. Is that her?" "Yes, yes," the woodman said. "She's a sage and she has this treasure that puts out fire. Because she protects the people who live over yonder they call her the Iron Fan Immortal. We have no need of her here, so we just call her Raksasi. She's the wife of the Bull Demon King."

唐僧路阻火燄山

The Tang Priest's Way is Blocked at the Fiery Mountains

Monkey went pale with shock at the news. "Another person who's got it in for me," he thought. "When I subdued the Red Boy the other year he said this bitch was his mother. Now I'm up against his parents. How am I ever going to borrow the fan?"

Brother Monkey then took his leave of the woodcutter and went straight to the mouth of the Plantain Cave. Both doors were tightly shut, and the scenery outside was magnificent. When the door opened a young girl came out.

Monkey went up to her with his hands together in front of his chest and said, "Would you kindly tell the princess that I'm a monk going to the west to fetch the scriptures. I'm here to beg the loan of her plantain fan as we can't get across the Fiery Mountains." "What monastery are you from," the girl asked, "and what is your name? Please tell me so that I can announce you." "I'm from the east," Monkey replied, "and my name is Sun Wukong."

The girl went back into the cave, knelt to the princess, and said, "Your Highness, there's a monk from the east called Sun Wukong outside who would like to see you to ask for the loan of the plantain fan to cross the Fiery Mountains." The name Sun Wukong was like a pinch of salt thrown into a flame, or oil poured on a fire. Her face went bright red and evil anger flared up in her heart. "So that damned monkey's here at last," she said with hatred. "Girl," she shouted, "fetch me my armour and my weapons." She then put on her armour, tied her pair of blue-tipped swords at her waist, fastened it all firmly, and went out.

"Where's Sun Wukong?" Raksasi shouted as she came out of her cave. Monkey stepped forward, bowed, and replied, "Monkey offers his respectful greetings, sister-in-law." "I'm no sister-in-law of yours," she shouted angrily, "and I'll have no greetings from you." "Your worthy husband the Bull Demon King was once my sworn brother," Monkey replied. "There were seven of us altogether. As I learn that you are my brother Bull's good lady, of course I must call you sister-in-law."

"Damned ape," said Raksasi, "if you're my husband's sworn

brother why did you have to do that terrible thing to our boy?" "Who is your son?" Monkey asked, as if he did not know. "He's the Red Boy, the Boy Sage King of the Fire-cloud Cave by Withered Pine Ravine on Mount Hao," Raksasi replied. "You ruined him, and now you've come to our door to pay with your life. We've been longing to get our revenge on you but didn't know where to find you. You'll get no mercy from me." Putting on the broadest of smiles, Monkey replied, "You haven't gone into it thoroughly enough, sister-in-law. You've no reason to be so angry with me. Your good son had captured my master and would have steamed or boiled him if the Bodhisattva hadn't taken the boy as his disciple and rescued my master. He's now the page Sudhana on the Bodhisattva's island and he's accepted the pursuit of the true reward from her. He is now beyond life and death and above filth and purity. He will live as long as heaven, earth, the sun and the moon. But so far from thanking me for saving his life you're getting at me. That's wrong of you."

"You smooth-tongued ape," Raksasi snapped back. "My boy may be alive, but when is he ever going to come here? When am I going to see him again?" "It'll be easy for you to see your son again," Monkey replied, still smiling. "Just lend me the fan to put the fires out. When I've taken my master across the mountains I'll go to the Bodhisattva's place in the Southern Ocean and ask him to come here to see you and give your fan back. No problem. Then you'll be able to see that he's completely unharmed. If he'd been wounded at all you'd have had every right to be angry with me. But he's as handsome as ever. You ought to be thanking me." To this Raksasi's reply was: "Shut up, ape fiend! Stick your head out for me to hack with my sword. If you can stand the pain I'll lend you the plantain fan. If you can't you'll be going straight down to Hell to see King Yama." Monkey then clasped his hands together in front of him and replied with a smile, "Enough said, sister-in-law. I'll stretch my bald head out and you can take as many hacks as you like until you're exhausted. But you must lend me the fan." With no more argument Raksasi swung both of her swords around and brought them down with loud thunks a dozen or more times on Monkey's head. He was not bothered at all. Raksasi was so frightened by this that she turned to run away. "Where are you going, sister-in-law?" Monkey said. "Hurry up and lend me that fan." "My treasure isn't something to be lent out casually," Raksasi replied. "Well," said Monkey, "if you refuse now you'll just have to try a taste of your brother-in-law's cudgel."

The splendid Monkey King held on to her with one hand while pulling his cudgel out from his ear with the other. With one wave it became as thick as a ricebowl. Raksasi broke free from his grip and raised her swords to strike back at him. Monkey started swinging his cudgel to hit her with and the fight began in front of Mount Turquoise Cloud. All talk of kinship was forgotten and their minds were full of hatred alone.

Raksasi and Monkey fought it out till evening. As Monkey's cudgel struck so hard and his technique was so flawless she realized that she would never be able to beat him. She brought out her plantain fan and with a single wave blew Monkey right out of sight. There was no way he could stand his ground. With that she went back to her cave in triumph.

The Great Sage was thrown around in the air, unable to come down to earth or find any refuge. He was like a dead leaf in a whirlwind or a fallen blossom carried along by a torrent.

Only after a whole night's buffeting did he manage to land on a mountain the next morning and hold on hard to a rock by putting both arms round it. He needed a long time to calm himself and take a good look around before he realized that he was on Little Mount Sumeru. "What a terrible woman," he said to himself with a deep sigh. "How ever did she get me here? I'll go down and find out some more from the Bodhisattva Lingji before I go back."

Just as he was making his mind up he heard a resounding gong, so he hurried down the mountain and straight to the dhyana monastery. The lay brother on the gate recognized Monkey and went in to announce, "The hairy-faced Great Sage is here again." Realizing that this must be Sun Wukong, the Bodhisattva hurried down from his throne to greet him and lead

him inside with the words, "Allow me to congratulate you. I
suppose you have fetched the scriptures now." "It'll be a long
time yet," said Monkey, "a long time." "But why are you
visiting my mountain if you have yet to reach the Thunder
Monastery?" the Bodhisattva asked. "In your great
kindness you subdued the Yellow Wind Monster for me
some years ago," Monkey replied. "Now we are at the Fiery
Mountains, but we can't cross them. When I asked the local
people they told me about an Iron Fan Immortal who had an
iron fan that could put the fires out. I went to visit the
immortal, only to discover that she's the wife of the Bull Demon
King and the Red Boy's mother. I told her that her son is now
Bodhisattva Guanyin's page, but she has it in for me because
she can't see him. She refused to lend me her fan and fought me.
When she realized that my cudgel was too much for her she
waved her fan and sent me hurtling through the air till I landed
here. That's why I've come blundering into your monastery to
ask the way back. How far is it from here to the Fiery
Mountains?"

"The woman is called Raksasi, or Princess Iron Fan," replied Lingji with a smile. "That plantain fan of hers is a miraculous treasure formed by heaven and earth behind Mount Kun-
lun ever since primal chaos was first separated. This leaf is the
very essence of the negative Yin principle, which is why it can
put out fire. If she fans somebody with it he'll be blown 27,000
miles before that negative wind drops. But this mountain of
mine is only some 17,000 miles from the Fiery Mountains. You
must have stopped here because you have the power to delay
clouds, Great Sage. No ordinary mortal would have been able to
stop." "She's terrible," said Monkey. "How ever is my master
going to get across those mountains?" "Don't worry, Great
Sage," Lingji replied. "The Tang Priest is fated to succeed on
this journey with you." "How can you tell?" Monkey asked.
"Many years ago when the Tathagata gave me his instructions,"
Lingji replied, "he presented me with a Wind-fixing Pill and a
Flying Dragon Staff. The Flying Dragon Staff was used to subdue the Yellow Wind Monster, but I haven't yet tried out the

Wind-fixing Pill and I'll give it to you today. It'll stop the fan from being able to move you. You'll just have to ask to get it and put the fire out with it. You'll have an instant success." Monkey bowed deeply and expressed profound thanks. The Bodhisattva then produced a brocade bag from his sleeve and took out of it the Wind-fixing Pill. This he gave to Monkey to sew up securely inside the lapel of his tunic. "I won't detain you here any longer," Lingji said as he saw Monkey out through doors. "Head northwest and that will get you to Raksasi's mountain."

Taking his leave of Lingji Monkey rode his somersault cloud straight back to Mount Turquoise Cloud and was there in a moment. "Open up, open up!" he shouted, hammering on the doors with his iron cudgel. "Monkey's here to borrow the fan." This so alarmed the servant girl inside the doors that she ran back and reported, "Your Highness, he's here to borrow the fan again." The news frightened Raksasi, who thought, "That damned monkey really has got some powers. If I fan anyone else with my treasure they go 27,000 miles before stopping. How can he be back so soon after being blown away? This time I'll fan him two or three times and he'll never be able to find his way back here." She sprang to her feet, tied all her armour firmly on, and went out of the cave with her swords in her hands shouting, "Sun the Novice, aren't you afraid of me? Why have you come back here to get yourself killed?" "Don't be so stingy, sister-in-law," said Monkey with a smile. "You've got to lend me the fan. I'll bring it back as soon as I've escorted the Tang Priest across the Fiery Mountains. I give you my word as a gentleman. I'm not the sort of low creature who borrows things but doesn't give them back."

"Damned macaque," Raksasi shouted back. "You're outrageous, and you understand nothing. I've got to avenge the loss of my son, so how could I possibly be prepared to lend you my fan? Clear off if you don't want a taste of my sword." The Great Sage, not at all afraid, struck back at her hands with his iron cudgel, and the two of them fought six or seven rounds. By then Raksasi's arms were becoming too tired to wield the swords, while Brother Monkey was feeling strong and fighting well. Seeing that the balance of the fight was tilting against her, Raksasi took out the fan and fanned it once in Monkey's direction. He stood unmoved, put his iron cudgel away, and said with a chuckle, "This time it's different. Fan as much as you like. If I move an inch I'm no man." She fanned twice more and still he did not move. By now she was so alarmed that she put her pride and joy away at once, went straight back into the cave, and shut the doors firmly.

When Monkey saw this he used magic. He tore the lapel of his tunic open, put the Wind-fixing Pill in his mouth, shook himself, turned into the tiniest of insects, and squeezed in through the crack between the doors, where he saw Raksasi shouting, "I'm thirsty, I'm thirsty. Quick, bring me some tea." The servant girl who attended her fetched a pot of the best tea and poured a large cup of it so noisily that the surface was frothy. Monkey was delighted. With a quiet buzz of his wings he flew under the froth. Raksasi was so parched that she drained the tea in two gulps.

Once inside her stomach Monkey reverted to his own form and shouted at the top of his voice, "Sister-in-law, lend me the fan." Raksasi went pale with shock. "Little ones," she called to her underlings, "are the front doors shut?" "Yes," they all said. "If the doors are shut then how can Sun the Novice be inside the cave and shouting?" she asked. "He's shouting from inside you," the servant girl replied. "Where are you playing your conjuring tricks, Sun the Novice?" Raksasi asked. "I've never been able to do conjuring tricks in all my life," Monkey replied. "My magic and my powers are all real. I'm fooling around in your own insides, good sister-in-law. I've just seen your lungs and your liver. I know you're very hungry and thirsty, so I'll give you a bowlful to quench your thirst." With that he stamped his foot, giving Raksasi an unbearable cramp in her stomach that left her sitting groaning on the floor. "Don't try to say no, sister-in-law," Monkey then said. "I'm giving you a pastry in case you're hungry." He butted upwards, causing such a violent heart pain that she could only roll around on the ground, her face sallow and her lips white with agony "Spare me, brother-in-law, spare me," was all she could say.

Only then did Monkey stop hitting and kicking. "So you call me brother-in-law now, do you?" he said. "I'll spare your life for my brother Bull's sake. Get me the fan, and quick." "You shall have it, brother-in-law, you shall have it," she said. "Come out and get it." "Fetch it and show it to me," Monkey said. She told the servant girl to fetch a plantain fan and stand holding it beside her. Monkey poked his head up her throat to see it and said, "As I'm sparing your life, sister-in-law, I won't smash my way out under your ribs. I'll come out through your mouth. Open wide three times." With that Raksasi opened her mouth and Monkey turned back into the tiny insect to fly out and alight on the fan. Not realizing what had happened Raksasi went on to open her mouth twice more. "Come out, brother-in-law," she said. Monkey turned back into himself, took the fan, and said, "Here I am. Thanks for the loan." With that he strode forward while the underlings opened the doors to let him out of the cave.

The Great Sage then turned his cloud around and headed back east. A moment later he had landed the cloud and was standing by the red brick wall. Pig was very pleased indeed to see him. "Master," he said, "Monkey's here! He's back!" Sanzang went out with the old man of the farm and Friar Sand to greet him, and they all went back inside. Propping the fan against the wall, Monkey asked, "Tell me sir, is this the fan?" "Yes, yes," the old man said. "This is a great achievement, disciple," said Sanzang. "Fetching this treasure cost you a great deal of trouble." "No trouble at all," said Monkey. He then told them how he borrowed the fan. When Sanzang heard this he was extremely grateful.

Master and disciples then took their leave of the old man and travelled about fifteen miles west. The heat was becoming unbearable. "The soles of my feet are being roasted," Friar Sand complained. "My trotters are getting burnt and it hurts," said Pig. The horse was going much faster than usual too. The ground was so hot that they could not stop, but every step was

painful. "Please dismount, Master," said Monkey, "and brothers, stay here while I use the fan to put the fire out. When
the wind and the rain come the ground will be a lot cooler and
we'll be able to get across the mountains." He then raised the
fan and fanned it hard once in the direction of the fire: tongues
of flame rose above the mountains. He fanned again, and they
were a hundred times as high. He fanned a third time, and now
they were a couple of miles high and beginning to burn him.
Monkey fled, but not before two patches of fur had been burnt
away. He ran straight back to the Tang Priest and said, "Hurry
back, hurry back, the flames are coming."

The master remounted and headed back east with Pig and
Friar Sand some seven miles before stopping and asking, "What
happened, Wukong?" "It's the wrong one," Monkey said, flinging the fan down, "it's the wrong one. The damned woman
fooled me." When Sanzang heard this he frowned and felt
thoroughly depressed. "What are we to do?" he sobbed, the
tears flowing freely down his cheeks. "Brother," said Pig, "why
did you come back in such a mad rush and send us back here?"
"The first time I fanned there were flames," Monkey replied,
"the second time the fire got fiercer, and the third time the
flames were a couple of miles high. If I hadn't run fast all my
fur would have been burnt off."

"But you're always telling us that you can't be hurt by
thunder and lightning and that fire can't burn you," said Pig
with a laugh. "How come you're afraid of fire now?" "Idiot,"
said Monkey, "you don't understand anything. The other times
I was ready: that's why I wasn't hurt. Today I didn't make any
flame-avoiding spells or use magic to defend myself. That's why
two patches of my fur were singed." "If the fire's so fierce and
there's no other way to the west what are we going to do?"
Friar Sand asked. "We'll just have to find somewhere where
there isn't any fire," Pig replied. "Which way will that be?"
Sanzang asked. "East, north or south: there's no fire those
ways," said Pig. "But which way are the scriptures?" "Only in
the west," Pig replied. "I only want to go where the scriptures
are," Sanzang said. "We're well and truly stuck," said Friar

Sand. "Where there are scriptures there's fire, and where there's no fire there are no scriptures."

While master and disciples were talking this nonsense they heard someone call, "Don't get upset, Great Sage. Come and have some vegetarian food before you take your discussions any further." The four of them looked round to see an old man wearing a cloak that floated in the wind and a hat the shape of a half moon. In his hand he held a dragon-headed stick, and on his legs were boots of iron. With him was a demon with the beak of an eagle and the cheeks of a fish carrying on his head a copper bowl full of steamed buns, millet cakes, cooked millet and rice. The old man bowed to them on the road to the west and said, "I am the local god of the Fiery Mountains. As I know that you are escorting this holy monk, Great Sage, and can't go any further I have brought this meal as an offering." "Eating doesn't matter," Monkey replied. "When are these fires going to be put out so that my master can cross the mountains?" "If you want to put the fires out you must first ask Raksasi to lend you the plantain fan," the local god said. Monkey went to the side of the path, picked the fan up, and said, "This is it, isn't it? The more I fan the flames the more fiercely they burn. Why?" "Because it's not the real one," said the local deity with a laugh when he looked at it. "She fooled you." "Then how am I to get the real one?" Monkey said. The local god bowed again and had a slight smile on his face as he replied, "If you want to borrow the real plantain fan you will have to ask the Strongarm King."

"The Strongarm King is the Bull Demon King," the local god explained. "Did he set these mountains ablaze and pretend they were the Fiery Mountains?" Monkey asked. "No, no," the local god replied. "If you'll promise to forgive me for doing so, Great Sage, I'll speak frankly." "What's there to forgive?" Monkey said. "Speak frankly." "You started this fire, Great Sage," the local god replied. "That's nonsense," said Monkey angrily. "I wasn't here. Do you take me for an arsonist?" "You don't realize who I am," the local god said. "These mountains haven't always been here. When you made havoc in Heaven five hundred years ago and were captured by the Illustrious Sage Erlang you were escorted to Lord Lao Zi, put in the Eight Trigrams Furnace and refined. When the furnace was opened you kicked it over, and some of its bricks that still had fire in them fell here as the Fiery Mountains. I used to be one of the Taoist boys who looked after the furnace in the Tushita Palace, but Lord Lao Zi was so angry with me for failing in my duty that he sent me down to be the local god here." "I was wondering why you were dressed like that," said Pig forcefully, "you're a Taoist turned local god."

"Tell me why I need to find the Strongarm King," said Monkey, only half-convinced. "He's Princess Raksasi's husband," the local god said. "He's abandoned her now and gone to live in the Cloud-touching Cave in Mount Thunder Piled. A fox king there who'd lived for ten thousand years died leaving an only daughter, Princess Jade, with property worth a million but nobody to manage it. Two years ago she visited the Bull Demon King and found out about his tremendous magical powers. She decided to give him her property if he'd come to live in her cave as her husband. So the Bull Demon King abandoned Raksasi and hasn't been back to see her for ages. If you can find him, Great Sage, and persuade him to come here you'll be able to borrow the real fan. First, you'll be able to blow the flames out to take your master across the mountains. Second, you'll put an end to this disastrous fire so that the land here can come back to life. And third, I'll be pardoned and allowed to go back to Heaven and return to live under Lord Lao Zi's command." "Where is Mount Thunder Piled, and how far is it from here?" "Due south," the local deity said, "and over a thousand miles." Once he knew this Monkey told Friar Sand and Pig to look after the master and ordered the local god to stay with them. There was then a roaring like the wind as he disappeared.

In less than an hour he saw a high mountain that touched the sky. Bringing his cloud down he stood on the peak to look around.

After looking for a long time the Great Sage walked down from the towering peak to find his way through the mountain.

行者一調芭蕉扇

Monkey's First Attempt to Borrow the Plantain Fan

Just when he was feeling bewildered a slender young woman came towards him holding a spray of fragrant orchid. The Great Sage slipped behind a grotesque rock and took a good look at her. She was extremely beautiful.

As the young woman slowly approached the rock the Great Sage bowed to her and said, "Where are you going, Bodhisattva?" Before he spoke she had not noticed him; but when she looked up and saw how hideous the Great Sage was she was petrified, unable to move forward or back. All she could do was shiver and force herself to reply, "Where are you from? How dare you question me?" "If I tell her about fetching the scriptures and borrowing the fan," the Great Sage thought, "this damn woman might be some relation of the Bull Demon King's. I'd better pretend to be some kinsman of the Bull Demon King come to invite him to a banquet." When he would not answer her questions the woman turned angry and shouted, "Who are you and how dare you question me?" "I'm from Mount Turquoise Cloud," Monkey replied with a bow and a forced smile. "I don't know the way as it's my first time here. Could I ask you, Bodhisattva, if this is Mount Thunder Piled?" "It is," she replied. "Where might I find the Cloud-touching Cave?" the Great Sage asked. "What do you want to find it for?" the woman asked. "I've been sent by Princess Iron Fan in the Plantain Cave on Mount Turquoise Cloud with an invitation for the Bull Demon King," Monkey replied.

The moment the woman heard him speak of Princess Iron Fan sending an invitation to the Bull Demon King she flared into a rage and went crimson from ear to ear. "She ought to know better, the low bitch. It's less than two years since the Bull Demon King came here, and goodness only knows how much jewellery, gold, silver, fine silk and brocade I've given her since then. I send her firewood every year and rice every month. She's doing nicely thank you. So what's the shameless hussy doing, sending him an invitation?" When the Great Sage heard this and realized that she was Princess Jade he deliberately pulled out his iron cudgel and shouted at her, "You're a damned bitch, using your wealth to buy the Bull Demon King. You could only get him to marry you for your money. You ought to be thoroughly ashamed of yourself instead of being so insulting." At this all of her souls were sent flying, and she fled trembling with terror, stumbling and tripping over her shoes, while the Great Sage ran after her, shouting and roaring. Once they were out from under the shade of the pines they were at the entrance to the Cloud-touching Cave. She ran inside and the doors slammed shut behind her.

The young woman, dripping with sweat after running and with her heart pounding from terror, went straight to the study where the Bull Demon King was quietly perusing a book on cinnabar alchemy. She threw herself into his arms feeling thoroughly put out, scratched and tugged at his face and ears, and howled aloud. "Don't upset yourself so, my lovely," said the Bull Demon King, all smiles. "What do you want to tell me?" She then began to prance and jump about in her fury as she said abusively, "You're killing me, damned monster." "What makes you say that?" he asked, all smiles. "I brought you here to look after me and protect me because I'd lost my parents and people who'd been around all said that you were a tough guy," she said. "But you're just another henpecked hack." The Bull Demon King took her in his arms and said, "How've I done you wrong, my lovely? Take your time and tell me about it. I'll make it up to you." "I was taking a stroll among the flowers outside the cave just now picking orchids," she said, "when a monk with a face like a thunder god rushed up to me and started bowing. I was so scared I couldn't move. When I calmed down enough to ask him who he was he said he'd been sent by that Princess Iron Fan with an invitation for you. I was so angry I had something to say about that, and he started abusing me and chased me with his cudgel. He'd have just about killed me with it if I hadn't run so fast. So you see, bringing you here was a disaster. It's killing me." At this the Bull Demon King apologized to her very earnestly. It took a long time and many tender attentions from him before she finally calmed down. "I tell you the truth, my lovely," the demon king said forcefully. "The Plantain Cave may be rather out of the way, but it's a place of purity and elegance. That wife of mine has had the highest moral principles since childhood, and she's also an immortal who has attained the Way. She runs her household very strictly. There's not even a page there. She couldn't possibly have sent a monk with a face like a thunder god. I wonder what evil fiend he is. He must have used her name to come and see me. I'm going out to have a look."

The splendid demon king strode out of the study and into the hall to put on his armour and take his iron cudgel. "Who are you, and why are you behaving so outrageously?" he shouted as he went out through the doors. Monkey, who was watching from one side, saw that he now looked quite different from the way he had five hundred years earlier.

The Great Sage then tidied his clothes, stepped forward and asked, "Can you still recognize me, eldest brother?" "Are you Sun Wukong, the Great Sage Equalling Heaven?" the Bull Demon King replied, returning his bow. "Yes, yes," said Monkey. "It's such a long time since last we met. I only got here to see you because I asked a woman some questions just now. I must congratulate you on how well everything is growing." "Cut that out," the Bull Demon King shouted back. "I heard about you making havoc in Heaven and being crushed under the Five Elements Mountain by the Lord Buddha. Then you were released from your heavenly punishment to protect the Tang Priest on his way to worship the Buddha and fetch the scriptures in the Western Heaven. Why did you have to destroy my son? I'm very angry with you. Why are you here looking for me?" "Please don't misjudge me, brother," said the Great Sage with another bow. "Your good son captured my master and was going to eat him. I was no match for him. Luckily the Bodhisattva Guanyin rescued my master and converted your boy. He's now the page Sudhana. He's even taller than you. He lives in a temple of great bliss and enjoys eternal ease. There's nothing wrong with any of that, so why be angry with me?" "Smooth-tongued macaque," retorted the Bull Demon King. "Even if you can talk your way out of having ruined my son, what do you mean by upsetting my beloved concubine and chasing her up to my doors?"

"Let me be honest with you," the Great Sage replied. "I'm stuck at the Fiery Mountains on my journey escorting the Tang Priest, and we're not getting anywhere. The local people told me that your good lady Raksasi has a plantain fan. I tried to borrow it. I went to visit my sister-in-law, but she refused to lend it me, which is why I've come to see you. I beg you, brother, in the greatness of your heart to come with me to sister-in-law's place and borrow the fan for me so that I can blow out the fires and get my master across the mountains. Then I'll return it right away."

At this the Bull Demon King's heart blazed with wrath. "You told me you knew how to behave," he said, noisily gnashing his teeth of steel. "I suppose all this was not just to borrow the fan. I'm certain my wife has refused to lend it you because you've mistreated her. So that's why you came to see me. On top of that you send my beloved concubine fleeing in terror. As the saying goes,

> Don't push around
> Your best friend's wife,
> Don't try to destroy
> The joy of his life.

You've been pushing my wife around and trying to destroy the concubine who's the joy of my life. It's an outrage. Take this!" "If you want to hit me, brother, I'm not afraid," said Monkey. "All I want is the treasure. I beg you to lend it me." "If you can last out three rounds with me," the Bull Demon King said, "I'll make my wife lend it to you. And if you can't I'll kill you and have my revenge." "Good idea, brother," Monkey replied. "I've been so lazy. I haven't been to see you for ages, and I don't know how your fighting powers now compare with the old days. Let's have a match with our cudgels." The Bull Demon King was in no mood for further argument, and he hit at Monkey's head with his mace. Monkey hit back with his gold-banded cudgel.

The Great Sage and the Bull Demon King fought over a

hundred rounds without either emerging as the victor. Just as they were becoming locked in their struggle a voice called from the peak, "King Bull, my king sends his respects and invites you to honour him with your presence at a banquet." At this the Bull Demon King blocked the gold-banded cudgel with his iron mace and called out, "You stay here, macaque. I'm going to a friend's house for a meal. I'll be back." With that he landed his cloud and went straight back into the cave. "My lovely," he said to Princess Jade, "the man you saw with a face like a thunder god is the macaque Sun Wukong. A bout with my mace has sent him packing: he won't be back. Stop worrying and enjoy yourself. I'm going to a friend's place for some drinks." He then took off his helmet and armour, donned a duck-green jacket of cut velvet, went outside and mounted his water-averting golden-eyed beast. Telling his underlings to look after the palace he headed northwest in clouds and mist.

While the Great Sage watched all this from the peak he thought, "I wonder who the friend is and where he's gone for his banquet. I'll follow him." Splendid Monkey then shook himself and turned into a clear breeze to follow him. He soon reached a mountain, but the Bull Demon King was nowhere to be seen. The Great Sage turned back into himself and started to search the mountain. He found a deep pool of pure water beside which was inscribed in large letters on a tablet of stone

RAGGED ROCK MOUNTAIN
GREEN WAVE POOL

"Old Bull must have gone into the water," Monkey thought. "I'd better go down and have a look."

Making a hand-spell and saying the magic words the splendid Great Sage shook himself, turned into a medium-sized crab weighing thirty-six pounds, jumped into the water with a splash, and went straight down to the bottom of the pool. He saw an ornamental arch of delicate tracery to which was tethered a water-averting golden-eyed beast. On the other side of the arch there was no more water. Monkey crawled through and took a careful look.

The Bull Demon King was sitting in the seat of honour with three or four lesser dragon spirits on either side. Facing him was an ancient dragon, surrounded by dragon sons, dragon grandsons, dragon wives and dragon daughters. Just as they were feasting and drinking the Great Sage Sun marched straight in, to be spotted by the ancient dragon, who ordered, "Arrest that vagrant crab." The dragon sons and grandsons fell upon him and seized him. "Spare me, spare me," said Monkey, suddenly reverting to human speech. "Where are you from, crab vagrant?" the ancient dragon asked. "How dare you come into my hall and behave in this disgraceful way in front of my distinguished guests? Tell me this moment if you want to be spared the death penalty." The splendid Great Sage said that he was Sideways Man-at-arms, a crab who had never been taught correct social behaviour. "I beg Your Majesty to show me mercy."

When the spirits at the banquet heard this they all bowed to the ancient dragon and said, "This is the first time that the Sideways Man-at-arms has come to your palace of jasper, and he does not understand royal etiquette. We beg Your Excellency to spare him." The ancient dragon thanked the spirits and ordered, "Release the wretch. Put a beating on record against his name, and have him wait outside." The Great Sage acknowledged his kindness, then fled for his life till he reached the archway outside. "That Bull Demon King is drinking for all he's worth in there," he thought. "I'm not going to wait till the feast breaks up. And even if I did he still wouldn't lend me the fan. I'd do better to steal his golden-eyed beast and turn myself into a Bull Demon King. Then I can trick Raksasi into lending me the fan and I'll be able to escort my master across the mountains. That'll be best."

The splendid Great Sage then reverted to his original form, untied the golden-eyed beast, leapt into the carved saddle, and rode straight up from the bottom of the water. Once out of the pool he made himself look like the Bull Demon King. Whipping on the beast he set his cloud moving and was soon at the mouth of the Plantain Cave in Mount Turquoise Cloud. "Open up!" he shouted, and at the sound of his voice the two servant girls inside the gates opened them for him. Taking him for the Bull Demon King they went in to report, "Madam, His Majesty's come home." At the news Raksasi quickly neatened her hair and hurried out on her little lotus feet to meet him. Climbing out of the saddle the Great Sage led the golden-eyed beast inside. Raksasi's mortal eyes failed to see who he really was as she led Monkey inside, hand in hand. The maids were told to prepare places and bring tea, and as the master was back the whole household tried its hardest.

The Great Sage and Raksasi were soon talking. Raksasi told the serving girls to lay on wine and a feast to welcome him back.

After they had each had several cups Raksasi was feeling a little drunk and rather sexy. She started to press herself against the Great Sage, stroking and pinching him. Taking him by the hand, she whispered tender words to him; leaning her shoulder against him, she spoke quietly and submissively. They shared the same cup of wine, drinking a mouthful each at a time, and she fed him fruit. The Great Sage pretended to go along with this and smile. He had no choice but to lean against her.

Watching her get drunk the Great Sage had kept his wits about him, and he tried to lead her on by saying, "Where have you put the real fan, wife? You must watch it very carefully all the time. I'm worried that Sun the Novice will trick it out of you with some of his many transformations." At this Raksasi tittered, spat it out of her mouth, and handed it to the Great Sage. It was only the size of an apricot leaf. "Here's the treasure," she said.

The Great Sage took it but could not believe that it really was. "How could a tiny little thing like this blow a fire out?" he wondered. "It must be another fake." Seeing him looking at the treasure so deep in thought, Raksasi could not restrain herself from rubbing her powdered face against Monkey's and saying, "Put the treasure away and have another drink, darling.

What are you looking so worried about?" The Great Sage took the chance to slip in the question, "How could a little thing like this blow out 250 miles of fire?" She was now drunk enough to have no inhibitions about speaking the truth, so she told him how it was done: "Your Majesty, I expect you've been overdoing your pleasures day and night these last two years since you left me. That Princess Jade must have addled your brains if you can't even remember about your own treasure. You just have to pinch the seventh red silk thread with the thumb of your left hand and say, 'Huixuhexixichuihu.' Then it'll grow twelve feet long. It can do as many changes as you like. It could blow 250,000 miles of flame out with a single wave."

The Great Sage committed all this very carefully to memory, put the fan in his mouth, rubbed his face and turned back into himself. "Raksasi!" he yelled at the top of his voice. "Have a careful look: I'm your brother-in-law. What a disgusting way you've been carrying on in with me, and for what a long time too. You're shameless, quite shameless." In her horror at realizing it was Sun Wukong she pushed the dining table over and fell into the dust, overcome with shame and screaming, "I'm so upset I could die, I could die."

Not caring whether she was dead or alive, the Great Sage broke free and rushed straight out of the Plantain Cave. He was indeed not lusting after that female beauty, and glad to turn away with a smiling face. He sprang on his auspicious cloud that took him up to the top of the mountain, spat the fan out of his mouth, and tried the magic out. Pinching the seventh red tassel with the thumb of his left hand, he said "Huixuhexixichuihu", and indeed it grew to be twelve feet long. On close examination he found it quite different from the false one he had borrowed before. It glittered with auspicious light and was surrounded by lucky vapours. Thirty-six threads of red silk formed a trellis pattern inside and out. But Brother Monkey had only asked how to make it grow and had not found out the spell for shrinking it. So he had to shoulder it as he went back by the way he had come.

The Second Attempt to Borrow the Fan

When the Bull Demon King's feast with all the spirits at the bottom of the Green Wave Pool ended he went outside to find that the water-averting golden-eyed beast was missing. The ancient dragon king called the spirits together to ask them, "Which of you untied and stole the Bull Demon King's golden-eyed beast?" The spirits all knelt down and replied, "We wouldn't dare steal it. We were all waiting, singing or playing at the banquet. None of us was out here." "I am sure that none of you palace musicians would have dared to take it," the ancient dragon said. "Have any strangers been here?" "A crab spirit was here not long ago during the banquet, and he was a stranger."

At this the Bull King suddenly realized what had happened. "Say no more," he exclaimed. "When you sent your messenger with the invitation this morning there was a Sun Wukong there who'd come to ask to borrow my plantain fan as he couldn't get the Tang Priest he's escorting to fetch the scriptures across the Fiery Mountains. I refused. I was in the middle of a fight with him that neither of us was winning when I shook him off and came straight here to the banquet. That monkey's extremely quick and adaptable. I'm sure that the crab spirit was him here in disguise to do a bit of spying. He's stolen my beast to go and trick the plantain fan out of my wife." This news made all the spirits shake with fright. "Do you mean the Sun Wukong who made havoc in Heaven?" they asked. "Yes," the Bull Demon King replied. "If any of you gentlemen have any trouble on the road west keep your distance from him whatever you do." "But if all that's true, what about Your Majesty's steed?" the ancient dragon asked. "No problem," the Bull Demon King replied with a smile. "You gentlemen may all go home now while I go after him."

With that he parted his way through the waters, sprang up from the bottom of the pool and rode a yellow cloud straight to the Plantain Cave on Mount Turquoise Cloud, where he heard Raksasi stamping her feet, beating her breast, howling and moaning. He pushed the doors open to see the water-averting golden-eyed beast tethered by them. "Where did Sun Wukong go, wife?" the Bull Demon King said. Seeing that the Bull Demon King was back, the serving girls all knelt down and said, "Are you home, Your Majesty?" Raksasi grabbed hold of him, banged her head against his, and said abusively, "Damn and blast you, you careless fool. Why ever did you let that macaque steal the golden-eyed beast and turn himself into your double to come here and trick me?" "Which way did the macaque go?" the Bull Demon King asked, grinding his teeth in fury. Beating her breast Raksasi continued to pour out abuse: "The damn monkey tricked me out of my treasure, turned back into himself, and went. I'm so angry I could die." "Do look after yourself, wife," the Bull Demon King said, "and don't be so upset. When I've caught the macaque and taken the treasure off him I'll skin him, grind his bones to powder, and bring you his heart and liver. That'll make you feel better." He then called for weapons. "Your Majesty's weapons aren't here," the serving girls replied. "Then bring your mistress' weapons," the Bull Demon King replied. The servants brought her pair of blue-tipped swords, and the Bull Demon King took off the duck-green velvet jacket he had worn to the banquet and tied the little waistcoat he wore next to his skin more tightly. He then strode out of the Plantain Cave, a sword in each hand, and headed straight for the Fiery Mountains in pursuit of Monkey.

CHAPTER 28
The Monkey King Battles with
the Bull Demon King

The story tells how the Bull Demon King caught up with the Great Sage Sun and saw him looking very cheerful as he went along with the plantain fan over his shoulder. "So the macaque has also tricked the art of using the fan out of her," the demon king thought. "If I ask him for it back to his face he's bound to refuse, and if he fans me with it and sends me sixty thousand miles away that would be just what he wants. Now I know that the Tang Priest is sitting waiting by the main road. When I was an evil spirit in the old days I used to know his second disciple the Pig Spirit. I think I'll turn myself into a double of the Pig Spirit and play a trick back on him. That macaque will no doubt be so pleased with himself that he won't really be on his guard." The splendid demon king could also do seventy-two transformations and his martial skills were on a par with those of the Great Sage: it was just that he was rather more clumsily built, was less quick and penetrating, and not so adaptable. First he hid the swords then he said the words of the spell, turned himself into the exact likeness of Pig, went down, and met Monkey face to face. "I'm here, brother," he called.

The Great Sage was indeed delighted, and called out, "Where are you going, brother?" The Bull Demon King made up an answer on the spot: "You'd been away for so long that the master wondered if the Bull Demon King's magic powers were too much for you and you couldn't get the treasure. So he sent me to meet you." "There was no need to worry," said Monkey. "I've already got it." "How did you manage that?" the Bull Demon King asked. " Old Bull and I fought over a hundred rounds without either of us getting the upper hand till he broke off the fight and went to the bottom of the Green Wave Pool in Ragged Rock Mountain for a banquet with a whole lot of lesser dragons and dragons. I tailed him there, turned into a crab, stole the water-averting golden-eyed beast, made myself look like him, and went to the Plantain Cave to trick Raksasi. She as good as married me on the spot and I conned it out of her." "You had to go to a lot of trouble, brother," the Bull Demon King replied. "Can I hold the fan?" Not realizing that this Pig was an impostor, or even considering the possibility, the Great Sage Sun handed him the fan.

Now the Bull Demon King knew the secret of making the fan shrink or grow, and as soon as he had the fan in his hands he made a spell with them that nobody could see, shrunk it back to the size of an apricot leaf, and reverted to his true form. "Bloody macaque," he swore, "do you know who I am now?" As soon as he saw this Monkey regretted making so terrible a mistake. With a cry of anguish he stamped his feet and yelled, "Aagh! After all these years I've been hunting wild geese a gosling has pecked out my eye!" He was now leaping around in a thunderous fury, and he took a crack at the Bull Demon King's head with his iron cudgel. The demon king then fanned him with the fan, not realizing that the Great Sage had inadvertently swallowed the wind-fixing pill he had in his mouth when he turned himself into a tiny insect to go into Raksasi's stomach. This had made all his entrails, his skin and his bones so solid and firm that no matter how hard the Bull Demon King fanned he could not move him. This alarmed the Bull Demon King, who put the treasure in his mouth and fought back, swinging a sword in each hand.

The story now tells not of those two locked in their struggle but of the Tang Priest sitting by the road and finding the heat unbearable. He was also very anxious and thirsty. "May I ask you," he said to the local deity, "what that Bull Demon King's powers are like?" "He has very great magic," the local god replied, "and his dharma powers are unlimited. He and the Great Sage Sun are well matched." "Wukong is a very good traveller," Sanzang replied. "He can normally go six or seven hundred miles and back in an instant. Why has he been away all day? I'm sure he must be fighting the Bull Demon King." With that he called for Pig and Friar Sand and asked, "Which of you will go to meet your elder brother? If he is up against an enemy you will have to help him in the fight, get the fan, and come back. I am very impatient to cross these mountains and continue along our way." "It's getting late," Pig replied, "and I'd like to go to meet him. The only thing is that I don't know the way to Mount Thunder Piled." "But I do," the local god said. "Tell the Curtain-lifting General to keep your master company while you and I go there." Sanzang was delighted. "I am most grateful to you for going to such trouble," he said, "and I shall thank you again when you have succeeded."

Pig then summoned up his spirits, tightened the belt round his black brocade tunic, and took his rake in his hands as he rose up on his cloud with the local god and headed due east. As they were going along they heard great shouts and were buffeted by strong winds. Stopping his cloud for a good look he saw that it was all caused by Monkey and the Bull Demon King fighting. "Why don't you join in, Marshal Tian Peng?" the local deity asked. "What are you waiting for?" At that the idiot brandished his rake and said with a great shout, "Brother, I'm coming." "Idiot," said Monkey bitterly, "you've ruined things for me." "But the master told me to come to meet you," Pig protested. "He asked the local god to guide me as I don't know the way. That's why I'm a bit late. How can you say I've ruined things for you?" "I'm not angry with you for being late," Monkey replied. "It's this damned bull who's a thorough disgrace. I'd got the fan off Raksasi, but he turned himself into your double and came to meet me. I was so pleased to see you that I passed him the fan. He turned back into himself and we've been fighting it out ever since. That's why I said you'd ruined things for me."

猪八戒助力破魔王

Pig Helps in the Fight Against the Bull Demon King

This news put Pig into a flaming temper. Raising his rake he shouted abuse to the Bull Demon King's face: "I'll get you, you pox-ridden bag of blood! I'll get you for pretending to be me, your own ancestor, to trick my brother and stir up trouble between us." Watch as he starts lashing out wildly with the rake. The Bull Demon King, who had been fighting Monkey all day, was tiring, and he also realized that he would never be able to withstand the onslaught of Pig's rake, so he fled in defeat. But his way was blocked by a force of spirit soldiers led by the local god of the Fiery Mountains. "Wait, Strongarm King," the local deity said. "All the gods and heavens are protecting Tang Sanzang on his journey west to fetch the scriptures. The Three Worlds all know about him, and the Ten Directions are supporting him. Please lend him your plantain fan to blow out the flames so that he can cross the mountains without danger or disaster. Otherwise Heaven will hold you criminally responsible and you're bound to be executed." "You haven't looked into the rights and wrongs of this at all," King Demon Bull replied. "That damned ape has done one evil thing after another: he's stolen my son, bullied my concubine, and defrauded my wife. I wish I could swallow him whole and turn him into shit to feed to the dogs. I'll never lend him my treasure."

Before the words were all out of his mouth Pig had caught up with him and was saying abusively, "I'll get you, you poxy bull. The fan or your life!" The Bull Demon King had to turn round to fight Pig off with his swords while the Great Sage Monkey wielded his cudgel to help him.

The demon king fought hard and courageously for mastery, falling back all the while. When the dawn came after a whole night of battle there was still no victor, and in front of them now was the entrance to the Cloud-touching Cave on Mount Thunder Piled. The ear-splitting noise that the three of them, the local god and the spirit soldiers were making alarmed Princess Jade, who sent her serving girls to see who was causing the din. The little demons on the doors came in to report, "It's our master. He's fighting the man with a face like a thunder god, another monk with a long snout and big ears, and the local god of the Fiery Mountains and his men." The moment Princess Jade heard this she ordered the senior and junior officers of the guard to take their swords and spears and help their lord. "Good to see you," said the Bull Demon King with delight, "good to see you." All the demons rushed wildly into the attack. It was more than Pig could cope with and he fled in defeat, trailing his rake behind him. The Great Sage sprang aloft out of the multiple encirclement on a somersault cloud; the spirit soldiers broke and ran. Old Bull led his host of demons back to the cave in victory and the doors were shut tightly behind them.

"He's tough, damn him," said Monkey. "He started fighting me at about four yesterday afternoon and we were nowhere near a result when you two came along to help last night. He fought for half a day and a whole night without showing any sign of tiring. And that bunch of little devils who came out just now were a rough lot too. Now he's shut the doors of his cave and won't come out. What are we to do?" "It was about ten yesterday morning when you left the master, brother," Pig said, "so why was it four in the afternoon when you started fighting him? What were you doing for the six hours in between?" Monkey then told him what had happened.

"As the saying goes," Pig replied, "it's just like a boatful of beancurd sinking: it came out of the wet and it disappeared into the wet. Easy come, easy go. But how are we going to take our master across the mountains if we're having so hard a time getting the fan? We'll just have to go back and make a bloody detour." "Don't get impatient, Great Sage," the local god said, "and don't try to be lazy, Marshal Tian Peng. If you make a detour that will mean leaving the straight and narrow: you'll never cultivate your conduct that way. As the old saying goes, 'In walking never take a short cut.' You mustn't talk about detours. Your master is waiting by the main road, desperate for your success." "Yes, yes," said Monkey, his resolve stiffened, "don't talk nonsense, idiot. The local deity is right." These words braced Pig's spirits too.

The two of them led the local deity and his spirit soldiers forward, then battered the doors of the Cloud-touching Cave to pieces with the rake and the cudgel. This so terrified the guard commanders that they rushed inside to report, "Your Majesty, Sun Wukong's brought his troops here and has smashed down our front doors." The Bull Demon King was just then telling Princess Jade what had happened and feeling thoroughly fed up with Monkey. The news of the front doors being smashed made him beside himself with fury, so he put his armour on immediately and went outside with his iron mace in his hands shouting abusively, "Damned macaque! You must think you're a very big shot indeed, coming here to play the hooligan and smash down my front door." "Old skinflint," retorted Pig, going forward, "who do you think you are, trying to put other people in their place? Don't move! Take this!" "Idiot!" the Bull Demon King replied. "Chaff-guzzler! You're not worth bothering with. Tell that monkey to come here." "You don't know what's good for you, cud-chewer," called Monkey. "Yesterday you were still my sworn brother, but today we're enemies. Watch this carefully!" The Bull Demon King met their onslaught with spirit, and the ensuing fight was even finer than the one before.

With death in their hearts and no thought of survival the three of them fought another hundred or so rounds till Pig took advantage of Monkey's miraculous powers to put all his brute strength into a rain of blows from his rake that were more than the Bull Demon King could withstand. He turned and fled defeated back to his cave, only to find the entrance blocked by the local god and his spirit troops. "Where do you think you're going, Strongarm King?" the local god shouted. "We're here." As he could not get into his cave the Bull Demon King fled, only to be pursued by Pig and Monkey. In his panic the Bull Demon King tore off his helmet and armour, threw away his mace, shook himself, turned into a swan and flew away.

Monkey looked around and said with a grin, "Pig, Old Bull's gone." The idiot had not the faintest idea of what had happened and neither had the local god as they looked all around and aimlessly searched Mount Thunder Piled. "Isn't that him flying up there?" said Monkey, pointing. "It's a swan," Pig replied. "Yes," said Monkey, "it's what Old Bull turned himself into." "So what are we going to do about it?" the local god asked. "You two charge in there, wipe all the demons out without quarter and tear down his den," Monkey replied. "That will cut off his retreat while I go and match transformations with him." We shall say no more of Pig and the local god smashing their way into the cave as they had been instructed.

Putting away his gold-banded cudgel and saying the words of a spell while making the necessary hand movements, Monkey shook himself and turned into a vulture who soared up into the clouds with his wings beating noisily, then swooped down on the swan, seizing its neck and gouging at its eyes. Realizing that this was Sun Wukong transformed the Bull Demon King braced himself and turned into a golden eagle who gouged back at the vulture. Then Monkey turned into a black phoenix to chase the eagle, only to be recognized by the Bull King, who turned into a white crane and flew off south with a loud call. Monkey stopped, braced his feathers, and turned into a red phoenix, who called loudly too. At the sight of the phoenix, the king of all the birds whom no bird dared treat with disrespect, the white crane swooped down beside the precipice with a beat of his wings, shook himself, and turned into a river-deer grazing in a timid, stupid way at the foot of the cliff. Monkey spotted him, came swooping down too, and turned into a hungry tiger that came running after the river-deer, swishing his tail hungrily. The demon king had to move fast as he transformed himself into a huge leopard with spots like golden coins who turned to savage the hungry tiger. Seeing this, Monkey faced the wind, shook himself, and turned into a golden-eyed lion with a voice like thunder, a brazen head and an iron brow. He spun round to devour the leopard, at which the Bull Demon King immediately became a giant bear that ran after the lion. Monkey then rolled himself up and became an elephant with tusks shaped like bamboo shoots, and a trunk like a python that he stretched out to wrap round the bear.

The Bull Demon King chuckled and switched back into his own original shape as a great white bull with a craggy head and flashing eyes. Each of his horns was like an iron pagoda, and his teeth were rows of sharp swords. He was about ten thousand feet long from head to tail and stood eight thousand feet high at the shoulder. "What are you going to do to me now, damned macaque?" he shouted to Brother Monkey at the top of his voice; at which Monkey too reverted to his own form, pulled out his gold-banded cudgel, bowed forward and shouted "Grow!" He then grew to be a hundred thousand feet tall with a head like Mount Taishan, eyes like the sun and moon, a mouth like a pool of blood and teeth like doors. He raised his iron cudgel and struck at the Bull Demon King's head; and the Bull Demon King hardened his head and charged Monkey with his horns. This was a ridge-rocking, mountain-shaking, heaven-scaring, earth-frightening battle.

The two of them gave such a great display of their magic powers as they fought on the mountain that they alarmed all the deities around there, who surrounded the demon king. He was not in the least afraid as he butted to east and west with his straight, shining, iron horns, and lashed to north and south with his strong and hairy tail. Sun Wukong stood up to him head-on while all the other gods surrounded him till in his despair the Bull Demon King rolled on the ground, turned back into his usual form, and headed for the Plantain Cave. Monkey too put away his magical form and joined in the chase with all the gods, but once in the cave the demon king shut the doors fast. The gods then threw a watertight encirclement around Mount Turquoise Cloud.

Just when they were all about to storm the doors they heard the shouts of Pig arriving with the local god and his spirit soldiers. "How are things in the Cloud-touching Cave?" Monkey asked, greeting him. "I finished off Old Bull's woman with one blow from my rake," grinned Pig, "and when I stripped her I found she was a jade-faced fox spirit. Her demons were all donkeys, mules, bulls, badgers, foxes, racoon dogs, river-deer, goats, tigers, elk, deer and things like that. We killed the lot of them and burnt down all the buildings in the cave. The local god tells me he's got another woman who lives here, so we've come here to wipe her out too." "You've done well, brother," said Monkey. "Congratulations. I tried competing with Old Bull in transformations, but I couldn't beat him. He turned into a simply enormous white bull, and I made myself as big as heaven and earth. We were just battling it out when all the gods came down and surrounded him. After a long time he turned back into himself and went into the cave." "Is this Plantain Cave?", Pig asked. "Yes, yes," Monkey replied, "Raksasi's in here." "Then why don't we storm the place and wipe the lot of them out to get the fan?" said Pig, his blood still up. "Are we going to let the two of them live to be any older and wiser and love each other with tender passion?"

The splendid idiot then summoned up his strength to bring his rake down on the doors so hard that doors, rockface and all collapsed with a mighty rumble. The serving girls rushed inside to report, "Your Majesty, someone's smashed the doors in and we don't know who he is." The Bull Demon King himself had just run panting in and was still telling Raksasi about his fight with Monkey for the fan when he heard this report, which made him very angry indeed. At once he spat out the fan and gave it to Raksasi, who took it in her hands and said tearfully, "Your Majesty, give the macaque the fan if he'll call his troops off." "Wife," the Bull Demon King replied, "it may only be a little thing in itself, but I hate and loathe him. Wait here while I have it out with him again." Once more the demon put on his armour, chose another pair of swords, and went out to find Pig smashing the doors down with his rake. Without a word Old Bull raised his swords and cut at Pig's head. Pig parried with his rake and fell back a few paces till he was outside the doors, where Monkey swung his cudgel at the Bull Demon King's head. The Bull Monster then mounted a storm wind and sprang away from the cave to fight Monkey once more on Mount Turquoise Cloud. All the gods surrounded him, while the local god's soldiers joined in the fray from either side. The Bull Demon King fought over fifty rounds till he abandoned the field, unable to hold out. He tried to flee but every way he turned he was blocked by the heavenly army. The Old Bull was now trembling with fear, but it was too late for regrets. On all sides he was surrounded by the Buddha's troops and heavenly generals. It really was as if he were caught in a high net from which there was no escape. In his despair he heard Monkey coming after him at the head of his forces, so he sprang on his cloud and went up.

At just that moment Heavenly King Li the Pagoda-carrier was encamped in the sky with Prince Nezha. "Not so fast," he shouted, "not so fast. I am here on mandate of the Jade Emperor to exterminate you." In his extremity the Bull Demon King shook himself, turned back into the giant white bull, and tried to gore the Heavenly King with his iron horns, while the Heavenly King hacked at him with his sword. Soon Brother Monkey arrived. "Great Sage," Prince Nezha shouted at the top of his voice, "I can't greet you properly as I'm in armour. Yesterday my father and I went to see the Tathagata Buddha, who sent a note to the Jade Emperor. It said that the Tang Priest was held up by the Fiery Mountains and that you couldn't subdue the Bull Demon King, Great Sage. The Jade Emperor then ordered my father to bring his forces here to help." "But this damned creature's magical powers are tremendous," Monkey replied, "and he's turned himself into this. What are we going to do about him?" "Have no doubts," replied Nezha with a smile. "Watch me catch him."

The prince then shouted, "Change!" gave himself three heads and six arms, and took a flying leap upon the Bull Demon King's back. With one swing of his demon-beheading sword he had the bull's head off before he even realized he had done it. The Heavenly King threw down his sword and went to meet Monkey. But another head grew out from the Bull Demon King's throat, its mouth breathing black vapours and its eyes flashing golden light. Nezha cut again, but as the head fell a new one appeared. Nezha's sword cut a dozen heads off and a dozen new heads immediately grew again. Nezha then hung his fire-wheel on the bull's horns, blew on the magic fire, and made it blaze so fiercely that the Bull Demon King bellowed in desperate pain, shaking his head and tail and trying for all he was worth to escape. Just when he was about to do another transformation and get away his true image was fixed in Heavenly King Li's demon-revealing mirror. Now he could make no more changes and he had no way of escape. He could only call out, "Spare my life! I wish to be converted to the Buddhist faith." "If you value your life, hand the fan over at once," said Nezha. "My wife is looking after it," the Bull Demon King replied.

Hearing this reply, Nezha undid the demon-binding rope and slipped it round his neck, then took him by the nose, ran the rope through it, and led him along by hand. Monkey meanwhile gathered together all the gods, to crowd around the white bull and lead him back to the entrance to the Plantain Cave. "Wife," Old Bull called, "bring the fan out and save my life." As soon as she heard this Raksasi took off her jewellery and bright-coloured clothing, dressed her hair like a Taoist nun and put on a white silk habit like a Buddhist one. She came out through the doors carrying the twelve-foot fan with both hands, and at the sight of the vajrapanis, the gods, the Heavenly King and Nezha she fell to her knees in terror, kowtowing in worship and saying, "I beg you Bodhisattvas to spare my husband and me. I present the fan to my brother-in-law Monkey for him to win his glory with." Monkey went forward, took the fan, and rode back east by auspicious cloud with the others.

The Great Sage Sun took the fan close to the Fiery Mountains, waved it as hard as he could, and put the flames out. Their glare disappeared. He waved the fan again and the rustle of a cool breeze could be heard; and at the third wave the sky was overcast with cloud and a fine rain began to fall. Having been relieved of his cares Sanzang stopped worrying and thanked all the gods. The Heavenly King and Nezha led the bull back to hand him over to the Buddha. This left only the local mountain god waiting there with Raksasi under his guard.

"Why aren't you on your way, Raksasi?" Monkey asked.

346

Monkey Borrows the Fan for the Third Time

"What are you standing there waiting for?" "I beg you in your mercy, Great Sage," she replied, "to give me back the fan." "You've got a cheek, damned bitch," roared Pig. "We've spared your life and that should be enough for you. What do you want the fan for? When we've crossed the mountains we'll be able to sell it for food. Do you think we're going to give it to you after all the trouble and effort we've been to? It's raining, so be off home with you." She bowed again and said, "But the Great Sage promised to give it back when he'd put the fire out. I'm very sorry about all that has happened. It was only because I was feeling so upset that I put you to all that trouble. We too have learned to live like human beings. The only thing is that we had not been converted to the pursuit of the true achievement. Now our true bodies have turned to the west, and we will not dare do anything wicked again. I beg you to return the fan so that I can reform and cultivate myself." "Great Sage," said the local deity, "let us make full use of this woman's knowledge of the art of extinguishing fire to put these fires out for good, and give her back her fan. Then I will be able to live here in peace, help the people who live here, and be given offerings of blood and food. This would truly be a great kindness to me." "I heard the local people saying that when the fan puts the flames out in these mountains they can only gather one harvest before they start burning again," said Monkey. "How are we going to be able to put them out forever?" "All you have to do to put the flames out forever," said Raksasi, "is wave the fan forty-nine times. Then they'll never burn again."

Now that Brother Monkey knew this he took the fan and fanned the mountains with it forty-nine times as hard as he possibly could, whereupon heavy rain began to pour down. The fan really was a treasure: where there were flames it rained, and where there were not the sky was clear. By standing where there were no flames master and disciples avoided getting wet. After spending the night sitting there they got the horse and luggage ready the next morning and returned the fan to Raksasi. "If I don't give you it back," Monkey said, "people might say I don't keep my word. Take the fan with you, go back to your mountain and don't make any more trouble. As you've achieved human form I'll spare your life." Taking the fan from him Raksasi said the words of the spell, pinched the thread so that it shrank back to the size of an apricot leaf and put it in her mouth. She then thanked them all and prepared to cultivate her conduct as a hermit. Later she too achieved the true reward. As Monkey, Pig and Friar Sand escorted Sanzang along his way their bodies felt cool and the ground under their feet was pleasantly damp.

CHAPTER 29
The Tang Priest Is Captured in the Gossamer Cave

The story tells how Sanzang and disciples got everything ready, saddled the horse and headed westwards, having many more adventures along the way. Before they realized it autumn and winter were over and spring's brightness and charm were back. Master and disciples were enjoying the scenery as their way led them across the greenery when they suddenly noticed a building amid trees. Sanzang dismounted and stood beside the main track. "Master," Brother Monkey asked, "the road is easy and there is no evil about, so why have you stopped?" "You aren't at all understanding, brother," Pig said. "The master is feeling sleepy after being in the saddle for so long. You ought to let him come down and have a rest." "It's not that," Sanzang said. "I can see a house over there. I was thinking of going there myself to beg for some food."

"What a thing for the master to say," said Monkey with a smile. If you want some food I'll go and beg some for you. As the saying goes, 'Your teacher for a day is your father for the rest of your life.' It would be outrageous for me, your disciple, to sit here idly and let my master go begging." "There's no need to say that," Sanzang replied. "Usually you three have to cross enormous distances as far as the eye can see to beg for our food. Today there's a house so close it's in shouting distance, so let me beg this time."

Pig accepted this suggestion and brought out the begging

bowl and a change of hat and cassock for the master, who went straight to the farm building to look at it. It really was a fine place. As there were no males but only four girls to be seen there the reverend gentleman did not dare to go inside.

He stood there for an hour. The silence was complete, unbroken by dog or cock. "If I'm not even capable of begging us a meal my disciples will laugh at me," he thought. "If the master can't beg a meal, what hope do his disciples have of ever getting to see the Buddha?"

He did not know what to do, but it seemed wrong to stay there any longer, so he went back towards the bridge, only to notice a pavilion inside the compound of thatched cottages. In the pavilion three more girls were juggling a ball with their feet.

After watching for a long time Sanzang could only go to the bridge and call loudly, "Bodhisattvas, fate brings me here as a poor monk to beg for the gift of some food." As soon as the women heard him they cheerfully put aside their needlework and balls to come out smiling and giggling through the gates to greet him. "Reverend sir," they said, "we're sorry we didn't welcome you sooner. As you have come to our poor farm we couldn't possibly feed you on the path. Please come inside and sit down." When Sanzang heard this he thought, "Splendid, this is splendid. The West really is Buddha's land. If even these womenfolk are so diligent about feeding monks the men are bound to be pious followers of the Buddha."

Sanzang stepped forward to greet the women and followed them into the thatched cottages. As he passed by the pavilion he looked and saw one of the women come forward to push the stone gates open and invite him to come inside and sit down. All he could do was go inside. When he looked up he saw that the tables and seats were all of stone, and the atmosphere was oppressively cold. This alarmed the venerable elder, who thought, "This is a thoroughly sinister place. I'm sure it's evil." "Please sit down, venerable elder," the women all said with simpering smiles. He had no choice but to sit down. A little later he found himself shuddering.

"What monastery are you from, reverend sir?" the women

asked. "For what purpose are you collecting alms? Are you repairing roads and bridges, founding monasteries, worshipping at pagodas, or having Buddha statues made and sutras printed? Won't you show us your donation book?" "I am not a monk collecting donations," the venerable elder replied. "If you're not here to ask for charity then why are you here?" the women asked. "We have been sent by Great Tang in the east to the Thunder Monastery in the Western Heaven to fetch the scriptures," Sanzang replied. "As our stomachs were empty when we happened to be passing this distinguished place I have come to beg a vegetarian meal from you in your kindness. After that we poor monks will be on our way again." "Splendid, splendid," the women all said. "As the saying goes, monks from afar most love to read the scriptures. Sisters! We must treat them well. Let's give them some vegetarian food as quickly as we can."

Sanzang was horrified when what they cooked for him was human flesh. They refused to let him go. "Business bringing itself to our door!" they all said. "You've no more chance of getting away from here than of covering up a fart with your hands. Where do you think you're going?" They were all quite skilled in the martial arts and quick movers too, and after they had grabbed Sanzang they dragged him like a sheep and threw him to the ground. Then they all held him down, tied him up, and suspended him from the rafters. The three ropes had him suspended from a beam with his back on top and his belly pointing down. As Sanzang endured the agony and held back this tears he thought with bitter regret, "How evil my destiny is. I thought I was coming to beg for a vegetarian meal from good people. I never imagined I'd be falling into the fiery pit. Disciples! Rescue me as soon as you can if I am ever to see you again. If you don't get here within four hours I shall be dead."

Despite his misery Sanzang kept a careful eye on the women. When they had him tied up securely and hanging there they started to remove their clothes. The women unbuttoned their gauze blouses, exposing their stomachs. Then each of them produced a silken rope about as thick as a duck egg from her navel. These they made move like bursting jade or flying silver as they fastened the farm gates with their silk.

We leave them and go back to Monkey, Pig and Friar Sand, who were all still waiting by the main road. While the other two were pasturing the horse and looking after the baggage Monkey was amusing himself by leaping from tree to tree and climbing around the branches as he picked leaves and looked for fruit. Suddenly he turned round and saw a sheet of light. This so alarmed him that he jumped out of the tree with a shout of, "This is terrible! Terrible! The master's luck is out." He pointed as he continued, "Look at the farm. What do you think?" When Pig and Friar Sand both looked they saw a sheet of something like snow but brighter and like silver but shinier. "That's done it," said Pig, "that's done it. The master's run into evil spirits. We'd better go and rescue him straight away." "Stop yelling, brother," said Monkey. "Neither of you can see just what's there. Wait while I go and take a look." "Do be careful, brother," said Friar Sand. "I can cope," Monkey replied.

The splendid Great Sage tightened his tigerskin kilt, pulled out his gold-banded cudgel and took a few strides forward to see that the silken ropes had formed something like a web with thousands of strands. When he felt it with his hands it was somewhat soft and sticky. Not knowing what it was, Monkey raised his cudgel and said, "Never mind thousands of strands. This cudgel could break through tens of thousands of them." He was just about to strike when he stopped to think, "If they were hard I could certainly smash them, but then soft ones would only be knocked flat, and if I alarm the demons and get caught myself that would be a disaster. I'd better make some enquiries before I do any hitting."

He made a spell and called out an old local god. Brother Monkey asked, "Tell me where this is." "Which way have you come, Great Sage?" the local deity asked. "I've come from the east and I'm heading west," said Monkey. "Which mountain have you reached on your journey from the east?" the local deity asked. "That ridge there," Monkey replied. "Our baggage and the horse are there, aren't they?" "That is Gossamer Ridge," the local deity replied. "Under the ridge there's a cave called Gossamer Cave where seven evil spirits live." "Male or female ones?" Monkey asked. "She-devils," the local deity replied. "How powerful is their magic?" Monkey asked. "I'm much too weak and insignificant to know that," the local god replied. "All I can tell you is that a mile due south of here there is a natural hot spring called the Filth-cleansing Spring," the local god said, "where the Seven Fairies from on high used to bathe. When the seven evil spirits settled here and took over the Filth-cleansing Spring the good spirits didn't try to fight them for it. They let the spirits have it for nothing. I reckon that if even good spirits from Heaven don't dare offend them the evil spirits must have tremendous powers." "Go back now, local god," Monkey said when he heard all this, "and wait while I capture them." The old local god kowtowed to him and went back to his shrine all of a tremble.

The Great Sage then gave a solo display of his magical powers, shaking himself, turning into a fly, and landing on the tip of a blade of grass to wait beside the path. A little later he heard a rustling, hissing sound like that of silkworms eating leaves or an ocean tide coming in. In the time it takes to drink half a cup of tea the silken ropes had all gone, and the farm looked just the same as it had before. Then there was a creaking noise as the wicker gate opened and the seven women came out laughing and talking noisily. Monkey watched carefully from where he was hiding and saw them talking and laughing as they held each other by the hand and walked shoulder to shoulder across the bridge.

The splendid Great Sage flew over with a high-pitched buzz and landed on the topknot of the woman who was walking in front. When she was over the bridge the women behind her caught up with her and called out, "Sister, let's have a bath before we steam the fat monk and eat him up." The women walked south, picking flowers and throwing grass at each other, and were soon at the bathing pool, where a very magnificent wall and gateway appeared, with fragrant flowers, among them a bed of orchids, growing all around. One of the women behind him stepped forward and with a whistling sound pushed the double gates open, revealing the pond of naturally hot water inside.

The bathing pool was about fifty feet across, a hundred feet long and four feet deep. The water was pure and translucent, and from the bottom of it came up bubbles like rolling pearls or floating jade. In the four sides of the pool there were six or seven pipes through which the water flowed out, keeping warm even when it reached fields up to a mile away. Beside the pool was a three-roomed pavilion, next to the back wall of which stood an eight-legged bench. At each end of the pavilion was a clothes stand painted in coloured lacquers. All this secretly delighted Monkey, who flew straight to one of the stands and landed on it.

When the women saw how clear and warm the water was they wanted to bathe in it, so they all took their clothes off and hung them on the stands before going into the pool together.

The women all jumped into the water and enjoyed themselves as they frolicked in the waves. "If I wanted to hit them," Monkey thought, "I'd only need to stir the water with my cudgel. It would be like pouring boiling water on a nest of mice: I could kill the lot of them. What a pity. If I hit them I'd kill them, but it wouldn't do my reputation any good. As they say, a real man doesn't fight women. It'd be hopeless if a man like me killed these girls. If I'm not going to hit them I'll have to make things difficult for them so that they can't move." The splendid Great Sage made a spell with his hands, said the words of it, shook himself and turned into a hungry eagle.

With a whoosh of his wings he flew towards them, stretched his sharp talons to seize all seven sets of clothes that were hung on the stands and flew straight back to the ridge with them. Here he reverted to his own form to see Pig and Friar Sand.

Just look at the idiot as he comes up to Brother Monkey and says with a grin, "The master must have been taken to a pawnbroker's." "How can you tell?" asked Friar Sand. "Can't you see all those clothes our brother's grabbed?" Pig replied. "These are the evil spirits' clothes," said Monkey. He explained what had happened. "If you ask me we should kill the demons then rescue the master," said Pig. "That's what's called cutting down weeds and digging them out by the roots." "I'm not going to hit them," Monkey replied. "If you want them hit go and do it yourself."

Pig then summoned up his spirits and in high delight rushed straight there, his rake held aloft. As he suddenly pushed the gates open and looked inside he saw the seven women squatting in the water. He tore off his clothes and jumped in with them.

The idiot was thoroughly rough and crude and wanted to show off his powers. He was unmoved by their fragrant feminine beauty. Raising his rake he charged them, lashing out wildly without caring what he was doing. The demons jumped out of the water and ran naked into the pavilion. Standing there they used magic to make thick silken ropes come out of their navels, filling the sky with a huge silken canopy under which Pig was caught. When the idiot looked up he could not see the sun in the heavens. He tried to run outside, but he could not lift his feet, which were tangled in silken ropes that covered the ground. When he tried to move his feet he tripped and staggered. He tried going left, but his head crashed to the ground, then tried going right and came a cropper. So he turned round as quickly as he could and kissed the dirt, got himself back on his feet, and collapsed head first once more. Goodness only knows how many times he stumbled and fell till his whole body was numb, his feet sore, his head aching and his eyes blurred. He could no longer even crawl, but lay groaning on the floor. Then the demons tied him up. They neither beat him up nor wounded him, but sprang outside to rush back to their cave, leaving the silken canopy to blot out the daylight.

The demons went back to their bedrooms carved out of the rock, put on their old clothes and went straight to the back door of the cave, where they stood and called, "Where are you, children?"

Now each she-devil had a child, not one that she had borne, but an adopted child who had taken her as a mother. They were called Bee, Hornet, Cockroach, Spanish-fly, Grasshopper, Wax-insect and Dragonfly, for such they were. The evil spirits had spread their nets across the sky, caught these seven insects and been on the point of eating them. The insects had pleaded for their lives and volunteered to take the spirits as their own mothers. Ever since then they had gathered blossoms in the spring and summer flowers for the evil spirits, and as soon as they heard the shouts they appeared and asked, "What orders do you have for us, mothers?" "Sons," the demons replied, "this morning we made a mistake and provoked the monk from Tang. His disciples trapped us in the pool and disgraced us. We were almost killed. You must do your utmost. Go outside and drive them away. When you've beaten them come to your uncle's to meet us." The she-devils then fled for their lives and went to the home of their teacher's senior disciple. Watch as the insects rub their fists in their hands and go out to confront their enemies.

Pig, meanwhile, whose head was spinning after falling over so often, looked up and suddenly saw that the silken canopy and ropes had all disappeared. Groping around he picked himself up, and despite his pain he made his way back the way he had come. As soon as he saw Monkey he grabbed him and said, "Brother, is my head bulging? Is my face all blue?" "What happened to you?" Monkey asked. "Those damned creatures caught me under a silken net and tripped me up goodness knows how many times with silk ropes," Pig replied. "My waist was twisted, my back felt broken and I couldn't move an inch. Then the silk canopy and the ropes all disappeared, so I could escape and come back." "Forget about it," said Friar Sand when he saw him, "forget about it. You asked for trouble. I'm sure the demons have all gone back to the cave to harm the master. We must go and rescue him straight away."

When Monkey heard this he set out at once as fast as he could and rushed back to the farm while Pig led the horse. Here the seven little devils could be seen standing on the bridge, blocking their way and saying, "Not so fast, not so fast. We're here." "What a joke!" said Pig when he saw them. "They're just a bunch of kids. They're only two foot five or six, well under three foot, and they can only weigh eight or nine pounds, not even ten." "Who are you?" he shouted. "We're the sons of the seven immortal ladies," the little devils replied. "You've insulted our mothers, and now you've got the effrontery to attack us, you ignorant fools. Stay where you are, and watch out." The splendid monsters then launched a wild onslaught on Pig, who was in a flaming temper after falling over so often. Seeing how tiny the insects were he lifted his rake to strike furious blows at them.

When the little devils saw how ferocious the idiot was they all reverted to their original forms, flew into the air and shouted, "Change!" In an instant each of them became ten, each ten became a hundred, each hundred became a thousand, and each thousand became ten thousand. Every one became a countless number.

"Brother," said Pig in alarm, "you can say what you like about it being easy to fetch the scriptures, but on this road to the west even the insects give you a bad time." "Don't be afraid, brother," said Monkey. "Go for them." "But they're flying into my head and my face and all over my body," replied Pig. "They're at least ten layers deep and all stinging me. How can I go for them?" "No problem," said Monkey, "no problem. I know a trick." "Whatever it is, brother," said Friar Sand, "use it right now. His shaven head has swollen up with those bites in no time at all."

The splendid Great Sage pulled out a handful of hairs, chewed them into little bits and blew them out, telling them to turn to golden eagles, falcons, hawks, white eagles, vultures, ospreys and sparrowhawks." "Brother," said Pig, "what's that jargon about goldens and all that?" "Something you don't know about," Monkey replied. "Golden eagles, falcons, hawks, white eagles, vultures, ospreys and sparrowhawks are the seven birds of prey that my hairs turned into. That's because the she-devils' children are insects." Because the birds were so good at catching insects they got one every time they opened their beaks, grabbed at them with their claws or struck them with their wings. They wiped all the insects out in an instant, leaving no trace of them in the sky. The ground was piled over a foot deep with their bodies.

Only then could the three brothers charge across the bridge and into the cave, where they found their master hanging groaning and sobbing in mid-air. "Master," said Pig, going up to him, "are you hanging around here for fun? I don't know how many times I've had to fall over on your account." "Untie the master before we take this conversation any further," said Friar Sand. Brother Monkey then snapped the ropes and set the master free, asking, "Where did the evil spirits go?" "All seven of them ran stark naked to the back," the Tang Priest replied. "They were calling for their sons." "After them, brothers!" said Monkey. "Follow me!"

The three of them, each holding his weapon, went searching in the back garden, but no sign of them could be found. They looked for them without success under all the peach and plum trees. "They've gone," said Pig, "they've gone." "We can stop looking for them," said Friar Sand. "I'm going to help the master away from here." The three brothers then went back to the front, where they asked the Tang Priest to mount up. "You two help the master along the way," said Pig. "I'm going to smash these buildings to the ground with my rake. Then they'll have nowhere to live when they come back." "Smashing the place would be too much effort," said Monkey. "The best way to cut off their roots would be to find some firewood." The splendid idiot then gathered some dead pine, broken-off bamboo, dried-out willow and withered creepers that he set alight. The roaring blaze destroyed everything. Only then did master and disciples feel easy enough to be on their way and hurried along the main road to the west.

The story tells how the Great Sage Sun supported the Tang Priest as they hurried west together with Pig and Friar Sand. Within a few hours they were in sight of a compound with many tall towers and imposing buildings. When master and disciples reached the gates to look there was a stone tablet set over the gateway on which was written YELLOW FLOWER

TEMPLE. Sanzang dismounted. "Yellow Flower Temple means it's a Taoist place," said Pig, "so it's all right for us to go in and see them. Although we wear different clothes we cultivate our conduct the same way."

The master accepted their suggestions and the four of them went inside. Next Sanzang went in through the inner gate, where he found the doors of the main hall shut tight and a Taoist master sitting under a covered walkway making elixir pills.

As soon as he saw him Sanzang shouted at the top of his voice, "My respectful greetings, venerable Taoist master." The Taoist looked up with a start and was so alarmed by what he saw that he dropped the elixir on which he was working. Then he neatened his hair-pins and clothes, came down the steps and greeted Sanzang: "Venerable sir, excuse me for failing to meet you. Please come inside and sit down." The venerable elder happily went up into the main hall. On pushing the doors open he saw the statues of the Three Pure Ones and an altar on which stood incense burners and incense, so he planted some joss-sticks in the burner and performed a triple set of obeisances to the Pure Ones before bowing to the Taoist master. He then went to the guest seats, where he sat down with his disciples. Immortal boys were told to bring tea at once.

Now the seven devils from Gossamer Cave had been fellow-students of the Taoist master here, and it was here that they had hurried after putting on their old clothes and calling for their sons. They were making themselves new clothes at the back of the temple when they noticed the boys preparing the tea and asked, "What visitors have arrived, boys? What are you in such a rush for?" "Four Buddhist monks have just turned up," the boys replied, "and the master has told us to prepare tea for them." "Is one of the monks pale and fat?" the she-devils asked. "Yes." "Does one of them have a long snout and big ears?" they asked again. "Yes." "Then take the tea in as quickly as you can," the she-devils said, "and tip your master a wink to come in here. We've got something urgent to say to him."

When the Taoist master went back to the abbot's lodgings

the seven women all fell to their knees and said, "Brother, brother, please listen to what we have to say. Does one of the four monks who are the guests outside have a pale, fat face, and one of them a long snout and big ears? Did you ask them where they're from?" "Yes," the Taoist said, "there are two like that among them. How did you know? I suppose you've seen them somewhere."

"You don't know the terrible things that have happened, brother," the devils said. "That monk was sent by the Tang court to fetch the scriptures from the Western Heaven. He came to our cave this morning begging for food. We captured him because we'd heard of this Tang Priest." "Why did you capture him?" the Taoist asked. "We've long known that the Tang Priest has a pure body because he has cultivated his conduct for ten successive incarnations," the devils replied. "Anyone who eats a piece of his flesh will live for ever. That's why we captured him. Later the monk with a long snout and big ears kept us in the Filth-cleansing Spring. He obviously had some very naughty ideas. As we weren't going to let him have his way he tried to kill us all with his nine-pronged rake. If we hadn't known a thing or two he'd have murdered the lot of us. We fled in fear and trembling and sent your nephews into battle. We don't know whether they are alive or dead. We have come here to fling ourselves on your mercy and beg you to avenge your fellow-students from long ago."

On hearing this the Taoist was furious, as could be seen from his changed expression. "What outrageous monks!" he exclaimed. "What hooligans! Don't you worry: I'm going to sort them out." "If you're going to fight them," said the she-devils in gratitude, "you must let us help you." "There'll be no need to fight," said the Taoist, "no need. As the saying goes, you have to lower yourself to fight someone. Come with me."

The women went with him into his room, where he carried a ladder behind the bed, climbed up to the rafters and brought down a leather box. In it was a packet containing a drug.

"Sisters," said the Taoist master, "any mortal who eats one

grain of this treasure of mine will be dead when it reaches his stomach. Only three grains would be enough to kill a god or an immortal. As these monks may have mastered something of the Way they'll need three grains. Fetch my balance." One of the women brought a balance at once. "Weigh out twelve grains," he said, "and divide that into four portions." Then he took twelve red jujubes, pinched holes in them, stuffed a grain of the drug in each, and put them into four teacups. These were then placed with a fifth cup containing two black jujubes on a tray. "Let me question them," he said. "If they aren't from Tang that'll be the end of it; but if they are I'll ask for fresh tea and you can give this tea to the boys to bring in. Once they drink it they'll all die and you'll be avenged. That'll cheer you up." The seven women were beside themselves with gratitude.

The Taoist changed into another robe and walked out again with a great show of feigned courtesy. He urged the Tang Priest and the others to sit down in the guest seats again. "Please excuse me, venerable sir," the Taoist said. "The reason why I neglected you just now was because I was at the back telling my disciples to choose some greens and radishes to cook as a vegetarian meal for you." "We Buddhist monks came empty-handed," said Sanzang. "We could not possibly trouble you for a meal." "We are all men of religion," replied the Taoist master with a smile. "Whenever we go to a monastery or temple we are entitled to three pints of rice, so why talk of being empty-handed? May I ask you, reverend sir, what monastery you are from, and why you are here?" "I have been sent by His Majesty the Great Tang emperor to fetch the scriptures from the Great Thunder Monastery in the Western Heaven," Sanzang replied. "As we were passing your Taoist temple we came in to pay our respects." At this news the Taoist's face was full of animation, as he said, "It was only because I did not realize you were so faithful to the most virtuous Buddha that I failed to come out a long way to meet you. Please forgive me. Please forgive me." Then he told the boys to bring fresh tea at once and get a meal ready as soon as possible, at which the boys went straight inside to fetch the tea. "Here's some good tea that's all ready," the women called to them. "Take this in." The boys did indeed take the five cups in, and the Taoist master hurriedly passed a cup of red jujube tea to the Tang Priest. As Pig was so big the Taoist took him for the senior disciple, and he thought Friar Sand was the next senior. Thinking that Monkey was the junior one the Taoist only handed him his cup fourth.

By the time the sharp-eyed Brother Monkey took his cup he had already noticed that there were two black jujubes in the cup left on the tray. "Let's change cups, sir," he said. "To be honest with you," the Taoist replied with a smile, "as a poor Taoist living out here in the wilds I am rather short of tea and food at the moment. I was looking for fruit out at the back just now and I could only find these twelve red jujubes to put into four cups of tea to offer you. As I had to take something with you I made another cup with these inferior jujubes to keep you company. This is just a gesture of respect." "What nonsense," said Monkey with a smile. "As the ancients said, 'You are never poor if you are at home; but poverty on a journey is killing.' You're at home here, so why all this talk about being poor? It's wandering monks like us who are really poor. I'll swop with you. I insist." "Wukong," said Sanzang when he heard this, "this immortal gentleman is being very hospitable. You have yours. There is no need for a swop." Monkey had no choice. Taking the cup with his left hand he covered it with his right and watched them.

Pig, however, who apart from feeling hungry and thirsty had an enormous appetite at the best of times, picked the three red jujubes out of the cup as soon as he saw them and swallowed them noisily. The master ate his too, as did Friar Sand. In that very instant Pig's face changed colour, tears started pouring from Friar Sand's eyes and the Tang Priest began to foam at the mouth. Unable to sit upright, all three of them fainted and fell to the floor.

Realizing that they had been poisoned, the Great Sage raised his teacup in his hands and threw it at the Taoist master's face. The Taoist stopped it with his sleeve and it shattered noisily as it fell to the floor. The splendid Great Sage felt in his ear for his gold-banded cudgel, waved it to make it as thick as a rice-bowl, and struck at the Taoist master's face. The Taoist rapidly turned and dodged the blow, then produced a fine sword with which he fought back.

Their cursing and fighting had by now disturbed the seven she-devils inside, who all rushed out shouting, "Spare yourself the trouble, elder brother. Let us catch him." At the sight of them Monkey became angrier than ever. Whirling his iron cudgel around with both hands he dropped his guard and tumbled in among them, lashing out wildly. The seven women then undid their clothes, revealing their white stomachs, and from their navels they produced by magic thick silken ropes that came reeling out in such abundance that they formed a canopy under which Brother Monkey was confined.

Seeing that things were going badly Monkey got up, said the words of a spell, did a somersault, smashed through the canopy and escaped. Then he stood gloomily in mid-air, con-trolling his temper and watching as the flashing silken ropes criss-crossed like the warp and weft of cloth on the loom. Within a moment the Yellow Flower Temple's towers and halls were all completely concealed.

The splendid Great Sage brought his cloud down to land, made a spell with his fingers, said the sacred syllable *Om*, and forced the old local god to come to him again. The old deity knelt beside the path, trembling with fear and kowtowing as he said, "Great Sage, you went to rescue your master. Why are you back again?" "I rescued him this morning," Monkey re-plied, "and a little way ahead from there we reached a Yellow Flower Temple. When I went in with the master to look around, the head Taoist of the temple greeted us, and in the middle of our conversation he knocked out my master and the other two with poisoned tea. And the seven she-devils produced their magic silken ropes from their bodies. I reckon that as you're a god who lives round here you're bound to know their background. What sort of evil spirit are they? Tell me the truth if you don't want to be hit." "It's less than ten years since those evil spirits came here," said the local deity, kowtowing. "When I was making an inspection three years ago I saw what they really are: seven spider spirits. The silken ropes that come out of them are spiders' webs." The news thoroughly delighted Monkey, who said, "From what you tell me they're no problem. Very well then. You can go back while I use magic to subdue him." The local god kowtowed and went.

Monkey then went to the outside of the Yellow Flower Temple, pulled seventy hairs out of his tail, blew on them with magic breath and shouted, "Change!" The hairs turned into seventy little Monkeys. He then blew a magic breath on his gold-banded cudgel, called "Change!" and turned it into seventy two-pronged forks, one of which he gave to each of the little Monkeys. Monkey himself used one of the forks to twist the silken ropes as he stood outside, then they all attacked together to the rhythm of a tune, tearing the ropes to pieces, each of them tearing off over ten pounds of rope. They dragged seven spiders out from inside. Each was about the size of a wicker basket. All of them held their hands and feet together and had ropes round their necks. "Spare us, spare us," they said. The seventy little Monkeys then pressed the seven spiders to the ground, refusing to let them go. "Don't hit them," said Monkey. "All we want is to make them give my master and my brothers back." "Elder Brother," shrieked the demons at the tops of their voices, "give the Tang Priest back and save our lives." The Taoist master rushed outside saying, "Sisters, I'm going to eat the Tang Priest. I can't save you."

This infuriated Brother Monkey. "If you won't give my master back just watch what happens to your sisters." The splendid Great Sage waved his fork, turned it back into an iron cudgel that he lifted with both hands and smashed the seven spider spirits to pulp. Then he shook his tail a couple of times, put the hairs back on it and charged inside alone, swinging his cudgel to fight the Taoist master.

When the Taoist master saw Monkey kill his seven fellow-students it was more than he could bear. Goaded to fury, he raised his sword to fight back.

盤絲洞七情迷本

Sanzang In the Gossamer Cave

When the Taoist master had fought fifty or sixty rounds with the Great Sage he felt his hand weakening and his sinews getting slack, so he undid his belt and with a loud flapping noise took off his black robe. "Well, my lad," said the Great Sage with a laugh, "if you can't beat me you still won't be able to when you strip off." Once the Taoist master had stripped off his clothes he raised both hands to reveal under his ribs a thousand eyes flashing golden light. They were dazzling bright.

Monkey started lashing out desperately with his hands and feet, but could only spin around inside the golden light, unable to take a step either forwards or backwards. It was as if he were turning round and round in a bucket. It was hopeless. He was unbearably hot. In his anxiety he leapt into the air, smashing against the golden light, and crashing head first to the ground. His head ached where he had hit it. He felt it anxiously to find that the top of his scalp was tender.

The splendid Great Sage said the words of a spell, shook himself, and turned into one of those scaly diggers called pangolins. He burrowed into the ground with his head, not coming out again till he had covered over six miles. The golden light could only enclose about three miles. When he emerged and turned back into himself he was exhausted. His muscles ached, his whole body was in pain, and he could not help weeping.

Just as the Handsome Monkey King was feeling miserable the sound of sobs could suddenly be heard from the other side of the mountain. Leaning forward and drying his tears he turned to look. A woman appeared, dressed in deep mourning and sobbing at every step as she came from the other side of the mountain. She was holding a dish of cold rice gruel in her left hand and several pieces of yellow paper money for burning to the dead in her right. Monkey sighed and nodded as he said to himself, "This is a case of

Weeping eyes meeting weeping eyes,
One broken heart coming across another.

I wonder what this woman is crying about. I'll ask her." Before long the woman was coming along the path towards him.

"Lady Bodhisattva," asked Brother Monkey with a bow, "who are you weeping for?" Through her tears the woman replied, "My husband was murdered by the master of the Yellow Flower Temple with poisoned tea because he got into a quarrel with him over the purchase of some bamboo poles. I'm going to burn this paper money as a mark of my love for him." This made Monkey's tears flow. The sight made the woman say angrily, "You ignorant fool. I'm grieving over my husband, but what business do you have to be weeping and looking so miserable? Are you mocking me?"

"Please don't be angry, Bodhisattva," said Monkey with a bow. He then told her who he was and what had happened to his Master and brothers.

Putting down the gruel and the paper money the woman returned Brother Monkey's bow and said, "Please forgive me. I didn't realize that you were a sufferer too. From what you've just said you don't know who that Taoist is. He's really the Demon King Hundred-eye, who's also known as the Many-eyed Monster. You must have tremendous magical powers to have escaped from the golden light and fought so long, but you couldn't get near him. I'll tell you about a sage you can send for who would be able to smash the golden light and defeat the Taoist."

Monkey's immediate response was to chant a noise of respect and say, "If you know the sage's background, Lady Bodhisattva, may I trouble you to tell me about it? If there is such a sage I'll fetch him to rescue my master and avenge your husband." "I'll tell you," the woman said, "and you can fetch the sage, who will subdue the Taoist, but that will only bring revenge. I'm afraid the sage won't be able to rescue your master." "Why not?" Monkey asked. "His poison is truly lethal," the woman replied. "When people are laid low by it the very marrow of their bones rots within three days. I'm afraid that by the time you've been to see the sage and come back again you'll be too late to save him." "I know how to travel," Monkey replied. "However far it is I'll only take half a day." "If you can travel then listen to this," the woman said. "About three hundred miles from here there's a mountain called Mount Purple Clouds, and in the mountain there's a Thousand Flower Cave where there lives a sage called Vairambha who will be able to defeat that demon." "Where's the mountain?" Monkey asked. "Which direction should I take?" "It's due south of here," the woman replied, pointing; and by the time Brother Monkey looked back at her she had disappeared.

Monkey quickly did a kowtow and said, "Which Bodhisattva was that? After all that burrowing your disciple was feeling too stupid to recognize you. I beg you to tell me your name so that I can thank you." At this there came a shout from mid-air, "Great Sage, it's me." Monkey quickly looked up to see that it was the Old Lady of Mount Li. Catching up with her in the sky he thanked her with the words, "Where have you come from to give me these instructions?" "On my way back from Dragon Flower Assembly I noticed that your master was in trouble," the Old Lady replied. "It was to save his life that I pretended to be a woman in mourning for her husband. Hurry up and fetch the sage. But don't tell her I sent you: she is rather difficult."

Thanking her, Monkey took his leave and set off straight away on his somersault cloud. Once at Mount Purple Clouds he brought his cloud down and saw the Thousand Flower Cave.

The Great Sage was delighted as he went inside, seeing boundless beauty at every stage. He went straight on, but found it deserted and completely silent. Not even a chicken or a dog could be heard. When he had gone a mile or two further on he saw a Taoist nun sitting on a couch.

Monkey went straight up to her without stopping and said, "Greetings, Bodhisattva Vairambha." The Bodhisattva then came down from her couch, put her hands together to return his greeting and said, "Great Sage, it was remiss of me not to come out to greet you. Where have you come from?" "How do you know that I'm the Great Sage?" Monkey asked. "When you made havoc in Heaven the other year," Vairambha replied, "your picture was circulated everywhere. That's why everyone can recognize you." "How true it is," Monkey said, "that

While good deeds stay at home
Bad deeds are known far and wide.

Take my conversion to Buddhism, for example. You didn't know about that." "Congratulations," said Vairambha. "When did that happen?" "Not long ago my life was spared to escort my master the Tang Priest on his journey to the Western Heaven to fetch the scriptures," Monkey replied. "My master has been laid low with poisoned tea by the Taoist of the Yellow Flower Temple. When I was fighting with him he caught me in his golden light, and I had to use magic to escape. I have come here to pay you my respects, Bodhisattva, and ask your help because I've heard that you are able to destroy his golden light." "Who told you that?" the Bodhisattva asked. "I have not left here since the Ullambana Assembly over three hundred years ago. I've lived in complete secrecy and nobody has heard of me, so how is it that you know of me?" "I'm an underground devil," Monkey replied, "and I can make my own enquiries anywhere at all." "Never mind," Vairambha said, "never mind. I shouldn't really go, but as you have honoured me with a visit, Great Sage, and as the great cause of fetching the scriptures must not be allowed to fail I'll go with you."

Monkey thanked her and said, "It's very ignorant of me to hurry you along in this way. I wonder what weapon you use." "I have an embroidery needle that will put an end to that damned creature," said the Bodhisattva.

This was too much for Monkey. "Old Lady, you've been wasting my time," he said. "Had I known it was an embroidery needle I wouldn't have had to trouble you. I could have provided a hundredweight of them." "Your embroidery needles are all made of iron, steel or gold," the Bodhisattva replied. "They're no use. My treasure isn't iron and isn't steel and isn't gold. It was tempered by my son in the sun." "Who is he?" asked Monkey. "He is the Star Lord of the Mane," Vairambha replied. This came as a shock to Monkey, who gazed at the golden light then turned to Vairambha and said, "The Yellow

Flower Temple is where that golden light is coming from."
Vairambha then took from the lapel of her gown an embroidery
needle about the thickness of an eyebrow hair and half an inch
long. Holding it between her fingers she threw it into the air.
A few moments later there was a loud noise and the golden light
was shattered. "That's wonderful, Bodhisattva, wonderful!"
exclaimed a delighted Monkey. "Let's find your needle now."
"Isn't this it here?" asked Vairambha, who was holding it in her
hand. Brother Monkey brought his cloud down to land with
hers and went into the temple, where he found the Taoist with
his eyes shut, unable to move. "Stop playing blind, damned
demon," he said abusively, taking his cudgel from his ear ready
to hit the Taoist with. "Don't hit him, Great Sage," said
Vairambha. "Go and see your master."

On going straight to the reception room at the back Monkey
found the three of them bringing up mucus and spittle where
they lay on the floor. "What am I to do?" wept Monkey.
"What am I to do?" "Don't grieve, Great Sage," said
Vairambha. "As I've come out today I think I might as well
accumulate some merit by giving you three of these pills that are
an antidote to the poison." Monkey turned round to bow down
and beg her for them, whereupon she produced a torn paper
packet from her sleeve containing three red pills that she
handed to Monkey, telling him to put one in each of their mouths.
This he did, forcing their teeth apart. A few moments later
they all started vomiting as the drug reached their stomachs,
bringing up the poison and coming back to life. Pig was the
first to scramble to his feet. "I feel suffocated," he said. Sanzang and Friar Sand both came round too, saying that they felt
very dizzy. "Your tea was poisoned," Brother Monkey explained. "It was the Bodhisattva Vairambha who saved you.
Hurry up and bow to her in thanks." Sanzang bowed to her to
show his gratitude as he straightened up his clothes.

"We are deeply indebted to your great power," Monkey
replied, "and we will of course obey. But we would like you to
turn him back into his real self so that we can have a look at
him ." "Easily done," said Vairambha, stepping forward and

pointing at the Taoist, who collapsed into the dust and reverted to his real form of a giant centipede spirit seven feet long. Picking him up with her little finger Vairambha rode her auspicious cloud straight back to the Thousand Flower Cave. "That old lady's a real terror," said Pig, looking up ."How did she manage to subdue that evil creature?" "When I asked her what weapon she had to smash the golden light with," Monkey replied,"she told me about a golden embroidery needle of hers that her son had tempered in the sun. When I asked her who her son was she told me he was the Star Lord of the Mane. As I remember, the Mane Star is a cock, so his mother must be a hen. Hens are very good at dealing with centipedes, which is why she could subdue him."

On hearing this Sanzang performed no end of kowtows. "Disciples," he ordered, "go and get things ready." Friar Sand then went inside to find some rice and prepare a vegetarian meal, so that they could all eat their fill. Then they led the horse up, shouldered the carrying-pole, and asked the master to set out. Monkey started a blaze in the kitchen that in an instant burnt the whole temple to ashes. They then set out on their way.

CHAPTER 30
The Tathagata Subdues the Monsters

The story tells how Sanzang and his disciples let the horse travel west. Before they had been going for very long the summer was over and the new coolness of early autumn was refreshing their bodies.

As Sanzang was travelling along a high mountain appeared in front of him. Its peak thrust up into the azure void, touching the stars and blocking out the sun. In his alarm the venerable elder said to Monkey, "Look at that mountain in front of us. It's very high. I don't know whether the path will take us across." "What a thing to say, Master," said Monkey with a smile. "As the old saying goes,

> However high the mountain there will be a way across;
> However deep the river there's always a ferryman.

There's no reason why we shouldn't get over it. Stop worrying and carry on." When Sanzang heard this his face broke out in smiles and he whipped his horse forward to climb straight up the high crag.

After a mile or two an old man appeared. His white hair was tangled and flying in the wind while his sparse whiskers were being blown about like silver threads. He wore a string of prayer-beads round his neck and held a dragon-headed walking-stick as he stood far away at the top of the slope shouting,

"Venerable gentleman travelling west, stop your worthy steed. Rein in. There is a band of demons on this mountain who claim to have eaten all the people in the world. Go no further!" At this Sanzang turned pale with terror.

Monkey said, "Don't be afraid, don't be afraid. I'm here. Sit there while I go and ask him." "With your ugly face and coarse language I'm afraid you may shock him," said Sanzang, "so you won't get the truth from him." "I'll make myself a bit better looking before questioning him," laughed Brother Monkey, and turned himself into a very neat little monk.

The splendid Great Sage left them behind as he went straight up to the old man, bowed to him and said, "Greetings, venerable sir." Seeing how young and cultivated he looked, the old man returned his greeting and stroked his head in an offhand way. "Little monk," the old man said with a smile, "where have you come from?" "We are from the Great Tang in the east," Monkey replied, "going to worship the Buddha and fetch the scriptures. When we came here and heard you tell us that there are demons here my master was terrified. He sent me to ask you about them. What sort of evil spirits are they?"

"You're much too young, little monk," said the old man with a smile, "to know what's good for you. Those evil spirits have tremendous magical powers!" Getting no details from the old man, Monkey gave him a terrible fright by turning back into his true self and went back.

Pig next swaggered up to the old man. The old man found that Pig looked even worse than Monkey, but was reassured by what Pig had to say to him.

Leaning on his stick, he said to Pig, "This is Lion Ridge, and it is 250 miles around. In it there is a Lion Cave where there are three demon chieftains. Those three demon chiefs have the most tremendous magic powers. As for the little demons under their command, there are five thousand on the southern end of the ridge, five thousand on the northern end, ten thousand on the road east, ten thousand on the road west, four or five thousand patrollers, and another ten thousand on the gates. Then there are any number who work in the kitchen and gather firewood. There must be 47,000 or 48,000 altogether.

They all have names and carry passes, and all they do is eat people."

On learning this the idiot ran back, shivering and shaking.

As Master and disciples were discussing the matter, the old man disappeared. "He must have been an evil spirit himself," said Friar Sand, "deliberately coming to frighten us with cunning and intimidation." "Take it easy," said Monkey. "I'm going to take a look." The splendid Great Sage leapt up to a high peak but saw no trace of the old man when he looked around. Then he suddenly turned back to see a shimmering coloured glow in the sky, shot up on his cloud to look, and saw that it was the Great White Planet. The planet hastened to pay Monkey his respects and said, "Great Sage, I beg you to forgive me for being late in reporting to you. Those demon chiefs really have tremendous magical abilities and their powers are colossal. With your skill in transformations and your cunning you may just be able to get over, but if you slight them it will be very hard." "I'm very grateful," Monkey thanked him, "very grateful. If I really can't get across this ridge I hope that you'll go up to Heaven and put in a word with the Jade Emperor so he'll lend me some heavenly soldiers to help me." "Yes, yes, yes," said the Great White Planet. "Just give the word and you can have a hundred thousand heavenly troops if you want them."

The Great Sage then took his leave of the planet and brought his cloud down to see Sanzang and say, "The old man we saw just now was actually the Great White Planet come to bring us a message." "Disciple," said Sanzang, putting his hands together in front of his chest, "catch up with him quick and ask him where there's another path we could make a detour by." "There's no other way round," Monkey replied. "This mountain is 250 miles across, and goodness knows how much longer it would be to go all the way around it. How ever could we?" At this Sanzang could not restrain himself from weeping. "Disciple," he said, "if it's going to be as hard as this how are we going to worship the Buddha?" "Don't cry," Monkey said, "don't cry. If you cry you're a louse. I'll take a look round."

The Great Sage used his powers of transformation to find

out about the demons, their powers and their armies. Suddenly
he heard shouts and whinnies. As he looked up he saw tens of
thousands of little devils drawn up outside the entrance to the
Lion Cave with their spears, sabres, swords, halberds, flags and
banners. Monkey was delighted. "The Great White Planet was
telling the truth," he thought. "He wasn't lying at all." The Great
Sage brought his cloud down, disguised himself as a patroller,
told the little devils that Monkey was going to kill them, and set
them all running for their lives. He then walked into the Lion
Cave.

When Monkey entered the cave, he saw hills of skeletons and
forests of bones. There was a mountain of corpses and an
unbearable stench of corruption.

He was soon inside the second gates, and when he looked
around here he saw that things were different from outside.
Here was purity, quiet elegance, beauty and calm. To left and
right were rare and wonderful plants; all around were tall pines
and jadegreen bamboo. After another two or three miles he
reached the third gates, slipped inside for a peep, and saw the
three old demons sitting on high. They looked thoroughly evil.
The one in the middle was the Blue-haired Lion Monster. The
one on the left was the Ancient Yellow-tusked Elephant. The one
on the right was the Mighty Roc.

Beneath these two were ranged a hundred and ten
commanders high and low, all in full armour and looking most
imposing and murderous. The sight delighted Brother Monkey,
who strode inside, quite unafraid, put down his clappers and
bell, and called, "Your Majesties." The three old demons
chuckled and replied, "When you were patrolling what did you
find out about where Sun the Novice is?" "Your Majesties,"
Monkey replied, "I don't dare tell you." "Why not?" the senior
demon chief asked. "I was walking along sounding my clappers
and ringing my bell following Your Majesties' orders," Monkey
said, "when all of a sudden I looked up and saw someone
squatting and polishing a pole there. He looked like one of the
gods that clear the way. If he'd stood up he'd have been well
over a hundred feet tall. He'd scooped up some water in his
hand and was polishing his iron bar on the rocky scar. He was

saying to himself that his cudgel still hadn't the chance to show its magical powers here and that when he'd shined it up he was coming to attack Your Majesties. That's how I realized he was Sun the Novice and came here to report."

On hearing this the senior demon chief broke into a sweat all over and shivered so that his teeth chattered as he said, "Brothers, I don't think we should start any trouble with the Tang Priest. His disciple has tremendous magical powers and he's polishing his cudgel to attack us. Whatever are we to do?" "Little ones," he shouted, "call everybody, high and low, who's outside the cave to come inside and shut the gates. Let them pass." "Your Majesty," said one of the subordinate officers who knew what had happened, "the little devils outside have all scattered." "Why?" the senior demon asked. "They must have heard about his terrible reputation. Shut the gates at once! At once!" The hosts of demons noisily bolted all the front and back gates firmly.

"Now they've shut the gates they might ask me all sorts of questions about things in here," Monkey thought with alarm "If I don't know the right answers I'll give the game away and they'll catch me. I'd better give them another scare and get them to open the gates to let me out." "Your Majesty," he said, stepping forward, "there were some other wicked things he said." "What else?" the senior demon chief asked. "He said he was going to skin Your Senior Majesty," replied Brother Monkey, "slice up the bones of His Second Majesty, and rip out His Third Majesty's sinews. If you shut the gates and refuse to go out he can do transformations. He might turn himself into a fly, get in through a crack between the gates and catch us all. Then we'll be done for." "Be very careful, brothers," said the senior demon. "We haven't had a fly here for years, so any fly that gets in will be Sun the Novice." "So I'll change into a fly and frighten them into opening the gates," thought Monkey, smiling to himself. The splendid Great Sage then slipped aside, reached up to pull a hair from the back of his head, blew on it with a magic breath, called "Change!" and turned it into a golden fly that flew straight into the old demon's face. "Brothers," said the old demon in a panic, "this is terrible! He's inside!" All the demons great and small were so alarmed that they rushed forward to swat the fly with their rakes and brooms.

The Great Sage could not help giggling aloud, which was just what he should not have done as it revealed his true face. The third demon chief leapt forward, grabbed him and said, "Brothers, he almost had us fooled." "Who had who fooled?" the senior demon asked. "The young devil who reported just now was Sun the Novice himself." the third chief replied, "He did this transformation to trick us." The officers were ordered to fetch ropes immediately.

The third demon chief knocked Monkey over and tied his hands and feet together. When his clothes were stripped off he was most evidently the Protector of the Horses. The third demon chief said, "Sun the Novice is a slippery customer and is good at escaping by magic. I'm worried he might get away. Tell the juniors to bring the jar out and put him inside. Then we can drink."

"Yes, yes," said the senior demon chief with a smile, who then chose thirty-six little demons to go inside, open the storerooms, and carry the jar out. Before long the precious jar had been carried out, set down outside the third pair of gates, cleaned up and opened. Monkey was untied, stripped bare and sucked inside the jar with a hiss by magical vapour that came out of it. The lid was then put back on and sealed on with a label, after which the demons went off to drink.

Once inside the jar the Great Sage, who was very cramped, decided to transform himself and squat down in the middle. Fires began to burn. The jar was soon full of flame. Luckily he could use the knack of making fire-averting magic with his hands as he sat in the middle of the jar completely unafraid. When he had endured the flames for an hour forty snakes emerged from all around to bite him. Swinging his arms about him Monkey grabbed hold of all of them, twisted with all his strength, and broke them into eighty pieces. A little later three fire dragons appeared to circle above and below Monkey, which was really unbearable. It drove Monkey into a helpless desperation of which he was only too conscious. "The other things were no trouble," he said, "but these three fire dragons are a real problem. If I don't get out soon the fire will attack my heart, and what then? I'll make myself grow," he went on to think, "and push my way out." The splendid Great Sage made a spell with his hands, said the words of a spell and called out, "Grow!" He made himself over a dozen feet tall, but as he grew the jar grew with him, enclosing him tightly. When he made himself smaller, the jar shrank too. "This is terrible," Brother Monkey thought with alarm, "terrible. It grows when I grow and shrinks when I get smaller. Why? What am I to do?" Before he had finished speaking his ankle began to hurt. Putting his hand down at once to feel it he found that it had been burnt so badly it had gone soft.

Just when he was feeling thoroughly miserable he suddenly remembered, "Years ago the Bodhisattva gave me three life-saving hairs on the Coiled Snake Mountain. I wonder if I've still got them. I'd better look for them." He felt all over his body and found three very rigid hairs on the back of his head. "All the other hair on my body is soft except for these three that are as hard as spears," he said with delight. "They must be my life-savers." Gritting his teeth against the pain, he pulled the three hairs out, blew on them with magic breath and called, "Change!" One of them turned into a steel drill, one into a strip of bamboo, and one into a silken cord. He made the bamboo strip into a bow to which he fixed the drill. After a noisy spell of drilling at the bottom of the jar he made a hole through which the light came in. "I'm in luck," he said with glee, "I'm in luck. Now I can get out."

The splendid Great Sage put his hairs back, made himself small by turning into the tiniest of insects, a very delicate creature as thin as a whisker and as long as an eyebrow hair, and slipped out through the hole, and then turned back into himself. He went back on his cloud to where the Tang Priest was. Here he found the venerable gentleman making symbolic incense with a pinch of earth and praying to the sky.

Putting his cloud away Monkey went up to Sanzang and called, "Master, I'm back." Sanzang held him as he said,

"Wukong, you have been to great trouble. I was very concerned because you had gone so far into these high mountains and not come back for so long a time. How dangerous is the mountain in fact?" Monkey told the whole story of how he had been drawn into the jar and escaped. "Now I've seen your face again, Master, it's like having a second life."

Sanzang expressed endless thanks and asked, "Did you not fight the evil spirits this time?" "No, I didn't," replied Brother Monkey. "Then you won't be able to escort me safely across this mountain," Sanzang said, at which Monkey, who hated to admit he was beaten, shouted, "What do you mean, I won't be able to escort you?" "If you and they have not yet had it out and you can only give me evasive answers I will never dare press ahead," the venerable elder replied. "Master," laughed the Great Sage, "you really don't understand. As the saying goes, you can't spin a thread from a single strand of silk, and you can't clap one-handed. There are three demon chiefs and thousands of the little devils. How could I fight them all single-handed?" "If you are that outnumbered you would indeed find it hard by yourself," Sanzang replied. "Pig and Friar Sand also have their talents. I shall tell them to go with you to help you clean up the path across the mountain and escort me over it." "What you say is completely right, Master," replied Monkey with a smile. "Tell Friar Sand to protect you while Pig comes with me."

The idiot braced himself and set off a gale with Monkey that carried them by cloud up to the top of the mountain where the entrance to the cave was. They saw at once that the gates were shut tight. There was nobody in sight anywhere around. Monkey went forward, his iron cudgel in his hands, to shout at the top of his voice, "Open up, evil monsters! Come out right now and fight Monkey!" When the young devils in the cave went inside to report the senior demon kitted himself out in his armour, had the gates opened, went out and roared in a voice like thunder, "Who is that knocking at my gates?"

"Your grandfather, Lord Sun, the Great Sage Equalling Heaven," said Monkey, turning to face the gate. "Are you Sun the Novice?" asked the demon with a laugh. "You've got a cheek, ape. I never gave you any trouble, so why are you here challenging me to battle?" " 'No waves come without a wind; without the tide the waters are still,' " Monkey replied. "Would I have come looking for you if you hadn't given me trouble? The reason why I'm here to fight is because your gang of foxes and dogs is plotting to eat my master." "Come over here," the senior demon shouted, "and be a chopping block for me. Let me hack you three times as hard as I can with sword on your bare head. After that I'll let your Tang Priest pass. If you can't take it then hand your Tang Priest over at once. He'll be a tasty morsel to help our rice down." "Bring out a brush and some paper if you have them in your cave and I'll give you a bond. You can hack at me from today till next year, but it'll be nothing to me."

The old demon then summoned up all his might, took up a stance with his feet apart, lifted his sword with both hands and hacked at the top of the Great Sage's head. The Great Sage raised his head, and though there was a mighty crash his scalp did not even go red. "That monkey really does have a hard head," exclaimed the old demon with shock. "Take two more blows from my sword. I'm most certainly not going to spare your life."

The senior demon raised his sword for another hack, which the Great Sage moved his head forward to meet. With a loud bang his head was split into two, whereupon the Great Sage rolled on the ground and gave himself a second body. The sight so alarmed the demon that he lowered his sword. Watching all this from a distance Pig said with a laugh, "Give him a couple more hacks, old devil, then there'll be four of him." Pointing at Brother Monkey the senior demon said, "I'd heard that you can use self-dividing magic. Why are you showing it off to me now?" "What self-dividing magic?" Monkey asked. "Why was it that the first time I hacked you it made no impact, but this time I cut you in two?" the senior demon asked. "Don't worry, evil spirit," said the Great Sage with a smile. "If you cut me ten thousand times there'll be twenty thousand of me." "You ape," the demon said, "you may be able to divide yourself but you can't put yourself together again. If you can, hit me with your cudgel." "Don't talk nonsense," said the Great Sage. "You asked to take three cuts at me but only took two. Now you've invited me to hit you once I'm not Monkey if I hit you one and a half times." "Very well," said the senior demon.

The splendid Great Sage hugged his two bodies together, rolled, became one body again and struck with his cudgel at the demon's head. The monster lifted his sword and struck with all his strength. Chuckling, Monkey blocked the blow with his iron cudgel. At first the two of them struggled in front of the cave, but then they both sprang up and fought in mid-air.

The senior demon and the Great Sage fought over twenty rounds without either emerging the victor while Pig admired their magnificent battle from down below until, unable to restrain himself, he grabbed his rake and leapt up into the air, riding on the wind to strike at the evil monster's face. The demon panicked, not realizing that Pig had no staying power, but could only rush recklessly in and give people a fright. All the demon could see was that Pig had a long snout, big ears and a vicious way with his rake, so he abandoned the struggle, threw his sword away, turned and fled. "After him," the Great Sage shouted, "after him!" The idiot raised his rake and went down in all his ferocious might straight after the monster. Seeing how close Pig was to him the old demon stood still in front of the mountainside, faced the wind, shook himself, resumed his real appearance and opened his mouth to devour Pig. This so terrified Pig that he fled as fast as he could into the undergrowth, not caring that brambles and thorns were tearing his head. He sat there trembling and listening out for the sound of the cudgel. When Monkey caught up with him the monster opened his jaws to eat Monkey up too. This was just what Monkey intended. Putting his cudgel away he went straight towards the demon, who swallowed him in a single gulp. This gave idiot such a fright as he was hiding in the undergrowth that he grumbled to himself, "You've got no common sense, Protector of the Horses. Why did you go towards the monster when he wanted to eat you up instead of running away? Now he's swallowed you. Today you're still a monk, but tomorrow you'll be a turd." Only when the monster had departed in triumph did Pig emerge from the undergrowth and slip back by the way he had come.

We shall leave Pig and return to the senior demon chief. When he had swallowed Monkey he thought he had won, so he went straight back to his cave, where all the other demons came out to ask him how the fight had gone. "I've got one of them," the senior demon said. "Which one is that?" asked the second demon with delight. "Sun the Novice," the senior demon replied. "Where have you got him?" the second demon chief said. "In my stomach," said the senior demon, "I swallowed him." "Elder brother," said the third demon chief with horror, "I forgot to tell you that Sun the Novice wasn't worth eating." "I'm delicious," said the Great Sage from inside the demon's stomach, "and I'll stop you from ever feeling hungry again." This caused the junior devils such a shock that they reported, "This is terrible, Your Senior Majesty. Sun the Novice is talking inside your stomach." "That doesn't frighten me," said the senior demon. "If I'm clever enough to catch him do you think I'm not clever enough to deal with him? Make me some hot salty water at once. I'll pour it into my stomach, vomit him out, and have him fried at my leisure to eat as a snack with some drinks."

The junior devils soon had ready half a bowl of hot salty water that the old demon drained in one, filling his mouth. He then really did vomit, but the Great Sage, who had taken root in his stomach, did not even move. The monster then pressed his throat and vomited again till his head was spinning, his eyes in a daze and his gall-bladder split, but still Monkey would not be shifted. By now the senior demon was gasping for breath. "Sun the Novice," he called, "won't you come out?" "Not yet," Monkey replied. "I don't want to come out now." "Why not?" the old demon asked. "You really don't understand, evil spirit," said Monkey. "Ever since I've been a monk I've had scant food and clothing. Although it's autumn now and getting cool I'm still only wearing a thin tunic. But it's warm in your stomach and there are no draughts down here. I think I'll spend the winter here before coming out."

The old demon heard this and was most alarmed despite saying that he was not afraid. All he could do was to summon up his courage and call, "Don't be scared, brothers. Bring me some of that drugged wine. When I down a few goblets of that the drugs will kill the monkey." At this Monkey smiled to himself and thought, "When I made havoc in Heaven five hundred years ago I drank the Jade Emperor's wine and ate Lord Lao Zi's elixir, the Queen Mother's peaches, the marrow of phoenix bones and dragon livers. I've eaten everything. What kind of drugged wine could do me any harm?" By then the junior devils had strained two jugfuls of drugged wine, a goblet of which they handed to the senior demon chief, who took it in his hands. Monkey, who could smell it from inside the demon's belly, called out, "Don't give it to him!" The splendid Great Sage then tipped his head back and turned it into the bell of a trumpet that he placed wide open below the demon's throat. The demon gulped the wine down noisily and Monkey noisily received it. The demon swallowed the second cupful and Monkey noisily drank that too. This went on till Monkey had drunk all of the seven or eight cupfuls that the demon downed. "That's enough," the demon said, putting the goblet down. "Normally my stomach feels as if it's on fire after a couple of cups of this wine," he said, "but this time my face hasn't even gone red after seven or eight." Now the Great Sage was not a heavy drinker, so after taking these seven or eight cupfuls he started to act drunk in the demon's stomach, propping himself up, falling flat on his face, kicking about him, swinging on the demon's liver, doing headstands and somersaults, and dancing wildly. This caused the monster such unbearable pain that he collapsed.

The monster made no sound and was not breathing either. As he said nothing Monkey thought the demon was dead, so he stopped hitting him. When the demon chief recovered his breath he called out, "Most merciful and most compassionate Bodhisattva, Great Sage Equalling Heaven." "My boy," said Monkey when he heard this, "don't waste your effort. You could save yourself a few words by simply calling me Grandpa

Sun." Desperate to save his skin, the evil monster really did call out, "Grandpa! Grandpa! I was wrong. I shouldn't have eaten you, and now you're destroying me. I beg you, Great Sage, in your mercy and compassion to take pity on my antlike greed for life and spare me. If you do I'll escort your master across the mountain."

The Great Sage decided once more to be kind. "Evil monster," he shouted, "I'll spare your life. How are you going to escort my master?" "My two brothers and I will carry him in a rattan chair across the mountain." "If you could carry him in a chair that would be better than treasure," said Monkey with a smile. "Open your mouth: I'm coming out." The demon then opened his mouth, whereupon the third chief went over to him and whispered in his ear, "Bite him as he comes out, brother. Chew the monkey to bits and swallow him. Then he won't be able to hurt you."

Now Monkey could hear all this from inside, so instead of coming straight out he thrust his gold-banded cudgel out first as a test. The demon did indeed take a bite at it, noisily smashing one of his front teeth in the process. "You're a nice monster, aren't you!" exclaimed Monkey, pulling his cudgel back. "I spare your life and agree to come out, but you try to murder me by biting me. I'm not coming out now. I'm going to kill you. I won't come out! I won't!" "Brother," the senior demon chief complained to the third one, "what you've done is destroy one of your own kind. I'd persuaded him to come out but you would have to tell me to bite him. Now I'm in agony from my broken tooth. What are we to do?"

In the face of the senior demon chief's complaints the third demon chief tried the method of making the enemy lose his temper. "Sun the Novice," he yelled at the top of his voice, "you have a thundering reputation. They tell of how mighty you were outside the Southern Gate of Heaven and at the Hall of Miraculous Mist. I'd heard that you've been capturing demons along your way to the Western Heaven. But now I see that you're only a very small-time ape." "What makes me small-time?" Monkey asked. " 'A hero who only roams three hundred miles around will go three thousand miles to make his fame resound," the third chief replied. "Come out and fight me if you're a real tough guy. What do you mean by messing about in someone else's stomach? If you're not small-time what are you?" "Yes, yes, yes," thought Monkey when he heard this. "It wouldn't be at all difficult for me to tear this demon's bowels to bits, rip up his liver, and kill him. But I'd destroy my own reputation in the process. I'll have to forget about it. Open your mouth and I'll come out and fight you. The only problem is that this cave of yours is much too cramped for me to use my weapons. We'll have to go somewhere where there's more room." On hearing this the third demon chief mustered all the demons young and old from all around. There were over thirty thousand of them armed with the finest and sharpest weapons who came out of the cave to form a line of battle symbolizing heaven, earth and mankind. They were all waiting for Monkey to come out of the senior demon's mouth before crushing him. The second demon chief then helped the senior demon out through the entrance of the cave, where he shouted, "Sun the Novice! If you're a tough guy come out. There's a good battlefield here for us to fight on."

The Great Sage could tell that this was an open area from the calls of crows, magpies and cranes that he could hear in the monster's belly. "If I don't come out I'll be breaking faith with them," he thought. "But if I do these demons are beasts at heart behind their human faces. They tried to lure me out and bite me when they promised to carry the master across the ridge. Now they've got their army here. Oh well! I'll let them have it both ways. I'll go out but I'll leave a root in his stomach too." With that he put his hand behind him to pluck a tiny hair from his tail, blew on it with magic breath, called "Change!" and made it into a string as fine as a hair but some four hundred feet long. As the string came outside it grew thicker in the wind. One end Monkey fastened round the evil monster's heart in a slip-knot that he did not tighten — if he had it would have caused great pain. The other end he held in his hand as he said to himself, "If they agree to escort my master across the ridge when I come out this time I'll leave it at that. But if they refuse and go for me with their weapons so hard that I can't cope with them I'll just need to pull this rope. I'll get the same results as if I were still inside." He then made himself tiny and crawled up as far as the throat, from where he could see that the evil spirit had opened his mouth wide. Rows of steel teeth were set above and below like sharp knives. "This is no good," he thought at once, "no good at all. If I take this rope out through his mouth and he can't stand the pain he'll be able to cut through it with a single bite. I'll have to go out where there aren't any teeth." The splendid Great Sage paid out the string as he crawled up the demon's upper palate and into his nostril, which made his nose itch. The demon sneezed with a loud "atishoo", blowing Monkey out.

As he felt the wind blowing him Monkey bowed and grew over thirty feet long, keeping the string in one hand and holding the iron cudgel in the other. The wicked monster raised his steel sword as soon as he saw Monkey appear and hacked at his face. The Great Sage met the blow one-handed with his cudgel. Then the second demon chief with his spear and the third chief with his halberd went for him furiously. The Great Sage relaxed his pull on the rope, put his iron cudgel away and made off at speed by cloud, afraid that he would be unable to fight properly when surrounded by so many young devils. Once he had leapt out of the demons' camp he brought his cloud down on a spacious and empty mountain top and pulled with both hands on the rope as hard as he could. This gave the senior demon a pain in the heart. The demon struggled upwards in agony, whereupon the Great Sage pulled him down again. As they all watched from afar the junior demons all shouted, "Don't provoke him, Your Majesty! Let him go. That ape has no sense of when things ought to be done. He's flying a kite before the beginning of April." When the Great Sage heard this he gave a mighty stamp, at which the senior demon came whistling down out of the sky like a spinning-wheel to crash into the dust, making a crater some two feet deep in the hard earth at the foot of the mountain.

This gave the second and third demon chiefs such a fright that they landed their clouds together and rushed forward to grab hold of the rope and kneel at the foot of the mountain. "Great Sage," they pleaded, "we thought you were an immortal of vast and boundless generosity. We'd never dreamed that you would be as small-minded as a rat or a snail. It's true that we lured you out to give battle, but we never expected that you would tie a rope round our eldest brother's heart." "You're a thorough disgrace, you damned gang of demons," said Monkey with a laugh. "Last time you tried to trick me into coming out so you could bite me and this time you've lured me out to face an army ready for battle. It's obvious that you've got tens of thousands of soldiers here to tackle me when I'm alone. Most unreasonable. I'll pull him away. I'm going to drag him off to see my master." "If in your mercy and compassion you spare our lives, Great Sage," the demons said, all kowtowing together, "we vow to escort your master across this mountain."

"If you want to live all you have to do is cut the rope with your sword," said Monkey with a laugh. "My lord," the senior monster said, "I can cut the rope outside, but it's no good having the length inside that's tied round my heart. It sticks in my throat so uncomfortably that it makes me feel sick." "In that case," said Monkey, "open your mouth and I'll go back inside to undo the rope." This alarmed the senior demon, who said, "If you don't come out when you go in this time I'll be in a mess, a real mess." "I know how to undo the end of the rope that's in you from the outside," Monkey replied. "But when I've undone it will you really escort my master across?" "We will as soon as you've undone it," the senior demon chief replied. "I wouldn't dare lie about this." Now that he had satisfied himself the demon was telling the truth Monkey shook himself and put the hair back on his body, whereupon the monster's heart pains stopped. It was the Great Sage Sun's transforming magic that had tied the hair round his heart in the first place, which was why the pain ended as soon as the hair was put back on Monkey. The three demon chiefs then rose up into the air to thank him with the words, "Please go back now, Great Sage, and pack your luggage. We will carry a chair down to fetch him." The demon horde then all put their weapons down and went back into the cave.

Having put his rope away the Great Sage went straight back to the eastern side of the ridge, and when he was still a long way away he saw the Tang Priest lying on the ground, rolling around and howling. Pig and Friar Sand had opened the bundles of luggage and were dividing it up. "Don't tell me," thought Monkey with a quiet sigh. "No doubt Pig has told the master that I've been eaten up by evil spirits. The master's sobbing his heart out because he can't bear to be without me and the idiot's dividing the things ready for us all to split up. Oh dear! I can't be sure, so I'd better go down and give the master a shout." Bringing his cloud down, Monkey shouted, "Master!" As soon as Friar Sand heard this he started complaining to Pig, saying "Our elder brother wasn't killed but you said he was and started this business here. Of course he's bound to kick up a row." "But I saw him with my own eyes being eaten up by the evil spirit in one mouthful," Pig replied. "I'm sure we're just seeing that ape's spirit because it's an unlucky day." Monkey then went up to Pig and hit him in the face with a slap that sent him staggering. "Cretin!" he said. "Is this my spirit you can see?" Rubbing his face, the idiot replied, "But the monster really did eat you up, brother. How can you, how can you have come back to life?" "Useless gumboil!" said Monkey. "After he ate me I grabbed his bowels, twisted his lungs, tied a rope round his heart and tore at him till he was in horrible agony. Then they all kowtowed and pleaded with me, so I spared his life. Now they're bringing a carrying-chair here to take the master over the mountain." As soon as Sanzang heard this he scrambled to his feet, bowed to Monkey and said, "Disciple, I've put you to enormous trouble. If I had believed what Wuneng said we would have been finished." "Chaff-guzzling idiot," said Monkey, taking a swing at Pig with his fist, "you're thoroughly lazy and barely human. But don't get upset, Master. The monsters are coming to take you across the mountain." Friar Sand too felt deeply ashamed, and quickly trying to cover it up he packed up the luggage and loaded the horse to wait on the road.

The story returns to the three demon chiefs, who led their devilish hosts back into the cave. "Elder brother," said the second demon, "I'd imagined that Sun the Novice had nine heads and eight tails, but he turns out to be nothing but that pipsqueak of a monkey. You shouldn't have swallowed him. You should have fought him. He'd have been no match for us. With our tens of thousands of goblins we could have drowned him in our spit. But by swallowing him you let him use his magic and cause you agony, so that you didn't dare have it out with him. When I said we'd take the Tang Priest across the mountains just now I didn't mean it. It was only a way of luring him out because your life was in danger. I most certainly won't escort the Tang Priest." "Why not, good brother?" the senior demon chief asked. "If you and I draw up three thousand junior devils ready for battle I can capture that ape," the second demon replied. "Never mind about three thousand," the senior demon chief said. "You can have our whole force. If we capture him it'll be a credit to us all."

The second demon chief then mustered three thousand junior demons whom he led to a place beside the main road, where they were put into battle formation. He sent a herald with a blue flag to carry a message. "Sun the Novice," the herald said, "come out at once and fight His Second Majesty." When Pig heard this he said with a laugh, "As the saying goes, brother, liars don't fool the people at home. You lied to us when you came back, you trickster. You said you'd beaten the evil spirits and that they'd be bringing a carrying-chair to take the master across. But here they are challenging you to battle. Why?" "The senior demon did surrender to me," Monkey replied, "and he wouldn't dare show his face. The sound of my name alone is enough to give him a headache. The second demon chief must be challenging me to battle because he can't bring himself to escort us across. I tell you, brother, those three evil spirits are brothers and they have a sense of honour. We're three brothers but we don't. I've beaten the senior demon, so the second demon's come out.　There's no reason why you shouldn't fight him." "I'm not scared of him," Pig said. "I'll go and give him a fight."

The idiot lifted his rake and rushed up the steep slope shouting, "Come out, evil spirit! Come and fight your ancestor Pig!" The herald with the blue flag rushed back to report, "Your Majesty, there's a monk with a long snout and big ears here." The second demon chief came out of the encampment, saw Pig, and without a word thrust his spear straight at Pig's face.　The idiot raised his rake and went forward to parry the blow.　The two of them joined battle in front of the mountainside, and before they had fought seven or eight rounds the idiot began to weaken. He was no longer able to hold the evil spirit off. The idiot started to run back now that he was defeated before falling face-down into the dust. The evil spirit caught up with him, unwound his trunk that was like a python, wrapped it round Pig and carried him back in triumph to the cave. The demons put him to soak off his bristles in a pool at the back.

"Disciple," said Sanzang, "Pig was born clumsy and can't transform himself, which makes this a very dangerous business. You must go and rescue him." "Don't worry, Master," said Brother Monkey. "I'll go and save him."

Monkey then made magic with his hands, said the words of a spell, shook himself, turned into the tiniest of insects and flew into the cave. He saw the idiot with his four limbs pointing upwards and his snout downwards as he half floated and was half sinking, grunting through his snout. He really was a ridiculous sight.

Monkey turned back into himself and used his cudgel to bring Pig close enough to grab him by his feet, drag him out and untie him. Pig then sprang up, took off his clothes, wrung them out, shook them, and draped them, still dripping wet, over his shoulders. "Brother," he said, "open the back gates. Let's go." "There's no glory in sneaking out the back way," replied Monkey. "We'll leave by the front gates." "My feet are still numb after being tied up." said Pig. "I can't run." "Buck up and come with me," said Monkey.

The splendid Great Sage charged out, clearing his way by

swinging his cudgel. The idiot had no choice but to endure the pain and keep close to him. When he saw the rake propped up by the second pair of gates he went over to it, pushed the junior devils aside, retrieved it and rushed forward, lashing out wildly. He and Brother Monkey charged through three or four pairs of gates, and goodness only knows how many junior devils they killed. When the senior demon chief heard all this he said to the second chief, "You captured a fine one! A fine one indeed! Look! Sun the Novice has rescued Pig and they've wounded or killed the juniors on the gates." The second demon at once sprang to his feet and rushed out through the gates brandishing his spear. "Damned macaque," he shouted at the top of his voice. "What a bloody cheek! How dare you treat us with such contempt!" As soon as the Great Sage heard this he stopped still. The monster thrust his spear straight at him without allowing any argument. With the unhurried skill of the expert Monkey raised his iron cudgel to hit back at the demon's face.

When he saw the Great Sage start fighting the evil spirit, Pig stood on the spur, his rake upright. Instead of joining in to help, he watched with stupefied amazement: Monkey's cudgel was so powerful and his martial skills so faultless. The evil spirit used his spear to parry Monkey's blows while unrolling his trunk to wrap round him. As Monkey knew about this trick he held his gold-banded cudgel out horizontally in both hands and raised them. The evil spirit's trunk caught Monkey round the waist but missed his hands.

Monkey waved his cudgel to make it as thick as a hen's egg and over ten feet long and actually did shove it hard up the monster's trunk. This gave the evil spirit such a shock that he unravelled his trunk with a swishing noise. Monkey brought his hand round to grab the trunk and drag it forcefully towards him. To spare himself any more agony the monster stepped out and moved with Monkey's hand. Only then did Pig dare approach, raising his rake to hit wildly at the monster's flanks. "No," said Brother Monkey, "that's no good. The prongs of your rake are so sharp they might break his skin. If he starts bleeding heavily and the master sees it he'll say we've been killing again. You'd better turn it round and hit him with the handle."

The idiot then raised the handle of his rake and struck the monster at every step while Monkey dragged him by the trunk. They looked like a pair of elephant boys as they led him down to the foot of the mountain. Friar Sand at once rushed straight towards them shouting, "The master says you mustn't kill the monster if he's really willing to escort him across the mountain." As soon as he heard this the demon fell to his knees and promised to do so in a very nasal voice. his voice was like this because Monkey was pinching his nostrils shut, making it sound as though he had a heavy cold. "Lord Tang," he said, "I'll carry you across by chair if you spare my life." "My master and we disciples are good people," Monkey replied. "As you've said this we'll spare your life. Fetch the chair at once. If you break your word again we most certainly won't spare your life when we catch you next time." The freed monster kowtowed and left.

The second demon chief returned trembling and shaking to the cave. Even before his return some junior devils had reported to the senior and the third demon chiefs that Monkey had dragged him off by the trunk. In his anxiety the senior demon had led his hosts out with the third demon when they saw the second chief coming back alone. As they brought him inside and asked him why he had been released the second chief told them all about Sanzang's words of mercy and goodness. They looked at each other, at a loss for words.

The third demon chief smiled again and said, "Elder brothers, it would have been luckier for those monks if they hadn't asked us to escort them but had slipped quietly across instead. By asking us to escort them they've fallen in with our plan to lure the tiger down from the mountain." "What do you mean by 'luring the tiger from the mountain'?" the senior demon asked. The third demon then told them his plan.

The senior demon was beside himself with delight on hearing this. It was as if he had recovered from a drunken stupor or woken up from a dream. "Excellent, excellent," he said, whereupon he mustered the demons, chose thirty to whom he gave the food and another sixteen to carry a rattan chair. As they set out the senior demon gave the following instructions to the rest of the demons: "None of you are to go out on the mountain. Sun the Novice is a very cautious ape, and if he sees any of you around he'll be suspicious and see through our plan."

The senior demon then led his underlings to a place beside the main road, where he called aloud, "Lord Tang, today's not an unlucky one, so please come across the mountain straight away." "Who is that calling me, Wukong?" Sanzang asked when he heard this. "It's the demons I beat," Monkey replied. "They're bringing a chair to carry you." Putting his hands together in front of his chest Sanzang looked up to the sky and said, "Splendid, splendid! But for my worthy disciple's great abilities I could not proceed on my journey." He then walked forward to greet the demons with the words, "I am most grateful for the consideration you gentlemen are showing. When my disciples and I return to Chang'an we will praise your admirable achievements." "Please get into the carrying-chair, my lord," the demons said, kowtowing. Having mortal eyes and body Sanzang did not realize that this was a trick. The Great Sage Sun, a golden immortal of the Supreme Monad with a loyal nature, thought that because he had captured and released the demons they were now won over. He never imagined that they had other plots in mind, so he did not investigate closely but went along with his master's ideas. He told Pig to tie the luggage on the horse and keep close to the master with Friar Sand while he cleared the way with his iron cudgel, watching out to see if all was well. While eight devils carried the chair and eight shouted in turn to clear the way the three demon chiefs steadied the poles of the chair. The master was delighted to sit in it and go up the high mountain by the main track.

The band of demons worked with one mind to escort them and serve them diligently at all times. After ten miles there was a vegetarian meal and after fifteen more miles another one.

Asking Lord Buddha to Lend a Hand

They were invited to rest before it grew late, and everything along their way was neat and tidy. Each day they had three most satisfactory and delightful meals and spent a comfortable night where they were able to sleep well.

When Master and disciples had travelled about 150 miles west they found themselves near a walled city. Raising his iron cudgel the Great Sage, who was only a third of a mile ahead of the carrying-chair, was so alarmed by the sight of the city that he fell over and was unable to rise to his feet. Do you know why someone of his great courage was so frightened by what he saw? It was because he saw a very evil atmosphere hanging over the town.

Just as he was being overcome by terror the Great Sage heard a wind from behind him and turned quickly to see the third demon chief raising a heaven-square halberd with a patterned handle to strike at his head. Springing to his feet, the Great Sage struck back at the monster's face with his gold-banded cudgel. Both of them were snorting with rage and fury as they ground their teeth and fought a wordless struggle. Monkey then saw the senior demon chief giving out orders as he lifted his steel sabre to hack at Pig. Pig was in such a rush that he had to let the horse go as he swung his rake around to hit wildly back. Meanwhile the second demon chief was thrusting with his spear at Friar Sand, who parried with his demon-quelling staff.

The three demon chiefs and the three monks were now all fighting in single combat, ready to throw away their lives. The sixteen junior devils obeyed their orders, each giving play to his talents as they grabbed hold of the white horse and the luggage and crowded round Sanzang, lifting up his chair and carrying him straight to the city. "Your Senior Majesty, please decide what to do now we've captured the Tang Priest," they shouted. All the demons of every rank on the city walls came rushing down to throw the city gates wide open. Every battalion was ordered to furl its flag, silence its drums, and on no account shout war-cries or strike gongs. "His Senior Majesty has given orders that the Tang Priest is not to be frightened. He can't endure being scared. If he is, his flesh will turn sour and be inedible." The demons were all delighted to welcome Sanzang, bowing and carrying him into the throne hall of the palace, where he was invited to sit in the place of honour. They offered him tea and food as they bustled around him in attendance. The venerable elder felt dizzy and confused as he looked about and saw no familiar faces.

The three demon chiefs were still in strenuous combat with the Great Sage and his two fellow disciples in the low hills to the east of the city.

After the six of them had been fighting for a long time evening was drawing in, and as the wind was also bringing cloud it became dark very quickly. Pig was finding it harder and harder to see as his big ears were covering his eyelids. His hands and feet were besides too slow for him to be able to hold off his opponent, so he fled from the fight, dragging his rake behind him. The senior demon chief took a swing at him with his sword that almost killed him. Luckily Pig moved his head out of the way, so that the blade only cut off a few of his bristles. The monster then caught up with Pig, opened his jaws, picked Pig up by the collar, carried him into the city and threw him to the junior demons to tie up and take to the throne hall. The senior demon chief then rose back into the air by cloud to help the other two.

Seeing that things were going badly Friar Sand feinted with his staff and turned to flee only to be caught, hands and all, when the second demon unravelled his trunk and noisily wrapped it round him. The demon took him too into the city, ordering the junior demons to tie him up in the palace before rising up into the sky again to tell the others how to catch Monkey. Seeing that both his brother disciples had been captured Monkey realized that it was going to be impossible for him to hold out single-handed. Indeed,

A couple of fists can defeat a good hand,
But cannot a competent foursome withstand.

With a shout Brother Monkey pushed the three demons' weapons aside, set off his somersault cloud and fled. When the third demon chief saw Monkey ride off by somersault he shook himself, resumed his real form, spread his wings and caught up with the Great Sage. You may well ask how the demon could possibly catch up with him. When Monkey made havoc in heaven all that time ago a hundred thousand heavenly soldiers had failed to capture him. Because he could cover 36,000 miles in a single somersault of his cloud, none of the gods had been able to catch up with him. But this evil spirit could cover 30,000 miles with one beat of his wings, so that with two beats he caught up with Monkey and seized him. Monkey could not get out of the demon's talons no matter how hard he struggled or how desperately he longed to escape. Even when he used his transformation magic he still could not move. If he made himself grow the demon opened his grip but still held firmly to him; and if he shrank the demon tightened his clutch. The demon took him back inside the city, released his talons, dropped him into the dust, and told the fiendish hordes to tie him up and put him with Pig and Friar Sand. The senior and the second demon chiefs both came out to greet the third chief, who went back up into the throne hall with them.

It was now the second watch of the night, and after all the demons had exchanged greetings the Tang Priest was pushed out of the throne hall. When he suddenly caught sight in the lamplight of his three disciples all lying tied up on the ground the venerable master leaned down beside Brother Monkey and said through his tears, "Disciple, when we meet with trouble you normally go off and use your magic powers to subdue the monsters causing it. Now that you too have been captured can I survive, poor monk that I am?" As soon as Pig and Friar Sand heard their master's distress they too began to howl together. "Don't worry, Master," said Monkey with a hint of a smile, "and don't cry, brothers. No matter what they do they won't be able to hurt us. When the demon chiefs have settled and are asleep we can be on our way." "You're just making trouble again, brother," replied Pig. "We're trussed up with hempen ropes. If we do manage to work them a bit loose they spurt water on them to shrink them again. You might be too skinny to notice, but fat old me's having a terrible time. If you don't believe me take a look at my arms. The rope's cut two inches deep into them. I'd never get away." "Never mind hempen ropes," said Monkey with a laugh, "even if they were coir cables as thick as a rice-bowl they'd be no more than an autumn breeze to me. What's there to make a fuss about?"

As master and disciples were talking the senior demon could be heard saying, "Third brother, you really are strong and wise. Your plan to capture the Tang Priest was brilliant and it worked." "Little ones," he called, "five of you carry water, seven scrub the pans, ten get the fire burning and twenty fetch the iron steamer. When we've steamed the four monks tender for my brothers and me to enjoy we'll give you juniors a piece so that you can all live for ever."

Before long a junior devil came in to report that the water was boiling. The senior chief ordered that the monks be carried in, and all the demons acted together to carry Pig to the lowest shelf of the steamer and Friar Sand to the second shelf. Guessing that they would be coming for him next Brother Monkey freed himself and said, "This lamplight is just right for some action." He then pulled out a hair, blew on it with magic breath, called, "Change!" and turned it into another Monkey he tied up with the hempen rope while extracting his real self in spirit form to spring up into mid-air, look down and watch. Not realizing that he was an imitation the crowd of demons picked up the false Monkey they saw and carried him to the third tray of the steamer, near the top. Only then did they drag the Tang Priest to the ground, tie him up, and put him into the fourth tray. As the dry firewood was stacked up a fierce fire blazed. "My Pig and Friar Sand can stand a couple of boilings," sighed the Great Sage up in the clouds, "but that master of mine will be cooked tender as soon as the water boils. If I can't save him by magic he'll be dead in next to no time."

The splendid Great Sage made a hand-spell in mid-air, and summoned the Dragon King of the Northern Ocean to him. A black cloud appeared among the other clouds, and from it there came at once an answering shout, "Ao Shun, the humble dragon

of the Northern Ocean, kowtows in homage." "Arise, arise,"
said Monkey. "I would not have ventured to trouble you for
nothing. I've now got this far with my master the Tang Priest.
He's been captured by vicious monsters and put into an iron
steamer to be cooked. Go and protect him for me and don't let
the steam harm him." The dragon king at once turned himself
into a cold wind that blew underneath the cooking pot and
coiled around to shield it from all the heat of the fire. Thus were
the three of them saved from death.

As the third watch was drawing to an end the senior demon
chief announced a decision. "My men," he said, "we have worn
out brains and brawn to capture the Tang Priest and his three
disciples. Because of the trouble we went to in escorting them
we have not slept for four days and nights. I don't think that
they'll be able to escape now that they're tied up and being
steamed. You are all to guard them carefully. Ten of your junior
devils are to take it in turns to keep the fires burning while we
withdraw to our living quarters for a little rest. By the fifth
watch, when it's about to get light, they're bound to be cooked
tender. Have some garlic paste, salt and vinegar ready and
wake us up; then we'll be able to eat them with a good appetite."
The devils did as they had been ordered while the three demon
chiefs returned to their sleeping chambers.

Up in the clouds Brother Monkey clearly heard these
instructions being given. A memory came back to him. "When
I was the Great Sage in the old days I once played a guessing
game with the Heavenly King Lokapala at the Northern Gate
of Heaven and won some of his sleep insects off him. I've got
a few left I can use on them." He felt around his waist inside
his belt and found that he had twelve of them left. "I'll give
them ten and keep two to breed from," Monkey thought. Then
he threw the insects into the ten junior devils' faces, where the
insects went up their nostrils, so that they all started feeling
drowsy, lay down and went to sleep. One of them, however, who
was holding a fire-fork slept very fitfully, kept rubbing his head
and face, pinching his nose and continuously sneezing. "That
so-and-so knows a trick or two," thought Monkey. "I'll have to

give him a double dose." He threw one of his remaining insects into the demon's face. "With two insects the left one can go in when the right one comes out and vice versa," Monkey thought. "That should keep him quiet." With that the junior demon gave two or three big yawns, stretched himself, dropped the fork and slumped down, fast asleep. He did not get up again.

"What marvellous magic; it really works," said Monkey, turning back into himself. Then he went close to the steamer and called, "Master." "Rescue me, Wukong," said the Tang Priest when he heard him. "Is that you calling to us from outside?" Friar Sand asked. "If I weren't out here would you prefer me to be suffering in there with you?" Monkey replied. "Brother," said Pig, "you sloped off and left us to carry the can. We're being closed-steamed in here." "Stop yelling, idiot," said Monkey with a laugh. "I'm here to rescue you." "Brother," said Pig, "if you're going to rescue us do it properly. Don't get us put back in here for another steaming." Monkey then took the lid off, freed the master, shook the hair of his that he had turned into an imitation Monkey and put it back on his body, then released Friar Sand and Pig, taking one tray at a time. As soon as he was untied, the idiot wanted to run away. "Don't be in such a hurry!" said Monkey, who recited the words of a spell that released the dragon before going on to say to Pig, "We've still got high mountains and steep ridges ahead of us on our way to the Western Heaven. The going's too heavy for the master — he isn't a strong walker. Wait till I've fetched the horse."

Watch him as with light step he goes to the throne hall, where he saw that all the demons young and old were asleep. He undid the rope attached to the horse's reins, being even more careful not to alarm him. Now the horse was a dragon horse, so had Monkey been a stranger he would have given him a couple of flying kicks and whinnied. But Monkey had kept horses and held the office of Protector of the Horses, and this horse was besides their own. That was why the animal neither reared nor whinnied. Monkey led the horse very quietly over, tightened the girth and got everything ready before inviting his master to mount. Trembling and shaking, the Tang Priest did so. He too wanted to go. "Don't you be in such a hurry either," Monkey said. "There'll be plenty more kings along our journey west and we'll need our passport if we're to get there. What other identity papers do we have? I'm going back to find the luggage." "I remember that when we came in the monsters put the luggage to the left of the throne hall," said the Tang Priest. "The load must still be there."

"Understood," said Monkey, who sprang off at once to search for it by the throne hall. When he suddenly saw shimmering lights of many colours Brother Monkey knew that they came from the luggage. How did he know? Because the light came from the night-shining pearl on the Tang Priest's cassock. He rushed towards it and found that their load was unopened, so he took it out and gave it to Friar Sand to carry, while Pig led the horse and he took the lead.

Sanzang was not yet free of his unlucky star. The three demon chiefs who had been fast asleep in their living quarters suddenly awoke and heard that the Tang Priest had escaped, got up, threw on their clothes and hurried to the throne hall of the palace. "How many times has the Tang Priest been steamed?" they asked. The junior devils who were looking after the fires were all so soundly asleep because the sleep insects were in them that not even blows could wake them up. The chiefs woke up some others who were not on duty, who answered rashly, "Ss ... ss ... seven times." Then they rushed over to the steamer to see the steamer trays lying scattered on the floor and the cooks still asleep. In their alarm they rushed back to report, "Your Majesties, th ... th ... they've escaped."

The three demon chiefs came out of the throne hall to take a close look around the cauldron. They saw that the steamer trays were indeed scattered on the floor, the water was stone-cold and the fire completely out. The cooks supposed to be tending the fire were still so fast asleep that they were snoring noisily. The fiends were all so shocked that they all shouted, "Catch the Tang Priest! At once! Catch the Tang Priest!" Their yells woke up the demons senior and junior all around. They rushed in a crowd to the main front gates carrying their swords and spears. Seeing that the sealed locks had not been touched and that the night watchmen were still sounding their clappers and bells they asked the watchman, "Which way did the Tang Priest go?" "Nobody's come out," the watchmen all replied. They hurried to the back gates of the palace, only to find that the seals, locks, clappers and bells were the same as at the front. With a great commotion they grabbed lanterns and torches, making the sky red and the place as bright as day. The four of them were clearly lit up as they climbed over the wall. "Where do you think you're going?" the senior demon chief shouted, running towards them and so terrifying the reverend gentleman that the muscles in his legs turned soft and numb and he fell off the wall to be captured by the senior demon. The second demon chief seized Friar Sand and the third knocked Pig over and captured him. The other demons took the luggage and the white horse. Only Monkey escaped.

The monsters took the Tang Priest into the throne hall but did not steam him again. The second demon chief ordered that Pig was to be tied to one of the columns supporting the eaves in front of the hall and the third chief had Friar Sand tied to one of the columns holding up the eaves at the back. That very night the poor Tang Priest was taken inside the palace, put into an iron chest and locked up in the pavilion. A rumour that the Tang Priest had been eaten was spread around the town.

When Monkey had wiped out all the junior demons in the Lion Cave he hurried back to the city, turned himself into a demon in palace uniform, and went into the palace. On being told by Pig and Friar Sand that the Master had been eaten he flew to the Vulture Peak to ask the Buddha's help.

The Tathagata Buddha was sitting on his nine-level lotus throne expounding the sutras to his eighteen arhats when he said, "Sun Wukong is here. You must all go out to receive him." In obedience to the Buddha's command the arhats went out in two columns with their banners and canopies. "Great Sage Sun," they said in greeting, "the Tathagata has commanded us to summon you to his presence." Only then did the four vajrapanis at the monastery gates step aside to let Monkey enter. The arhats led him to the foot of the lotus throne, where he went down to kowtow on seeing the Tathagata. He was sobbing and weeping. "Wukong," said the Buddha, "what makes you weep so miserably?"

"Your disciple has often received the grace of your instruction," Brother Monkey replied, "and has committed himself to the school of Lord Buddha. Since being converted to the true achievement I have taken the Tang Priest as my master and been protecting him on our journey. No words could describe what we have suffered. We have now reached the city of Leonia near Lion Cave on Lion Mountain where three vicious monsters, the Lion King, the Elephant King and the Great Roc, seized my master. All of us disciples of his were in a very bad way too, tied up and put in a steamer to suffer the agony of fire and boiling water. Fortunately I was able to get away and summon a dragon king to save the others. But we could not escape our evil star: the master and the others were recaptured when I was trying to sneak them out last night. When I went back into the city this morning to find out what had happened I learned that those utterly evil and ferocious monsters ate my master raw during the night. Nothing is left of his flesh and bones. On top of that my fellow-disciples Wuneng and Wujing are tied up there and will soon be dead too. I'm desperate. That's why your disciple has come to visit the Tathagata. I beg you in your great compassion to recite the Band-loosening Spell so that I can take the band off my head and give it back to you. Let your disciple go back to the Mountain of Flowers and Fruit and enjoy himself." Before he had finished saying this the tears welled up again. There was no end to his howls of misery.

"Don't upset yourself so, Wukong," said the Tathagata with a smile. "You can't beat those evil spirits. Their magical powers are more than you can handle. That is why you are so unhappy." Monkey knelt below the Buddha and beat his breast as he replied, "Truly, Tathagata, I made havoc in Heaven all those years ago and was called Great Sage. Never in all my life had I been beaten before I met these vicious monsters."

"Stop being so sorry for yourself," said the Tathagata. "I

know those evil spirits." "Tathagata!" Monkey suddenly blurted out. "They say those evil spirits are relations of yours." "Wicked macaque!" said the Tathagata. "How could an evil spirit be any relation of mine?" "If they're not relations of yours how come you know them?" retorted Monkey with a grin. "I know them because I see them with my all-seeing eyes," the Buddha replied. "The senior demon and the second demon have masters. Ananda, Kasyapa, come here. One of you is to take a cloud to Mount Wutai and the other to Mount Emei. Summon Manjusri and Samantabhadra to come and see me." The two arhats left at once as they had been commanded. "They are the masters of the senior and the second demon chiefs. But the third demon does have some connection with me." "On his mother's or his father's side?" Monkey asked. "When the primal chaos was first separated the heavens opened up in the hour of the rat and the earth at the hour of the ox," the Buddha replied. "Mankind was born at the tiger hour. Then heaven and earth came together again and all living creatures were born, including beasts that walk and birds that fly. The unicorn is the most senior of the beasts that walk and the phoenix is the most senior of the birds that fly. When the phoenixes combined their essential spirit they gave birth to the peafowl and the Great Roc. When the peafowl came into the world she was the most evil of creatures and a man-eater. She could devour all the people for fifteen miles around in a single mouthful. When I was cultivating my sixteen-foot golden body on the peak of the snowy mountain she swallowed me as well. I went down into her belly. I wanted to escape through her backside, but for fear of soiling my body I cut my way out through her backbone and climbed Vulture Peak. I would have killed her, but all the Buddha host dissuaded me: to kill the peahen would have been like killing my own mother. So I kept her at my assembly on Vulture Peak and appointed her as the Buddha-mother, the Great Illustrious Peahen Queen Bodhisattva. The Great Roc was born of the same mother as she was. That is why we are relations of a kind." When Monkey heard this he said with a smile, "By that line of argument, Tathagata, you're the evil spirit's nephew." "I shall have to go and subdue that demon in person," the Tathagata said.

The Tathagata then came down from his lotus throne and went out through the monastery gates with all the Buddha host just as Ananda and Kasyapa arrived bringing Manjusri and Samantabhadra. These two Bodhisattvas bowed to the Tathagata, who asked them, "How long have your animals been away from your mountains, Bodhisattvas?" "Seven days," said Manjusri. "A mere seven days on your mountains is several thousand years in the mortal world," the Tathagata replied. "Goodness knows how many living beings they have destroyed there. Come with me to recapture them at once." The two Bodhisattvas travelled at the Buddha's left and right hand as they flew through the air with the host.

It was not long before the city was in sight. "Tathagata," said Monkey, "that's Leonia, where the black vapours are coming from." "You go down into the city first," said the Tathagata, "and start a fight with the evil spirits. Do not win. You must lose and come back up. Leave it to us to recapture them."

The Great Sage then brought his cloud straight down to land on the city wall, where he stood on the battlements and shouted abusively, "Evil beasts! Come out and fight me at once!" This caused such consternation among the junior demons in the towers on the wall that they jumped straight down into the city to report, "Your Majesties, Sun the Novice is on the wall, challenging us to battle." "That ape hasn't been here for two or three days," the senior demon replied. "Now he's back challenging us to battle. Can he have fetched some reinforcements?" "He's nothing to be scared of," said the third demon chief. "Let's all go and have a look." The three chieftains, all carrying their weapons, hurried up on the wall where they saw Monkey. Without a word they raised their weapons and thrust at him. Monkey held them off by swinging his iron cudgel. When they had fought seven or eight rounds Monkey feigned defeat and fled. "Where do you think you're going?" the demon king asked with a mighty shout, and with a somersault Monkey sprang up into mid-air. The three spirits went after him on clouds, but Monkey slipped aside and disappeared completely in the Lord Buddha's golden aura.

All that could be seen were the images of the Three Buddhas of Past, Future and Present, the five hundred arhats and the three thousand Protectors of the Faith who spread all around, encircling the three demon kings so closely that not even a drop of water could leak through. "This is terrible, my brother," said the senior demon chief, lashing out wildly, "that ape is a really sharp operator. How did he manage to bring my master here?" "Don't be afraid, elder brother," said the third demon. "If we all charge together we can cut down the Tathagata with our swords and spears and seize his Thunder Monastery." The demons, who had no sense of proper behaviour, really did raise their swords to charge forward, hacking wildly. Manjusri and Samantabhadra recited the words of a spell and shouted, "Won't you repent now, evil beasts? What else do you hope for?" The senior and the second demon chiefs gave up the struggle, threw down their weapons, rolled and reverted to their true images: a blue lion and a white elephant.

Now that the blue lion and the white elephant had been captured only the third evil monster was still unsubdued. Spreading its wings it dropped its heaven-square halberd and rose straight up to try to catch the Monkey King with a swing of its sharp talons, but as the Great Sage was hiding in the golden aura the demon dared get nowhere near him. When the Tathagata realized what it was trying to do he made his golden aura flash and shook his head, which was the supreme meditator, in the wind to turn it into a bright red lump of bloody meat. The evil spirit seized it with a flourish of its sharp talons, whereupon the Lord Buddha pointed upwards with his hand, destroying the muscles in the monster's wings. It could not fly or get away from the top of the Buddha's head, and it reverted to its true appearance as a golden-winged vulture.

Only then did Monkey emerge to kowtow to the Tathagata and say, "Lord Buddha, today you have captured the evil spirits and removed a great bane, but my master is dead." At this the

Great Roc said bitterly as it ground its teeth, "Damned ape! Why did you have to bring these ferocious men here to persecute me? I never ate that old monk of yours. He's in the Brocade Fragrance Pavilion now, isn't he?" When Monkey heard this he quickly kowtowed to thank the Lord Buddha. Not daring to release the Great Roc, the Buddha made him into a guardian of the dharma in his brilliant halo, then led his host back to his monastery on their clouds.

Monkey landed his cloud and went straight into the city, where there was not a single junior demon left. They had all fled for their lives when they saw the Buddha capturing their evil kings. Monkey then freed Pig and Friar Sand, found the luggage and the horse, and said to his fellow-disciples, "The master hasn't been eaten. Come with me." He took the two of them straight into the inner compound where they found the Brocade Fragrance Pavilion. Opening the door and looking inside they saw an iron trunk from which could be heard the sound of Sanzang weeping. Friar Sand used his demon-quelling staff to open the iron cage over the chest and raise its lid. "Master," he called. At the sight of them Sanzang wept aloud and said, "Disciples, how were the demons beaten? How did you manage to find me here?" Monkey told him all the details of what had happened from beginning to end and Sanzang expressed boundless gratitude. Then master and disciples found some rice in the palace and ate their fill of it before packing their things and leaving the city along the main road west.

CHAPTER 31
Monkey Shows His Powers in Dharmadestructia

As Tang Sanzang and three disciples headed westwards they did not notice that it was already summer: warm breezes were beginning to blow, and the early summer rain was falling.

As the master and his three disciples travelled along enduring the heat they suddenly noticed two rows of tall willows, from under the shade of which an old woman emerged, leaning on a small boy. "Don't go any further, monk," she called out. "Stop your horse and go back east as soon as you can." Pointing westwards, the old woman continued, "If you go that way you will come to the capital of Dharmadestructia in a couple of miles. The king formed a hatred of Buddhism in an earlier existence, and in his present life he is punishing it without just cause. Two years ago he made a monstrous vow to kill ten thousand Buddhist monks. In that time he's killed 9,996 unknown monks in succession. He's just waiting for four famous monks to make up his ten thousand so that he will fulfil the vow. If you go into the city you will be throwing away your lives for nothing." At the sound of this Sanzang was so terrified that he shivered and shook as he replied, "Venerable Bodhisattva, I am deeply moved by your great kindness and infinitely grateful too. But, tell me, is there a suitable way I could take that does not go into the city?" "There's no way round," the old woman replied with a laugh, "no way round. The only way you'll get past it is if you can fly."

Monkey's fiery eyes with their golden pupils really could distinguish good from evil, and he saw that the old woman and the little boy on whom she was leaning were in fact the Bodhisattva Guanyin and the page Sudhana. He hastily flung himself to the ground and began to kowtow, calling out, "Bodhisattva, your disciple failed to welcome you. I'm sorry." The Bodhisattva then rose slowly on her multicoloured cloud, so startling the venerable elder that his legs gave way under him and he kowtowed as he knelt there for all he was worth. Pig and Friar Sand also fell to their knees in alarm and kowtowed to heaven.

"It was lucky the Bodhisattva told us that Dharmadestructia, where they kill monks, is ahead of us," Pig and Friar Sand said to Monkey. "Whatever are we to do?" "Don't be afraid, idiot," Monkey replied. "We've come to no harm from any of the vicious demons and evil monsters we've met already or in the tigers' dens and dragons' pools we've been in. This is just a country of ordinary people. What's there to be so scared of? The only thing is that we can't stay here. It's getting late in the day and some of the villagers are coming back from market in the town. It will be no good if they see we're monks and raise a hue and cry. We'd better take the master away from the main road to some quiet and secluded spot where we can discuss things." Sanzang accepted Monkey's suggestion and they slipped away from the main road to a hollow in the ground where they sat down. "Brother," said Monkey, "you two look after the master while I turn myself into something and go into town to take a look around. I'll find a side road that we can get away along tonight." The Great Sage leapt whistling up into the air. As he stood in the clouds looking down he saw that the city was full of the most happy and auspicious atmosphere.

Watch him as he flutters and flies straight to the main streets and the markets, keeping close to the eaves and the corners of the buildings he passes. As he was flying along he noticed that on a square lantern outside the middle house was written, "Accommodation for Commercial Travellers", with "Wang the Second's Inn" beneath it. Only then did Monkey realize that this was an inn. Stretching his head forward for a closer look he saw eight or nine men inside who had all eaten their supper, taken off their clothes and hats, washed their hands and feet and gone to bed. "The master will get through," Monkey thought with secret delight. How did he know that? Because he was having a wicked idea: he would wait till they were all asleep, then steal their clothes and hats so that he and his companions could go into the city dressed as laymen.

The Great Sage used his magic powers to take the clothes from the inn. Then he escaped on his cloud, which he turned round to go straight back to the hollow by the road. Sanzang was looking out for him fixedly by the bright light of the moon and the stars, and as soon as he saw Monkey approaching he called out, "Can we get through the capital of Dharmadestructia, disciple?" Coming up and laying the clothes down in front of him, Monkey replied, "Master, you won't get through Dharmadestructia as a monk. The king is wicked and does kill monks. I've just borrowed these hats and clothes from an inn for us to dress ourselves up as laymen in. We'll go into the city, put up for the night, get up at the fourth watch and ask the innkeeper to fix us some vegetarian food. At the fifth watch we'll go out through the gate and head west along the main road. If we meet anyone who tries to stop us we can talk our way out of it. I'll tell him we were sent by the ruler of their suzerain state. The king of Dharmadestructia won't dare hold us up. He'll let us go on our way." "Our big brother has arranged things very well," said Friar Sand. "Let's do as he suggests." Although he was not happy about it the Tang Priest had to go along with this.

Under Monkey's instruction, all of them put on the laymen's clothes and hurried to the city, leading the horse and carrying the luggage. As this was a very peaceful place the city gates were still open although it was already night. They went straight into the city, and as they passed the gateway of Wang the Second's inn, a man came out to take the horse. Monkey handed him the horse to take inside. He then led the master into the building in the shadow of the lamp. Upstairs there were tables and chairs conveniently arranged, and when the window was opened they all sat down in the clear moonlight. When someone came with a lighted lamp Monkey blocked the doorway, blew it out and said, "No need for a lamp on a bright night like this."

No sooner had the man with the lamp gone down than a maid came up with four bowls of tea. Monkey took the bowls from her, only for her to be followed by a woman who looked to be about fifty-six or fifty-seven coming up the stairs. Standing beside Monkey she asked, "Where are you gentlemen from? What fine goods do you have?" "We're from the north," Monkey replied, "and we've got a few poor horses to sell." "You're very young to be a horse dealer," the woman said. "This gentleman is Tang the Eldest," Monkey explained, "this is Hogg the Third, and this is Sand the fourth. I'm Sun the Second, an apprentice."

The old woman said, "My late husband was called Zhao, but I'm afraid he died long ago, so this is now called Widow Zhao's Inn. We have three classes of entertainment for our guests. Let's get sordid money matters out of the way, then we can be more civilized later. The first thing is to discuss the tariffs and agree on one so that we know where we stand when it's time to settle the accounts." "Quite right," Monkey replied. "Give us the first-class treatment."

"Make some good tea," the woman said with great delight, "and tell the kitchen to get the food ready quickly." "Don't kill any living creatures today: we're eating vegetarian food today," Monkey said. "Are you gentlemen permanent vegetarians, or just vegetarians for this month?" asked the woman in surprise. "Neither," replied Monkey. "We're vegetarians on *gengshen* days.* Today's one, so we have to eat meatless food. But after the third watch tonight it'll be a *xinyou* day and the restrictions won't apply. Kill them tomorrow. Lay on some vegetarian food today, and make it first-class." She was delighted to be spared the expense of meat, and they ate soon after.

---

* A *gengshen* day, like the *xinyou* day that follows it, occurs once in every cycle of sixty days.

"Where are we going to sleep?" Sanzang whispered in Monkey's ear. "Upstairs," Monkey replied. "Too dangerous," Sanzang replied. "We have all had so hard a journey that we may well fall fast asleep. If any of the inn people come in to tidy up and our hats have rolled off they will see our bald heads, realize that we are monks, and raise a hue and cry. That would be a disaster." "You're right," said Monkey, going out to stamp his foot again. "What instructions do you have this time, Mr. Sun?" the woman asked, coming upstairs once more. "Where are we to sleep?" Monkey asked. "Upstairs is best," she replied. "There are no mosquitoes and there's a south wind. Open the windows wide and you'll sleep beautifully." "We won't be able to," said Monkey. "Our Mr. Hogg the Third has a touch of gout, Mr. Sand the Fourth has some rheumatism in his shoulder, Brother Tang can only sleep in the dark, and I don't like the light myself. So this is no place for us to sleep."

The woman said, "Mr Sun, if you won't have our poky little room there's nowhere darker here than our big trunk. It'll keep out light and draughts. So why don't you sleep in the trunk?" "Splendid," Monkey replied. She then told several of the retainers to carry the trunk out and open the lid, while inviting her guests to come downstairs. Monkey led the master and Friar Sand carried the luggage as they went to the trunk, following in the lantern's shadow. The reckless Pig was the first to climb inside. Friar Sand lifted the luggage in then helped the Tang Priest in before getting in himself. "Where's our horse?" Monkey asked. "Tied up eating hay in the stables at the back," replied the servant who was attending them. "Bring it here," said Monkey, "and bring the trough too. Tether the animal next to the trunk." Only then did he get inside himself and call out, "Shut the lid, Mrs. Zhao, fasten the hasp and padlock it. And look it over for us. Glue paper wherever it lets in the light. Open it again early tomorrow morning." "You're very particular," the widow said. After that the doors were fastened and everyone went to bed.

The story switches to the four of them in the chest. Poor

things! They were wearing hats, the weather was very hot and it was airless and stuffy. They took off their hats and clothes, and fanned themselves with their monastic hats for lack of fans. They were all crowded in next to each other and did not fall asleep till the second watch.

Now the floor staff, the water-carriers and the kitchen porters were in league with bandits. After hearing Brother Monkey talking about all the money they had, several of them slipped off to fetch twenty or more armed bandits to come with torches to rob the four horse traders. As they charged in through the gates they gave Widow Zhao and her daughter such a fright that shivering and shaking they fastened the doors of their room and let the robbers take whatever they wanted outside. Now the bandits were not after the inn's property but were looking for the guests. When they went upstairs and found no sign of them there, they lit their torches and held them out while they looked all around. All they could see was a large trunk in the courtyard, to the bottom of which was tethered a white horse. The lid was tightly locked and could not be prized open. "Travelling merchants all know what they're about," the bandits said. "This trunk looks so strong that it's bound to be full of purses, valuables and silk. Let's steal the horse, take the trunk out of town, open it up and share out what's inside. That would be the best thing, wouldn't it?" The bandits then found some rope with which they lifted the box and carried it off, swinging and swaying. "Brother," said Pig, woken up by this, "go to sleep. Why are you rocking us?" "Shut up," Monkey replied. "Nobody's rocking us." Sanzang and Friar Sand had been abruptly awoken too, and they asked, "Who's carrying us?" "Keep quiet," said Monkey, "keep quiet. Let them carry us. If they carry us to the Western Heaven we'll be saved the trouble of walking."

But the successful bandits were not heading west. Instead they headed towards the east of the city, killing the soldiers on the city gate, opening it and letting themselves out. This caused a sensation in the streets and the markets, where the watchmen of all the shops reported it to the commander-in-chief of the city garrison and the east city commissioner. As this was their responsibility the commander-in-chief and the east city commissioner mustered a force of infantry, cavalry and bowmen that left the city in pursuit of the bandits. Seeing that resistance to so powerful a government force would have been pointless, the bandits abandoned the trunk and the white horse, scattered into the undergrowth and disappeared. The government troops did not catch even half a robber: all they captured was the trunk and the white horse, with which they returned in triumph.

The commander-in-chief rode the white horse instead of his own steed as he led his men back into the city. The trunk was carried to his headquarters, where he and the east city commissioner sealed it with strips of paper on which they wrote and set a guard over it till morning, when they would submit a memorial to the king and request a decision on what to do with it. After that the other troops were dismissed.

In the third watch Monkey used one of his magic powers. Slipping his cudgel out he blew on it with a magic breath, called "Change!" and turned it into a triple auger with which he drilled two or three holes near the bottom of the chest, forming a single larger hole. He put the auger away, shook himself, turned into an ant and crawled out. Then he turned back into himself and rode his cloud straight to the palace gates. The king was fast asleep at the time, so Monkey used his Great All-powerful Body-dividing Magic. Plucking all the hairs out of his left arm he blew on them with a magic breath, called "Change!" and turned them into little Monkeys. Then he pulled all the hairs out from his right arm, blew on them with a magic breath, called "Change!" and turned them into sleep-insects. Next he recited the magic word *Om* and told the local deity of the place to take the little Monkeys to distribute them throughout the palace to all the officials in every office and department of government. Each holder of official rank was given a sleep-insect to ensure that he or she would sleep soundly and not get up. Monkey then took his gold-banded cudgel in his hands, squeezed it, waved it, called, "Change, treasure!" and turned it into over a thousand razors of the sort used for shaving the head. Taking one himself, he told all the little monkeys to take one each and shave the heads of everyone in the inner quarters of the palace and in all the government departments and offices.

That night the head-shaving was completed, so Monkey said another spell to dismiss the local deity, shook himself to bring all the hairs back to his arms, then touched all the razors to turn them back into their true form as the gold-banded cudgel, which he made much smaller and hid in his ear again. Finally he reverted to being an ant and crawled back into the trunk.

When the palace ladies in the inner quarters got up to wash and do their hair before dawn the next morning they all found that their hair had gone and went to wake the king. When the king suddenly opened his eyes wide and saw the queen's bald head he got straight out of bed and said, "Why are you like that, my queen?" "You're the same, Your Majesty," she replied. The king then rubbed his head, which gave him such a fright that the three souls in his body groaned, and his seven spirits flew off into the air. "We think this must be because of all the monks we have killed," he said. He then gave these orders: "None of you are to say anything about the loss of our hair as, if you do, the civil and military officials may slander our country and say that it has been badly governed. Let us now hold court in the throne hall."

The story tells how when the king held his dawn audience the civil and military officials all carried memorials. "Sovereign Lord," they reported, "we beg you to forgive your servants for their lack of decorum." "Gentlemen," the king replied, "you are all as courteous as ever. What lack of decorum are you showing?" "Sovereign Lord," they said, "we do not know why, but all of your servants lost their hair last night." Holding in his hand these memorials about the lost hair, the king descended from his dragon throne to say to the officials, "Indeed, we do not know why either, but everyone in the palace, young and old, lost their hair last night." King and ministers alike all wept as they said, "From now on we will not dare kill any more monks." The king then returned to his throne and the officials took their places in their proper ranks. The king then said, "Let those with business here come forward from their ranks to report. If there is no other business the curtain may be rolled up and the audience ended." The commander-in-chief of the capital's garrison then moved forward from the ranks of military officials and the east city commissioner moved forward from the ranks of the civil officials to kowtow at the steps of the throne and report, "We were patrolling the city on Your Majesty's orders last night when we recaptured a trunk of bandits' booty and a white horse. As we do not dare take unauthorized action over these we beg Your Majesty to issue an edict." The king was delighted. "Bring it here, trunk and all," he ordered.

On being invited by the two officials to have the trunk opened and look inside the king ordered that this be done. No sooner was the lid lifted than Pig, who could restrain himself no longer, sprang outside, giving all the officials such a fright that they shivered, unable to speak. Next Brother Monkey could be seen helping the Tang Priest out, while Friar Sand lifted the luggage out. This so terrified the official that he collapsed head over heels. The four pilgrims all stood upright in the middle of the steps, and when the king saw that they were monks he came down at once from his dragon throne, sent for his queen and consorts from the inner quarters, descended the steps of the throne hall, bowed to them along with all his officials and asked, "What brings you venerable gentlemen here?" "I have been sent by His Majesty the Great Tang Emperor to go to the Great Thunder Monastery in India in the West to worship the living Buddha and fetch the true scriptures," Sanzang replied. "Venerable Master," the king said, "you have come from far away. But why did you sleep in this trunk last night?" "I knew that Your Majesty had sworn a vow to kill Buddhist monks," Sanzang replied, "which is why I did not dare to visit your illustrious country openly, but disguised myself as a layman to arrive late at night to find lodging in one of your inns. We slept in the trunk because we were afraid that our real identity would be discovered. Unfortunately the trunk was stolen by bandits, then brought back here by the commander-in-chief. Now that I have been able to see Your Majesty's dragon countenance, the clouds have cleared away and the sun has come out. I hope that Your Majesty will pardon and release me, ascetic monk that I am: my gratitude will be as deep as the ocean."

"Venerable Master," the king replied, "you are a distinguished monk from our suzerain heavenly dynasty. It was wrong of us not to go out to welcome you. For years we have been fulfilling a vow to kill monks because a monk once maligned us. The vow we made to heaven was to kill ten thousand monks to make up a round number. We never imagined that today we would return to the truth and that we would all be turned into monks. Now all of us, king, officials, queen and consorts, have had our hair shaved off. I beg, Venerable Master, that you will not be grudging with your lofty virtue and will take us as your disciples." When Pig heard this he started roaring with laughter: "If you're going to be our disciples what introductory presents have you got for us?" "If you will accept us as your follower, Master," the king replied, "we will present you with all the wealth in our kingdom." "Don't talk about wealth to us," said Brother Monkey, "as we're proper monks. As long as you inspect and return our passport and escort us out of the city I can guarantee that your monarchy will last for ever and that you will enjoy a long and happy life." On hearing this the king ordered his office of foreign relations to arrange a great feast at which monarch and officials together returned to the one truth. The passport was immediately inspected and returned, after which Sanzang was asked to change the name of the country. " 'Dharma' in the name of Your Majesty's country is excellent," Monkey said, "but the 'destructia' part is nonsense. Now that we've come here you should change the name to 'Dharmarespectia'. This would guarantee

Clear waters and victory for a thousand generations;
Timely winds and rain with universal peace."

The king thanked them for their gracious kindness, had the royal carriage prepared and escorted the Tang Priest and his three disciples westwards out of the city.

CHAPTER 32
Meeting the Primal Sage
of Ninefold Numinosity in Yuhua City

When the four of them had been travelling for a long time they saw the towering shape of a city wall. "Wukong," said Sanzang, waving his riding-crop, "you can see there's another city there. I wonder where it is."

Before the words were out of his mouth an old man appeared from among some trees. He was leaning on a stick, lightly dressed with coir sandals on his feet and had a sash round his waist. The Tang Priest hastily dismounted and went over to greet the old man. Returning his greeting as he leant on his stick, the old man asked, "Where are you from, reverend sir?" "I am a poor monk sent by the Tang court in the east to worship the Buddha in the Thunder Monastery and fetch the scriptures," the Tang Priest replied, putting his hands together in front of his chest. "Now that I have come to this distinguished place I wonder which city it is that I can see in the distance, and I would ask you, venerable benefactor, to inform me." When the old man heard this he replied, "Enlightened master of the dhyana, this humble place of ours is Yuhua County in one of the prefectures of India. The lord of our city is a member of the king of India's royal family who has been made prince of Yuhua. He is a very worthy prince who respects both Buddhist and Taoist clergy and cares deeply for the common people. If you go to see him he will certainly treat you with great respect." Sanzang thanked the old man, who went off through the woods.

Master and disciples were happy to hear this. They decided to walk into the city. Once over the drawbridge they found the main roads bustling and prosperous with bars and houses of entertainment. It was indeed a city in a divine region.

When they learned that a bushel of hulled rice cost only four tenths of an ounce of silver and a pound of sesame oil only eight thousandths of an ounce of silver they realized that this truly was a place where crops grew in abundance.

After walking for quite a long time they reached the prince of Yuhua's palace. "Disciples," said Sanzang, "here is the palace. Wait at the government hostel while I go inside for the prince to inspect our passport and let us on our way."

Thereupon the master changed his habit and hat and went straight into the prince's palace with the passport in his hands. Soon he was met by a protocol officer who asked, "Where are you from, reverend sir?" "I am a monk sent by the Great Tang in the east to worship the Lord Buddha and fetch the scriptures in the Great Thunder Monastery," Sanzang replied. "Now that I have reached this distinguished place I would like to have my passport inspected and returned, which is why I have come to seek an audience with His Royal Highness." The protocol officer passed this on, and as the prince was indeed an enlightened one he sent for Sanzang at once.

Sanzang bowed in greeting before the prince's hall, and the prince invited him into the hall to sit down. When the prince read the passport that Sanzang handed him and saw the seals and signatures from so many countries on it he signed it himself, folded it up and put it on his table. "Venerable Teacher of the Nation," he said, "you have passed through many countries on your way here from Great Tang. How long has your journey taken?" "I have kept no record of the distance," Sanzang said, "but some years ago the Boddhisattva Guanyin appeared to me and left an address in verse in which it was said that the road would be sixty thousand miles long. I have already seen fourteen winters and summers on my journey." "That means fourteen years," the prince replied. "I should imagine that there were many delays along the way." "It would be hard to tell of them all," said Sanzang. "There were thousands of monsters and I don't know how much suffering to be endured before I could reach here." The prince was so pleased with his visitor that he ordered his kitchens to prepare a vegetarian meal for him. "I wish to inform Your Royal Highness that I have three disciples," Sanzang said. "As they are waiting outside I will not be able to delay our journey by accepting the meal." The prince then ordered his aides to go straight out to invite the venerable elder's three disciples into the palace to share the meal.

Monkey, Friar Sand and Pig were led to the palace. When the prince looked up and saw how ugly they were he too was frightened. "Do not be alarmed, Your Royal Highness," said Sanzang, putting his hands together in front of his chest. "Although my rough disciples are ugly they have good hearts." Pig intoned a noise of respect and said, "How do you do?" This made the prince feel even more alarmed. "All my rough disciples are from the wilds and the mountains and they do not know how to behave," Sanzang explained, "so please forgive them." Overcoming his fear, the prince told the superintendent of his kitchens to take the monks to eat in the Gauze Pavilion.

When the prince withdrew from the palace hall to his living quarters his three sons noticed his pallor and asked, "What has given you such a fright today, Father?" "A most remarkable monk has arrived," the prince replied. "He has been sent by the Great Tang in the east to worship the Buddha and fetch the scriptures, and he came to present his passport. When I invited him to take a meal he told me that he had some disciples outside the palace, so I asked them in. When they came in a moment later they didn't kowtow to me but just said, 'How do you do?' That was upsetting enough. Then when I looked at them I saw that they were all as ugly as demons, which gave me quite a shock. That's why I'm looking pale." Now the three young princes were no ordinary boys. They were all fond of the martial arts, so they stretched out their hands, rolled up their sleeves and said, "They must be evil spirits from the mountains disguised as humans. Wait while we fetch our weapons and take a look at them."

Splendid young princes! The eldest wielded a brow-high rod, the second a nine-toothed rake and the third a black-painted cudgel, and the three of them strode with great valour and spirit out of the palace, shouting, "What's this about monks fetching scriptures? Where are they?" "Young prince," replied the superintendent of the kitchens and the others on their knees, "they're eating in the Gauze Pavilion." The young princes then charged straight in without stopping to think as they shouted, "Are you men or monsters? Tell us at once and we'll spare your lives."

The second prince strode forward wielding his rake in both hands to strike at Pig, which made him say with a chuckle, "That rake of yours is only fit to be the grandson of mine." With that he stripped down, pulled his own rake out from his belt and swung it, making ten thousand beams of golden light, then went through some movements, leaving a thousand strands of auspicious vapour. The second prince was so terrified that his hands went weak and his muscles turned numb and he lost the nerve for any more showing off.

When Monkey saw that the oldest of the young princes was leaping about with a brow-high rod he brought his own gold-banded cudgel out from his ear and shook it to make it as thick as a bowl and twelve or thirteen feet long. Ramming it into the ground, he made a hole about three feet deep in which it stood upright, then said with a smile, "I'm giving you this cudgel." As soon as the prince heard this he threw his own rod down and went to take the cudgel, but though he pulled at it with all his strength he couldn't move it by as much as a hair's breadth. Then he straightened himself up and shook it, but it was as if it had taken root. At this the third prince started acting wild, moving into the attack with his black-painted cudgel. Friar Sand dodged the blow then brought out his own demon-quelling staff, and as he fingered it brilliant light and glowing, coloured clouds came from it, leaving the superintendent of the kitchens and the rest of them wide-eyed and speechless.

The three young princes hurried back into the palace to

report to their father, "The three hideous disciples of the monk who's going to fetch the scriptures are in fact divine teachers. We must make them our teachers and learn their skills to protect the country with." When the prince, their father, heard this he was convinced and agreed.

Father and sons then went straight to the Gauze Pavilion, going on foot instead of by carriage, and without any parasols. The four travellers had by now packed up their luggage and were just about to go to the palace to thank the prince for the meal and start out on their journey again when they saw the prince of Yuhua and his sons come into the pavilion and prostrate themselves before them. The venerable elder hurriedly rose and prostrated himself to return the courtesy, while Monkey and the rest of them moved aside with a hint of a mocking grin. When the kowtowing was over the four travellers were happy to go into the palace on being invited to do so and take seats of honour. Then the senior prince got up and said, "Tang Master, there is one thing I would like to ask of you, but I do not know whether your three illustrious disciples will grant it." "My disciples will obey any instruction that Your Royal Highness gives them," Sanzang replied. "When I first saw you gentlemen," said the prince, "I took you for pilgrim monks from distant Tang, and because I am a mere mortal with fleshly eyes I treated you in a most offhand way. It was only when I saw Teacher Sun, Teacher Zhu and Teacher Sand whirling around in the sky that I realized you are immortals and Buddhas. My three wretched sons have been fond of the martial arts all their lives and they now wish most sincerely to be accepted as your disciples and learn some of your skills. I beg that in the greatness of your hearts you will agree to be the salvation of my boys. I wil certainly reward you with all the wealth of the city."

When Brother Monkey heard this he could not restrain himself from replying with a chuckle, "You really don't understand, Your Royal Highness. As monks we'd love to have disciples, and your fine sons have their hearts set on goodness. But you mustn't talk about material benefits. As long as they can get on with us we'll look after them." This delighted the prince, who ordered a great banquet in the main hall of the palace. The three young princes kowtowed to Monkey, Pig and Friar Sand and addressed them as their teachers.

The next day the three princes came and said, "We would like to get smiths to make lighter copies of your weapons, but don't know whether you would agree, Teachers." "Great, great," said Pig. "That's the way to talk. You ought to have your own made because you can't use our weapons, and anyhow we need them to protect the Dharma and beat monsters." The princes then sent for smiths who bought ten thousand pounds of iron and steel, set up a workshop with a furnace in the front courtyard of the prince's palace, and began to cast the weapons. On the first day the steel was made, and on the second Monkey and the other two were asked to bring out their gold-banded cudgel, nine-toothed rake and demon-quelling staff and put them under the matting shelter to be copied. The work went on by night and day without stopping.

These weapons were the treasures they always carried with them that they could not be parted from for a moment. Normally they hid them about their persons. Now the weapons were protected by coloured light, so that when they were put in the yard of the workshop for several days many beams of radiance reached up to the heavens, while every kind of auspicious vapour blanketed the earth. That night an evil spirit, who was sitting out on a night watch in a cave called Tigermouth Cave on a mountain called Mount Leopard Head that was only some twenty-five miles from the city, noticed the glow and the auspicious vapours. Going up on his cloud to investigate he saw that the light came from the city, whereupon he brought his cloud down and went closer for a better look. Discovering that the light was coming from the weapons, he thought with delight and desire, "What wonderful weapons, what splendid treasures. I wonder whose they are and why they've been left here. This must be my lucky chance. I'll take them, I'll take them." His covetousness now moved, he created a mighty wind, scooped up all three weapons and took them back to his cave.

The story tells how after days on end of hard work the

smiths all went to sleep that night, only to get up at dawn to start again and find that the three weapons had disappeared from under the matting shelter. Dumbfounded with horror, they started looking for them everywhere, and when the three young princes came out of the inner quarters to watch, the smiths all kowtowed to them and said, "Young masters, we don't know where the divine teachers' three weapons have all gone."

When the young princes heard this news they trembled and said, "We expect our masters put them away last night." Rushing to the Gauze Pavilion, they found the white horse still tethered in the walkway and could not help shouting, "Teachers, are you still asleep?" "We're up," Friar Sand replied, and opened the door of their room to let the young princes in. When they saw that the weapons were not there they asked with alarm, "Masters, have you put your weapons away?" "No," replied Monkey, springing up. "The three weapons disappeared during the night," the princes explained.

Amid all this commotion the senior prince came out, and when he asked what had happened the colour drained from his face too. After muttering to himself in a low voice for a while he said, "Divine teachers, your weapons were not mere mortals' ones. Even if there had been a hundred or more people they would never have been able to move them. Besides, my family has been ruling this city for five generations. I'm not boasting, but I do have a certain reputation for being a good man. The soldiers, civilians and artisans who live here fear my laws, and I am certain that they could never have had so wicked an idea. I hope that you divine teachers will think again." "No need for any more thinking about it," replied Brother Monkey with a smile, "and no need to make the smiths suffer for what's not their fault. I would like to ask Your Royal Highness if there are any evil monsters in the mountains and forests around the city." "That's a very good question," the prince replied. "There is a mountain north of the city called Mount Leopard Head, with a Tigermouth Cave in it. People often say that immortals, or tigers and wolves, or evil spirits live there. As I've never been there to find out the truth I am not sure what kind of creatures there are." "No need to say any more," replied Monkey with a laugh. "It must be someone wicked from there who knew they were treasures and came during the night to steal them. Pig, Friar Sand," he ordered, "stay here to guard the master and the city while I go for a look round." He then told the smiths to keep the furnace burning and carry on forging the new weapons.

The splendid Monkey King took his leave of Sanzang and whistled out of sight. Soon he was on Mount Leopard Head, which took him but an instant as it was only ten miles from the city. As he climbed to the summit to look around he saw that there was quite an air of evil about it.

Just as he was surveying the scene Monkey heard voices on the other side of the mountain, turned quickly round to look, and saw a couple of wolf-headed ogres climbing towards the north-west and talking loudly as they went. "They must be monsters patrolling the mountain," Monkey guessed. "I'm going to listen to what they have to say."

Making magic with his hands and saying the words of a spell Monkey shook himself, turned into a butterfly, spread his wings and fluttered after them.

He flew to a spot right above the evil spirits' heads, where he hovered and listened to what they had to say. "Brother," one of them shouted suddenly, "our chief's struck it lucky again. Last night he got three weapons which really are priceless. Tomorrow there's going to be a Rake Banquet to celebrate, so we're all going to benefit." "We've been quite lucky too," the other replied, "being given these twenty ounces of silver to buy pigs and sheep. When we get to Qianfang Market we can have a few jugs of wine to start with, and then fiddle the accounts to make ourselves two or three ounces of silver to buy ourselves padded jackets for the winter. It's great, isn't it?" As they laughed and talked the two monsters hurried along the main path at a great speed.

When Monkey heard about the banquet to celebrate the rake he was quietly delighted. He would have liked to kill the devils, but it was not their fault and, besides, he had no weapon. So he flew round till he was in front of them, turned back into himself and stood at a junction along the path. As the devils gradualiy came closer he blew a mouthful of magic saliva at them, recited the words *Om Humkara* and made a fixing spell that held the two wolf-headed spirits where they were. Their eyes were fixed in a stare, they could not open their mouths, and they stood upright, both legs rigid. Monkey then knocked them over, undid their clothes and searched them, finding the twenty ounces of silver in a purse carried by one of them in the belt of his kilt. Each of them was also carrying a white lacquered pass. One of these read "Wily Freak" and the other read "Freaky Wile".

Having taken their silver and undone their passes the splendid Great Sage went straight back to the city, where he told the princes, the Tang Priest, the officials high and low and the smiths what had happened. "I reckon my treasure's the one that shone the brightest," said Pig with a grin. "That's why they're buying pigs and sheep for a slap-up meal to celebrate. But how are we going to get it back?" "We'll all three of us go," said Monkey. "This silver was for buying pigs and sheep. We'll give it to the smiths: His Royal Highness can provide us with some animals. Pig, you turn yourself into Wily Freak, I'll turn into Freaky Wile, and Friar Sand can be a trader selling pigs and sheep. We'll go into Tigermouth Cave, and when it suits us we'll grab our weapons, kill all the monsters, come back here to pack up and be on our way again." "Terrific," said Friar Sand. "No time to lose. Let's go." The senior prince agreed with the plan and told his steward to buy seven or eight pigs and four or five sheep.

The three of them left their master and gave a great display of their magic powers once outside the city. Monkey helped Pig turn into Wily Freak's double with a white pass to wear at his waist. Monkey then turned himself into Freaky Wile with a pass at his waist too, and Friar Sand made himself look like a travelling dealer in pigs and sheep. Then they drove pigs and sheep together along the path west towards the mountain.

Before long, they were near the Tigermouth Cave. As they came closer to the mouth of the cave they saw a crowd of evil spirits of every age and kind playing under the blossoming trees, and when they heard Pig's shouts of "Hey! Hey!" as he drove the pigs and sheep they all came out to meet them. The pigs and sheep were caught and trussed up. The noise had by now disturbed the demon king inside, who came out with ten or more junior demons to ask, "Are you two back? How many animals did you buy?" "Eight pigs and seven sheep — fifteen altogether," Monkey replied. "The pigs cost sixteen ounces of silver and the sheep nine. We were only given twenty ounces, so we still owe five. This is the dealer who's come with us for the silver." "Fetch five ounces of silver, little ones," the demon king ordered on hearing this, "and send him on his way." Before he could finish speaking a junior devil came out with five ounces of silver that he gave to Monkey, who in turn handed it to Friar Sand with the words, "Take your silver, stranger, then come round to the back for something to eat with us."

Taking his courage in his hands, Friar Sand went into the cave with Pig and Monkey. When they reached the second hall inside they saw on a table in the middle of it the nine-toothed iron rake set up in all its dazzling brightness to receive offerings. At the eastern end of the table was leant the gold-banded cudgel, and at the western end the demon-quelling staff. "Stranger," said the demon king who was following them in, "that's the rake shining so brightly in the middle. You're welcome to look, but don't tell anyone about it, whatever you do." Friar Sand nodded in admiration.

Pig had always been a rough customer, and once he saw his rake he was not going to talk about the facts of the case, but charged over, pulled it down and swung it around as he turned back into himself. He struck straight at the evil spirit's face, not caring now about the proper ways of using his weapon. Monkey and Friar Sand each rushed to one end of the table to grab his own weapon and turn back into himself. As the three brothers started lashing out wildly the demon king had to get out of their way in a hurry, go round to the back and fetch his four-bright halberd with its long handle and sharp, pointed butt. Rushing into the courtyard, he used this to hold off the three weapons and shout at the top of his voice, "Who do you think you are, tricking me out of my treasures by impersonation?" "I'll get you, you hairy beast," Monkey cursed back. "You don't realize who I am. I'm a disciple of Tang Sanzang, the holy monk from the east. When we came to Yuhua to present our passport the prince told his three sons to take us as their teachers of fighting skills. They were having weapons copied from ours. That was why ours were left in the courtyard for you to sneak into the city and steal in the middle of the night. And you accuse us of tricking them out of you by impersonation! Stay right there and try a taste of our three weapons." The evil spirit at once raised his halberd to fight back.

After their long fight on Mount Leopard Head the evil spirit shouted at Friar Sand, "Watch this halberd!" As Friar Sand fell back to dodge the blow the evil spirit escaped through the opening he left and fled by wind to the Xun quarter to the southeast. Pig started rushing after him to catch him, but Monkey said, "Let him go. As the old saying goes, 'never chase a desperate robber.' Let's leave him nothing to come back to."

Pig agreed, and the three of them went back to the entrance of the cave, where they killed all the hundred and more evil spirits great and small. It turned out that they were all really tigers, wolves, tiger cats, leopards, red deer and goats. Monkey used one of his powers to bring all the valuables and fabrics, as well as the bodies of all the animals they had killed, the pigs and the sheep out of the cave. Friar Sand used some dry wood he found to start a fire that Pig fanned with both his ears. The cave was soon burnt out, and they took what they had brought with them back to the city.

The story now tells of how the evil spirit really did head southeast to Bamboo Mountain, in which there was a cave called the Nine-bend Twisty Cave where the evil spirit's grandfather, the Primal Sage of Ninefold Numinosity, lived. That night the demon did not stop treading the wind until he reached the cave's entrance in the last watch. When he knocked on the gates and went in a junior devil greeted him with the words, "Your Majesty, Greenface brought the invitation last night, and the old gentleman invited him to stay till this morning to go to your Rake Banquet with him. Why have you come here so very early to invite him yourself?" "I hate to have to say it," the evil spirit replied, "but the banquet is off." As they were talking Greenface came out from the inner part of the cave to say, "What are you doing here, Your Majesty? As soon as His Senior Majesty's up he's coming to the celebration with me." The evil spirit was so distraught that he could say nothing, but only wave his hands.

A little later the old demon got up and called for the evil spirit, who dropped his weapon and prostrated himself on the ground to kowtow, tears streaming down his cheeks. "Worthy grandson," the old demon said, "you sent me an invitation yesterday, and this morning I'm on my way to the celebration. So why have you come yourself, looking so miserable and upset?" The evil spirit told him what had happened and continued, still kowtowing, "Those three monks are very good fighters. As I was no match for them by myself I had to run away and come here. If you have any love for your grandson I beg you to lend me your arms in order to get my revenge on those monks." The old demon replied with a smile, "I'll go with you and capture those so-and-sos and the prince of Yuhua to avenge you." On hearing this the evil spirit kowtowed again in thanks.

The senior demon immediately mustered his grandsons Monkey Lion, Snowy Lion, Leo, Gryphon, Racoon-dog Lion and Elephant-fighter, each of whom carried a sharp weapon. With Tawny Lion leading the way each of them set off a powerful gale that carried them straight to Mount Leopard Head.

Here they saw that the place had been set on fire and all the buildings burnt down. The evil spirit could not stop his tears from gushing forth as he stamped his feet in fury, let loose heaven-shaking roars and howled in his hatred and anger. The old demon then said, "Grandson, what's done is done. Upsetting yourself won't do you any good. What you must do now is summon up all your energy to catch those monks in the city."

With a roaring wind and in a thick fog they approached the

city, so frightening all the people living outside the city wall that they abandoned their belongings and dragged or carried their children with them as they fled into the city. Once the people were all inside the gates were shut. A report was then made to the palace that a disaster was upon them. When the prince, who was taking a vegetarian breakfast in the Gauze Pavilion with the Tang Priest and the others, heard this report he went out to ask about it. "A whole crowd of evil spirits are heading for the city with sandstorms, flying stones, fogs and wind." "Whatever shall we do?" asked the prince, deeply alarmed. "All stop worrying," said Brother Monkey, "all stop worrying. It's the evil spirit from Tigermouth Cave who ran away when he was beaten yesterday. He went to the southeast to gang up with the Primal Sage of Ninefold Numinosity or whatever he's called and now he's here. We brothers are going out. Tell them to shut all the city gates, and send men to hold the city wall." The prince ordered that the city gates be shut, sent men to the wall, and went with his sons and the Tang Priest to inspect. The army's banners blotted out the sun, and the cannon fire reached the sky as Monkey, Pig and Friar Sand left the city amid wind and clouds to give battle.

The story tells how the Great Sage Sun left the city with Pig and Friar Sand and looked the monsters in the face to see that they were all lions of various kinds. The Tawny Lion Spirit was leading, with Leo and Elephant-fighter Lion on his left, Gryphon and Racoon-dog Lion on his right and Monkey Lion with Snowy Lion behind him. In the middle of them all was a nine-headed lion. The ogre Greenface was holding a canopy of brocade embroidered with flowers just behind the nine-headed lion.

In his rough way Pig went up to them to shout abusively, "Ogres! Thieves! Treasure-stealers! What did you go there and gang up with that hairy lot for?" To this the Tawny Lion Spirit retorted, gnashing his teeth in fury, "Vicious baldies! When I was alone yesterday the three of you beat me and I had to run away. You should have done right, instead of burning my cave palace, destroying my mountain home and murdering my family.

My hatred for you is as great as the ocean. Stay where you are and take this from my halberd!" The splendid Pig raised his rake to parry the blow. When the two of them had just started fighting and neither was yet coming out on top Monkey Lion joined in, swinging his spiked iron club, as did Snowy Lion with his three-edged mace. "Welcome," shouted Pig. Watch him as he charges straight forward to meet their onslaught and fight with them all. Friar Sand quickly pulled his demon-quelling staff out from where he was at the side and hurried forward to help Pig, at which the monsters Leo, Gryphon, Elephant-fighter and Racoon-dog all piled in. The Great Sage Monkey held the evil spirits at bay with his gold-banded cudgel. Leo fought with a club, Snowy with a bronze hammer, Elephant-fighter with a steel spear and Racoon-dog with a battleaxe.

After the evil spirits had been fighting the Great Sage and the two others for half a day, night fell. Pig by now was dribbling and his legs were going weak, so he feinted with his rake and fled in defeat. "Where do you think you're going?" Snowy Lion and Monkey Lion shouted. "Take this!" The idiot could not dodge them, and he took a heavy blow from the mace on his spine that laid him flat on the ground crying out, "I'm done for, I'm done for!" The two lion spirits grabbed Pig by the bristles on his neck and by his tail and carried him over to see the nine-headed lion. "Grandfather," they reported, "we've caught one of them."

Before the words were out of their mouths Friar Sand and Monkey also had to fall back, beaten. When the evil spirits all came after them Monkey pulled out a handful of hairs, chewed them to pieces, spat them out, shouted, "Change!" and turned them into more than one hundred little Monkeys who went round and round, surrounding Snowy, Leo, Elephant-fighter, Racoon-dog and Tawny Lion. Friar Sand and Monkey then came forward to join in the fight again. Later that night they caught Leo and Gryphon and put Racoon-dog and Elephant-fighter to flight. When Tawny Lion reported to the old demon that two of the lions had been lost the demon ordered, "Tie Pig up but don't kill him. When they give our lions back we'll return Pig to them. If they're stupid enough to kill them we'll make Pig pay with his life." That evening all the fiends slept outside the city.

The story now turns to the Great Sage Sun, who carried the two lion spirits to beside the city wall, from where the senior prince saw him and ordered that the gates be opened. Twenty or thirty officers were sent out with rope to tie the lion spirits up and carry them into the city. The Great Sage then put his magic hairs away and went straight with Friar Sand to the wall tower, where he saw the Tang Priest. "This is a terrible business," the Tang Priest said. "Is Wuneng still alive?" "No problem," Brother Monkey replied. "As we've captured a couple of the evil spirits they won't possibly dare harm him. Have them tied up tight. I'll swop them for Pig tomorrow morning."

Soon it was dawn, and the old demon sent for Tawny Lion Spirit to make a plan of action: "You must all use your wits to capture Sun the Novice and Friar Sand while I make a secret flight up onto the wall to capture their master, the old prince and his sons. I'll take them back to the Nine-bend Twisty Cave and wait for you to come back in triumph." Accepting this plan, Tawny Lion took Monkey Lion, Snowy Lion, Elephant-fighter and Racoon-dog back to beside the city wall, all carrying their weapons and demanding battle amid winds and fog. On the other side Monkey and Friar Sand jumped on the wall, where Monkey yelled abusively at the top of his voice, "Thieving damned ogres! Give me my brother Pig back this moment and I'll spare your lives. If you don't I'll smash your bones to powder and chop you all into little pieces." With no further argument the evil spirits all charged into the attack. The Great Sage and Friar Sand had to use skill and cunning to hold the five lions at bay.

While the five lion spirits with coats of different colours were fighting really well with Monkey and Friar Sand the old demon flew on a black cloud straight to the wall tower, where he shook his heads, which gave the military and civil officials, Sanzang, the senior prince and the soldiers guarding the wall such a fright that they all fell off. The demon then charged into the tower, opened his mouths, took Sanzang, the senior prince and his sons in them one by one, and went back to the hollow ground, where he took Pig in another mouth, one of the nine he had in his nine heads. One mouth held the Tang Priest, one Pig, one the senior prince, one his eldest son, one the second son and one the third son. With six mouths full of six people he still had three mouths empty and wide open as he roared, "I'm going back ahead." The five junior lion spirits all fought more bravely than ever now that they had seen their grandfather's triumph.

As soon as Monkey heard the yells from the wall and realized he had fallen for a trick, he gave Friar Sand a quick shout to be careful then pulled all the hairs off his arms, put them in his mouth, chewed them up and spat them out as well over a thousand little Monkeys who swarmed into the attack. They knocked Monkey Lion over, took Snowy alive, captured Elephantfighter, laid Racoon-dog Lion low and killed Tawny Lion. They returned to the city wall with a great hubbub. When the officers on the wall saw what had happened they opened the gates, tied up the five lion spirits with ropes and carried them into the city. But before they could deal with them the princess appeared, sobbing and weeping, to say, "Holy teachers, His Royal Highness the prince, our sons and your master are all dead. How ever is this isolated city to survive?" Putting his magic hairs away, Monkey bowed to her and said, "Don't upset yourself, Princess. It was only because I'd captured seven of his lion spirits that the old demon carried off my master, His Royal Highness and your sons with catching magic. I'm certain they'll come to no harm. My brother-disciple and I will go to his mountain first thing tomorrow morning, and I can guarantee that we'll catch the old demon and bring your four princes back to you."

The next morning the Great Sage took Friar Sand up on an auspicious cloud. Before long they were at the top of Bamboo Mountain. Greenface suddenly appeared in a ravine between cliffs. He was holding a short cudgel. "Where do you think

you're going?" Monkey shouted. "I'm here." This gave the
young devil such a fright that he went running and tumbling
down the ravine. Monkey and Friar Sand went straight after
him but could find no sign of where he had gone. When they
went further and searched around they found a cave palace with
double gates of mottled stone that were firmly closed. Above the
gates a stone tablet was set on which was written in large block
letters:

NINE-BEND TWISTY CAVE,
MIGHTY BAMBOO MOUNTAIN

Now when the junior devil ran inside the cave he had shut
the gates firmly behind him. Once inside he reported to the old
demon, "My lord, those two monks are outside." "Have your
lord, Monkey Lion, Snowy Lion, Elephant-fighter and Racoon-
dog come back yet?" the old demon asked. "I haven't seen
them," the junior demon replied. "There were just the two monks
looking around from high up on the peak. As soon as I saw
them I turned and ran. As they came after me I shut the gates."
The old demon bowed his head in silence at this news. After a
while his tears began to flow as he called out, "This is terrible.
My grandson Tawny Lion is dead. My grandsons Monkey Lion
and the rest of them have all been captured by those monks and
taken into the city. How am I to get my revenge? Little ones,
guard the place well while I go out to catch those other two
monks. Then we can punish them all together."

Watch him as he strides off without armour or weapons.
When he heard Monkey shouting he threw the gates of the cave
wide open and went straight for him, not deigning to answer.
Monkey raised his iron cudgel to stop him with a blow to the
head while Friar Sand swung his staff at him. As the demon
shook his principal head the eight other heads to left and right
of it all opened their mouths, with which they gently picked Monkey and Friar Sand up and carried them into the cave. He
ordered that the two of them be tied up securely. "Impudent
ape," said the old demon, "you captured my seven grandsons.

But now I've caught you four monks and the four princes I've got enough to ransom them with. Little ones, get some thorns and willow rods and beat this ape for me to avenge my grandson Tawny Lion."

The three junior devils then beat Monkey with willow rods, but Monkey's body had been so toughened that all the rods could do was to scratch his itches. He made no sound and was not in the least bothered, no matter how hard they hit him. The beating continued for a while as night slowly fell. "Little ones," the old demon called, "stop for now. Light the lamp and go for something to eat and drink. I'm off to my Brocade Cloud Den for a little shut-eye. You three have all had a hard time, so keep a close watch on them. We'll carry on with the beatings tomorrow." The three junior devils moved a lamp over and hit Monkey some more on the top of his head with their willow rods, tic-tic-toc, toc-toc-tic, like the rhythm of a wooden clapper, sometimes fast and sometimes slow. By then it was very late and they all fell asleep.

Monkey now used escaping magic to shrink himself, wriggled out of his bonds, shook his fur, straightened up his clothes, took the cudgel out of his ear and shook it till it was the width of a well-bucket and about twenty feet long. Then he said to the three junior devils, "You animals, you hit me an awful lot of times, and now I'm going to return the compliment. I'll just shove this at you and see how you like it." One gentle push from the cudgels turned the three devils into three lumps of minced pork. Monkey then turned up the lamp and released Friar Sand. Pig, who was feeling desperate about being tied up, could not stop himself from yelling at the top of his voice, "My hands and feet are tied up so tight they're swollen. Why don't you come and free me?" The idiot's shout at once woke up the old demon, who rolled straight out of bed and called out, "Who's setting them free?" The moment Monkey heard this he blew out the lamp, smashed his way through several sets of doors with his cudgel and fled, not bothering about Friar Sand and the rest of them, while the old demon went into the main hall shouting, "Little ones, why's there no light? Don't let them get away!" He shouted once without getting an answer, then again, and still no answer. When he fetched a lantern and looked all he could see were three gory lumps of minced meat on the floor. The prince, his sons, the Tang Priest and Pig were still there, but Monkey and Friar Sand had disappeared. He lit a torch, searched the front and the back and could find only Friar Sand, who was still standing pressed against the wall of a corridor. The demon knocked him down, tied him up as before, and carried on looking for Monkey. Seeing that pair after pair of his doors had been smashed down, he realized that Monkey had destroyed them in his flight. Instead of giving chase he patched up and blockaded the doors and guarded his home.

The story now tells how Monkey left the Nine-bend Twisty Cave and rode by auspicious cloud straight back to the city of Yuhua, where all the local deities and spirits as well as the god of the city could be seen bowing in mid-air to greet him.

"The old demon came down to Bamboo Mountain the year before last," one of them who was the local diety of the Bamboo Mountain said, shivering and shaking as he kowtowed. "The Nine-bend Twisty Cave used to be the den of six lions. Once the old demon came the six lions all took him as their grandfather. He is a nine-headed lion called the Primal Sage of Ninefold Numinosity. If you want to deal with him you must go to the Wonderful Crag Palace in the uttermost east and fetch his master here to subdue him. Nobody else can possibly do it." When Monkey heard this he thought for a long time before saying, "The Wonderful Crag Palace in the uttermost east is where the Heavenly Honoured Saviour of the Great Monad lives. Yes, he does have just such a nine-headed lion under his throne. Protector, Jias," he ordered, "go back with the local deity and keep a secret watch on the master, my brother-disciple, the prince of the city and his sons. The city god must guard the wall and moat. Off you go." The gods all took up guard as instructed.

The Great Sage set off his somersault cloud and travelled through the night till it was about the last watch, when he reached the Eastern Gate of Heaven. Monkey went in through the Eastern Gate of Heaven and was soon at the Wonderful Crag Palace.

There was an immortal boy wearing a rainbow mantle standing at the palace gates, and as soon as he noticed the Great Sage he went in to report, "My lord, the Great Sage Equalling Heaven who made havoc in Heaven is here." When the Heavenly Honoured Saviour of the Great Monad heard this he ordered all the immortals in attendance on him to go out to welcome Monkey and bring him into the palace. Here the Heavenly Honoured One was sitting on a nine-coloured lotus throne amid countless rays of auspicious light, and when he saw Monkey he came down from his throne to greet him while Monkey bowed to him from below. "Great Sage," the Heavenly Honoured One said, returning his bow, "I haven't seen you for years, but I did hear that you have abandoned the Way for Buddhism and are escorting the Tang Priest to fetch the scriptures from the Western Heaven. I presume that you have now succeeded." "Not yet," Monkey replied, "but near enough. I have escorted the Tang Priest as far as Yuhua, where the prince told his three sons to take me and the other two as their teachers of martial arts and had copies of our three magic weapons made. The weapons were, to our surprise, stolen one night. When I searched for them the next day I found that they had been stolen by a spirit turned by a golden-haired lion from Tiger-mouth Cave on Mount Leopard Head. I tricked them back from him by cunning, whereupon the spirit ganged up with some other lion spirits to give me a tremendous fight. One of them is a nine-headed lion with enormous magic powers who carried my master, Pig, the prince and his three sons to the Ninebend Twisty Cave on Mount Bamboo. When Friar Sand and I went to look for them the next day we were carried off too. He had me tied up and hit so often I lost count. Luckily I was able to make my get-away by magic, but they're still suffering there. When I questioned the local deity I found out that you were his master, Heavenly Honoured One, which is why I'm here to ask you to subdue the lion and rescue them."

As soon as the Heavenly Honoured One heard this he sent

his immortal officers to the lion house to call out his lion-keeper slave and question him. The lion-keeper slave was sleeping so deeply that the officers had to push and shake him before they could wake him up and drag him into the main hall. Here the Heavenly Honoured One asked him, "Where is the lion?" All the slave could do was to kowtow with tears streaming down his face, pleading, "Spare me, spare me." "The Great Sage Sun is here," the Heavenly Honoured One replied, "so I won't have you beaten just yet. You must explain this instant your carelessness in letting the nine-headed lion escape." "My lord," the lion-keeper replied, "I stole and drank a jug of wine I saw in the Sweet Dew Palace of the Great Chiliocosm. Before I realized what had happened I was dead drunk. It must have slipped its chains and got away." "That wine was given me by Lord Lao Zi of the Supreme Ultimate," the Heavenly Honoured One replied. "It's called Cyclical Nectar, and after drinking that you would have slept for three days. How many days has the lion been gone?" "What the local deity said was that he went down there the year before last, which would mean two years or more," the Great Sage said. "That's right," the Heavenly Honoured One said with a smile, "A day in the palaces of Heaven is a year in the mortal world. Get up," he said to the lion-tamer. "I'll spare your life. Come down to the lower world with the Great Sage and me to recapture him. You immortals can all go back. None of you need come with us."

The Heavenly Honoured One, the lion-keeper slave and the Great Sage all went by cloud straight to Bamboo Mountain, where the Protectors of the Four Quarters and the Centre, the Six Dings, the Six Jias and the local deity of the mountain all knelt to greet them. "Has my master been harmed while you people have been protecting him?" Brother Monkey asked. "The evil spirit was so angry that he went to sleep," the gods replied. "He didn't torture them any more." "That Primal Sage of mine is a true soul who has long cultivated the Way," the Heavenly Honoured One remarked. "A single call from him will go up to the Three Sages and down to the Underworld. He wouldn't kill anyone lightly. Great Sage

Sun, go to his gates, challenge him to battle and draw him outside for us to catch."

As soon as Monkey heard this he sprang towards the mouth of the cave, brandishing his cudgel and shouting loudly and abusively, "Damned evil spirit, give me my people back! Damned evil spirit, give me my people back!" He shouted several times, but the old demon was fast asleep and nobody answered. Monkey lost his patience, swung his cudgel and smashed his way inside, still cursing. Only then did the old demon wake up, rise to his feet and yell with great fury, "I'm coming for you!" He shook his heads and opened his jaws to pick Monkey up. As Monkey turned and fled the evil spirit chased after him till they were outside the cave, shouting, "Where do you think you're going, you thieving ape?" "How dare you go on behaving so dreadfully!" said Monkey with a grin from where he was standing on the top of a high cliff. "You haven't even got the sense to realize that your life's at stake. Don't you see your master's here?" By the time the evil spirit reached the cliff in pursuit of Monkey the Heavenly Honoured One had said a spell and shouted, "I'm here, my little Primal Sage." Recognizing his master, the monster gave up the struggle and lay down with all four feet on the ground, kowtowing. The lion-keeper then ran over to him, took hold of his mane, and punched him hundreds of times on the neck, saying abusively, "Why did you run away, animal? You got me into terrible trouble." The lion kept his mouths shut and said nothing, not daring to move, and the lion-keeper only stopped hitting him when his fist was tired out. When a brocade saddlecloth had been put on the animal's back the Heavenly Honoured One mounted and shouted to it to go. They then rose up on coloured clouds and went straight back to the Wonderful Crag Palace.

After addressing his thanks skywards the Great Sage went into the cave and freed first the prince of Yuhua, then Sanzang, then Pig, Friar Sand and the three young princes. After this they made a leisurely search of the cave and led everyone outside. Pig then fetched some dry brushwood, piled it at the front and the back, and started a fire that left the Nine-bend Twisty Cave looking like a ruined, burnt-out kiln. Monkey released all the gods, ordered the local deity to keep guard on it, and told Pig and Friar Sand to use their magic to carry the four princes back to the city while he helped the Tang Priest along. They were soon back at the city, where the princess and the officials all came out to greet them. It was now getting dark, and a vegetarian feast was provided for everyone to enjoy. The venerable elder and his disciples slept in the Gauze Pavilion once more.

The next day the prince issued an order for another great vegetarian banquet to be laid on. Each of the officials high and low in the palace expressed his gratitude. After the banquet, the people accompanied master and disciples for a long while on the journey before returning to the city. Only thus did the four travellers manage to leave the city and head west.

CHAPTER 33
In India the Tang Priest
Faces a Royal Marriage

The story tells how the Tang Priest and his three disciples fed on the wind and slept in the open, travelling uneventfully for the best part of a month. After crossing a high mountain, they saw a big monastery beside the road. Above the gates was written, 'Spread Gold Dhyana Monastery'. The tablet was inscribed, 'Ancient relic'.

As they went in through the monastery gates they saw people carrying loads with shoulder-poles or on their backs, pushing carts, or sitting in loaded carts. Others were sleeping or talking. The sight of the master, who was so handsome, and his three hideous disciples rather frightened them, so they drew back to make way. Worried that his disciples would provoke trouble, Sanzang kept saying, "Behave yourselves! Behave yourselves!" They were all very restrained. As they went round the Vajra Hall a Dhyana monk of most unworldly appearance came out to meet them.

When Sanzang extended a monastic greeting to him the monk returned his courtesy and asked, "Where are you from, teacher?" "I am Chen Xuanzang," Sanzang replied, "sent to the Western Heaven at the command of the Great Tang emperor in the east to worship the Buddha and fetch the scriptures. As my journey brings me here I am paying you this hasty visit to request a night's shelter before continuing on my way tomorrow." "This monastery of ours is one that receives people from all quarters," the monk replied. "Everyone is welcome to visit, and we would be especially happy to provide for so holy a monk from the east as your reverend self." Sanzang thanked him and called to his three disciples to come with him as they crossed the cloister and refectory and went to the abbot's lodgings. When they had exchanged courtesies they sat down as befits host and guests. Monkey and the other two sat down as well, their hands at their sides.

The story tells how, on learning that monks from Great Tang in the east who were going to fetch the scriptures had arrived, all in the monastery, young and old alike, whether permanent inmates, itinerant monks, elders or novices came to see them. After tea had been drunk a vegetarian meal was brought in.

When the monks asked about why they had come from the east, Sanzang told them all about it and asked, "Why did I see so many travelling merchants with horses, mules, carts and carrying-poles resting here when I came in through the gates of your monastery?" "This mountain is called Mount Hundredfoot," the monks replied. "We used to live in peace and prosperity here, but with the cyclic progression of the natural forces a number of centipede spirits have for some inexplicable reason appeared. They attack people on the roads and though nobody gets killed people don't dare to travel. At the foot of the mountain there's a Cock-crow Pass that people only dare to cross after cock-crow. As all these strangers arrived late they are worried that it would not be safe and are putting up here tonight. They'll set out at cock-crow." As master and disciples were talking a vegetarian meal was brought in that they ate.

Sanzang and Monkey were strolling in the light of the rising half moon when a lay brother came to announce, "Our ancient master would like to meet the gentlemen from China." Sanzang at once turned to see an ancient monk holding a bamboo cane who came forward to greet him and ask, "Are you the teacher come from China?" "You do me too great an honour," Sanzang replied, returning his greeting. The old monk was full of admiration for him, asking how old he was. "I have wasted forty-five years," Sanzang replied. "May I ask how old you are?" "Just one sixty-year cycle older than you, teacher," the other answered. "Then you're a hundred and five this year," Brother Monkey said. "How old do you think I am?" "Teacher," the old monk replied, "your appearance seems so ancient and your spirit so pure that I could not tell in a hurry, especially by moonlight with my poor eyes." After talking for a while they walked to the back cloister for a look round.

After a leisurely stroll enjoying the moonlight they sat down for a while on a terrace, where they heard the sound of sobbing. As Sanzang listened with a still heart he turned to the monks and asked, "Who is it being so sad, and where?" On hearing this question the ancient monk sent all the others away to prepare tea, and when nobody else was around he kowtowed to the Tang Priest and Brother Monkey. "Venerable abbot," said Sanzang, helping him to his feet again, "why do you pay me this courtesy?"

"As I am over a hundred," the ancient monk replied, "I do know a little of the ways of the world; and in between periods of meditation and stillness I have seen some things. I know a certain amount about you, my lord, and your disciples, and you are not like other people. The only teachers here who would be able to analyse this most painful business are you." "Tell me what it's all about," said Monkey. "A year ago today," the ancient monk replied, "I was concentrating my mind on the nature of the moon when I suddenly heard a gust of wind and the sound of someone grieving. I got out of bed, went into the Jetavana and saw a beautiful girl there. 'Whose daughter are you?' I asked her. 'Why are you here?' 'I am a princess, the daughter of the king of India,' the girl replied. 'The wind blew me here when I was looking at the flowers by moonlight.' I locked her up in an empty room that I bricked up like a prison cell, just leaving a gap in the door big enough to pass a bowl through. That day I told the other monks that she was an evil spirit I had captured. But as we monks are compassionate I couldn't kill her, and every day she is given two meals of simple food and drink to keep her alive. The girl is clever enough to understand what I mean, and to prevent herself from being sullied by the other monks she has pretended to be deranged and slept in her own piss and shit. During the day she talks nonsense or just sits there in silence, but in the still of the night she cries because she misses her parents. I've been into the city several times to make enquiries about the princesses, but not a single one is missing. So I have put her under stronger locks, and I am even more determined not to let her go. Now that you have come here, teacher, I beg you to go to the capital and use your dharma powers to find out the truth. You will thus be able both to rescue the good and display your magical powers." When Sanzang and Monkey heard this they noted it very carefully. As they were talking two junior monks came in to invite them to take tea and go to bed, so they went back inside.

They had not slept long that night when they heard the cocks crowing. The traders in front of the monastery all got up noisily and prepared their breakfast by lamplight. The venerable elder woke up Pig and Friar Sand to bridle the horse and pack up, while Monkey called for lamps to be lit. The monks of the monastery, who were up already, set out tea, soup and snacks, and waited on them. Pig ate a plate of steamed buns with delight then took the luggage and the horse outside while Sanzang and Brother Monkey took their leave of all the monks. "Please don't forget about that very tragic business," said the ancient monk. "I'll give it all my attention," Monkey replied, "all my attention. Once I'm in the city I'll be able to find out the truth from what I hear and see." They traders noisily set off together. By the last watch of the night they were through Cock-crow Pass, and by ten in the morning the walls of the city were in sight. It was indeed a powerful city as strong as an iron cauldron, the heavenly capital of a divine region.

That day they reached the streets of the eastern market, where the traders all put up at inns. As Sanzang and his disciples were walking in the city they came to a government hostel and went inside. The hostel manager went to report to the hostel superintendent that there were four strange-looking monks outside who had arrived with a white horse. On being told about the horse the superintendent realized that they must be on an official mission, so he went out to welcome them. "I have been sent by the Tang court in the east to the Great Thunder Monastery on Vulture Peak to see the Buddha and seek the scriptures," Sanzang replied with a bow. "I have a passport to present at court for inspection. I would be grateful if I could spend the night in Your Excellency's distinguished hostel. I will be on my way when my business has been done." "This hostel has been established to entertain envoys and travellers," the superintendent replied, returning his bow, "so it is only right that we should entertain you. Please come in, please come in."

A delighted Sanzang invited his disciples to come in to meet the superintendent, who was quietly appalled by their hideous faces. He did not know whether they were men or demons, so he trembled as he saw to tea and a vegetarian meal for them. Noticing his fright, Sanzang said, "Don't be afraid, Your Excellency. My three disciples look hideous, but they are good at heart. As the saying goes, the faces are ugly but the men are kind. There's nothing to be afraid of about them."

The hostel superintendent's worries were eased when he heard this. "Where is your Tang court, Teacher of the Nation?" "In the land of China in the continent of Jambu," Sanzang replied. "When did you leave home?" was the next question. "In the thirteenth year of *Zhenguan*, fourteen years ago," Sanzang replied. "I had to cross thousands of rivers and mountains — it was very hard — to arrive here." "You are a holy monk," the hostel superintendent said. "How old is your exalted dynasty?" Sanzang asked. "This is the great land of India," the superintendent replied, "and the dynasty has endured for over five hundred years since our High Ancestor. Our reigning sovereign, who is a lover of landscapes and flowers, is known as the Happy Emperor. His reign-period is called *Jingyan* and is now in its twenty-eighth year." "I would like to have an audience with His Majesty today to have the passport inspected and returned," said Sanzang. "When does he hold court?" "Splendid," the superintendent said, "absolutely splendid. Today is the twentieth birthday of Her Royal Highness, the king's daughter. A decorated tower has been built at the crossroads, where the princess is going to throw down an embroidered ball to let heaven decide who her husband is to be. Today is a very lively one, and I believe that His Majesty will not yet have finished his morning audience. This would be a good time to go if you wish to have your passport inspected and returned." Sanzang was just about to set happily off when the meal was brought in, so he ate it with the superintendent, Monkey and the other two.

By now it was past midday, and Sanzang said, "I had better be going." "I'll escort you, Master," said Brother Monkey. Sanzang then put on his cassock. Monkey took the passport case and accompanied him. In the streets everyone — gentleman, peasant, artisan, trader, scholar, pen-pusher, dim-wit, or common man — was exclaiming, "Let's go and see the embroidered ball being thrown."

The story now explains that two years earlier the king of India had taken his queen, consorts and daughter into the royal garden to enjoy a moonlit night because he so loved landscapes and flowers. This had provoked an evil spirit, who had carried the princess off and turned herself into the girl's double. When she learned that the Tang Priest was coming at this time, day, month and year the evil spirit had used the wealth of the kingdom to build the decorated tower in the hope of winning him as her mate and absorbing his true masculine primal essence to make herself a superior immortal of the Great Monad. At the third mark of the noonday hour, when Sanzang and Monkey had joined in the crowd and were approaching the tower, the princess lit some incense and prayed to heaven and earth. She was surrounded by five or six dozen exquisitely made-up beauties who were attending her and holding her embroidered ball for her. The tower had many windows on all sides. As the princess looked around she saw the Tang Priest approaching, so she took the embroidered ball and threw it with her own hands at the Tang Priest's head. It knocked his Vairocana mitre askew, giving him such a start that he immediately reached with both hands to steady the ball, which rolled down his sleeve. At once there were great shouts from everyone on the tower of, "She's hit a monk! She's hit a monk!"

All the travelling merchants at the crossroads pushed and shouted as they rushed to grab the embroidered ball, to be met by Monkey with a shout and bared teeth as he bent forward and grew to the majestic height of thirty feet. The hideous face he made gave them all such a fright that they collapsed and crawled about, not daring to come closer. A moment later they had all scattered and Monkey resumed his true form. The maids, palace beauties and senior and junior eunuchs who had been in the tower all came up to the Tang Priest, kowtowed to him and said, "Your Highness, we beg you to come to the palace to be congratulated." Sanzang was quick to return their greetings and help them all back to their feet.

He then turned back to grumble at Monkey, "Ape! You've been trying to make a fool of me again." "It was your head the embroidered ball landed on," Monkey replied with a laugh, "and your sleeve it rolled into. Nothing to do with me, so what are you moaning at me for?" "What are we going to do?" Sanzang asked. "Stop worrying, Master," Monkey said. "While you go to the palace to see the king I'll go back to the hostel to tell Pig and Friar Sand to wait. If the princess doesn't want you, that'll be that. You submit the passport and we can be on our way. If the princess insists on marriage you must say to the king, 'Please send for my disciples so that I can take my leave of them.' When we three are summoned to court I'll be able to tell whether the princess is real or an impostor. This is the trick called 'subduing a demon through marriage'." The Tang Priest had nothing to say as Monkey turned away and went back to the hostel.

The story tells how Monkey, after taking his leave of Sanzang at the foot of the decorated tower, went happily back to the hostel, laughing aloud as he walked. "Why are you laughing so cheerfully, brother," Pig and Frair Sand asked as they greeted him, "and why's the master disappeared?" "The master has found happiness," Monkey replied. "What happiness?" Pig asked. "He hasn't reached the end of the journey, he hasn't seen the Buddha and he hasn't fetched the scriptures." "The master and I only got as far as the foot of a decorated tower at the crossroads," Brother Monkey replied. "Just then the king's daughter hit the master with an embroidered ball, so he was hustled by palace beauties, pretty girls and eunuchs to the front of the tower, where he climbed into a carriage to go to the palace with the princess. He's been invited to become the king's son-in-law. Isn't that something to be cheerful about?"

When Pig heard this he stamped, beat his chest and said, "If I'd known beforehand, I'd have gone too. It was all Friar Sand's fault for making trouble. I'd have run straight to the foot of the decorated tower, the embroidered ball would have hit me first time, and the princess would have taken me for her husband. That would have been marvellous, terrific. I'm handsome and good-looking: I'd have been just the man. We'd all have been in luck and have had a good time. It'd have been real fun." "Stop talking nonsense, idiot," Monkey retorted, "and pack the baggage. I expect the master will get anxious and send for us, so we must be ready to go to protect him at court." "You're wrong again, brother," said Pig. "If the master's the king's son-in-law, he won't be climbing any more mountains, or tramping along the road, or running into monsters. He's old enough to know what happens in bed. He won't need your help." Monkey grabbed Pig by the ear and said, "You're as dirty-minded as ever, you cretin."

While they were in the middle of their quarrel the hostel superintendent came to report, "His Majesty has sent an official here with a request for you three holy monks to present yourselves." "What's he really asking us to go for?" "The senior holy monk had the good fortune to be hit by the princess's golden ball and be taken as her husband," the superintendent replied, "which is why the official has come with invitations for you." "Where is the official?" Monkey asked. "Send him in." The official then bowed in greeting to Monkey, after which he did not dare look straight at Monkey as he muttered to himself, "Is it a ghost? a monster? a thunder god? a yaksha?" "Why are you mumbling instead of saying whatever you have to say, official?" Monkey asked. Trembling with terror, the official raised the royal edict with both hands as his words came tumbling out in confusion: "Her Royal Highness — invitation — meet her new relations — Her Royal Highness — meet her relations — invitation. . . ." "We've got no torture equipment here and we're not going to beat you," Pig said, "so don't be frightened and take your time telling us." "Do you think he's scared you're going to beat him?" Monkey said. "What he's scared of is your ugly mug. Get the carrying-pole load packed up at once. We're taking the horse and going to court to see the master and talk things over."

The story tells how Brother Monkey and the other two disciples went with the official who had brought the invitation to outside the Meridional Gate of the palace, where the eunuch gate officer immediately reported their arrival and brought back a summons for them to enter. The three of them stood in a row, not bowing. "Are you three gentlemen the illustrious disciples of the holy monk? What are your names? Where do you live? Why did you become monks? What scriptures are you going to fetch?" Monkey then came closer, intending to enter the throne hall. "Don't move," one of the king's bodyguards shouted. "If you have anything to say, say it standing down there." "We monks like to step forward whenever we're given an opening," Monkey said with a smile, at which Pig and Friar Sand too approached the king. Worried that their rough manners would alarm the king, Sanzang stepped forward and called out, "Disciples, His Majesty has asked you why you have come here. You must submit your reply." Seeing his master standing in attendance beside the king, Monkey could not restrain himself from calling aloud, "Your Majesty is treating yourself with respect but others with contempt. If you are taking my master as your son-in-law, why do you make him stand in attendance on you? The normal custom is for a king to call his son-in-law Your Excellency, and an Excellency really ought to be sitting down." This gave the king so bad a fright that he turned pale and wished he could leave the throne hall. But as this would have looked very bad he had to summon up his courage and tell his attendants to fetch an embroidered stool on which he invited the Tang Priest to sit. Monkey, Pig and Friar Sand then told how they were former monsters who had become monks.

The king was both most alarmed and most delighted to hear this. Delighted because his daughter had found herself a living Buddha, and alarmed by three veritable evil gods. Just as the king was being torn between alarm and delight the chief astrologer submitted this memorial: "The wedding has been set for the twelfth day of this month, the day of water-rat, a lucky time at which all will be auspicious for nuptials." This greatly pleased the king, who sent his officials in attendance to have the halls and pavilions in the royal garden swept clean. Here he invited his future son-in-law with his three distinguished disciples to stay while they waited for the nuptial feast at which the princess would marry him. The underlings all carried out their instructions, the king ended the audience and the officials withdrew.

The story now tells how when Sanzang and his disciples reached the imperial garden night was falling. A vegetarian meal was laid on. Pig ate many bowls of rice and pasta. A little later the lamps were lit and the bedding laid out, after which everyone went to bed. As soon as the venerable elder saw that there was nobody around he started to shout angrily at Monkey, telling him off. "You macaque, Wukong! You keep ruining me. I said we were just going to present the passport and told you not to go near the decorated tower. Why did you keep demanding to take me there to have a look? Well, did you have a good enough look? Whatever are we to do about this trouble you have got us into?" "Master," replied Monkey, putting on a smile, "it was you who said, 'My late mother married after throwing an embroidered ball to make the match she was destined for.' I only took you there because you seemed to want to enjoy something of the past. Besides, because I remembered what the ancient monk in the Almsgiver's Spread Gold Monastery said I came here to find out whether she's an impostor or not. When I saw the king just now there was something a bit sinister about the way he looked, but I haven't yet seen what the princess is like."

"What will happen when you see the princess?" the venerable elder asked. "My fiery eyes with their golden pupils can tell whether someone's true or false, good or evil, rich or poor," Monkey replied. "I'll know what to do and be able to sort out right and wrong." Sanzang was not at all pleased and threatened to say the Band-tightening spell again.

Before long they had been staying in the palace for three or four days, by when it was that splendid day, the twelfth. The officials of the three sections of the Department of Foreign Relations all submitted a memorial that said, "Since we received the edicts on the eighth the palace for the Royal Son-in-law has been built, and all that we are waiting for is for the trousseau to be installed. The nuptial banquet has been prepared, with meat and vegetarian food for over five hundred guests." This greatly pleased the king, who was just going to invite his future son-in-law to come to the banquet when a eunuch from the inner quarters of the palace reported to him, "Your Majesty, Her Majesty the Queen asks you to come." The king then withdrew to the inner quarters of the palace, where the queens of the three palaces and the consorts of the six compounds brought the princess to the Sunlight Palace to talk and joke together.

When the king arrived his queens and consorts led the princess and the other palace ladies out to meet him. The delighted king took them into the Sunlight Palace to sit down. When the queens, consorts and others had made their obeisances the king said, "Princess, my good daughter, we think that your heart's desire was fulfilled when you had the good fortune to find the holy monk by throwing your ball from the decorated tower on the eighth. The officials of all the departments have been most understanding of our wishes, so that everything is now ready. As today is a lucky one let us hurry to the nuptial banquet and not be late." The princess stepped forward, went down in a kowtow, and submitted this petition: "Your Majesty my father,

452

I beg you to forgive your daughter for her effrontery, but I have a request to make. In the last few days it has been reported in the inner quarters of the palace that the Tang Priest has three extremely hideous disciples. I couldn't bring myself to see them: I'm afraid the sight would terrify me. So I beg you, Father, to send them out of the city. Otherwise the shock might be too much for my frail health and lead to disaster." "If you had not mentioned them, child," the king replied, "we would have very nearly forgotten about them. They are indeed rather ugly, and for the last few days we have had them entertained in the Lingering Spring Pavilion. When we go into the throne hall this morning we will return their passport and tell them to leave the city so that we can hold our banquet." The princess then kowtowed again in thanks, after which the king left in his carriage to enter the throne hall and issue a decree inviting his son-in-law and the other three gentlemen to attend.

Now the Tang Priest had been following the dates by counting on his fingers, so when he reached the twelfth he had a discussion with his three disciples before dawn. "It is the twelfth today," he said. "How are we to cope?" "I've already noticed something of an ill-omened air about the king," Brother Monkey replied, "but the evil hasn't actually infected him or done any great harm. The only thing is that I've not yet had a look at the princess. If she comes out and lets me take a peep at her I'll know whether she's an impostor or not, then I'll do something. Don't worry. He's bound to summon us now and send us three away from the city. Accept the invitation and don't be afraid. I'll slip back and stay close to you to protect you." As master and disciples were talking a royal equerry did indeed come with officials from the protocol office to bring an invitation. "Let's go," said Monkey, "let's go. I'm sure they're going to see us three on our way and keep you here, Master, for the wedding."

They then followed the officials to the foot of the throne hall steps, taking baggage and horse with them. When the king had greeted them he commanded Monkey and the other two to come forward. "Hand your passport up," he said, "and we shall seal it, sign it and return it to you. You three gentlemen will be generously provided with funds for your journey and escorted on your way to see the Buddha on Vulture Peak. If you come back with the scriptures you will also receive generous rewards. We shall keep our son-in-law here: there will be no need for you to worry about him." Monkey thanked the king, then told Friar Sand to take the passport out and hand it over. The king read it, sealed and signed it, then brought out ten ingots of gold and twenty of silver that he wanted to present to them as gifts for his in-laws. Pig, who always had been very keen on money and sex, stepped forward to accept them.

As Brother Monkey and the other two went out through the palace gates they each took their leave. "Are we really going?" asked Pig. Monkey said nothing, and just walked back to the hostel, where the superintendent received them and provided tea and a meal. "You two stay here," Monkey said to Pig and Friar Sand, "and whatever you do, don't show your faces. If the hostel superintendent asks what's happening, give him vague answers. Don't say anything. I'm going off to look after the master."

The splendid Great Sage pulled out one of his hairs, blew on it with magic breath, called "Change!" and turned it into his own double to stay in the hostel with Pig and Friar Sand, while he himself leapt up into mid air in a flash, turning himself into a bee.

Monkey then flew into the palace, where he saw the Tang Priest sitting on an embroidered stool at the king's left, frowning and worried at heart. Flying up to his master's Vairocana mitre, Monkey crept stealthily to his ear and said, "I'm here, Master, so don't fret." These words were heard by the Tang Priest alone, — none of the ordinary mortals had any hope of hearing them — so he felt relief at last. Before long a eunuch came with an invitation: "Your Majesty, the nuptial banquet is set out in the Jay Palace. Her Majesty and the princess are awaiting you in the inner quarters. They invite Your Majesty and His Excellency to go in for the wedding." Overwhelmed with happiness, the king went into the inner quarters with his son-in-law.

The story tells how the Tang Priest was feeling thoroughly miserable as he accompanied the king into the inner quarters, from where a great sound of drums and music arose and fine perfumes could be smelt. He kept his head bowed, not daring to look up. Monkey, secretly very pleased, had fixed himself to the Vairocana mitre, from where he used his magic light to look around with his fiery eyes and golden pupils. There were two ranks of court ladies, making it seem like a palace of flowers or immortals, and finer than a spring breeze blowing past a brocade screen.

A little later the princess came out of the Jay Palace surrounded by the queens and consorts to greet the king with cheers of "Long live the king! Long live the king!" This so alarmed the venerable elder that he trembled, not knowing what to do. By now Monkey had already noticed a touch of the demonic — though nothing very vicious — that could just be made out in the aura above the princess's head. Monkey crawled quickly to Sanzang's ear and said, "The princess is a fake, Master." "If she is a fake," the venerable elder replied, "then how are we to make her turn back into her real form?" "I'll give myself a magic body and catch her right here," said Monkey. "That would terrify His Majesty," said Sanzang. "Wait till he and his queens have withdrawn before using your magic."

Now Monkey had been impatient by nature all his life, so he could not restrain himself. With a great and angry roar he resumed his true form, rushed up and grabbed the princess. "You're a fine, evil beast," he said abusively. "You've had no end of luxury here, you impostor, but it wasn't enough for you. You're so sex-crazed you had to try to trick my master and destroy his primal masculinity." This struck the king speechless with fright, and made the queens and consorts fall about. The palace beauties all ran off to hide, fleeing for their lives.

Sanzang hastily put his trembling arms round the king and said, "Don't be afraid, Your Majesty. It is only my wicked disciple using his magical powers to find out whether she is an impostor or not."

Seeing that things were going badly for her, the evil spirit broke free, tore off her clothes, flung down her jewellery and hair ornaments and ran to the shrine of the local deity in the palace garden. From here she brought out a short club shaped like the head of a trip-hammer, with which she started hitting wildly at Monkey as she turned quickly towards him. Monkey, who had caught up with her at once, struck back at her face with his iron cudgel. Shouting and roaring at each other, the two of them started fighting in the palace gardens. Then each began a great display of magic powers, riding clouds as they battled in mid air.

As the two of them battled in mid air they terrified the common people of the city, and struck fear into all the officials at court. The venerable elder kept saying as he supported the king, "Don't be alarmed, and please tell Her Majesty and all the others not to be afraid. Your princess is an impostor pretending to be her. When my disciple has captured her you will be able to see whether she is good or evil." Some of the bolder consorts brought clothes and jewellery to show the queen. "These are what the princess wore. She tore them off and is fighting that monk up in the sky stark naked. She must be an evil spirit." Only then did the king, queens and consorts come to their senses and look up into the sky.

When the evil spirit and the Great Sage had been fighting for half a day without either emerging as victor Monkey threw his cudgel up and called "Change!" One turned into ten, ten into a hundred, and a hundred into a thousand. Half the sky was filled with writhing serpents and pythons striking wildly at the evil spirit. With a flurry of her hands and feet she turned into a pure wind and fled into the azure sky. Monkey said a spell, took all the iron cudgels back into a single cudgel, and went straight after her magic light. As he approached the Western Gate of Heaven and saw the dazzling flags and banners Monkey shouted at the top of his voice, "Heavenly gatekeepers, stop that evil spirit and don't let her get away." The gate was being held by the Heavenly King Lokapala with the four great marshals Pang, Liu, Gou and Bi, who did indeed use their weapons to block the way. As she could not get further she turned straight back and started fighting Monkey with her short club.

As he wheeled his iron cudgel the Great Sage looked carefully at her and saw that one end of her club was thick and one end thin, just like the head of a trip-hammer used for hulling with a mortar, so he gave a furious roar and shouted, "Beast! What's that implement you're holding? How dare you fight me with it? Surrender at once or I'll smash your skull with a single blow from my cudgel." Grinding her teeth, the evil spirit replied, "You don't know about this weapon of mine. It was a drug-pounding pestle in the Moon Palace."

When the evil spirit had fought another dozen or so rounds with Brother Monkey she could see how thick and fast his blows were coming, and realized that she could not win. Feinting with her pestle, she shook herself and fled due south in ten thousand beams of golden light with the Great Sage in pursuit. Suddenly they reached a great mountain, where the evil spirit landed her golden light and disappeared into a cave. Monkey, who was worried that she might escape, return to India and do some underhand harm to the Tang Priest, made sure he could recognize the mountain then turned his cloud round and went straight back to the capital.

It was now about four in the afternoon. The king was clinging to Sanzang, shivering and shaking as he kept saying, "Save me, holy monk!" The consorts and queens were all in a panic as the Great Sage came down from the clouds with a cry of, "Here I am, Master!" "Stand still, Wukong," said Sanzang. "You must not alarm His Majesty. Now, I am asking you what in fact happened about the imitation princess." Standing outside the Jay Palace, Monkey put his hands together in front of his chest and said, "The imitation princess was an evil spirit. First of all I fought her for half a day, and she couldn't beat me, so she turned into a pure wind and fled straight to the gates of heaven. I shouted to the gods to block her way. She turned back into her real self and fought another dozen or so rounds with me. Then she turned herself into golden light and fled due south to a mountain, beaten. I chased her as fast as I could till I got to the mountain, but I couldn't find her anywhere. Then I came back because I was worried she might come here to harm you." When the king heard this he grabbed hold of the Tang Priest and asked, "If the false princess was an evil spirit, where is my real princess?" "When I've caught the false princess your real princess will turn up by herself," Monkey replied straight away. When the queens and consorts heard this their fears vanished, and each of them came forward to bow and say, "We beg you to rescue our real princess, holy monk, and sort out the light from the dark. You will be richly rewarded." "This is no place for us to talk," said Monkey. "I beg Your Majesty to go from the inner quarters to the throne hall with my master. Her Majesty and the rest of them should all go back to the inner palace, and my fellow-disciples Pig and Friar Sand should be sent for to protect my master so that I can go and subdue the demon. That will keep a proper distinction between the inner and outer quarters of the palace, and spare me from worrying. I am going to sort this out to show my sincerity." The king accepted the suggestion and was boundlessly grateful. He led the Tang Priest out of the inner quarters and straight to the throne hall. All the queens and consorts returned to the inner palace. A vegetarian meal was ordered while Pig and Friar Sand were sent for. The two of them soon arrived. Monkey explained to them both about what had happened and told them to guard the master carefully. The Great Sage set off by his cloud somersault and flew up into mid air. All the officials in front of the throne hall looked up into the sky and bowed low.

The Great Sage Monkey went straight to the mountain that lay due south. When the evil spirit had fled in defeat to the mountain and gone into her den she blocked the entrance with boulders and lay hidden there, terrified. Having looked around for a while and seen no sign of life Monkey felt very impatient, so he made a spell with his hands and said the magic words, calling out the local deity and mountain god to be questioned. A moment later the two gods arrived, kowtowed and said, "We didn't realize, we didn't realize. If we had known we'd have gone a long way to meet you. We beg you to forgive us." "I won't hit you just now," Monkey said. "Tell me what this mountain's called. How many evil spirits are there here? Tell me the truth and I'll forgive you your crimes." "Great Sage," the two gods replied, "this mountain is called Mount Hairtip. There are three hare warrens in the mountain, but from remote antiquity there have never been any evil spirits here. This is a blessed land of five felicities. Great Sage, if you want to find an evil spirit, take the road to the Western Heaven." "I've reached the kingdom of India in the Western Heaven, where the king has a princess who was carried off by an evil spirit and abandoned in the wilds. The evil spirit turned herself into the princess's double to deceive the king into building a decorated tower from which she could throw an embroidered ball to find herself a husband. When I got to the foot of the tower while escorting the Tang Priest she deliberately hit the Tang Priest because she wanted to mate with him and lure his primal masculinity out of him. When I saw through her I turned back into myself in the palace to catch her. She threw off her human clothes and jewels and fought with me for half a day with a short club that she called a medicine-pounding pestle. Then she turned herself into a pure wind and disappeared. When I chased her as far as the Western Gate of Heaven and fought another dozen or more with her she realized she couldn't beat me, turned herself into golden light and fled here. Why didn't you see her!"

When the two gods heard this they led Brother Monkey to search the three warrens. When they first looked by the warren at the foot of the mountain a few frightened hares were startled and ran away. When their search reached the cave at the top of the mountain they saw that the entrance was blocked with two great boulders. "The evil spirit must have gone inside," the local god said, "when you were chasing her so hard." Monkey then prised the boulders apart with his iron cudgel. The evil spirit, who was indeed hiding in there, sprang out with a whoosh, raising her medicine pestle to strike him with. As Monkey swung his cudgel to parry her blow the mountain deity fell back in terror and the local god fled. From the demon's mouth came abusive grumbles: "Who told you to bring him here to find me?"

She continued to fend off the iron cudgel as she fled up into mid air in a fighting retreat.

Just at the moment of crisis, when it was getting late in the day, Monkey became more vicious than ever and his blows were even harder. He wished he could finish her off with a single stroke. Just then a call came from the ninefold azure sky of, "Don't strike, Great Sage! Don't strike! Be kind with your cudgel." When Monkey turned round he saw that it was the Star Lord of the Moon leading his beauties and immortals down on multicoloured clouds to stand in front of him. A flustered Monkey at once put his iron cudgel away, bowed and said, "Where are you going, Old Man? I'm sorry I didn't keep out of your way." "The evil spirit fighting you is the Jade Hare who pounds the immortal elixir of mysterious dew in my palace," the Moon replied. "A year ago she secretly opened the golden locks on the jade gates and absconded from the palace. As I reckoned that she would be in mortal peril I have come here to save her life. I do beg you, Great Sage, to spare her life out of considera-tion for me." Monkey assented, saying only, "I wouldn't dare harm her, I wouldn't dare. No wonder she's so good with a medicine-pounding pestle. She's the Jade Hare. What you don't know, Old Moon, is that she has kidnapped the king of India's daughter, made herself into the princess's double, and wants to ruin my master's primal masculinity although he's a holy monk. This is the truth. We can't stand for crimes like that. How can you possibly let her off so lightly?"

"There are things you don't know," the Moon replied. "That king's daughter is no ordinary mortal. She was the White Beauty from the Moon Palace. Eighteen years ago she slapped the Jade Hare, after which she longed for the human world and came down to it in a beam of magic light to the womb of the king's senior queen. She was born then. The Jade Hare was get-ting her own back for that slap when she ran away from the palace last year and threw White Beauty into the wilds. But she was wrong to want to marry the Tang Priest. That's an offence she mustn't get away with. It was a good thing you were careful enough to see through her before she ruined your master. But I plead with you to forgive her for my sake and let me take her back." "If that's why it happened," Brother Monkey replied with a smile, "I wouldn't dare to make any objections. But if you take the Jade Hare back I'm worried that the king might not believe it, so I'd like to trouble you and the immortal sisters to take the Jade Hare over there to prove it to the king. Then I'll be able to show off my powers and explain how White Beauty came down to earth. I'll make the king fetch Princess White Beauty to prove the truth of retribution. The Moon was persuaded, so he pointed at the evil spirit and shouted, "Repent and submit, evil beast!" The Jade Hare rolled on the ground and turned back into her real form.

When the Great Sage saw this he was delighted, and treading clouds and light he led the way as the Moon Lord brought all the beauties and immortals, taking the Jade Hare with them as they headed straight for India. It was now dusk, and the moon was slowly rising. When they reached the walls of the capital they heard the drums being beaten on the watch-towers. The king and the Tang Priest were still inside the throne hall, while Pig, Friar Sand and the officials were standing in front of the steps. They were just discussing whether the king should withdraw when a sheet of coloured cloud as bright as day was seen due south. When they all raised their heads to look they heard the Great Sage Monkey shouting at the top of his voice, "Your Majesty, King of India, ask your queens and consorts to come out and look. Under this canopy is the Star Lord of the Moon Palace, and the immortal sisters to either side of him are the beauties of the moon. This Jade Hare was the bogus princess of yours who has now turned back into her real form." The king then quickly called his queen, consorts, palace beauties and maids out, and they all kowtowed towards the sky. The king, the Tang Priest and the officials also bowed to the sky in thanks. There was nobody in any house throughout the whole city who did not set out an altar on which to burn incense, kowtow and recite the name of the Buddha. The Moon Lord had his celestial canopy turned about as he took the Jade Hare straight back to the Moon Palace with all his beauties.

The king then thanked Brother Monkey in the throne hall. When the king was told what had happened he said, "We are very grateful to you, holy monk, for using your great magical powers to capture the imitation princess. But where is our real daughter?" "She is no ordinary human either," Monkey replied, "but the immortal girl White Beauty from the Moon Palace. Because she slapped the Jade Hare in the face eighteen years ago she yearned for the lower world, came down to the womb of Your Majesty's senior queen and was born here. It was because the Jade Hare nursed her old grudge that she surreptitiously opened the golden lock on the jade gates, came down here, abandoned White Beauty in the wilds and made herself look like White Beauty to deceive you. The Moon Lord himself told me about this chain of events. Today we've got rid of the imposter, and tomorrow I'll invite Your Majesty to go in your royal carriage to fetch the real one." This came as rather a shock to the king, who said with the tears streaming down his cheeks, "Daughter! In all the time since we came to the throne as a child we have never even gone outside the city gates. Where are we to go to look for you?" "No need to upset yourself," said Monkey with a smile. "Your daughter is now in the Almsgiver's Spread Gold Monastery, pretending to be mad. Everyone can go home now. Tomorrow morning I'll bring your real princess back to you." "Please stop worrying, Your Majesty," the officials all said, kowtowing. "These holy monks are all Buddhas who can ride clouds and mists: they are sure to know all about causes and effects in the future and the past. If we trouble the holy monks to come with us tomorrow to look for her we will learn the truth." Accepting their suggestion, the king invited the monks to the Lingering Spring Pavilion, where a vegetarian meal was provided and they spent the night.

During the night the king lost his demonic aura, and his spirit grew with great speed, so that at three marks after the fifth watch he came out of the inner quarters to give audience once more. When the audience was over he ordered that the Tang Priest and his three disciples be fetched to discuss the search for the princess. Sanzang then came and did obeisance to the king, while the Great Sage and the other two also paid their respects. The king bowed to them and said, "Yesterday you spoke of our daughter the princess. May we trouble you divine monks to find and rescue her?" Sanzang then told him what they had seen and heard in the Spread Gold Garden.

The king then issued these commands: "Let the Queens of the Eastern and Western Palaces look after the court while the High Minister takes charge of the nation's business. We are going to the monastery with our Senior Queen, our officials and the four holy monks to fetch the princess."

Carriages were at once prepared and a line of them left the palace. Watch as Brother Monkey sprang up into the air and with a bend of his back was the first to reach the monastery. The monks all hastily knelt to greet him. "When you left, sir," they said, "you walked with the others, so why did you come down from the sky today?" To this Monkey replied with a smile, "Where is your ancient teacher? Ask him to come out straight away, and set out incense tables to welcome His Majesty. The king and queen of India, the officials and my master are all coming." The monks could not understand what he meant, so they asked the ancient monk to come out. When the ancient monk saw Monkey he prostrated himself before him with the words, "What has happened about the princess, sir?" Monkey told him all about how the imitation princess had thrown the embroidered ball, wanted to mate with the Tang Priest, been chased, fought, and been recaptured by the Moon Lord as the Jade Hare. The ancient monk kowtowed to him again in thanks. "Please stop kowtowing," said Monkey, helping him up, "please stop. Hurry up and get ready to receive His Majesty." Only then did the monks realize that it was a girl locked up in the garden at the back. Surprised and delighted, they all set out a row of incense tables outside the monastery gates, put on their cassocks and started striking the bell and the drum. Soon after this the king's carriage arrived.

When the king arrived outside the monastery gates the monks were all lined up on their knees in orderly ranks, bowing low in greeting. Monkey stood in the middle. "How did you arrive first, holy monk?" the king asked. "It just took a little bend of my waist for me to get here," Monkey replied. "Why were you such a long time coming?" After this the Tang Priest and the others all arrived. He led the royal carriage to the building at the back where the princess was still raving and pretending to be crazy. The ancient monk knelt down, pointed towards her and said, "This is Her Royal Highness the princess who was blown here by a wind the other year." The king ordered the cell opened. When the iron locks were undone and the door opened the king and queen saw and recognized the princess. Not caring about the filth, they went up to her and threw their arms round her. "Our poor child," they said, "how did you come to suffer these torments and have so terrible a time here?" How true it is that the meeting of parents and child is not like that of other people. The three of them sobbed aloud, their arms round each other's heads. When they had cried for a while and told each other what had happened since they were parted, scented hot water was sent for. The princess bathed and changed her clothes before they all climbed into carriages to go back to the capital.

Monkey then put his hands together in greeting to the king and said, "I have something else to put to you, Your Majesty." "Say it, whatever it is, holy monk," the king said, returning his greeting, "and we will do as you ask." "This mountain of theirs," Monkey replied, "is called Mount Hundredfoot. They tell me that centipedes have been turning into spirits here recently and injuring people by night. This is very awkward for travelling merchants. As I see it, only chickens can deal with centipedes, so a thousand extra-large cockerels should be chosen and then scattered across the mountainside to get rid of these venomous insects. The mountain could be renamed and you could make a land grant to these monks to thank them for looking after the princess." This suggestion pleased the king greatly, and he accepted it. Officials were then sent back to the city to fetch cocks, while the mountain was renamed Mount Splendour. The Department of Works was instructed to provide the materials for the monastery to be rebuilt, a deed of enfeoffment was written describing the mountain as "Mount Splendour, granted to the Almsgiver's Spread Gold Monastery", and the ancient monk was given the title National Benefactor Hierarch, a title that was to be handed on to his successors in perpetuity, together with a stipend of thirty-six bushels of grain. The monks all thanked the king for his kindness and saw him off on his way back to the capital. Here the princess returned to the inner palace and was greeted by all the ladies in turn. A banquet was then laid on to cheer the princess up and congratulate her on her deliverance.

Early the next morning the king ordered that painters make portraits of the countenances of the four holy monks to be kept in the Sino-Barbarian Hall. The princess was also invited to come out from the throne hall in her new finery to thank the Tang Priest and the other three for saving her from her suffering. When she had thanked them the Tang Priest took his leave of the king to continue his journey west. The king refused to let them go, but ordered great banquets at which they feasted for five or six days. The idiot really was given a good time, and he enjoyed putting as much food in his stomach as he possibly could. When the king saw how determined they were to visit the Buddha he realized that no matter how hard he tried he would not be able to keep them. He had two hundred ingots of gold and silver brought out, as well as a tray of jewels for each of them as an expression of thanks. Master and disciples refused to accept anything. The king then ordered the royal carriage prepared, invited the master to enter it, and instructed officials to escort them a long way. The queens, consorts, officials and common people all kowtowed endlessly in thanks. As they went along the way their monks all came out to kowtow to them in farewell; none of them could bear to be parted from the travellers. Seeing that the people seeing them off were unwilling to turn back, Monkey had no option but to make a spell with his hands and blow a magic breath in the direction of the trigram of the wind, Xun, so that a dark wind stopped all the escorts from seeing them. Only then did the travellers get away.

CHAPTER 34
The Pilgrims Finally Reach the West and Obtain the Scriptures

The Tang Priest and his three disciples continued along the road until they arrived at the Western land of the Buddha. It was unlike anywhere else. They saw precious flowers, rare grasses, ancient cypresses and hoary pines. In all the places they passed through every family was pious and fed monks. Under every mountain people cultivated their conduct; in all the forests travellers recited sutras. Master and disciples took shelter each night and set out at dawn, till six or seven days later a mass of high buildings and splendid halls suddenly came into view.

Sanzang raised his whip and pointed with it as he said, "What a fine place, Wukong." "Master," said Monkey, "why won't you dismount today when you've reached the real place where the true image of the Buddha is?" No sooner had he heard this than Sanzang sprang straight out of the saddle and went to the gateway. A young lay brother who stood to one side of the monastery gateway called out, "You must be the people from the east who have come to fetch the scriptures." The venerable elder quickly straightened his clothes and raised his head to look around.

The Great Sage Monkey recognized the young lay brother. "Master," said Monkey, "this is the Great Gold-crested Immortal who lives at the Jade Truth Temple at the foot of Vulture Peak. He is here to greet us." Only then did Sanzang realize who he was and step forward to salute him. "You have finally arrived here this year," replied the Great Immortal with a smile. "I was fooled by the Bodhisattva Guanyin. Ten years ago she went to the east at the Buddha's command to find the Pilgrim who would fetch the scriptures. She told me then he would be here within two or three years. I have been waiting for years on end with no news of you at all. I never thought that it would be this year before we met." Putting his hands together in front of his chest, Sanzang replied, "I am very grateful to you for your kindness, Great Immortal, very grateful." Sanzang and his three disciples led the horse and carried the baggage with them into the Taoist temple, where they were introduced to all the Great Immortals there. Tea and a vegetarian meal were then ordered, and the Taoist boys were told to heat scented water for the holy monks to bathe in before climbing to the Buddha land. By the time master and disciples had bathed the day was drawing to a close. They spent the night in the Jade Truth Temple.

The next morning the Tang Priest changed into his brocade cassock, put on his Vairocana mitre and grasped his monastic staff in his hand to climb the steps of the main hall and take his leave of the Great Immortal. "Yesterday you were in rags," the Great Immortal said with a smile, "but today you are dressed in splendour. I can see from your appearance that you are indeed a son of the Buddha." Sanzang then bowed in farewell. "Wait a moment," the Great Immortal said. "I will see you off." "There's no need for you to see us off," Monkey replied. "I know the way." "What you know," said the Great Immortal, "is the way by cloud. The holy monk has never gone by cloud. He must go by the overland way." "You're right," replied Monkey. "Although I've been here several times I've always come and gone by cloud. I've never come here on foot. If there's an overland route I'll trouble you to see us along it. My master is very serious about worshipping the Buddha, so I'd be very grateful if you could hurry up about it." The Great Immortal chuckled as he took the Tang Priest by hand and led the Incense to the gate of the Dharma. The way led not out by the temple's front entrance but through the main hall and out through the back gate. Pointing towards Vulture Peak, the Great

Immortal said, "Holy monk, do you see the auspicious light of many colours and the richly textured aura in the sky? That is the summit of Vulture Peak, the holy territory of the Lord Buddha." As soon as he saw it the Tang Priest bowed low. "Master," said Brother Monkey with a smile, "we haven't got to the place for bowing yet. As the saying goes, 'The mountain may be in view, but your horse will collapse before you get there.' We're still quite a long way from the place, so why start bowing now? If you bow all the way from here to the top, how ever many times will you have to hit your head on the ground?" "Holy monk," said the Great Immortal, "You, the Great Sage, Marshal Tian Peng, and the Curtain-raising General have now reached the blessed land and seen Vulture Peak. I am going back now." Sanzang took his leave of the Great Immortal and continued on his way.

The Great Sage led the Tang Priest and the others slowly up Vulture Peak. Within a couple of miles they reached a river of mighty rolling waves some three miles wide. There was no sign of anyone anywhere around. "Wukong," said Sanzang with alarm, "we have come the wrong way. I wonder if the Great Immortal misdirected us. This river is so wide and the waves so big, and there are no boats to be seen. How are we to cross it?" "He didn't send us the wrong way," replied Monkey with a smile. "Look over there. That's a bridge, isn't it? Once we're over that we'll have completed the true achievement." When the venerable elder and the others went closer to look they saw a tablet beside it on which were written the words CLOUD-TOUCHING CROSSING. Now this bridge was only a single log.

"Wukong," said Sanzang in fear and trembling, "no mortal man could cross that bridge. Let us look elsewhere to find the way." "But this is the way," replied Monkey with a smile, "this is the way." "Nobody's going to dare cross that even if it is the right way," said Pig with alarm. "The river's so wide, and there are those terrible waves, and all there is that narrow, slippery tree-trunk. We couldn't take a single step." "You all stand there while I go on it to show you," replied Monkey.

468

如真見滿行成功

The Pilgrims Finally See the Tathagata

The splendid Great Sage strode forward and sprang on the single-trunk bridge. He quickly ran across to the other side, swaying as he went, and called out, "Come over, come over." The Tang Priest waved in refusal, while Pig and Friar Sand bit their fingers and said, "It's much too hard." Monkey then ran back again from the far side and pulled at Pig. "Come with me, you idiot," he said, "come with me." "It's too slippery, it's too slippery," said Pig, lying down on the ground. "I could never cross it. Please spare me that and let me cross by wind and mist." Monkey held him down as he replied, "This is no place for you to be allowed to go riding wind and mist. You can only become a Buddha by crossing this bridge." "Brother," said Pig, "I'll never make it. Honestly, I can't walk across."

As the two of them were pulling at each other and fighting, Friar Sand went over to talk them round. Only then did they let go of each other. Sanzang then looked round to see a man poling a boat towards them from downriver and shouting, "Ferry! Come aboard." "Stop fooling around, disciples," said a delighted venerable elder. "There is a ferry-boat coming." The other three sprang to their feet and all watched together as the boat drew closer. It was a bottomless craft. Monkey had already spotted with the golden pupils in his fiery eyes that this was the Welcoming Lord Buddha, who is also known as Ratnadhvaja, the Royal Buddha of Brightness, but instead of giving this away he just kept calling, 'Over here, punt, over here." A moment later the ferryman had punted his boat up to the bank and was again shouting, "Ferry! Come aboard!" Sanzang was once more alarmed at the sight. "Your boat has no bottom," he said, "so how ever could you ferry anyone across?" The ferryman explained that his bottomless boat could ferry all living creatures.

Monkey thanked him with the words, "I am grateful to you for your generosity in coming to welcome my master. Step aboard, Master. That boat of his may have no bottom, but it's stable, and won't capsize even in wind and waves." The venerable elder was still very doubtful, but Monkey seized him by the arms and pushed him forward. Unable to keep on his feet, the master tumbled into the water, where the ferryman grabbed hold of him at once and stood him on the boat. The master shook his clothes and stamped his feet, complaining about Monkey, who led Friar Sand and Pig to stand on board bringing the luggage and the horse with them. Gently and strongly the Buddha pushed off, at which a corpse came floating downstream to the horror of the venerable elder. "Don't be frightened, Master," said Monkey. "That's you." "It's you, it's you," said Pig. Friar Sand clapped his hands as he said, "It's you, it's you!" The boatman gave a call, then also put in, too, "It's you! Congratulations! Congratulations!" The three of them all joined in these congratulations as the ferryman punted the boat quickly and steadily over the immortal Cloud-touching Crossing. Sanzang turned around and sprang lightly ashore on the opposite bank.

This was indeed what is meant by great wisdom, the boundless dharma of crossing to the other bank. When the four of them climbed the bank and looked back the bottomless boat had already disappeared, goodness knew where. Only when Brother Monkey explained that it had been the Welcoming Buddha did Sanzang find enlightenment. At once he turned round to thank his three disciples. "Let's not exchange thanks," said Monkey. "We've helped each other. You saved us three, Master, and showed us the way to win merit so as to complete the true achievement. And we have protected you, Master, holding to the faith and helping you happily to cast off your mortal body. Master, look at the magnificent scenery ahead. Flowers, grasses, pines and bamboo, as well as phoenixes, cranes and deer. Compare it with those places where evil beings created illusions through transformation. Ask yourself which is beautiful and good, and which ugly and evil." Sanzang was full of expressions of gratitude. All of them were now light of body and cheerful as they walked up Vulture Peak.

As master and disciples walked freely and at their ease up to the summit of Vulture Peak lay people could be seen under the green pines, and pious men and women amid the jade-coloured cypresses. The venerable elder bowed to them politely, whereupon all the lay men and women, monks and nuns all hastened to put their hands together and say to him, "Do not bow to us, holy monk. Come back and talk with us when you have seen Sakyamuni." "It's a bit early for that," replied Monkey with a grin. "Let's go and worship the boss."

The venerable elder waved his arms and performed a ritual dance as he followed Monkey straight to the gates of the Thunder Monastery, where four great vajrapanis greeted them with the words, "Have you arrived now, holy monk?" "Yes," Sanzang replied with a bow, "Your disciple Xuanzang has arrived." Having given this reply he was about to go in through the gateway. "Please wait for a moment, holy monk," the vajrapanis said. "Let us report before you come in." The vajrapanis sent a report of the Tang Priest's arrival to the four great vajrapanis on the middle gates, who in turn reported it to the inner gates, inside which were divine monks making offerings. As soon as they heard of the Tang Priest's arrival they all hurried to the Mahavira Hall, where they announced to the Tathagata Sakyamuni Buddha, "The holy monk from the Tang Court has arrived at your noble monastery to fetch the scriptures." The Lord Buddha was very pleased. He called together his Eight Bodhisattvas, Four Vajrapanis, Five Hundred Arhats, Three Thousand Protectors, Eleven Heavenly Shiners and Eighteen Guardians, who drew themselves up in two lines and passed on the Buddha's command summoning the Tang Priest to enter. Thus it was that the invitation was sent down from one level to the next: "Let the holy monk come in." Observing the requirements of ritual, the Tang Priest went in through the gate with Wukong and Wujing, who were leading the horse and carrying the luggage.

As the four of them arrived in front of the Mahavira Hall they all prostrated themselves and kowtowed to the Tathagata, then to their left and right. After they had each completed three rounds of worship they then knelt before the Buddha to present their passport. When the Tathagata had read it carefully he handed it back to Sanzang, who bowed his head low and reported, "Your disciple Xuanzang has made the long journey to your precious monastery at the command of the Great Tang emperor to beg for the true scriptures that will save all living beings. I implore the Lord Buddha in his goodness to grant them at once so that I may return to my country." The Tathagata then opened his compassionate mouth and in the great mercy of his heart said to Sanzang, "Your eastern land is in the Southern Continent of Jambu. As the sky is lofty there, the soil deep, its products many, and the people multitudinous there is much covetousness, murder, debauchery, lying, deception and dishonesty. They do not follow the Buddhist teaching, do not turn towards good destinies, and do not honour the sun, moon and stars or value the five grains. They are not loyal, filial, righteous or kind. In the delusion of their hearts they mislead themselves, cheating on weights and measures, taking life and killing animals, thus creating such boundless evil karma and such a superabundance of sin and evil that they bring the catastrophe of hell on themselves. I have Three Stores of scriptures that offer deliverance from suffering and release from disaster. Ananda, Kasyapa, take the four of them to the foot of the jewel tower and give them a vegetarian meal. After the meal open up the pavilion, select a few rolls from each of the thirty-five scriptures in my Three Stores, and tell them to propagate these scriptures in the east, where they may eternally grant their great goodness."

Acting on the orders of the Buddha the two arhats then led the four pilgrims to the bottom of the tower, where no end of rare and wonderful jewels and treasures were set out. Here the divinities who made offerings set out a vegetarian banquet, with immortal food, immortal delicacies, immortal tea, immortal fruit, and every kind of culinary delight not to be found in the mortal world. Master and disciples bowed their heads to the ground in thanks for the Buddha's kindness and proceeded to eat to their hearts' content.

This was a piece of good fortune for Pig, and a great benefit to Friar Sand as they ate their fill of the food in the Buddha's land that gave eternal life and new flesh and bones for old. The two arhats kept the four of them company till the meal was over, after which they went to the treasure pavilion, where the doors were opened for them to go in and look. Over this all was a thousandfold aura of coloured light and auspicious vapours, while brilliant mists and clouds of good omen wafted all around.

Ananda and Kasyapa led the Tang Priest to read the titles of all the scriptures. "You have come here from the East, holy monk," they said to him. "Have you brought us any presents? Hand them over right now, then we can give you the scriptures." When Sanzang heard this he said, "Your disciple Xuanzang has come a very long way, and I did not bring any with me." "That's very fine," the two arhats said with a laugh. "If we hand the scriptures over for nothing, they'll be passed down through the ages and our successors will have to starve to death." Monkey could not stand hearing them talking tough like this and refusing to hand the scriptures over, so he shouted, "Let's go and report them to the Tathagata, Master. We'll get him to give me the scriptures himself." "Shut up!" said Kasyapa. "Where do you think you are, acting up like this? Come here and take the scriptures." Pig and Friar Sand, who were keeping their own tempers under control, calmed Monkey down. They turned back to accept the scriptures, which were packed one by one into the luggage. Some of it was put on the horse's back, and the rest tied up as two carrying-pole loads that Pig and Friar Sand shouldered. They all then returned to the Buddha's throne, kowtowed, thanked the Tathagata and went straight out. They bowed twice to every Buddha and every Bodhisattva they met. When they reached the main entrance they bowed to the bhiksus, the bhiksunis, the laymen and the laywomen, taking their leave of each one. Then they hurried back down the mountain.

The story tells not of them but of the Ancient Buddha Dipamkara, who had been quietly listening in the library when the scriptures were handed over. He understood perfectly well that Ananda and Kasyapa had handed over wordless scriptures. "Those stupid monks from the East didn't realize that those were wordless scriptures," he thought with a smile to himself. "The holy monks' journey across all those mountains and rivers will be a complete waste. Who is in attendance here?" he called, and the arhat Suklavira stepped forward. "Use your divine might," Dipamkara instructed him, "and go after the Tang Priest like a shooting star. Take the wordless scriptures from him and tell him to come back to fetch the true scriptures." The arhat Suklavira then flew off on a storm wind that roared away from the Thunder Monastery as he gave a great display of his divine might.

The Tang Priest was walking along when he smelt the fragrant wind, but he paid no attention to it, taking it for an auspicious sign of the Lord Buddha. Then a noise could be heard as a hand reached down from mid-air to lift the scriptures lightly off the horse's back, which gave Sanzang such a shock that he beat his chest and howled aloud. Pig scrambled along in pursuit, Friar Sand guarded the carrying-poles loaded with scriptures, and Brother Monkey flew after the arhat. Seeing that Monkey had almost caught up with him, and frightened that the merciless cudgel would make no bones about wounding him badly, the arhat tore the bundle of scriptures to shreds and flung it into the dust. When Monkey saw the bundle falling in pieces that were being scattered by the fragrant wind he stopped chasing the arhat and brought his cloud down to look after the scriptures. The arhat Suklavira put the wind and the clouds away, then went back to report to Dipamkara.

When Pig, who was also in pursuit, saw the scriptures falling he helped Monkey to collect them up and carry them back to the Tang Priest. "Disciples," the Tang Priest exclaimed, tears pouring from his eyes, "even in this world of bliss evil demons cheat people." After gathering up the scattered scriptures in his arms Friar Sand opened one of them up and saw that it was as white as snow: not a word was written on it. Quickly he handed it to Sanzang with the remark, "There's nothing in this scroll, Master." Monkey opened out another scroll to find that it had nothing written in it either. Pig opened another and. it too had nothing in it. "Open them all for us to examine," said Sanzang. Every single scroll was blank paper. "We Easterners really do have no luck," he said, sighing and groaning. "What point is there in fetching wordless scriptures like these? How could I ever face the Tang emperor? I will have no way of avoiding execution for the crime of lying to my sovereign." Monkey, who already understood what had happened, then said to the Tang Priest, "Say no more, Master. Ananda and Kasyapa gave us these scrolls of blank paper because we hadn't got any presents to give them when they asked for them. Let's go back, report them to the Tathagata and get them accused of extortion." "That's right," shouted Pig, "that's right. Let's report them." The four of them then hurried up the mountain again, and after a few steps they were rushing back to the Thunder Monastery.

Before long they were once more outside the gates of the monastery, where everyone raised their clasped hands in greeting. "Have you holy monks come to exchange your scriptures?" they asked with smiles. Sanzang nodded and expressed his thanks. The vajrapanis did not block them, but let them go straight in to the Mahavira Hall. "Tathagata," yelled Monkey, "our master and the rest of us have had to put up with endless monsters, demons, troubles and hardships to get here from the east to worship you. You gave the orders for the scriptures to be handed over, but Ananda and Kasyapa didn't do so because they were trying to extort things from us. They conspired and deliberately let us take away blank paper versions without a single word written on them. But what's the point in taking those? I beg you to have them punished, Tathagata." "Stop yelling," replied the Lord Buddha with a smile. "I already know that they asked you for presents. But the scriptures cannot be casually passed on. Nor can they be taken away for nothing. In the past bhiksus and holy monks went down the mountain and recited these scriptures to the family of the elder Zhao in the land of Sravasti. This ensured peace and safety for the living and deliverance for the dead members of the family. All that was asked for was three bushels and three pecks of granular gold. I said they had sold the scriptures too cheap, so I saw to it that Zhao's sons and grandsons would be poor. You were given blank texts because you came here to fetch them empty-handed. The blank texts are true, wordless scriptures, and they really are good. But as you living beings in the east are so deluded and have not achieved enlightenment we'll have to give you these ones instead. Ananda, Kasyapa," he called, "fetch the true scriptures with words at once. Choose a few rolls from each title to give them, then come back here and tell me how many."

The two arhats then led the four pilgrims to the foot of the library building and once again asked the Tang Priest for a present. Having nothing else to offer, he ordered Friar Sand to bring out the begging bowl of purple gold and presented it with both hands. "Your disciple is poor and has come a very long way," he said, "and I did not bring any presents with me. This bowl was given to me by the Tang emperor with his own hands to beg for food with on my journey. I now offer it to you as a token of my heartfelt feelings. I beg you arhats not to despise it but to keep it. When I return to my court I shall report this to the Tang emperor, who will certainly reward you richly. I only ask you to give me the true scriptures that have words to save me from failing in my imperial mission and making this long, hard journey for nothing."

Ananda accepted the bowl with no more than a hint of a smile. The warriors guarding the precious library building, the kitchen staff responsible for the spices and the arhats in charge of the library rubbed each other's faces, patted each other's backs, flicked each other with their fingers and pulled faces. "Disgraceful," they all said with grins, "disgraceful. Demanding presents from the pilgrims who've come to fetch the scriptures!" A moment later Ananda was frowning with embarrassment but still holding the bowl and not letting go. Only then did Kasyapa go into the library to check the scriptures through one by one and give them to Sanzang. "Disciples," called Sanzang, "take a good look at them, not like last time." The three of them took the rolls and examined them one by one. All had words. 5,048 rolls were handed over, the total in a single store. They were neatly packed up and put on the horse, and those left over were made into a carrying-pole load for Pig to take. Friar Sand carried their own luggage, and as Brother Monkey led the horse the Tang Priest took his staff, pushed his Vairocana mitre into position, shook his brocade cassock, and went happily into the presence of the Tathagata. Kowtowing in thanks, the Tang Priest did three circuits of homage round the Lord Buddha. He and his three disciples then took their leave and returned to the Great Tang in the East.

As Sanzang had lost his mortal body he too could now fly, and in a few days they were back in the Tang capital Chang'an, where they delivered the scriptures and installed them in the Monastery of the Wild Goose Stupa. When this was done master and disciples rose up to the ninth level of clouds to return to the Vulture Peak, where they were all assigned new posts: Sanzang as the Candana-punya Buddha, Monkey as the Victorious Fighting Buddha, Pig as the Altar Cleanser, Friar Sand as the Golden Arhat, and the white horse as a Heavenly Dragon. Now that he was a Buddha, Monkey's golden band disappeared.

Here ends the *Journey to the West.*